D1131189

THE ANNOTATED

PETER PAN

The Annotated Secret Garden
by Frances Hodgson Burnett, edited with an introduction
and notes by Gretchen Holbrook Gerzina

The New Annotated Dracula
by Bram Stoker, with an introduction by Neil Gaiman,
edited with a preface and notes by Leslie S. Klinger

The Annotated Wind in the Willows
by Kenneth Grahame, edited with a
preface and notes by Annie Gauger, with an introduction by Brian Jacques

ALSO BY MARIA TATAR

The Grimm Reader: The Classic Tales of the Brothers Grimm

Enchanted Hunters: The Power of Stories in Childhood

Secrets beyond the Door: The Story of Bluebeard and His Wives

The Classic Fairy Tales

Lustmord: Sexual Murder in Weimar Germany

Off with Their Heads! Fairy Tales and the Culture of Childhood

The Hard Facts of the Grimms' Fairy Tales

Spellbound: Studies on Mesmerism and Literature

J·M·BARRIE

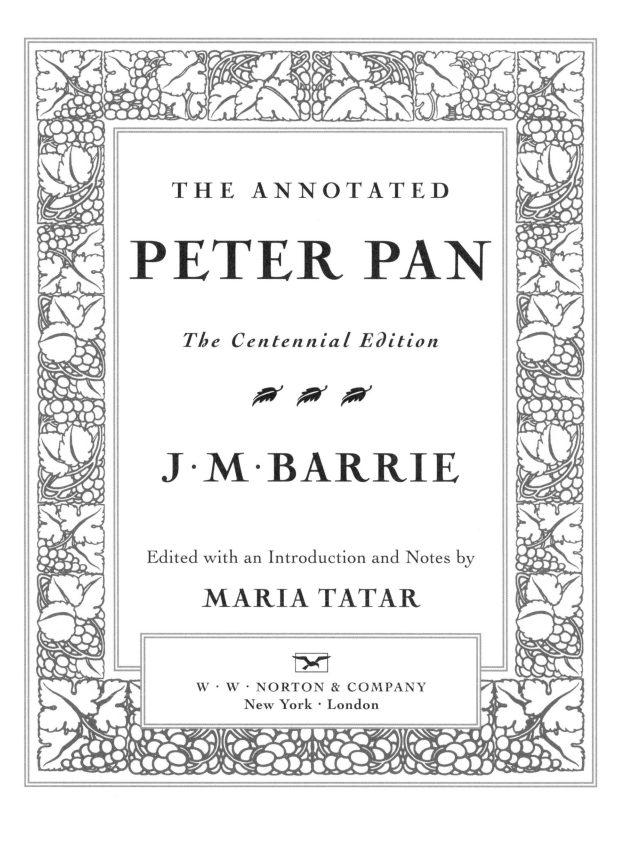

THE ANNOTATED

PETER PAN

The Centennial Edition

J·M·BARRIE

Edited with an Introduction and Notes by

MARIA TATAR

W·W·NORTON & COMPANY

New York · London

Frontispiece: Sir William Nicholson, *James Barrie*, 1904. Oil on canvas.
(Courtesy of the Bridgeman Art Library. Reproduced by permission of Desmond Banks)

For information about permission to reproduce selections from this book,
write to Permissions, W. W. Norton & Company, Inc.,
500 Fifth Avenue, New York, NY 10110

For information about special discounts for bulk purchases, please contact
W. W. Norton Special Sales at specialsales@wwnorton.com or 800-233-4830

Manufacturing by Courier Kendallville
Book design by JAM Design
Production manager: Anna Oler

ISBN: 978-0-393-06600-5

W. W. Norton & Company, Inc.
500 Fifth Avenue, New York, N.Y. 10110
www.wwnorton.com

W. W. Norton & Company Ltd.
Castle House, 75/76 Wells Street, London W1T 3QT

1 2 3 4 5 6 7 8 9 0

To the Five:
For Lauren and Daniel,
as always,
and for the boys in the next generation,
Ben, Sam, and Grant

Contents

PETER AND WENDY by J. M. Barrie

Acknowledgments

cknowledgments often stop writers short. They are usually the last and can often be the most challenging piece in the process of producing a manuscript. Writing a book takes us away from the world. Books and papers occupy every available surface; our plants languish; the laundry piles up; faucets drip; dust settles; and coffee begins to feel like a best friend. J. M. Barrie once created a literary alter ego named Bookworm, and, in a series of notes jotted down for the play about him, he wrote: "B[ookworm] realizes he has been leading a selfish life engrossed in own work & not playing citizen's part in world." Those words hit home when I read them while writing this volume.

It may be true that books require solitude, but they are worldly both in their origins and their destinations. Mine have given me much to talk about, and without that talk those books would be shadowy, anemic versions of themselves. Since the time that Bob Weil of W. W. Norton called me to ask if I was interested in editing an *Annotated Peter Pan*, I have talked ceaselessly, perhaps interminably, about J. M. Barrie and Peter Pan. There was so much more to both their stories than I could ever have imagined, and everyone I knew had an autobiographical memory to share about Peter Pan—save Lani Guinier, who instead urged me to consider the history of flight in connection with Peter Pan. And then there were the scholars and experts on Barrie—from the earliest biographer, Denis Mackail, with his encyclopedic *Story of J.M.B.*, to creative geniuses like Andrew Birkin, with his authoritative *J. M. Barrie and the Lost*

Boys and his BBC documentary *The Lost Boys*. Their voices, too, added to the chorus that I soon felt myself to be channeling as I tried to capture the magic of Peter Pan in his many incarnations.

Generosity is the term that comes to mind first when I look back on the many conversations that took place with family, friends, and colleagues over the past years. Tactfully steering me away from the arcane and esoteric while cheerfully drawing me back to the power of Barrie's story, brothers, sisters, children, nieces, and nephews will find their influence, along with bits and pieces of our conversations, in this book. My students always put me back on the right track with their unfailingly sharp instincts about the plausible and the far-fetched. Their responses to Peter Pan reassured me that the story had retained a vibrant cultural energy and that there would always be something new to say about its many complicated layers of meaning.

Without Andrew Birkin's monumental work on J. M. Barrie and his relationship to the Llewelyn Davies boys, I would have been lost in the archives and taken many more years to finish this book. Andrew's willingness to share the labors of many years is nothing short of astonishing, and the dog-eared copy of *J. M. Barrie and the Lost Boys* on my desk speaks volumes about my indebtedness to his groundbreaking work. I have especially valued the work of Jacqueline Rose, Jack Zipes, Lisa Chaney, and Jackie Wullschläger, who have provided new perspectives and insights on *Peter Pan*.

The staff at the Beinecke Rare Book and Manuscript Library at Yale University gave me access to papers and objects that brought my work alive in powerful ways. I feel grateful for their trust in allowing me to handle precious objects such as the only remaining copy of *The Boy Castaways of Black Lake Island* and Barrie's key to Kensington Gardens. The staff enabled me to work through the papers with maximum efficiency, and it gives me real pleasure to acknowledge their support as well as the love of books they displayed on a daily basis. Timothy Young, curator of Modern Books and Manuscripts, paved the way for my work, and I relied often on his expertise as I pored over the papers in the J. M. Barrie Manuscript Vault.

Christine De Poortere of Great Ormond Street Hospital Children's Charity has been an extraordinary partner in this enterprise. Sharing her expertise and her passionate commitment to Barrie's legacy, she has smoothed many rocky paths for me, and I send heartfelt thanks to her on the other side of the Atlantic. I am also grateful to her for writing the informative essay included in this volume about the hospital and its history.

Bob Weil has worked with me every step of the way, encouraging, prodding, inspiring, and reassuring. His modesty will prevent him from revealing the importance of his contributions, both editorial and intellectual. I do not exaggerate in saying that this book would not exist without his confidence in me and his willingness to push me out of my academic comfort zones. My thanks also go to Philip Marino at W. W. Norton, who understands the degree to which the devil is in the details and was always willing to participate in collective acts of exorcism.

At the very beginning of this project, Sarah Chalfant of the Wylie Agency and I shared our memories of Peter Pan and of reading the story when we were young. We marveled at illustrations by Attwell and Rackham, and it was at that point that I knew that Peter Pan was in my future.

Doris Sperber helped out in countless ways, tracking down books, catching errors, and printing out documents with lightning speed—with unfailing good cheer. My colleagues in the Folklore and Mythology Program at Harvard University—Deborah Foster, Holly Hutchison, and Steve Mitchell—provided a day-to-day working environment conducive to conversations and collaborations. Melissa Carden worked her magic with administrative matters and made sure that all the Peter Pan bills were paid. Many others will recognize their contributions to this volume, among them Owen Bates, Sarah Batista-Pereira, Kate Bernheimer, Lisa Brooks, Alexa Fishman, Ian Fleishman, Jenya Godina, Donald Haase, Heidi Hirschl, Elizabeth Hoffman, Adam Horn, Emily Hyman, Rick Jacoby, Emily Jones, Stephanie Klinkenberg, Sandy Kreisberg, Julia Lam, Kathy Lasky, Penny Laurans, Lois Lowry, Gregory Maguire, Hannah Milem, Madeline Miller, Garrett Morton, Christina Phillips, Isabella Roden, Lexi Ross, Ruth Sanderson, Alan Silva, Michael Sims, Ellen Handler Spitz, Corley Stone, Larry Wolff, and Jack Zipes.

And, Daniel and Lauren, as always, kept me from turning into Bookworm.

Alice B. Woodward, *The Peter Pan Picture Book*, 1907.

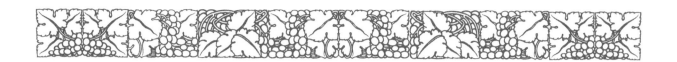

A Message for Those
Who Have Grown Up

All children, except one, grow up," J. M. Barrie tells us, in the famous first sentence of his novel *Peter and Wendy,* published seven years after Peter Pan's theatrical debut in London. That one rebellious child exists in many different versions today. There is Walt Disney's redheaded Peter Pan, animated in both senses of the term. There are the many nimble women of Broadway—Mary Martin, Sandy Duncan, and Cathy Rigby—who have soared across the stage as Peter Pan. There is the enchanting Peter Pan who magically appears at the home of the Llewelyn Davies boys, when their mother is ill, in Marc Forster's *Finding Neverland.* We encounter the boy who would not grow up on stage and screen, and also in fiction, with countless prequels, sequels, adaptations, and revisions. Peter Pan may refuse to grow up, but he also will not die.

When I rediscovered *Peter Pan* as an adult, I quickly learned that he existed in multiple textual forms even before he detached himself, to lead a life of his own, from the Scottish writer who dreamt him up. He was first brought to life in Barrie's 1902 novel *The Little White Bird*, a whimsical and elusive work (Barrie hated both those adjectives, in part because they captured his style so perfectly) about a bachelor who develops an attachment to a six-year-old boy named David. Embedded in that novel is the story of a seven-day-old Peter Pan and his adventures in Kensington Gardens ("All perambulators lead to the Kensington Gardens"). The chapters about Peter Pan were published separately in 1906, with only a few minor changes, under the title *Peter Pan in Kensington Gardens*. The volume was illustrated by the artist Arthur Rackham, perhaps the most acclaimed children's book illustrator of his day, best known today for images he created for fairy tales by the Brothers Grimm and by Hans Christian Andersen and for works ranging from *Aesop's Fables* to Kenneth Grahame's *The Wind in the Willows*.

Today, we know Peter Pan best in his role as lead of the 1904 play *Peter Pan, or The Boy Who Wouldn't Grow Up*. The play did not appear in print until 1928,

Program for the London production of *Peter Pan*. (Beinecke Rare Book and Manuscript Library, Yale University)

but in 1911 Barrie published the novel *Peter and Wendy*, which became known as *Peter Pan*. To recapitulate, we have:

The Little White Bird, 1902

Peter Pan, or The Boy Who Wouldn't Grow Up (stage premiere) 1904

Peter Pan in Kensington Gardens, illustrated by Arthur Rackham, 1906

Peter and Wendy, 1911 (later renamed *Peter Pan*)

Peter Pan, or, The Boy Who Would Not Grow Up, published in 1928

The play, which existed only in performance for many years, underwent multiple revisions. Barrie attended rehearsals and was constantly cutting, revising, and adding new material, collaborating with the actors and actresses to improve dialogue and staging. Many of the early scripts are preserved in the J. M. Barrie archive at the Beinecke Rare Book and Manuscript Library in New Haven, Connecticut, where the bulk of Barrie's papers are stored. To give one example: on onion-skin sheets in a small folder marked 1904/05, the third act of what was then a three-act play showed Wendy agreeing to become Peter's mother and to live with him in Kensington Gardens. The two discover a baby under some rubbish in the park, and a delighted Wendy, who realizes that Peter will need someone to take care of him once she grows up, takes the child in. The curtain falls on Peter, Wendy, and child as they wave from their perch in Kensington Gardens. Who knew that there were also performances in which anywhere from a dozen to twenty beautiful mothers compete with one another to adopt one of the lost boys? Or that Hook survived the crocodile attack on the high seas in an early version of the play but

Postcard of Cecilia Loftus and Hilda Trevelyan in *Peter Pan*. (Beinecke Rare Book and Manuscript Library, Yale University)

accidentally lowered himself into its gaping jaw while climbing down a tree in Kensington Gardens?

The conventional story of a Peter Pan who enters the nursery of the Darling family, abducts the children by teaching them how to fly, and escorts them with Tinker Bell to Neverland is far less stable than most of us realize. To be sure, in all versions the children and the lost boys on the island still come into conflict with pirates and "redskins," and Peter must always battle the wicked Captain Hook. But the return home is imagined in a variety of ways, and we do not always have a grown-up Wendy at the end of the play, with a daughter who will fly off to Neverland to help Peter with his spring cleaning. For Barrie, Peter Pan existed in performance, and the various typescripts reveal exactly how much he loved to see the character come alive onstage and transform and renew himself with each new production.

Barrie at first refused to fix his iconic character in print. "Mr. Barrie has often been asked to write a short narrative or libretto of his immortal child's play and

A scene from the first production of *Peter Pan*, showing the beautiful mothers and the boys they are hoping to adopt. (Courtesy of Great Ormond Street Hospital Children's Charity)

G. D. Drennan capitalized on the growing popularity of *Peter Pan* with a 1909 volume that promised to elaborate on what was in the play. (Beinecke Rare Book and Manuscript Library, Yale University)

has as often refused," the *Bookman* reported in 1907.[1] Barrie may have stalled, but others were quick to supply keepsakes, alphabets, and picture books. Daniel S. O'Connor's *Peter Pan Keepsake* appeared just in time to satisfy the desires

1. *The Bookman,* January 1907, 161.

TWO CHARMING MEMENTOS OF

"Peter Pan,"

PRODUCED BY

A. J. CALEY & SON, LTD.

NORWICH.

"Peter Pan at Home."

A reconstruction in miniature of Mr. J. M. Barrie's Play with the Principal Scenes, and over 520 coloured figures, &c. (singly and in groups), produced chiefly from photographs of the actual play, with the Story of Peter Pan, and directions and suggestions for reproducing it.   The whole enclosed in PETER PAN'S HOUSE ON THE TREE TOPS.

"An endless source of amusement for wet days and long evenings."
"Intelligent children will never tire of adding new figures and fresh stage effects.

Price - - - 12s. 6d. each

Peter Pan Crackers.

Containing Souvenirs of the Play, and Quotations, with Miniature Photographs of some of the principal characters in each Cracker, packed in PETER PAN'S HOUSE ON THE TREE TOPS.

Price - - 3s. 6d. per Box.

THESE PRODUCTIONS ARE ON SALE at the DUKE OF YORK'S THEATRE, LONDON, AND AT THE LEADING TOY SHOPS, CONFECTIONERS, STORES, Etc., THROUGHOUT THE KINGDOM.

Advertisement for a miniature Peter Pan theater for children and for Peter Pan Crackers. (Beinecke Rare Book and Manuscript Library, Yale University)

of young theatergoers, who wanted a print version of the story. It was followed in the same year by *The Peter Pan Picture Book*, also by O'Connor, with illustrations by Alice B. Woodward. Oliver Herford published a charming *Peter Pan Alphabet* in 1909, and G. D. Drennan fleshed out the story with his *Peter Pan: His Book, His Pictures, His Career, His Friends*.

Barrie finally gave in to requests for an official story, with a narrative entitled *Peter and Wendy*, published in 1911 and illustrated by F. D. Bedford (a gallery of those illustrations is included in this volume). Like Peter Pan himself, that novel is betwixt and between, forever shifting its orientation from children to adults and then back again. Readers today will not be surprised to learn that it was constantly reshaped, adapted, and rewritten in Barrie's own day, although mainly by writers authorized by Barrie to recast the story for "little people" or for "boys and girls." Still that version of the story is one that captures, crystallizes, and broadens what Barrie wanted to say with the figure of Peter Pan, and for that reason, I use it as the text for this annotated volume. Since it came to be published under the title *Peter Pan*, I have kept that appellation in the title for this volume, although I will differentiate (when necessary) between play and novel by referring to one as *Peter Pan* and the other as *Peter and Wendy*. Nearly all my annotations are relevant to the play as well, which exists in many print versions. Peter Hollindale offers an excellent introduction to the stage version in his *J. M. Barrie: Peter Pan and Other Plays*.

This volume aims to keep readers under the spell even as they learn more about *Peter and Wendy* and its author. Some will appreciate a dose of reality with their *Peter and Wendy*, while others may prefer to avoid the annotations and focus on Barrie's story alone and the illustrations that offer visual points of entry into it. My own years spent with J. M. Barrie and Peter Pan continue to expand my appreciation and understanding of a work that will not grow old and that becomes more magical with each new reading. The story behind Peter Pan is as moving as the novel and play itself, and readers will find in this volume two separate essays: an introduction to the novel annotated here and a second to its author. They will discover in the annotations both cultural context and critical response. And in "A Montage of Friends, Fans, and Foes: J. M. Barrie and Peter Pan in the World," they will learn how readers and audiences have responded to the author and to Peter Pan. Here's to that magic and its power to move us, transport us, and transform us with energy so radiant that we can experience, even as adults, the "ecstasies innumerable" of Neverland.

Sir George James Frampton, *Peter Pan*, 1912. Bronze statue in Kensington Gardens, London. (Courtesy of the Bridgeman Art Library)

A Note from the Author
about Peter Pan and J. M. Barrie

My first memory of Peter Pan goes back to a burst of color that entered my life when I was young. A school chum had invited me to view the musical *Peter Pan* (with the famed American singer and actress Mary Martin in the lead role) on her grandmother's brand-new color television set. The apparatus was hopelessly clunky by today's standards, but we watched the show breathlessly, with a sense of excitement and revelation. Never mind that static interrupted the performance from time to time or that the tiny screen failed to capture the vibrancy and depth of the theatrical set. Like generations of children before me, in London's Duke of York's Theatre or New York's Empire Theatre (where *Peter Pan* won fame and acclaim), I lost my heart to the boy who would not grow up. For weeks after that, I dreamed about fairy dust and flying.

Years later, as an adult, I was smitten once again. This time the encounter took place in London's Kensington Gardens, where I found myself one crisp autumn day, giddy with anticipation at the thought of visiting the celebrated statue of Peter Pan in that park. A map of the city was at hand, but it had not occurred to me that I might need something additional to guide my steps through a public park. After all, I had seen many pictures of the statue and knew something about its general location. The work was cast in bronze and showed Peter, planted on a solid hillock, holding a pipe to his lips to play

Michael Llewelyn Davies as Peter Pan, 1906. (Courtesy of Great Ormond Street Hospital Children's Charity)

a tune for an enchanted audience of rabbits, squirrels, mice, and fairies. And I had read that it was situated in a "green glade" about halfway down the west bank of the Long Water (the place where Peter Pan lands after flying out of the nursery).

I had also read up on the statue's history. Plans for it had developed over a century ago, in 1906, when J. M. Barrie took photographs of a six-year-old boy named Michael Llewelyn Davies in a Peter Pan costume. Six years later Barrie, who had by then become the adoptive father to the boy and his four brothers, commissioned Sir George Frampton, a renowned British sculptor, to make a statue of Peter Pan, based on those photographs of Michael. Frampton ended up using two other boys as models, and Barrie worried forever after that the sculptor had failed to capture any resemblance at all to Michael—"It doesn't show the Devil in Peter."[1]

Despite Barrie's reservations, the statue of Peter Pan, blowing on his pipe, appeared "like magic" in Kensington Gardens on the morning of May 1, 1912.[2] That same day, James Barrie had placed this announcement in the *Times*:

> There is a surprise in store for the children who go to Kensington Gardens to feed the ducks in the Serpentine this morning. Down by the little bay on the south-western side of the tail of the Serpentine they will find a May-day gift by Mr. J. M. Barrie, a figure of Peter Pan blowing his pipe on the stump of

1. Andrew Birkin, *J. M. Barrie and the Lost Boys: The Real Story behind Peter Pan* (New Haven, CT: Yale University Press, 2003), 202.

2. There were seven statues made from the original mold, and they are in Kensington Gardens, Sefton Park in Liverpool, and Egmont Park in Brussels; at Rutgers University in Camden, New Jersey; and in Bowring Park in St. John's Newfoundland, Glenn Gould Park in Toronto, and Queen's Gardens in Perth, Western Australia.

a tree, with fairies and mice and squirrels all around. It is the work of Sir George Frampton, and the bronze figure of the boy who would never grow up is delightfully conceived.[3]

New Zealand postage stamp with an image of the Peter Pan statue in Kensington Gardens. (Beinecke Rare Book and Manuscript Library, Yale University)

Knowing that Kensington Gardens was not a vast space and feeling the desire to prolong the joyful anticipation of seeing the statue, I meandered through the park, imagining how Frampton had installed the statue under the cover of darkness and wondering whether Barrie had been present that evening. I soon began encountering flocks of single-minded tourists, maps in hand. As they wound their way through the park, most skipped gleefully ahead of me, disappearing around a bend and dissolving into nothing but a collection of symphonic sounds and mellifluous voices. And then suddenly I heard it: a whispered chorus of voices in uncanny unison, uttering the words "Peter Pan" with hushed, barely contained excitement. Even before the statue came into view, I recognized that I was in the presence of something massive, even monumental. We all hailed from different corners of the earth, and yet, in Kensington Gardens, we were, *mirabile dictu*, also all turned into dazzled pilgrims, reverently united by our faith in fairies and our love for Peter Pan.

Those breathless tourists reminded me of Peter Pan's international appeal. We encounter him, after all, not only in J. M. Barrie's stagecraft and fiction but also at the movies, when he comes to be refashioned by Walt Disney Studios as an animated figure or by Steven Spielberg as a grown-up lawyer specializing in corporate takeovers. Peter Pan greets us from the label of peanut butter jars and winks at us from the sides of buses making runs from Boston to New York.[4] We discover his darker side when we view images of Michael Jackson

3. The Fine Art Society, *Sir George Frampton & Sir Alfred Gilbert. Peter Pan and Eros: Public & Private Sculpture in Britain, 1880–1940* (London: The Fine Art Society, 2002), 3.

4. Jacqueline Rose writes in *The Case of Peter Pan, or The Impossibility of Children's Fiction* (London: Macmillan, 1984) that Peter Pan has been monetized in England and converted into "toys, crackers, posters, a Golf Club, Ladies League, stained glass window in St. James's Church, Paddington, and a 5000-ton Hamburg–Scandinavia car ferry" (103). Consumer culture has always been expert at appropriating beloved characters from children's books, but Great Ormond Street Hospital does not in fact receive any royalties for Disney merchandise, nor has it received revenues from car ferries or a Ladies League. Barrie did profit, in his lifetime, from the sale of Peter Pan crackers and from a Peter Pan theater set design for children.

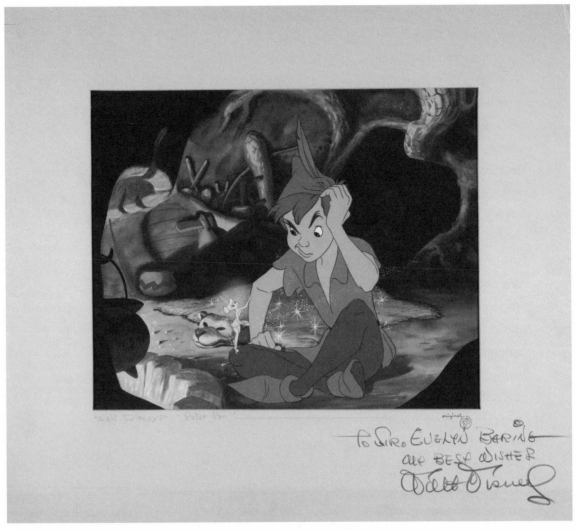

Signed animation cell from Walt Disney's *Peter Pan,* 1952. (Beinecke Rare Book and Manuscript Library, Yale University)

and his Neverland Valley Ranch, with its eerily life-size figures of Pan, Hook, and other Barrie characters. It was Michael Jackson who famously claimed, in an interview with Martin Bashir, that he *was* Peter Pan, in his heart, and that he would never grow up.

Peter Pan may appear to have been appropriated by corporate culture, but his image and likeness are still protected by Great Ormond Street Hospital for Children, to which J. M. Barrie willed the rights to the play and to the novel *Peter and Wendy*. (The House of Lords amended the Copyright, Designs and Patent Act in 1988 to extend the expired rights.) It goes without saying that he also belongs to everyone—child or adult—who has read his story or watched him onstage. And, as my experience in Kensington Gardens reminded me, their numbers are legion.

Mercurial and flighty, Peter Pan has imprinted himself on each of us in different ways. For that reason, it seemed important to include in this volume my own history with Peter Pan and, more importantly, the story of what felt like a close, personal encounter with J. M. Barrie. It did not take place in Kirriemuir, Scotland, where J. M. Barrie was born, nor in Edinburgh, where he studied, nor in London, which he set out to conquer as a talented young journalist. Instead it took place in the United States, which Barrie had visited on an impulse in 1914, with the hope of raising support for the war effort.

New Haven, Connecticut, seems an unlikely location to meet J. M. Barrie, but it was there that I found him, a living, breathing, spectral presence in the vast archive of papers and memorabilia housed in the Beinecke Library under the heading "MS VAULT BARRIE." "Nineteen linear feet of documents": that was how the collection had been described to me. Eager as I was to see those materials, I also shuddered inwardly at the thought of the musty typescripts, letters, and notebooks that awaited me. I also knew that I could not write *The Annotated Peter Pan* without studying what was at the Beinecke, even though I arrived there having read everything I could track down in print by Barrie or about him.

The Beinecke Library offers generous fellowships that enable scholars with projects pertaining to their collections to spend a month in residence. When I received the good news that there was interest in my project, I mentally divided the nineteen linear feet by the number of days in October and quickly realized that I had only about a day for each foot of documents (the library closes on Saturdays and Sundays). I would have to work quickly and efficiently if I wanted to see everything. And there were also the Llewelyn Davies Family papers, a collection of letters, diaries, and memorabilia left behind by the five boys adopted by J. M. Barrie after the death of both their parents.

The Beinecke Library at Yale University is a six-story rectangular building with walls made of translucent marble that protect the books from direct light but transmit some light into the tower of book stacks. Its sunken courtyard contains three sculptures representing time (a pyramid), the sun (a circle), and chance (a cube). When I entered the ground-level reading room for the first time, I could not help but feel those geometric shapes resonate with my anxieties and hopes about the Barrie papers. How could I possibly read, review, and reflect on everything in the Barrie archive, even with a ten-hour working day? Although the reading room had large glass panels, it felt sepulchral, with nothing to look at but the sun-dappled concrete of the courtyard. I would have to pin my hopes on chance—the possibility that proximity to the papers would produce an intimacy and understanding deeper than what I had found in Barrie's writings and in books about him.

One of the first boxes I opened contained Barrie's notebooks, handwritten in a scrawl that was frustratingly illegible. With effort, I was able to get most of the words making up each sentence or phrase, but one key word always resisted decoding, and each sentence was thereby doomed to remain a mystery (or at least unquotable), drawing me into a suffocating vortex of archival alienation. The first full sentence I managed to decipher was one I already knew by heart: "May God blast any one who writes a biography of me." Unintentionally it became the name of the file in which I was collecting aphorisms and observations from the notebooks.

Next came Barrie's letters—astonishingly often in their original envelopes—

Peter Scott, *J. M. Barrie in His Study*. (Beinecke Rare Book and Manuscript Library, Yale University)

preserved by correspondents who no doubt understood their value. Here I fared better, for Barrie knew just how unreadable his hand was and made the effort to be more legible when writing to friends and acquaintances. On my second day at the Beinecke, I came across a nondescript envelope directed to Barrie's personal secretary, Cynthia Asquith, with no address. It was dated June 24, 1937—the day Barrie died. In it was nothing but a small scrap of paper with the words "dangerously ill" written on it. That was my first archival epiphany, and

J. M. Barrie with Michael. (Beinecke Rare Book and Manuscript Library, Yale University)

those two words—in all their heartrendingly painful awareness of death— brought James Matthew Barrie to life for me. They were probably the last words he wrote. It is no accident that we make a distinction between dead letters and a living spirit, but on that day I experienced just how powerfully handwritten words can invoke a living spirit, one that became a spectral presence in that Reading Room.

There were many such days in the archive, and it was with awestruck excitement and reverence that I sat down each day to a new box of materials. In one I found Barrie's letters to his adopted son George Llewelyn Davies. George had attended Eton and distinguished himself in sports, academics, and drama. He volunteered for service in World War I and was struck down, at the age of twenty-one, by a stray bullet on the fields of Flanders. Somehow those letters, written to George at the western front, had found their way back to Barrie. I touched them, but I did not have the heart to open them, for I recalled not only Barrie's love for George but also the words of George's father, Arthur Llewelyn Davies, about his son. When Arthur had cancer of the jaw, he was unable to speak after a painful operation and could communicate only through handwritten notes. On his deathbed, he jotted down the following about his five boys—

what he remembered about them and how he visualized each one. Here's what I could make out: "Michael going to school. Porthgwarra and S's blue dress. Burpham garden. Kirkby view across valley. Buttermere. Jack bathing. Peter answering chaff. Nicholas in the garden . . . George always."[5] And then there was their mother, Sylvia's, declaration in her will about how grieved she was to leave her boys: "I love them so utterly." The letters felt sacred to me. I could not bring myself to open them, much as I also felt a powerful obligation to read everything available to me in an effort to make sense of the continuing enigma of J. M. Barrie and Peter Pan.

Like most scholars, I am a passionate reader and invariably develop a strong affective bond with what I write about. But the depth of feeling opened up by Barrie's papers remained a surprise. At first, I tried hard to resist the emotional overload invoked. But it was impossible to look at pictures of the boys fishing in Scotland, to open an envelope and find locks of Michael's hair, to read Sylvia's will and Barrie's transcription of it, or to look at Nico's school report without experiencing an opera of emotions. Occasionally I worried that one of the many guards monitoring security tapes of the reading room might report the presence of a mildly unhinged user who alternated between euphoric ecstasies and depleted gloom.

Biographers can be relentless about mastering the mysteries of their subject's life, and there is no shortage of accounts that try to pin down the exact nature of J. M. Barrie's relationship to Sylvia Llewelyn Davies and her five boys. Peter, the third son of Arthur and Sylvia, nearly drove himself mad while assembling what he would later call "The Morgue," a set of letters and documents, with his commentary, that tried to make sense of his family's past and how the lives of the five boys, their parents, and J. M. Barrie intersected, connected, and were intertwined. He even went so far as to quiz his former nanny, sending her a list of questions, and to interrogate family members, friends, and acquaintances in order to get to the bottom of things.[6]

The key question, for Peter Davies, turned on Barrie's feelings for Sylvia and the boys. Was his love for Sylvia romantic or platonic? Or was she noth-

5. Llewelyn Davies Family Papers, GEN MSS 554 4/120.

6. All quotations that follow are from "The Morgue," which can be found at the Beinecke Library, GEN MSS 554 / Box 4.

ing more to him than the gatekeeper for the five boys who were the real target of Barrie's love and affection? Perhaps Barrie was asexual and, as his wife, Mary Ansell, broadly hinted, incapable of intimate relations? One biographer, as Peter Davies notes, reported that Barrie met Sylvia at a dinner party and was "overwhelmed" by her beauty and "intrigued by the way she put aside some of the various sweets that were handed round, and secreted them" (the sweets were for Peter). A letter to Peter Davies from a friend claimed that Barrie fell in love with Sylvia at a formal tea: "He saw, fell a victim and was utterly conquered." Still, there is no evidence at all that their feelings for each other, even after Arthur's death, went beyond anything but deep friendship.

Peter Davies speculated endlessly about his father's reaction to Barrie's love for Sylvia. Was he "a shade vexed"? Were relations between the two "strained" by the "infiltrations of this astounding little Scotch genius of a 'lover'"? Was Arthur's "irritation" deep? Did he feel "resentment" toward Barrie or "gratitude" for the many kindnesses he showed the family? On the one hand, Peter himself seems vexed by the fact that his father was constantly upstaged by Barrie's wealth and fame; yet he also seems genuinely moved by Barrie's altruism and selflessness. "It would be interesting to have a list of all the impoverished authors and their families whom J. M. B. helped out of his own pocket at one time and another," he wrote.

Reading through "The Morgue" led me to the conclusion that Barrie took some secrets to the grave and that efforts to recover them are futile. A recent biography by Piers Dudgeon served as a cautionary example in substituting speculation for evidence. Focusing on the dark side of Neverland, Dudgeon paints a portrait of Barrie as a predatory monster who wormed his way into the affections of Sylvia Llewelyn Davies so that he would have access to her boys. In the archive, I discovered that nothing could be further from the truth (and reviewers of Dudgeon's book have not disagreed with my own assessment).

To be sure, there were moments (I counted two in my many years of research devoted to Barrie's life and works) when I worried that Barrie's generosity was tainted by ulterior motives. If you read *The Little White Bird*, the ur–Peter Pan, you will feel queasy going through a description of a sleepover involving the narrator and a young neighbor boy named David. And Barrie's replacement of his own name, "Jimmy," for "Jenny" (the hired nanny's sister) as the person designated by Sylvia Llewelyn Davies in her will to raise the boys with Mary

Hodgson feels wrong, although Barrie was in fact given guardianship and Sylvia no doubt linked Jenny to Mary for the purposes of day-to-day childrearing activities. Members of the extended family supported Barrie's guardianship, not having themselves the time or means to raise five boys.

As I pondered these matters, I remembered a meditation from 1910 in Barrie's notebooks. As soon as someone dies, he wrote, their face becomes "inscrutable—an enigma," and they preserve their secret forever. "All have one, which nobody knows, good or bad." Barrie no doubt had his share of secrets, good and bad. But much of him is an open book, and in it, there is love, affection, generosity, and imagination, mixed in with—as he was the first to admit—a good dose of dour moodiness and Scottish reserve. A man who fell in love with "work" at a young age (seeing his salvation in it later in life) and who declared early on that literature was his game, he loved solitude more than most. Yet he embraced real-world responsibilities, giving up his game for a time when he adopted the five Llewelyn Davies boys.

At his death, Barrie was said to have amassed a fortune greater than that acquired by any other writer through his work. Yet his philanthropic activities, in his lifetime, were also remarkable. During World War I, he subsidized a hospital and shelter for French children. He engaged in fund-raising activities, writing plays and sketches for various causes or allowing his works to be

J. M. Barrie, 1905. (Beinecke Rare Book and Manuscript Library, Yale University)

performed gratis for servicemen and war-connected charities. He even drafted a statement proposing small-scale daily economies for helping fund the war effort. For much of Barrie's life, the royalties from *Peter Pan* did not add to his personal wealth but were assigned to support London's Hospital for Sick Children on Great Ormond Street. After his death, the author bequeathed all proceeds from the work to the hospital. His legacy to that institution and to children everywhere continues and seems to grow with each new generation.

St. James's Church in Paddington, London, has a set of stained glass panels, four of which represent themes linked to the church: transportation (the first Great Western Railway built Paddington Station), leisure (Lord Baden-Powell, founder of the Boy Scouts, was baptized in the church), art (the statue of Peter Pan in Kensington Gardens is located nearby), and science (the biologist Alexander Fleming lived and worked in the neighborhood). The windows were destroyed during the Blitz and rebuilt in the 1950s. (Courtesy of Great Ormond Street Hospital Children's Charity)

Introduction to
J. M. Barrie's *Peter Pan*

How do we explain Peter Pan's enduring hold on our imagination? Why do we get hooked (and I use the term with all due deliberation) when we are children and continue to remain under the spell as adults? J. M. Barrie once observed that Huck Finn was "the greatest boy in fiction," and Huck, who would rather go to hell than become civilized, may have inspired the rebellious streak found in Peter Pan.[1] Like Dorothy, who does not want to return to Kansas in *The Emerald City of Oz*, Huck and Peter have won us over with their love of adventure, their streaks of poetry, their wide-eyed and wise innocence, and their deep appreciation of what it means to be alive. They all refuse to grow up and tarnish their sense of wonder and openness to new experiences.

Few literary works capture more perfectly than *Peter Pan* a child's desire for mobility, lightness, and flight. And it is rare to find expressed so openly and clearly the desire to remain a child forever, free of adult gravity and responsibility. Where else but in Neverland are there endless possibilities for adventure? There is, to be sure, also trouble in paradise, but before looking at unsettling and disturbing moments on the island, it is worth taking a look at what makes

1. J. M. Barrie, in Mark Twain, *Who Was Sarah Findlay, with a Suggested Solution of the Mystery by J. M. Barrie* (London: Clement Shorter, 1917), 10.

our hearts beat faster when the curtain rises for the play *Peter Pan* or when we turn the pages of the novel *Peter and Wendy*.

FAIRY DUST, ETERNAL YOUTH, AND PLAY: THE ATTRACTIONS OF *PETER PAN*

We can begin with fairy dust and flight. What child has not imagined the pleasures of soaring through the air and feeling alive with kinetic energy? Flying allows you to leave behind the safety of that nest known as home and, suddenly, to be above it all (for a change). You can make your way to the sublime—to the deep mysteries of the azure sky or to the misty beauty of fluffy clouds. Flight has its perils, as the Greek myth about Icarus makes clear. After ignoring the instructions of his father, Daedalus, about the dangers of flying too close to the sun, his wings of feather and wax melt, and he plunges into the ocean. Still, few children would pass up the opportunity to leave behind the weighty matters of daily life to experience the vertiginous pleasures of taking wing. And does any child in a book ever refuse the offer to mount a winged creature or take to the air in some other way?

Airborne children did not abound in books until after Peter Pan flew into the Darling nursery. There were magical carpets in *The Thousand and One Nights* and in some folktales (Baba Yaga gives one to Ivan the Fool and Yelena the Fair), but children remained earthbound on the whole, preferring travel by land or by sea. Hans Christian Andersen, with his love of avian creatures (ducklings, swans, and sparrows), is an exception, for he understood the euphoric delights of flight, and his little Kai is lifted into the air when he rides in the carriage of the Snow Queen, in the fairy tale of that title. After *Peter Pan*, stories proliferate about children given the chance to fly: in The Chronicles of Narnia on the back of Aslan, in Selma Lagerlöf's *Wonderful Adventures of Nils* on a goose, in *The Wizard of Oz* in a house, in the Harry Potter books on broomsticks, and in Madeleine L'Engle's *A Swiftly Tilting Planet* on a winged unicorn. These youthful aeronauts would all endorse what E. B. White's Louis says in *The Trumpet of the Swan*: "I never knew flying could be such fun. This is great. This is sensational. This is superb. I feel exalted, and I'm not dizzy."[2]

Barrie lived in an era when flight had finally become possible for humans. Wilbur and Orville Wright had flown their first glider in the fall of 1900 at Kitty Hawk, and by 1901 they had already developed the capacity to fly a distance of 400 feet. They soon added power and doubled that distance, but skeptics on the other side of the Atlantic were certain that the two were bluffing. The European press remained unconvinced by reports from the brothers themselves and from eyewitnesses: "They are in fact either fliers or liars. It is difficult to fly. It's easy to say, 'We have flown.' "[3] In an age when airplanes had not yet moved out of the realm of fantasy and science fiction, the power to fly was all the more exquisitely thrilling.

Fairy dust is of paramount importance to children, but even it has trouble competing with the mirage of eternal youth that finds embodiment in Peter Pan. The *puer aeternus* (Latin for "eternal boy") found in Ovid's *Metamorphoses* was a child-god named Iacchus, identified at various times with Dionysus (god of wine and ecstasy) and with Eros (god of love and beauty). Connected with the mysteries of death and rebirth, he is the god who remains forever young. The Swiss psychiatrist Carl Gustav Jung connected the *puer aeternus* with the archetype of the *senex*, or old man. Without doubt we can find that very pairing of archetypes in *Peter Pan*, with Hook as something of a shadow to Peter Pan, just as the *senex* is the dark double of the *puer aeternus*. Peter's story walks a fine line between indulging the fantasy of eternal youth and menacing readers with the specter of death—both our first death when childhood is over, and our second death when life comes to an end. What it does supremely well is to construct one boy who, by incarnating the dream of eternal youth, connects us viscerally to the human condition of mortality.

Just what makes eternal youth so appealing? In *Tuck Everlasting*, inspired no doubt by the story of Peter Pan, Natalie Babbitt's Tuck makes it clear that living forever can be a curse: " 'I want to grow again . . . and change. And if that

2. E. B. White, *The Trumpet of the Swan* (New York: HarperCollins, 2000), 60.

3. *New York Herald,* February 10, 1906.

Frank Gillett's illustrations from the 1905–6 production of *Peter Pan*. (Beinecke Rare Book and Manuscript Library, Yale University)

means I got to move on at the end of it, then I want that, too.' "[4] J. M. Barrie would answer that question differently, and he would point to the attractions of games, play, and adventure—forever fun.

4. Natalie Babbitt, *Tuck Everlasting* (New York: Farrar, Straus and Giroux, 1988), 64.

The nineteenth century invented the adventure story for children. There is not just *Treasure Island, Coral Island,* and *Kidnapped,* but also *Alice's Adventures in Wonderland, The Adventures of Pinocchio*, and *The Adventures of Tom Sawyer*. In serial fashion, one episode after another in these works provides the repetitive delights of peril, conflict, and return to safety. In Neverland, we have the same unending cycle, with constant conflict among redskins, pirates, beasts, and lost boys. Neverland, like Wonderland, is both psychic space and social space, with external conflicts often mirroring or refracting psychological processes.

Barrie's phantasmagoric adventures are more distinctly theatrical than those in earlier volumes for children. At times, the different camps suspend hostilities and simply parade around the island, in a kind of ceremonial display of their costumes. "The lost boys were out looking for Peter, the pirates were out looking for the lost boys, the redskins were out looking for the pirates, and the beasts were out looking for the redskins. They were going round and round the island, but they did not meet because all were going at the same rate." The boys form a "gallant band," "gay and debonair," as they dance and whistle while circling the island. "Let us pretend to lie here among the sugar-cane and watch them as they steal by in single file," the narrator writes, and proceeds to enumerate for us the dramatis personae of the play (in the double sense of the term) that will unfold before us. *Peter and Wendy* is filled with such theatrical moments, and it creates a spectacle dominated by masquerade, mimicry, disguise, performance, role playing, and masks. Theater was Barrie's game, as much as fiction.

In the ceremonial march around the island, each lost boy, pirate, redskin, and beast engages in what the noted cultural historian Johan Huizinga famously described as the essence of play: "*making an image* of something different, something more beautiful, or more sublime, or more dangerous than what he usually *is*."[5] Using "imagination" in the root sense of the term, the characters create new identities in that secret, sacred space known as Neverland. There they inhabit a zone where play rules supreme. Cut off from ordinary reality, they possess a certain freedom yet are also subject to the tensions and rules found in all games and activities that we characterize as play. That kind of play, more than the cultural work of adults in the real world, can create a space of

5. Johan Huizinga, *Homo Ludens: A Study of the Play-Element in Culture* (Boston: Beacon Press, 1955), 14.

orderly form and aesthetic beauty. When we describe play, we often draw terms from an aesthetic register that seeks to capture the beauty of its movements: poise, harmony, concentration, focus, balance, tension, contrast, and resolution. Players fall under the spell of the game, and spectators are often enchanted or captivated by the performance.

Neverland is a theater for the imagination, providing the lost boys with an opportunity to have endless adventures and "ecstasies innumerable." It is a space of beauty and imagination, but it seems at first to be a site of disorder rather than aesthetic order. Here is its description as the Darling children approach it:

> Neverland is always more or less an island, with astonishing splashes of color here and there, and coral reefs, and rakish-looking craft in the offing, and savages and lonely lairs, and gnomes who are mostly tailors, and caves through which a river runs, and princes with six older brothers, and a hut fast going to decay, and one very small old lady with a hooked nose.

This first inventory gives us the mythical and mysterious in all its complicated splendors. In the heterogeneous enumeration of everyday objects that follows this passage, we begin to understand that Neverland is no utopia or garden of earthly delights—nor is it a dystopic domain of horror. Instead it forms a kind of heterotopia that mirrors the real world even as it stands apart from it, creating a new order:

> It would be an easy map if that were all; but there is also first day at school, religion, fathers, the round pond, needlework, murders, hangings, verbs that take the dative, chocolate pudding day, getting into braces, say ninety-nine, threepence for pulling out your tooth yourself, and so on; and either these are part of the island or they are another map showing through, and it is all rather confusing, especially as nothing will stand still.

Neverland is presented in all its glorious variety—liberated from the tyranny of adult efforts (like those of Mrs. Darling, who "puts things straight" every night in the minds of her three children) to produce order. It gives us a higher order in which what looks like clutter and messiness turns out to have real imaginative content. Here, everything is touched by the wand of poetry, transforming itself into something new in the context of Neverland. By suspending the "real" laws of existence and of any interest at all in use-value or profit, Neverland gives us a symbolic order of true beauty with the added enchantments of play.

Historians have argued forcefully that the harsh disciplinary culture surrounding childhood finally yielded, in the eighteenth century, to opportunities for play and entertainment. Games, toys, and books were especially designed for children, and harsh childrearing practices gave way to more permissive modes and to expressive affection. Yet Victorian and Edwardian England were also known for their cruel economic exploitation of children. Small and agile, children were sent into coal mines and factories, and, most visibly, operated as chimney sweeps. At age ten, Charles Dickens famously had to leave school and work at Warren's Black Warehouse, pasting labels onto bottles of shoe polish.

Children entered the labor force at a very young age and often worked over ten hours a day in wretched conditions. They roamed the streets of London as beggars, street urchins, and prostitutes. But if the reign of Queen Victoria witnessed the Industrial Revolution and the rise of urban poverty, it also ushered in a new commitment to education, with a dramatic increase in the number of children attending schools and with a stronger personal and social investment in them. What had once been the worst of times for children was gradually becoming, through legislative attention, a better time, particularly in the years after 1860, when Barrie was growing up in Kirriemuir, the son of a manual laborer.

With the benefit of a first-rate education provided by a father wholeheartedly committed to educating his children, J. M. Barrie never experienced the harsh social practices of everyday life. He bemoaned the loss of the pastoral in the new industrial landscape and wrote poignantly about how it had slipped away before his boyhood eyes. But childhood remained a sacred preserve for the delights of the world that he and his contemporaries had lost. Children—"gay and innocent and heartless," as we learn at the end of *Peter and Wendy*—become the last refuge of beauty, purity, and pleasure. "Trailing clouds of glory," as Wordsworth had put it, they are the source of our collective salvation.

PETER PAN: BETWIXT AND BETWEEN

Peter Pan creates a true contact zone for young and old. In fact it is his story, as staged in the play *Peter Pan* and as told in *Peter and Wendy*, that helped break down the long-standing barrier—in literary terms—between adult and child. *Alice's Adventures in Wonderland*, with its enigmatic characters, allusive density, playful language, and sparkling wit, had already gone far in that direction, uniting children and adults in the pleasures of the reading experience. Earlier children's books, seeking to teach and preach, had not been designed to draw adults in. Even John Newbery's landmark *A Little Pretty Pocket-Book* (1744), which recognized the importance of "sport" and "play" in children's books, was not written to delight adults. And parents may have read James Janeway's lugubrious *A Token for Children* (1671) with their children—it dominated the children's book market for decades—but the unnatural rhetoric in the effusive declarations of faith by children on their deathbeds very quickly wore thin, and it is hard to imagine repeated readings of that gloomy volume.

Fairy tales and adventure stories, which flourished in the nineteenth century, reoriented children's literature in the direction of delight rather than instruction, and both literary forms inspired the narrative sorcery of *Peter Pan*. Drawing readers into exotic regions and magical elsewheres, they promised excitement and revelation where there had once been instruction and edification. The expansive energy of *Peter and Wendy* is not easy to define, but it has something to do with the book's power to inspire faith in the aesthetic, cognitive, and emotional gains of imaginative play. As sensation seekers, children delight in the novel's playful possibilities and its exploration of what it means to be on your own. In Neverland, they move past a sense of giddy disorientation to explore how children cope when they are transplanted from the nursery into a world of conflict, desire, pathos, and horror. Adults may not be able to land on that island, but they have the chance to go back vicariously and to repair their own damaged sense of wonder.

Barrie's refusal to serve as adult authority (manifested in his unwillingness to recall ever writing the play and in his attribution of the work to other children and to a nursemaid) paradoxically reveals just how determined he was to break with tradition and to write a story that appeared to be by someone whose allegiances were to childhood. In a book on Peter Pan, Jacqueline Rose famously proclaimed the "impossibility" of children's literature, claiming that fiction "for" children constructs a world in which "the adult always comes first (author, maker, giver) and the child comes after (reader, product, receiver)."[6] Basing her observations chiefly on J. M. Barrie's *Peter and Wendy*, she concludes that authors of children's fiction use the child in the book to take in, dupe, and seduce the child outside the book. She is particularly incensed by the narrator of *Peter and Wendy,* who refuses to identify himself clearly as child or adult: "The narrator veers in and out of the story as servant, author and child."[7] Undermining the very idea of authority and authorship, Barrie dared to disturb the notion of a strict divide between adult and child.

To be sure, much of what Rose has to say rings true, and, when we read about J. M. Barrie entertaining children in Kensington Gardens with his St. Bernard named Porthos, we cannot help but have the sneaking suspicion that children's fiction may indeed be "something of a soliciting, a chase, or even a seduction."[8] But it is equally true that Barrie's addiction to youth—his infatuation with its games and pleasures—enabled him to write something that, for the first time, truly was *for* children even as it appealed to adult sensibilities. And beyond that, Barrie turned a category that was once "impossible" (for Rose there is nothing but adult agency in children's literature) into a genre that opened up possibilities, suggesting that adults and children could together inhabit a zone where all experience the pleasures of a story, even if in different ways. Old-fashioned yet also postmodern before his time, Barrie overturned hierarchies boldly and playfully, enabling adults and children to share the reading experience in ways that few writers before him had made possible.

We do not know exactly what books constituted leisure reading for children in Barrie's day, although we have many autobiographies with detailed accounts of encounters with books ranging from the *Arabian Nights* (Barrie was disappointed that those nights turned out to be a time of day) to Mary Martha Sherwood's *The History of the Fairchild Family*. They may have picked up one of the many English translations of the German *Struwwelpeter* (in which Pauline goes

6. Rose, *The Case of Peter Pan*, 1–2.

7. Ibid., 73.

8. Ibid., 2.

up in flames for playing with matches), encountered the dull pieties of books like *Goody Two-Shoes* (whose heroine always shows "good sense" and "good conscience"), or immersed themselves in Ballantyne's *Coral Island* (a favorite of Barrie's). What we do know is that, in the waning days of the Victorian era, adults took an unprecedented interest in reading to and writing for children. Robert Louis Stevenson developed the idea for *Treasure Island* when he created a map of the island with his stepson Lloyd Osbourne. Kenneth Grahame wrote parts of *The Wind in the Willows* in the form of letters to his son, Alastair. And, later, A. A. Milne immortalized his son, Christopher Robin, in *Winnie-the-Pooh*.

With the rise of compulsory education and a newfound interest in a literate citizenry, parents and writers were at long last taking the trouble to puzzle out what it would take to recruit children as eager, enthusiastic readers. Unsurprisingly, writers absorbed in childhood and devoted to children were the ones best able to fashion high-wattage stories that would enable children to sit still and listen or read.

Like Lewis Carroll, who developed and refined his storytelling skills by conarrating (telling stories *with* children rather than *to* them), Barrie did not just sit at his desk and compose adventures. He spent time with young boys—above all, the five he adopted—playing cricket, fishing, staging pirate games, and, most important, improvising tales. Here is a description of the collaborative process from *The Little White Bird*, with the narrator describing how he and David coauthor stories:

> I ought to mention here that the following is our way with a story: First, I tell it to him, and then he tells it to me, the understanding being that it is quite a different story; and then I retell it with his additions, and so we go on until no one could say whether it is more his story or mine. In this story of Peter Pan, for instance, the bald narrative and most of the moral reflections are mine, though not all, for this boy can be a stern moralist, but the interesting bits about the ways and customs of babies in the bird-stage are mostly reminiscences of David's, recalled by pressing his hands to his temples and thinking hard.[9]

9. J. M. Barrie, *The Little White Bird, or Adventures in Kensington Gardens* (New York: Charles Scribner's Sons, 1902), 159.

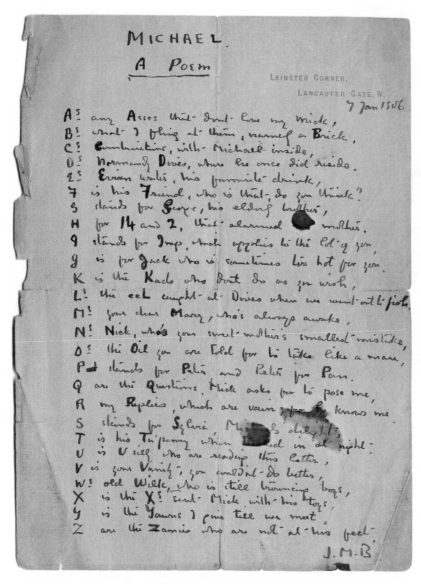

J. M. Barrie's 1906 acrostic alphabet poem for Michael Llewelyn Davies. (Beinecke Rare Book and Manuscript Library, Yale University)

In an interview, Barrie put a slightly different spin on the writing of *Peter Pan*, explaining his role as storyteller to the boys as well as their way of accepting the deeds described as the gospel truth:

It's funny . . . that the real Peter Pan—I called him that—is off to the war now. He grew tired of the stories I told him, and his younger brother became

J. M. Barrie with Michael Llewelyn Davies, circa 1912. (Beinecke Rare Book and Manuscript Library, Yale University)

interested. It was such fun telling those two about themselves. I would say: "Then you came along and killed the pirate" and they would accept every word as the truth. That's how *Peter Pan* came to be written. It is made up of only a few stories I told them.[10]

Perhaps, then, the fantasy of collaborative storytelling is a fiction, yet Barrie, more than any other author of children's books, attempted to level distinctions between adult and child, as well as to dismantle the opposition between creator and consumer (the hierarchical relationship that Jacqueline Rose finds so troubling in children's literature). He aimed to produce a story that would be sophisticated and playful, adult-friendly as well as child-friendly. At long last, here was a cultural story that would bridge the still vast literary divide between adults and children. Like *Alice's Adventures in Wonderland*, *Peter and Wendy* could be a shared literary experience, drawing two audiences together that had long been segregated into separate domains.

"If you believe," Peter shouts, "clap your hands; don't let Tink die." In urging suspension of disbelief, Peter not only exhorts readers young and old to have faith in fairies (and fiction) but also urges them to join hands as they enter a story world in a visceral, almost kinetic manner. Whether entering Neverland for the first time or returning to it, we clap for Tink and, before long, begin to breathe the very air of the island as we read the words describing it.

When Dorothy Ann Blank, an assistant in the story department at Walt Disney Studios, was asked in 1938 to review and report on the source material for the planned cinematic adaptation of *Peter Pan*, she was surprised to find that the book was less transparent and straightforward than she had imagined. "I am trying to formulate a straight, simple story line," she complained, "but

10. Birkin, *J. M. Barrie and the Lost Boys*, 225.

it's all over the place right now." The plot of *Peter Pan in Kensington Gardens* was a real challenge for her to summarize, and even *Peter and Wendy* had a plotline that was irritatingly difficult to capture. "It's a swell story," Blank observed, "but Mr. Barrie has scattered it around and made it as confusing as possible."[11]

Why this sense of disorientation? It is not just the terrors and enchantments of Neverland that create vertiginous moments. J. M. Barrie's narrator—with his frequent direct address of the reader (for example, "If you ask your mother")—may create a sense of cozy intimacy, but he is also forever flirting with readers without revealing an identity of his own. Shifting rapidly and with ease from the register of an adult narrator to that of a child, he seems sometimes to be a grown-up ("We too have been there [Neverland]; we can still hear the sound of the surf, though we shall land no more") and sometimes a child ("Which of these adventures shall we choose? The best way will be to toss for it").

Barrie's narrator uses sophisticated adult diction, but he is also playful, capricious, and partisan in ways that third-person narrators rarely are. In place of omniscience, we have only partial knowledge. "Now I understand what had hitherto puzzled me," he reports at one point, as if he were writing and experiencing at the same time. "Some like Peter best and some like Wendy best, but I like [Mrs. Darling] best," he declares elsewhere, only to denounce his favorite later as someone he positively detests. What are we to make of someone who is as fickle as the character about whom he writes? Is the strategy there to remind us about the degree to which the narrator wants to be the boy who will not grow up? In many ways, J. M. Barrie was forever straddling lines—betwixt and between in real life and as a narrator in his fictions.

THE MYTH OF PETER PAN

With Peter Pan, the boy who would not grow up, J. M. Barrie drew on both life and literature to do something massive and mysterious. He invented a new myth, one set in his own time and place—London at the turn of the twenti-

---

11. Donald Crafton, "The Last Night in the Nursery: Walt Disney's *Peter Pan*," *The Velvet Light Trap* 24 (1989): 33–52.

J. M. Barrie. (Beinecke Rare Book and Manuscript Library, Yale University)

eth century—yet also situated in another world, the made-up island of Never-land. Barrie borrowed much from literary forebears, creating a story that is not so much original as syncretic, uniting disparate, often contradictory bits and pieces from his own experience and from the foundational stories of Western culture. Philip Pullman, author of the trilogy His Dark Materials, was asked once what sort of daemon he would choose for himself (in his universe every human has an animal soulmate). His reply: "a magpie or a jackdaw . . . one of those birds that steals bright things."[12] It was Barrie's genius to use that same skill, what the anthropologists call *bricolage*, making resourceful use of materi-als close at hand to construct a new myth.

Few were as close at hand as the young Peter Llewelyn Davies, and it is not much of a stretch to imagine that Peter Pan was inspired by the middle of the five sons of Arthur and Sylvia Davies, the boys Barrie adopted after both

12. Millicent Lenz and Carole Scott, eds., *His Dark Materials Illuminated: Critical Essays on Philip Pullman's Trilogy* (Detroit: Wayne State University Press, 2005), 71.

parents succumbed to cancer, Arthur in 1907, Sylvia in 1910. (The boys were born in 1893, 1894, 1897, 1900, and 1903.) After all, Peter was just a baby when the aspiring playwright began telling his older brothers, George and Jack, about an infant who escapes from his mother to dwell in Kensington Gardens. Barrie had once jotted down notes for a "Fairy Play," about an ordinary boy who is taken in by the fairies: "Hero might be a poor boy of today with ordinary clothes—unhappy, &c, in Act I—taken into Fairydom still in everyday clothes which are

Peter, George, and Jack Llewelyn Davies. (Beinecke Rare Book and Manuscript Library, Yale University)

strange contrast to clothes worn by the people of fairydom—(a la Hans Xian [*sic*] Andersen)."[13] Part baby and part bird (all children were born as birds, according to Barrie), Peter Davies morphed into a boy named Peter Pan, who uses the power of flight to escape the nursery and live a carefree life with birds and fairies in Kensington Gardens.

But Peter Pan is also obviously far more than Peter Llewelyn Davies and the boy in Kensington Gardens. The name is a curious mix of Christian and pagan associations. The biblical Simon Peter is known as the apostle most passionate about his faith, and his story resonates with the conflict between faith and reason in *Peter Pan*. In Matthew 16, Jesus renames Simon and calls him Peter: founder of the church: "You are Peter, the Rock; and on this rock I will build my church, and the powers of death shall never conquer it. I will give you the keys of the Kingdom of Heaven." Still, it is Peter who denies his relationship to Jesus three times "before the cock crows," and he thereby becomes a figure who is both solidly faithful yet also lacking in faith. Barrie could not have found a better way to capture Peter Pan's loyalty to Neverland, on the one hand, and his capricious, volatile nature, on the other.

13. Beinecke Library, MS Vault BARRIE, A3.

One of many notebooks kept by Barrie to jot down everything from literary ideas to addresses. This entry contains the germ of the idea for *Peter Pan*, which was first called *Fairy*. (Beinecke Rare Book and Manuscript Library, Yale University)

If the name Peter initially provides a rock-solid foundation for J. M. Barrie's character, whose Christian name is indeed Christian, the biblical associations are immediately tempered by the pagan "Pan." Peter Pan has a rich mythological ancestry, with a deep kinship to figures ranging from Pan, Hermes, and Dionysus to Icarus, Narcissus, and Adonis. Like the mythical god Pan, whose name derives from the Greek word for "all," Peter Pan is a creature of nature, associated with pastoral delights. The god, half-goat and half-human, can be benign and destructive, delightful and terrifying. Pan is, tellingly, the son of Hermes, the trickster and thief renowned for his golden, winged feet and for his mercurial nature. He belongs also to the retinue of Dionysus, with his "ecstasies innumerable," and the terror he creates links him with that god as well. He is also the Greek god revived in the golden age of children's literature—by Rudyard Kipling in *Puck of Pook's Hill*, by Robert Louis Stevenson in "Pan's Pipes," and by Kenneth Grahame in *The Wind in the Willows*. The child who will not grow up comes to be endowed with all the pagan energy of the sylvan deity.[14]

Barrie toned down the pagan elements in the dense complexities of Peter Pan's mythological ancestry. In early productions of Barrie's play, Peter Pan evidently appeared onstage not only playing his pipes but also riding a goat. These undisguised references to "the chthonic, often lascivious and far from childlike goat-god" were soon removed from the play and did not find their way into the novel.[15]

14. Jean Perrot, "Pan and *Puer Aeternus*: Aestheticism and the Spirit of the Age," *Poetics Today* 13 (1992): 35.

15. Ann Yeoman, *Now or Neverland: Peter Pan and the Myth of Eternal Youth. A Psychological Perspective on a Cultural Icon* (Toronto: Inner City Books, 1999), 15.

Michael Llewelyn Davies in a Peter Pan costume. (Beinecke Rare Book and Manuscript Library, Yale University)

Barrie's Pan is not at all like the great god Pan, represented by Kenneth Grahame in *The Wind in the Willows* as the mysterious Piper at the Gates of Dawn. An appealingly mischievous and charmingly elusive boy, he has his own cult following but does not inspire anything close to the awe and dread felt by Mole and Rat when they row up the river in search of Otter's son Portly and answer the great god Pan's "imperious summons."

When Hook demands to know who Peter Pan is, the boy answers quickly: "I'm youth, I'm joy . . . I'm a little bird that has broken out of the egg." Mobile and nomadic, Peter Pan is truly all things—all things to everyone. And yet he is also, as the stage directions indicate, never "touched" by anyone else. In short, he is self-contained and so determined to resist connection that he comes to embody what the narrator describes as "heartlessness," a trait he shares with all children. He is not simply Pan but also Adonis and Narcissus—all those mythic figures, renowned for their beauty, who refuse to grow up, mature, and develop emotional attachments. And, as importantly, he is, precisely because he remains eternally young, a grim reminder that the rest of us must all grow up and one day die.

MORTAL COMBAT AND CHILD'S PLAY

Few critics have resisted the temptation to read the battle between Pan and Hook in Freudian terms, as a dramatic oedipal conflict, particularly since Hook (the evil father) and Mr. Darling (the benevolent father) are generally played by the same actor. They point out that the children fly to Neverland, encounter their father in symbolic form, and conspire with Peter Pan to kill him by proxy. There is, to be sure, real conflict between adults and children on Neverland, but, in all the battles, everyone, including the captain and the pirates, acts like a child. What seems far more significant than the overt rivalry between Hook and Pan or the children's possible covert resentment of their father is Hook's fear of death and Peter's immunity to that fear—for him everything becomes "an awfully big adventure." Hook is the only character in the work with a "dread" of crocodiles, and, when Smee predicts that the clock in the crocodile will one day run down, Hook replies, "that's the fear that haunts me." For Hook, death becomes alarmingly real in ways that it cannot be for those who have not yet grown up or for the boy who will never grow up.

When we were young, we could read Barrie's play and novel with a sense of breathless anticipation: "Which of these adventures shall we choose?" With confidence in the power to navigate and conquer the world of the book, we could cheerfully accept the occasional disturbances that unsettle the playfulness of the narrative—the ticking clock, the arrow that hits Wendy, the cavalier slaying of pirates, Tink's brush with death, and Wendy's flirtatiousness. The critic Timothy Morris, for example, recalls that when he watched *Peter Pan* as a preschooler, "I didn't get the sexuality that the play exudes. I was blissfully innocent about the images that shock me today. . . . Wendy in her nightgown, falling to earth pierced between the breasts with a gigantic rubber-tipped arrow."[16] As adults, we are more likely to feel a twinge of sorrow when we learn that the narrator can still hear the sound of Neverland's shores yet knows that he "shall land no more." Who will fail to think of Poe's raven, and the mournfully relentless *memento mori* captured by the word "Nevermore"?

Peter and Wendy is encoded with many adult matters, but children find them easy to ignore in their eagerness to follow the adventures of the Darling children. The adult content creates only minor disturbances in a rousing story about fairy dust, pirates, canine nursemaids, and mermaids. Adult readers, by contrast, are more likely to see the skulls littering the text, the many brushes with death and the constant reminder that, when children grow up, they are "done for."

J. M. Barrie, 1911. (Beinecke Rare Book and Manuscript Library, Yale University)

In the standoff between Hook and Peter, we have a form of mortal combat that divides adult and child, but in a manner both playful and parodic. A spirit of competition animates the two antagonists, who strut, preen, brag, show off, and parade before each other in a contest for respect. Hook and Peter are not competing for land, power, arms, or goods. Rather, they are both invested in commanding the respect of those on the island and winning games or competitions rather than military maneuvers. In their highly stylized encounters, they are enacting the rituals of boyhood—setting up dares, challenging each other, and undertaking adventures. These are akin to many of the rituals of tribal societies in which the dare and the challenge transcend all else. To the end, Hook remains a worthy opponent, focused on good form and "not wholly unheroic." Hook has one last "triumph" in making Peter resort to "bad form," then he surrenders to the crocodile and "perishes." Even Peter cries in his sleep that night.

16. Timothy Morris, *You're Only Young Twice: Children's Literature and Film* (Urbana and Chicago: University of Illinois Press, 2000), 114.

Child readers may also be moved to tears, but they are unlikely to begin speculating about why Peter sheds tears, for they will be distracted by Hook's missing hand, the swords flashing in battle, the leap into the waters, and the crocodile's open jaws. Adult readers, by contrast, will speculate at a deeper level about Peter's crying. Is it caused by the loss of a worthy opponent? Is there some small recognition that Peter is defeating a man who was also capable of feeling affection for him? Does Peter mourn human vulnerability and mortality? A remark about tears that feels trivial to children, often escaping their attention, becomes, in its stunning economy, a philosophical and psychological conundrum for the adult reader. It was Barrie's genius to encode the story in this double fashion without drawing attention to the effort to reach both child and adult.

PETER PAN ONSTAGE

Peter Pan's mutability becomes evident in the many adaptations, appropriations, prequels, sequels, and spin-offs of J. M. Barrie's work. A creature who embraces miming, improvisation, and role playing, Peter Pan belongs in the theater, for it is there that he inhabits the domain of play and performance, all the while retaining his manic energy, darting in and out, changing from season to season, never contained or fully defined by mere words on a page.

When Mark Twain attended a New York performance of *Peter Pan* in 1905, with Maude Adams playing the lead role, he was so deeply enamored of the play that he wrote in the *Boston Globe*: "It is my belief that *Peter Pan* is a great and refining and uplifting benediction to this sordid and money-mad age; and that the next best play on the boards is a long way behind it as long as you play Peter."[17] With an impressive string of theatrical successes behind him, most recently and famously *The Admirable Crichton*, Barrie began writing the first lines of the play on November 23, 1903. The original manuscript, now housed at Indiana University in Bloomington, was entitled *Anon. A Play*. It was

---

17. Mark Twain, *Boston Globe,* October 9, 1906. Twain met Barrie on several occasions and was frustrated by the fact that their conversations were always interrupted: "I have never had five minutes' talk with him that wasn't broken up by an interruption," he complained.

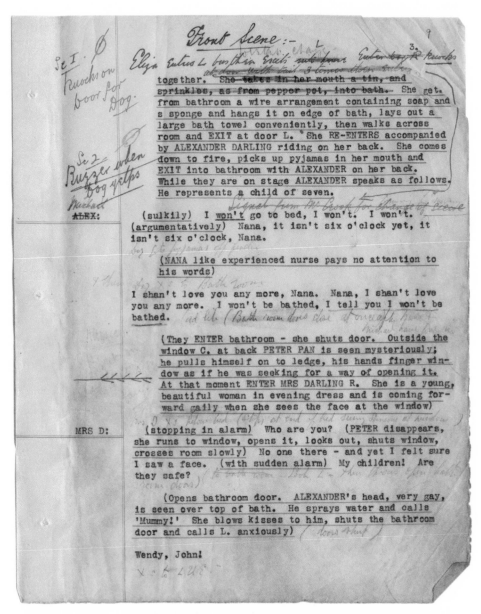

Typescript for the first scene of the 1904 *Peter Pan*. (Beinecke Rare Book and Manuscript Library, Yale University)

Nina Boucicault as Peter Pan. (Beinecke Rare Book and Manuscript Library, Yale University)

renamed *The Great White Father*, until Charles Frohman (known as the Napoleon of the theater world) took a look and urged Barrie to finish the play but with a new title. Frohman had great confidence in everything Barrie wrote—more confidence than Barrie himself had. "It will not be a commercial success," Barrie had written when Frohman first asked about his latest work. "But it is a dream-child of mine."[18] Barrie was so eager to see the play onstage that he offered Frohman a second work, *Alice-Sit-by-the-Fire*, to compensate for any losses incurred on *Peter Pan*. (*Alice-Sit-by-the-Fire* ran for only 115 performances before it was shut down.)

Frohman was enchanted by *Peter Pan* and not at all daunted by the challenges of staging a fantasy that required a cast of fifty playing everything from pirates and fairies to mermaids and ostriches. He could not resist describing the scenes from the play to his friends, and acted them out on the street. Frohman saw, far more clearly than did Barrie, the appeal of a play that allowed children to fly, brought wolves and crocodiles onstage, and had a father exchange places with his dog in the kennel. Barrie had the good fortune of working with famed director Dion Boucicault Jr. at the Duke of York's Theatre. The theater, with its seating capacity of nine hundred, was the ideal size for the production, with a stage large enough to accommodate the planned special effects but not so cavernous as to destroy all sense of magical intimacy. The actors and actresses had not been perfectly prepared for what was to come. "Rehearsal—10:30 for Flying" was the notice that an astonished actress playing Wendy received, only to learn that she had to have her life insured in case of an accident.

Flying was so important a part of the stage fantasy for Barrie that he hired George Kirby of the Flying Ballet Company to improve the harnesses that were used in his dance productions by making them less visible and less unwieldy.

18. Roger Lancelyn Green, *Fifty Years of Peter Pan* (London: Peter Davies, 1954), 70.

Satin program for the 1904 production of *Peter Pan* at the Duke of York's Theatre. (Beinecke Rare Book and Manuscript Library, Yale University)

Kirby created a completely new mechanism to be used by Peter and the Darling children, but it required special training, and cast members spent two weeks of precious rehearsal time mastering the art of taking off and landing. Stagehands began to protest the burden of trying to manage all of the mechanical gear, and a depressed man in overalls, as Barrie described him, kept popping up to announce, "The gallery boys won't stand it!" Barrie had rewritten the ending five times, and he was still making cuts and revisions just days before the play was to open.

Peter Pan, or The Boy Who Wouldn't Grow Up. A Play in Three Acts by J. M. Barrie made its theatrical debut on Tuesday, December 27, 1904. The production was shrouded in mystery, with actors and actresses sworn to secrecy. Newspapers made wild statements about what was to be onstage, including the claim (Barrie was their source) that one scene would show the birth of a fairy. The play was scheduled to open on December 22, 1904, but the challenges of staging led to a four-day delay—on the night before the show was to open, a mechanical lift collapsed, taking much of the scenery with it. No one felt ready for opening night (least of all Barrie, who spent most of Christmas Day rewriting the ending once again), and there was considerable anxiety among cast members that the play would not survive the season. But not long after the curtain went up, once the audience had been transported into the Darling nursery to witness the children's nighttime rituals, the spell was cast. The orchestra did not even have to lead the clapping to save Tink's life, as they had been prompted. Audience members—and most were adults, not children—burst into spontaneous applause as soon as Peter asked: "Do you believe in fairies?"

Critics felt the power surges in the theater. "*Peter Pan* is not so much a play as a spree," the *Morning Post* declared. And the *Daily Telegraph* described it as a play of "such originality, of such tenderness, and of such daring, that not even a shadow of doubt regarding its complete success was to be discerned in the final fall of the curtain. . . . It is so true, so natural, so touching."[19] And in *The Saturday Review*, the popular essayist Max Beerbohm revealed that he understood the real wizardry at work onstage: "Mr. Barrie is not that rare creature, a man of genius. He is something even more rare—a child who, by some divine grace, can express through an artistic medium the childishness that is in him."[20] George Bernard Shaw, the other leading playwright of the era, was less generous in his praise, calling *Peter Pan* "holiday entertainment for children but really a play for grown-up people."[21] In private, he called the

19. Janet Dunbar, *J. M. Barrie: The Man Behind the Image* (Newton Abbot, Devon: Readers Union, 1971), 142.

20. Ibid., 88.

21. Bernard Shaw, *Collected Letters, 1898–1910,* edited by Dan H. Laurence (London: M. Reinhardt, 1965), II, 907.

Four portraits of famous actresses who played Peter Pan: Maude Adams, Pauline Chase, Nina Boucicault, Cecilia Loftus. (Beinecke Rare Book and Manuscript Library, Yale University)

play an "artificial freak" that was being foisted on children. *Androcles and the Lion*, his answer to *Peter Pan*, ran for a mere eight weeks and is rarely revived on the stage. By contrast, in its first fifty years, *Peter Pan* has been performed thousands of times in England and revived every year but two—and then only because of the war.

Barrie's timing was perfect. Queen Victoria's patronage of the theater in the

Jean Arthur and Boris Karloff make an unlikely pairing for a Broadway version of *Peter Pan*, with incidental music by Leonard Bernstein. (By permission of Photofest)

1840s and 1850s, along with the efforts of theater owners to attract middle-class and upper-middle-class audiences, led to the transformation of London theatrical culture. With improved transportation systems in and around London, theater owners could run the same play for weeks, months, and even years on end, rather than constantly changing the fare to fill theater seats. On the West End playbills, J. M. Barrie, George Bernard Shaw, Oscar Wilde, and Henrik Ibsen were lifting the tone by supplanting prolific hacks such as Dion Boucicault Sr. (father of the stage manager for the 1904 *Peter Pan*), Tom Taylor, and H. J. Byron, who had dominated the Victorian stage with their melodramas and burlesques.

Over a century after his debut onstage, Peter Pan has attained iconic power in the world of children's literature. He even has a psychological medical syndrome named after him. *Webster's New World Medical Dictionary* now accepts the term Peter Pan Syndrome, coined by Dan Kiley in his 1983 book of that title to describe men who have "never grown up." More important, Peter Pan lives on at a variety of institutional and cultural sites. He is, understandably, the patron saint of Great Ormond Street Hospital, and the main attraction in Kensington Gardens. He once cast a spell on Robert Baden-Powell, founder of the Boy Scouts, who went to see the play on consecutive nights. He has had a starring role in films—silent and sound, animated and live-action.

Yet he also risks, through a process of cultural entropy, becoming a cartoon version of himself as his story is adapted, appropriated, and recycled. Each new version of *Peter Pan* seems to lose some of the luster of the original, especially when it migrates into commercial advertisements, comic books, and Disney sequels. Fortunately, we can still go back, and this book offers an opportunity to return to the original Neverland—the first one invented—the one that appears in J. M. Barrie's stories about Peter Pan. This is not to say that we should not keep reinventing Peter Pan—a figure who has gathered the storybook power of a Cinderella, Alice in Wonderland, or Winnie-the-Pooh. But copies are rarely as sharp, clear, and captivating as the original, and Barrie's Peter Pan gives us something that no one after him managed to capture fully.

At the end of his autobiographical poem *The Prelude*, William Wordsworth wrote: "What we have loved, / others will love, and we will teach them how." This volume is dedicated to that proposition, to the belief that stories like Barrie's can continue to work their magic and that we do not break the spell by knowing more about Peter Pan and his creator. *Peter and Wendy* serves as the perfect springboard for looking at the many different versions of Peter

Hayley Mills plays Peter Pan on the London stage in 1969. (By permission of Photofest)

At the London Palladium in 1936, Elsa Lanchester played Peter Pan, and her husband, Charles Laughton, took the role of Hook. (By permission of Photofest)

Pan's story that came to be written down in the course of Barrie's lifetime—from the *Boy Castaways of Black Lake Island* to the first filmscript for Peter Pan. Its presentation here serves also as an opportunity for meditations on many other matters: J. M. Barrie's own life story, the fortunes of the play *Peter Pan*, the illustrations created for stories about Peter Pan, and the impact of the boy who would not grow up on the lives not just of luminaries and literati but also of ordinary people. In *Peter and Wendy,* full chords are sounded on every page, and they resonate powerfully with Barrie's life, art, and cultural legacy.

ENTERING PARADISE THROUGH THE BACK DOOR

In a moving memoir about her encounters with C. S. Lewis's Chronicles of Narnia, the cultural critic Laura Miller tells us about her passionate devotion to reading as a child. As an adult, she found herself disappointed in some respects when she tried to go back, disillusioned by the many ideological wrong turns in books she had loved as a child. Yet she did not simply dismiss those stories and condemn them as outdated and obsolete. Instead she found a way to renew her love and appreciation of her childhood reading. "What if I decided to know even more, to learn more, about how the Chronicles came to be written and all the various ways they have been and can be read? Then I might arrive 'somewhere at the back' and find a door open. Not the original one, not the wardrobe itself, but another kind of door, perhaps, with a different version of paradise on the other side."[22] We would do well to approach *Peter Pan* with the same irreverent devotion, digging further in and deeper down to get at the true spirit of J. M. Barrie's book through an understanding of its genesis, cultural context, and effects.

22. Laura Miller, *The Magician's Book: A Skeptic's Adventures in Narnia* (Boston: Little, Brown, 2008), 175.

Like C. S. Lewis, J. M. Barrie was a child of the British Empire, though Lewis's real allegiances were to his Irish ancestry, while Barrie's were to his native Scotland. Neither was ever able to cut loose from the ideologies and biases of his day. Much as some critics have sought to prove that Barrie undoes racial stereotyping by overdoing his depiction of redskins and Piccaninnies, many adults will find themselves resorting to editing when reading the story to children. As adults, we may be clever enough to recognize that some of the excesses are part of a broader satirical strategy, but we will surely find ourselves wondering what children will make of the "wiliness" of the "redskin race" or the strange language of the Piccaninnies.

Toni Morrison has suggested that what we perceive as racial stereotyping may be nothing of the kind to a child's eyes. She tells us that Helen Bannerman's *Story of Little Black Sambo* was her favorite book as a child: "Little Black Sambo was a child as deeply loved and pampered by his parents as ever lived. Mumbo. Jumbo. Sambo. They were beautiful names—the kind you could whisper to a leaf or shout in the cellar and feel as though you had let something important fly from your mouth."[23] Nonetheless, once you read, say, Jean de Brunhoff's *The Story of Babar* with postcolonial eyes and observe how the Old Lady embarks on a European civilizing mission when it comes to African elephants (turning Babar into an educated elephant who introduces Western civilization to the natives he left behind), it can become challenging to claim that children's stories are all culturally innocent. It is precisely for that reason that we need the stories behind the story.

Do we want to lose Peter Pan? Should he fly off into oblivion? Should we invent a new character and story that conform more closely to the cultural values we embrace? Peter Pan's call to "Come away! Come away!" remains powerful and is unlikely to be silenced soon. His story remains a source of beauty and enchantment as well as terror and fright, taking hold in ways that are beyond our control. And so we continue to read it and to pass it on to the next generation, often without coming to terms with its content. Yet we also no longer read *Peter Pan* with innocent eyes, and part of growing up, for us as for our children, means historicizing and coming to terms with aspects of the text that grate on our own sensibilities. We owe it to our children to give them books

23. Jim Haskins, *Toni Morrison* (Springfield, MO: 21st Century, 2002), 24.

that do not put a politically correct dot on every "i" and that offer challenges, provocations, and an occasional sting that keeps us alive and thinking about those who lived before us. And they too will learn to search and explore, as did Laura Miller when she grew up.

As part of a precious cultural heritage, *Peter Pan* belongs to a special class of books designated as the canon of bedtime reading. Plunging us into the nighttime rituals of the Darling nursery, it takes the children to a land whose inhabitants—everyone from the lost boys to the pirates—crave stories. It is itself the consummate bedtime story, a tale that emerged at a time when parents in England needed potent substitutes for the soothing syrups (often containing narcotics) that they had used for some time to quiet children down at nighttime. *Peter Pan* may not have put children to sleep, but it did wake parents up to the idea of reading with their children, providing entertainment and comfort at a time when everything becomes "deathly still" and when children's thoughts can take an anxious turn. It has retained its bonding power even a century after its publication.

The Annotated Peter Pan is, as Barrie would have meant it to be, for both adults and children. It offers an opportunity to create a place where the child can be swept away by the story and where the adult can meditate on it, getting lost in a "good read" yet also pondering the genesis of J. M. Barrie's story, its architecture, its cultural codes and meaning, and its fortunes over time. Read it without the annotations, if you prefer, and savor the text and the illustrations. The commentary is there for those driven by the same addictive curiosity about pirates and lagoons, plays and parties of cricket, or Porthos and the Llewelyn Davies boys that led me to spend several years of my life with J. M. Barrie and his literary creation.

Barrie was not a philosopher, but he seems to have understood better than any writer the wisdom of Jean-Jacques Rousseau on childhood and its games. Like the philosopher, Barrie endorsed play and freedom from constraint. More important, both the French philosopher and the Scottish playwright understood the role of attentive affection in interactions with children. Rousseau, over two centuries ago, dispensed advice that may seem obvious to us but that rankled his contemporaries. "How people will cry out against me!" he grumbled. What he proposed will not sound revolutionary to our ears: "Love childhood, indulge its sports, its pleasures, its delightful instincts."[24] Barrie became the champion of Rousseau's philosophy, and he created, miraculously, a story that indulged the child's love of play yet also captured our adult tragic awareness of mortality and the fleeting nature of childhood pleasures.

Mia Farrow points the way to Neverland as she flies past Big Ben in a 1976 television production of *Peter Pan*. (By permission of NBC, Photofest)

24. Jean-Jacques Rousseau, *Emile: Or, On Education* (New York: Basic Books, 1979), 51.

J. M. Barrie in Neverland:
A Biographical Essay

Through *Peter Pan*, James Matthew Barrie will forever be linked with youth, joy, and the pleasures of childhood. The Scottish writer, born on May 9, 1860, in the village of Kirriemuir, had a boyish quality to him even in middle age. His delicate features, short stature, and lifelong habit of wearing an overcoat several sizes too large made him appear even younger than he was. On walks with his St. Bernard, Porthos, in Kensington Gardens, Barrie socialized with children more than with adults, stopping to perform tricks and tell stories, all the while endearing himself to everyone by wiggling his ears and raising one eyebrow while lowering the other. It was through Porthos that he met the boys who stood model for Peter Pan.

A man in a bulky overcoat, a large dog, small children, a public park—that combination is fraught with dark overtones, and our cultural associations with J. M. Barrie and Peter Pan are not, by any means, all positive. We do not have to look long and hard to come up with disturbances in the frequencies of the Peter Pan airwaves. There is Michael Jackson's Neverland Valley Ranch, pop psychologist Dan Kiley's *Peter Pan Syndrome*, and Jacqueline Rose's *The Case of Peter Pan, or The Impossibility of Children's Fiction*, each in its own way pointing to trouble in Neverland. All the more reason to look closely at the man who created the character of Peter Pan in an effort to understand the cultural stakes in his work and to identify the extent to which his own fears and

J. M. Barrie and Luath, 1904. William Nicholson took this photograph of Barrie with Luath in the garden of the Leinster Corner residence. Nana's costume for the first production of *Peter Pan* was modeled on Luath's coat. (Beinecke Rare Book and Manuscript Library, Yale University)

desires permeate a story about childhood innocence and adventure.[1]

Barrie's many acts of kindness and generosity—he often used the great wealth acquired from his success as a novelist and playwright to benefit those around him—suggest a man deeply committed to family, friendship, and community. Yet time and again his intimates describe him as "morose," "reticent," "withdrawn," and "gloomy." He would, from time to time, simply shut down, and a note to A. E. Housman, after an awkward encounter, speaks volumes: "I am sorry about last night when I sat next to you and did not say a word. You must have thought I was a very rude man: I am really a very shy man."[2] (Housman wrote back the exact same words with a curt postscript stating that Barrie had only made things worse by misspelling his last name.) Barrie himself acknowledged a dark, depressive side and worried that the "reserve" he had inherited from his mother closed him off from the world. Blaming his national heritage, he declared that, like the Scots in general, he was "a house with all the shutters closed and the doors locked."[3] And much as he tried to open those shutters from time to time and prop the door open, "they

1. Allison B. Kavey discusses some of the negative associations in her introduction ("From Peanut Butter Jars to the Silver Screen") to *Second Star to the Right: Peter Pan in the Popular Imagination* (New Brunswick, NJ: Rutgers University Press, 2009), 1–12.

2. Graham Chainey, *A Literary History of Cambridge*, 2nd ed. (Cambridge, MA: Cambridge University Press, 1995), 225.

3. J.M. Barrie, *Margaret Ogilvy, by Her Son, J. M. Barrie* (New York: Charles Scribner's Sons, 1923), 156.

The Allahakbarries cricket team in 1905 at Black Lake Island. Members included (back row) Maurice Hewlett, J. M. Barrie, Henry Graham, E. V. Lucas; (front row) H. J. Ford, A. E. W. Mason, Charles Tennyson, and Charles Turley Smith. (Courtesy of Great Ormond Street Hospital Children's Charity)

will bang to," he worried. By turns confessional and effusive (as in *Margaret Ogilvy, by Her Son, J. M. Barrie*, the biography he wrote of his mother), and both dour and withdrawn (as in his marriage), he remains an enigma even with the wealth of information we have about his family, his literary life, and his social activities.

James Barrie's childhood was haunted by the knowledge that, like every child, he would one day grow up. "The horror of my boyhood," he wrote, "was that I knew a time would come when I also must give up the games, and how it was to be done I saw not . . . I felt that I must continue playing in secret."[4] Barrie's descriptions of childhood games—playing cricket, staging shipwrecks, building fortresses—are full of light and joy, suggesting an intensity of sensation absent from most childhood recollections. All his life he characterized himself as a "man's man." With Arthur Conan Doyle, A. A.

4. Ibid., 30.

Milne, and other writers, he found one way to resurrect the intoxicating energy of childhood sports. Barrie organized a team that came to be known as the Allahakbarries (a friend returning from travels in Morocco told the team that "Allah Akbar" was the Arabic term for "God help us," and the suffix gave the term a relevant twist). But it was through the Llewelyn Davies boys, whom he first met in Kensington Gardens in 1897, that Barrie achieved what he was really after: summers filled with the seemingly endless daredevil thrills of pirate games and other escapades. "Nothing that happens after we are twelve matters very much," he wrote wistfully, even after success had come to him as playwright and author.[5]

In one of his earliest fictional works, *Tommy and Grizel*, Barrie reminds us that anxieties about growing up can be both alarmingly real and deeply felt. Tommy Sandys—unlike Peter Pan—has matured physically, but "he was so fond of being a boy" that he finds himself unable to attain emotional maturity and eventually, in a sequel, comes to a wretched end. In one charged episode, Tommy tries desperately to return to his childhood haunts: "He came night after night trying different ways, but he could not find the golden ladder, though all the time he knew that the lair lay somewhere over there."[6] As an adult, Barrie worried constantly that he might be caught by other adults while enjoying the pastimes of youth, his therapeutic alternative for dreary grown-up obligations.

Barrie was perpetually in search of golden ladders that could take him back to his childhood. There was much in that childhood that could be described as idyllic and euphoric, and yet quicksand also opens up when we take a closer look. Tragedy visited the Kirriemuir household on more than one occasion, and it is not hard to imagine why Barrie's boyish features later sank all too readily into what one critic describes as "the caved-in sadness of old age."[7] Tortured by nightmares ("in my early boyhood it was a sheet that tried to choke me in the night") and tormented by feelings of inadequacy ("the things I could have said to them if my legs had been longer"), he struggled all his life with the pall cast over his childhood self by trauma and loss. Later in life,

5. Ibid., 42.

6. J. M. Barrie, *Tommy and Grizel* (New York: Charles Scribner's Sons, 1911), 88.

7. Anthony Lane, "Lost Boys," *The New Yorker*, November 22, 2004, 98–103.

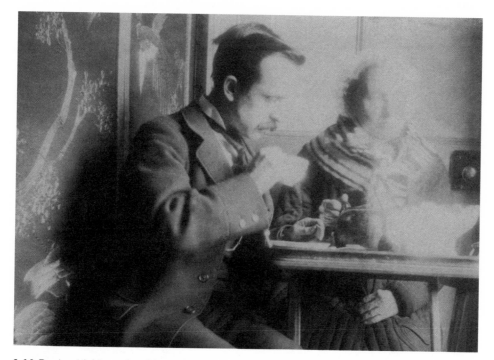

J. M. Barrie with his mother, Margaret Ogilvy, 1892. (Beinecke Rare Book and Manuscript Library, Yale University)

death continued to stalk his closest friends as well as members of his family, well before they reached their time. "[Barrie] has a fatal touch for those he loves. They die," D. H. Lawrence wrote, without any real malice, to Barrie's ex-wife, Mary Cannan.[8]

The youngest of three sons born to the handloom weaver David Barrie and his wife, Margaret Ogilvy (who kept her maiden name according to an old Scots custom), Jamie, as the young Barrie was called, lived to some extent in the shadow of his two older brothers, Alexander and David. Kirriemuir had evolved, by midcentury, into a textile center with 1,500 weavers. It had an astonishingly high literacy rate and a culture that valued education. David Barrie worked long hours and practiced thrift in ways that enabled him to support his large family and to educate them for a higher station in life than his own. Oddly, Barrie hardly ever wrote a word about his father except to extol him as a steadying force, even as he wrote a full appreciation of his mother.

8. Warren Roberts, Charles T. Boulton, and Elizabeth Mansfield, eds., *The Letters of D. H. Lawrence* (Cambridge: Cambridge University Press, 2002), 48.

In *Margaret Ogilvy*, Barrie gives us a heartbreaking account of the event that plunged his mother into a state of desolation and that was to affect him profoundly as a child and as an adult. Alick, the eldest of the three Barrie sons, had opened his own private school in Lanarkshire after a successful academic career at Aberdeen University. He was joined in the new enterprise by his sister Mary, who helped with the housekeeping and taught at the school. When Alick was appointed classics master at the Glasgow Academy, he encouraged his parents to send their second son, David, to study at the school. David, handsome, studious, athletic, and known to be his mother's favorite, was destined for the ministry, and the opportunity seemed impossible to pass up. Jamie remained the only son still at home.

The winter of 1867 was exceptionally cold, according to one account, and David had just received a pair of new skates from his brother Alick. Ever the generous spirit, David shared them with a friend. The friend tore across the ice and sped back, toppling David, who fell to the ground, hitting his head and fracturing his skull. "When the terrible news came," Barrie reported in *Margaret Ogilvy*, "I have been told the face of my mother was awful in its calmness as she set off to get between Death and her boy."[9] Just before Margaret's departure for Glasgow, a second telegram arrived with the mournful news: "He's gone!"

Margaret Ogilvy's life had never been easy, and she had been "delicate" after the birth of her fifth child, Agnes. Suffering then from what was likely puerperal fever (childbirth fever), she endured the death of a newborn and watched her daughter Elizabeth succumb to whooping cough. In this time of struggle, Margaret's father died, his lungs weakened by years of inhaling quarry dust as a stonemason. For months, the family cottage, on Brechin Road, was a site of hardship, tragedy, and mourning. But Margaret Ogilvy recovered her health in 1853, and within a period of seven years, she gave birth to five more children, three girls and two boys. Then came the news of David's accident. Losing him was more than she could bear, and she retreated to her bedroom, David's christening robe by her side. Jamie resorted to various strategies to draw her out, becoming adept, for instance, in the art of impersonation and pantomime. Barrie describes how he developed an "intense desire . . . to become so like

9. Barrie, *Margaret Ogilvy*, 30.

[David] that even my mother should not see the difference," and he practiced in secret until he had the boy's whistle and stance (legs apart and hands in the pockets of his knickerbockers) down pat.[10] Perhaps we can find here, as in his childhood games of acting out adventures, the beginnings of his love of play-acting, performance, and theater.

In an effort to brighten his mother's spirits by engaging her in conversation, the young Barrie exchanged stories—his tales of adventure alternating with her accounts of a childhood devoted to taking care of a younger brother and carrying out domestic chores after her own mother's death. Barrie read eagerly and voraciously with his mother. *Robinson Crusoe* and *Pilgrim's Progress* counted among his childhood favorites. In the lively exchanges between mother and son we can see a mirroring of the relationship between Peter and Wendy (albeit with some generational slippage): the boy enamored of adventure paired with the dutiful daughter who sews, scrubs, and tells stories. Storytelling, along with impersonating, served in the first instance as compensatory actions, helping young Jamie succeed in his "crafty way of playing physician" to the grieving mother. But they also developed into talents that served him well in adult life.

Margaret Ogilvy never really recovered from her son David's death, but she made an effort to return to a semblance of normal life. One day she proposed to her son that he write down some of his stories. As Barrie recalls it, "the glorious idea" seemed to be his own, but it was most likely devised by his mother, who was hoping at the time to make some progress on her "clouty hearth rug."[11] A schoolmate recalls his friend's unusual flair for storytelling:

> I remember one summer afternoon when I left school in his company. . . . We turned into the Back Wynd, where we were greeted with the ring of hammer on anvil, and stopped for a minute as all boys would to watch Forsyth the smith sharpening chisels. . . . After leaving the smith's door Jim began to tell me a story, and was fairly under way with it when we turned into The Limepots. . . . It was a "strange eventful history" told with sparkling eye, full of the minutest detail and entrancing to the listener. The story is long lost to my memory, but I recollect on my way home I pondered over the incident

10. Ibid., 16–17.

11. Ibid., 49.

and thought to myself, "He's a queer chap Jim. Where can he have got that story? It's not like any a boy ever told."[12]

Jamie was not only precocious but also prophetic. Storytelling came to be embraced as an antidote to loneliness, and he later described how, as a child, he would retreat into a dusty attic corner to write stories in order to prepare himself for the career of author:

> There were tales of adventure (happiest is he who writes of adventure), no characters were allowed within if I knew their like in the flesh, the scene lay in unknown parts, desert islands, enchanted gardens, with knights . . . on black chargers, and round the first corner a lady selling water-cress. . . . From the day on which I first tasted blood in the garret my mind was made up; there could be no hum-dreadful-drum profession for me; literature was my game.[13]

Writing sustained and nourished the young Barrie early on and later became the only satisfactory adult substitute for childhood games. His early novels in particular have an interesting oral quality to them, as if the narrator were recounting events to an intimate rather than sitting at his desk. Playful, expansive, and chatty, works like *Tommy and Grizel* and *The Little White Bird* hark back to Barrie as boy storyteller, always with an audience in mind and always aware of the performative element in narrative.

At age thirteen, Barrie attended the famous Dumfries Academy, where his brother was Inspector of Schools. The grown Barrie, in a speech given in 1924 at Dumfries, traces the origins of *Peter Pan* to the games played in the schoolyard there: "When the shades of night began to fall, certain young mathematicians shed their triangles and crept up walls and down trees, and became pirates in a sort of Odyssey that was long afterwards to become the play of *Peter Pan*. For our escapades in a certain Dumfries garden, which is enchanted land to me, were certainly the genesis of that nefarious work."[14]

12. J. A. Hammerton, *The Story of a Genius* (New York: Dodd, Mead & Co., 1929), 36.

13. Barrie, *Margaret Ogilvy*, 50–51.

14. Ibid.

It was at Dumfries that Barrie read R. M. Ballantyne's *The Coral Island*, a work that inspired him "to be wrecked every Saturday for many months in a longsuffering garden." And it was there that he also discovered drama, rarely missing a performance at the town's newly rebuilt theater: "I entered many times in my school days, and always tried to get the end seat in the front row of the pit. . . . I sat there to get rid of stage illusion and watch what the performers were doing in the wings."[15] The Dumfries Theatre Royal offered Shakespeare, and the young Barrie was treated to *Hamlet*, *Othello*, and *Macbeth*, along with melodramas and burlesques. Immersed in this theatrical culture, the boy scholar wrote his own play, *Bandelero the Bandit* (Bandelero, like Peter, was a composite of Barrie's "favorite characters in fiction"), which achieved some notoriety after being performed for the public. A clergyman who had attended one of the performances denounced it as "grossly immoral." Many local worthies rose to the defense of the young thespians against the fulminations of a "certain class of pulpit bigots," and a second successful season followed the first for the Dumfries Amateur Dramatic Club.[16] In one production (a play adapted from a story by James Fenimore Cooper), the young Barrie played six different roles. He later looked back at the five years at Dumfries as "probably the happiest of my life."

After finishing his education at the academy, Barrie went on, reluctantly, to the University of Edinburgh for the study of literature. Far more appealing than the drab academic life there ("students occasionally died of hunger and hard work combined") was the world of journalism. The offer of three pounds a week to write leaders for the *Nottingham Journal*, after completing his M.A. degree at Edinburgh, was irresistible.[17] Determined to make his living by the pen, Barrie was relentless in seeking outlets for his prose. A series of articles for the *St. James's Gazette* published under the title "Auld Licht Idylls" that described life in the fictional village of Thrums (modeled on his native Kirriemuir) gave Barrie the courage to move to London and begin the "hard campaign" of establishing himself as a writer. An auspicious sign came on

15. J. M. Barrie, *The Greenwood Hat, Being a Memoir of James Anon* (New York: Charles Scribner's Sons, 1938), 64.

16. Dunbar, *J. M. Barrie: The Man Behind the Image*, 35–36.

17. Ibid., 41.

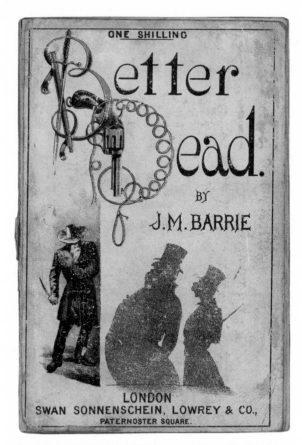

Book jacket for Barrie's 1887 first novel, *Better Dead*, which moved in the genre of the "shilling shocker." (Beinecke Rare Book and Manuscript Library, Yale University)

his arrival in the city: the first sight to greet him was a placard advertising his article "The Rooks Begin to Build" in the *St. James's Gazette*. "I remember," he reminisced in the third person, "how he sat on his box and gazed at this glorious news about the rooks." Barrie looked back on that moment as the beginning of the great romance of his life.

Working as a freelance journalist in London, Barrie developed a homespun style, taking up topics that cosmopolitan audiences had never before encountered in the pages of the *British Weekly*, the *Era*, or *Punch*. "On Running After One's Hat," "A Plea for Wild Flowers," "The Joys of Wealth by a Bloated Aristocrat," and "On Folding a Map" were among the projects he undertook. With quirky humor and wayward charm, he drew even sophisticated readers in. But Barrie himself recognized that his own voice rarely came through, for he had a habit of impersonating others: "Writing as a doctor, a sandwich-board man, a member of the Parliament, a mother, an explorer, a child . . . a professional beauty, a dog, a cat. He did not know his reason for this, but I can see that it was to escape identifying himself with any views. In the marrow of him was a shrinking from trying to influence anyone, and even from expressing an opinion."[18] Characteristic of Barrie is the resistance to using pronouns consistently. In his newspaper articles, as in his fiction, he moves seamlessly from "I" to "he" or from "we" to "you," never allowing himself to be pinned down to one identity or point of view.

Barrie's sprightly journalistic essays were collected under the title *Auld Licht Idylls* and published in 1888. The anthology formed a launching pad

18. Barrie, *Greenwood Hat*, 29.

for more sustained novelistic efforts, and *A Window in Thrums*, published to critical acclaim two years later, sold well. Both works sought to capture a world that was rapidly vanishing in the face of industrialization and urbanization. Thrums, a thinly disguised Kirriemuir, offered an opportunity for nostalgic meditation, reminding its readers that rural life had a kind of dignified communal rootedness even in the midst of hardship and poverty. Inspired by his observations of the daily lives of the weavers, artisans, and peasants in his own town, Barrie offered accurate, unsentimental portraits that rang so true that his mother hid the book whenever she received visitors.

Barrie's next novel established him as a major voice in the literary world, and suddenly his name began to appear in the company of Hardy, Kipling, and Meredith. *The Little Minister* tells the story of a scandalous relationship between Gavin Dishart, a cleric assigned to Auld Licht church in Thrums (with a pious mother named Margaret), and Babbie, a beautiful and mysterious Gypsy girl betrothed to the sinister Lord Rintoul. Torn between convention, piety, and responsibility and the lure of an exotic, forbidden romance, Dishart struggles to maintain his respectability even as he succumbs to the charms of a seemingly otherworldly creature—she had "an angel's loveliness."

The novel began its run as a serial in the periodical *Good Words* and was published in London in 1891 as one of the last "three deckers," works that appeared in a three-volume format. It was adapted for the stage six years later and made into five feature films (the last a 1934 melodrama starring Katharine Hepburn). *The Little Minister* featured what Barrie called "the shortest hero in fiction." In the preface, he added with a touch of pride that Dishart is in fact "the only short hero" ever. "Were all the heroes of the novels to meet on some vast plain, you could pick him out at once, not because he was preaching to the others (though that is what he would be doing), but solely because of his lack of inches."[19]

The Little Minister secured Barrie's literary reputation in the Anglo-American literary world. When the play was performed in the United States (where numerous pirated versions of the novel were in circulation), it broke records on Broadway at Frohman's Empire Theatre with Maude Adams in the lead. A number of plays followed in rapid succession, despite Barrie's

19. J. M. Barrie, *The Little Minister* (New York: Charles Scribner's Sons, 1921), vii.

The first installment of *My Lady Nicotine*, which begins by comparing smoking to matrimony. (Beinecke Rare Book and Manuscript Library, Yale University)

stated belief that drama was a "walk of literature I at first trod rather contemptuously,"[20] among them *Walker, London*, staged in 1892. For that work, Barrie had hired a young actress named Mary Ansell to play the second lead, and the two began dining together at fashionable restaurants. The courtship, followed closely by London gossip columnists, took many twists and turns. It was interrupted for a period of several months by another tragic event in Barrie's life, when his sister's fiancé was thrown from a horse and

20. Barrie, *Greenwood Hat*, 266.

Mary Ansell, 1896. (Beinecke Rare Book and Manuscript Library, Yale University)

died. The horse had been a gift from Barrie himself, who was stricken with grief and guilt in the months to come.

J. M. Barrie and Mary Ansell were both in their thirties at the beginning of their courtship, and Mary became increasingly perplexed that there was no proposal, no plan, no decisive turn in their relationship. Yet Barrie was all the while wrestling with questions about his future with Mary. He retreated at one point to the Cornwall estate of his friend Arthur Quiller-Couch to write a story about a character called Bookworm. There, while delighting in the company of the three-year-old Bevil Quiller-Couch, Barrie outlined the main features of a character in a play that was to be called *The Professor's Love Story*. In it he expressed some deep misgivings about a man who seeks to remain a lifelong

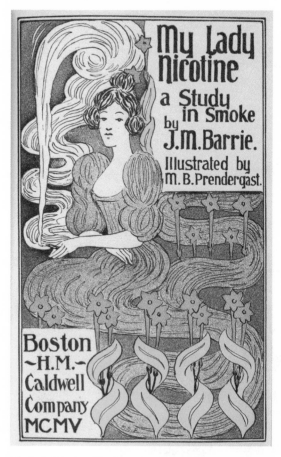

My Lady Nicotine offered a series of vignettes on smoking. Barrie himself smoked a pipe all his life and suffered from a persistent percussive cough. (Beinecke Rare Book and Manuscript Library, Yale University)

bachelor. Bookworm's doctor asserts that marriage will turn his life around and lead to his "remaking": "He has got so sunk in books, they'll drown him, he'll become a parchment, a mummy."[21]

A decade later, in 1904, even after his marriage to Mary, Barrie continued to fret about his sense of being more literary than real. He delivered a speech to the Royal Literary Fund and wondered "whether we are really here or whether this is only a chapter in a book; and if it is a chapter in a book I wonder which of us all is writing it."[22] He reflected often on the question of a divided self in ways that dovetail perfectly with modernist notions of split consciousness and existential anxieties about hyperintellectualization. Literature had truly become his game, and there is a sense in which scripts, roles, pantomimes, masks, and mimicry had taken over his life. There is no doubt that Barrie saw himself as self-contained in a way that few other people were—including his fellow Scots, with what he had described as their shuttered windows. If we add to that the fact that the marriage to Mary was more than likely never consummated, it becomes clear why Barrie hesitated for so long.

Years earlier, Barrie had felt misgivings of a different kind. In an article written for the *Edinburgh Evening Post* entitled "My Ghastly Dream," he describes a recurring nightmare that changed in content over the years and gradually took the form of anxieties about wedlock:

21. Birkin, *J. M. Barrie and the Lost Boys,* 25.

22. James Matthew Barrie, *McConnachie and J. M. B.: Speeches by J. M. Barrie* (London: Peter Davies, 1938), 13.

When this horrid nightmare got hold of me, and how, I cannot say, but it has made me the most unfortunate of men. . . . At school it was my awful bedfellow with whom I wrestled nightly while the other boys in the dormitory slept with their consciences at rest. It assumed shape at that time: leering, but fatally fascinating; it was never the same, yet always recognisable. One of the horrors of my dream was that I knew how it would come each time, and from where. . . . My weird dream never varies now. Always I see myself being married, and then I wake up with the scream of a lost soul. . . . My ghastly nightmare always begins in the same way. I seem to know that I have gone to bed, and then I see myself slowly wakening up in a misty world.[23]

Barrie came to a decision at last and traveled north in March 1894 to break the news to his mother that he was engaged to an actress. During the visit, he developed a case of pneumonia that turned into pleurisy, and he was more seriously ill than ever before in his life. Mary Ansell rushed to his bedside to assist in the convalescence, and when Barrie recovered, the couple set a wedding date. On July 9, 1894, James Matthew Barrie and Mary Ansell married and traveled to Switzerland for their honeymoon. There, Barrie purchased a St. Bernard puppy as a wedding present for his wife. The dog, shipped off to London, was named Porthos after the St. Bernard (in turn named after one of the three musketeers) in George du Maurier's novel *Peter Ibbetson*, and he became like a child to the couple. Their new home, at 133 Gloucester Road, in London, was conveniently close to Kensington Gardens, where Barrie and his large dog (who could stand on his hind legs and box with his master) became a prominent odd couple attracting the attention of children at play.

Porthos served more functions than one might imagine in the lives of the Barries. In her book *Dogs and Men*, Mary described painful "silent meals" at home, when "the mind of your man is elsewhere": "Just when the silence is becoming unbearable, your dog steps in and attracts your attention. . . . And with an adoring glance he rewards you for the titbits you pop into his mouth. Your heart begins at once to warm up again. The whole balance of life is restored."[24] With no children and with an acting career that had come to

23. J. M. Barrie, "My Ghastly Dream," *Edinburgh Evening Post*, 1887.

24. Mary Ansell, *Dogs and Men* (New York: Ayer, 1970), 42.

an end, Mary had to resort to the companionship of dogs and to the domestic pleasures of redecorating, focusing on homes and gardens, first in London, where she made improvements to the homes on Gloucester Road and, later, Leinster Corner. She would also refurbish a cottage in Surrey adjacent to Black Lake, the scene of her husband's pirate games with the Llewelyn Davies boys.

To celebrate their first wedding anniversary, the Barries returned to Switzerland in the summer of 1895 and enjoyed the elegant amenities of the Hotel Maloja and the fresh mountain air of the Engadine. On the first day of September, Barrie received word that his sister Jenann, who had been caring for their mother, had died suddenly. (She had been silently suffering from undiagnosed cancer for some time.) Just twelve hours before Barrie arrived in Kirriemuir, Margaret Ogilvy, too, passed away, and Barrie returned home to bury both sister and mother on Cemetery Hill. It was after his mother's death that he wrote *Margaret Ogilvy, by Her Son, J. M. Barrie*. Barrie seems almost unique in taking the attachment to his mother so far as to write her biography, particularly since she had done nothing of great social or cultural distinction and since mourning seems to have been her most passionate pastime. The mother-son relationship had always been paramount, with all others relegated to the sidelines. Mary Ansell's name was not mentioned at all in this exercise in maternal hagiography. It comes as no small surprise to learn that, despite some carping from the critics (the book was seen as exhibiting a "foetal complex"), *Margaret Ogilvy* sold well—nearly forty thousand copies rolled off the presses in Great Britain within a matter of weeks, with laudatory reviews and high sales in the United States as well.

With the publication of *Sentimental Tommy* in 1896, Barrie's work took an even stronger biographical turn. Setting out to write a coming-of-age tale about a boy who is resettled from London back to Thrums, Barrie found himself so fascinated by the character that he felt compelled to move backward rather than forward. "When we meet a man who interests us, and is perhaps something of an enigma, we may fall awondering what sort of boyhood he had," Barrie writes in the introduction to the novel. "And so it is with writers who become inquisitive about their own creations." Intending to summarize the childhood of his character, he discovers that he, as author, was "loth to leave him, or perhaps it was he who was loth to grow up, having a suspicion of what was in store for him." With this book Barrie revealed an idiosyncratic preoccupation with childhood that was particularly unusual in light of his success as a playwright who had addressed manners, morals, and marriage. Most adult writers become fascinated by coming-of-age stories or by the mysteries of adult behaviors, but Barrie saw adult characters as little more than opportunities for exploring the child that would become father to the man.

With *Margaret Ogilvy* and *Sentimental Tommy* behind him, Barrie made plans to travel to the United States, where he had a "roaring time," meeting the theatrical producer Charles Frohman, a "Niagara of a man." Frohman took an interest in Barrie's play *The Little Minister*, which had opened at London's Haymarket in 1897 to triumphant reviews. Barrie's financial future was now secure, and Frohman himself was fully confident of a promising new alliance. With astonishing swiftness, fame and fortune had come Barrie's way, finally leaving him with time for a range of favorite activities that had as much to do with play as with work.

Barrie now had plenty of time for walks in Kensington Gardens, and it was there, while walking Porthos, that the playwright encountered three boys, five-year-old George, three-year-old Jack, and Peter, still in a pram. Dressed in red tam-o'-shanters, the boys adored the St. Bernard who performed tricks with his master. They thrilled to the company of a man who could do amazing things with his eyebrows. "I alone of boys had been able to elevate and lower my eyebrows separately," he boasted. "When one was climbing up my forehead the other descended it, like the two buckets in the well." And he could tell stories—long, rambling tales that incorporated the boys into the adventures and showed them facing down and triumphing over evil adversaries.

It was most likely on New Year's Eve 1897 that Barrie met Sylvia Llewelyn Davies and her husband, the barrister Arthur Llewelyn Davies, at a dinner party given by the famous London solicitor Sir George Lewis. Sylvia was not only the mother of the boys but also the sister of the actor Gerald du Maurier and daughter of the writer and artist George du Maurier. A great beauty, she was always described as having unconventional good looks: "Without being strictly pretty, she has got one of the most delightful, brilliant sparkling faces I have ever seen. . . . She has pretty black fluffy hair, but her expression is what gives her that wonderful charm, and her low voice," as one contemporary

Arthur Llewelyn Davies, 1890. (Beinecke Rare Book and Manuscript Library, Yale University)

put it.[25] J. M. Barrie was "instantly conquered," as noted earlier.[26] And then came the discovery that the author had already encountered Sylvia's children in Kensington Gardens, where Barrie and Porthos constantly attracted the attention of children with their antics. Did her sons wear real red tam-o'-shanters? Yes, and they were made from their great-grandfather's judicial robes.

Barrie's relationship with the Llewelyn Davies family began as a romance—his infatuation with Sylvia and his affection for the boys—and ended in tragedy, with the death of the boys' parents and the adoption of "the Five." In between, the writer and dramatist in Barrie found ways to process what he—a married man with no children of his own—was experiencing. In *The Little White Bird*, first published in 1902, he gave literary expression to his affective life, documenting the pathological aspects of his desire to father a child by proxy. In the play *Peter Pan*, performed just two years later, he finally exorcized the demons (at least in his work), in large part through his success as father figure to the Llewelyn Davies boys and, as important, through the delivery of a boy who will never grow up.

Let us begin with *The Little White Bird*—in many ways Barrie's most deeply personal work. While writing it, Barrie kept notebooks in which he jotted down random remarks ("the queer pleasure it gives when George tells me to lace his shoes, &c.") and revealed that his greatest joy was to be taken for the father of the Llewelyn Davies boys—a joy shadowed by the fear that it might be revealed he was in fact not. The narrator of *The Little White Bird* is an eccentric bachelor, a thinly disguised version of J. M. Barrie, who is always

25. Dolly Ponsonby, *Diaries*, October 13, 1891, cited by Lisa Chaney, *Hide-and-Seek with Angels: Life of J. M. Barrie, The Author of Peter Pan* (New York: St. Martin's Press, 2005), 151.

26. Dunbar, *J. M. Barrie*, 115–16.

Sylvia Llewelyn Davies with George and Jack, 1895.
(Beinecke Rare Book and Manuscript Library, Yale University)

slipping back into the world of childhood, liquidating the boundary between fantasy and reality, and playing with fantasies about fatherhood. ("My white bird a book," he wrote when Sylvia Llewelyn Davies was pregnant with her fourth child, "hers a baby.")[27]

Barrie's bachelor does not have children of his own, but he spends a good deal of time with a boy named David, the son of a couple whose reconciliation and marriage he engineers. Mary may be the mother of David, but the narrator has endowed her child with a new identity through his stories and games. His attachment to the boy cannot but seem morbid and teetering

27. Beinecke Library, MS Vault BARRIE, A3.

on the edge of pedophilia to our eyes. Here is a partial description of an overnight visit by David:

> I knew by intuition that he expected me to take off his boots. I took them off with all the coolness of an old hand, and then I placed him on my knee and removed his blouse. This was a delightful experience, but I think I remained wonderfully calm until I came somewhat too suddenly to his little braces, which agitated me profoundly.
>
> I cannot proceed in public with the disrobing of David. Soon the night nursery was in darkness but for the glimmer from the night-light, and very still save when the door creaked as a man peered in at the little figure on the bed.

After the narrator turns in, David awakens and moves from his own bed to that of his adult friend. We are, to be sure, in the realm of fiction, but the description of boy and man together remains disturbing, even if it did not seem to have shocked Barrie's contemporaries with its open description of a boy's desire for comfort at nighttime from an adult who is not a parent and who is deeply overinvested in the child's movements at night:

> Without more ado the little white figure rose and flung itself at me. For the rest of the night he lay on me and across me, and sometimes his feet were at the bottom of the bed and sometimes on the pillow, but he always retained possession of my finger, and occasionally he woke me to say that he was sleeping with me. I had not a good night. I lay thinking. . . . of how I had stood by the open door listening to his sweet breathing, had stood so long that I forgot his name and called him Timothy.

Timothy is the name of the narrator's made-up son, a boy who is given an early fictional death to enable his father to donate clothing to David's parents. The last chapter of *The Little White Bird* takes us into a dizzying series of reversals and mirrorings, with the narrator writing the novel that David's mother had planned and then "aborted," and David's mother asserting that the narrator's book is in fact about Timothy rather than David. Each has conceived a child, with the mother possessing "the substance," and the narrator "having the shadow."[28] Maternity and paternity are pitted in a race against authorship, with parenthood losing out decisively when David decides to introduce his mother to the narrator, the man he calls "Father."

The Little White Bird proved therapeutic for Barrie in its eccentric expression of fantasies about playing father to a child. It was also the book that enabled him to conceive of a "lost" boy who runs away from home in order to avoid growing up: "His parents find him in a wood singing joyfully to himself because he thinks he can now be a boy for ever; and he fears that if they catch him they will compel him to grow into a man, so he runs farther from them into the wood and is running still, singing to himself because he is always to be a boy."[29] The "wandering child" who wants to be "a boy forever" appears in *The Little White Bird* as Peter Pan who, at the tender age of seven days, "escapes by the window" and flies back to Kensington Gardens. On outings with George and Jack, Barrie described this boy, who would eventually migrate from *The Little White Bird* into *Peter Pan in Kensington Gardens*. That volume was dedicated to Sylvia and Arthur Llewelyn Davies and to "their boys—my boys."

The man who was still a boy had finally found a way to become a father. In *Tommy and Grizel*, the sequel to *Sentimental Tommy*, Barrie bemoaned the fact that "he was still a boy, he was ever a boy, trying sometimes, as now, to be a man. . . . He was so fond of being a boy that he could not grow up."[30] Is it any wonder that there might be real marital trouble in the life of a man who creates a character who declares: "I seem to be different from all other men; there seems to be some curse upon me. I want to love you, dear one, you are the only woman I ever wanted to love, but apparently I can't"?[31] Mary was to protest some of the passages in *Tommy and Grizel* and even insisted on deleting a few, among them: "What God will find hardest to forgive in him, I think, is that Grizel never had a child."

Mary may never have had children, but James Barrie made sure that he would be surrounded by them all his life, first by the Llewelyn Davies brothers and then by the dream child he created in the many variants of the Peter Pan

28. Barrie, *Little White Bird*, 206.

29. Barrie, *Tommy and Grizel*, 399.

30. Ibid., 117.

31. Ibid., 179.

The Llewelyn Davies brothers: George, Jack, and Peter. (Beinecke Rare Book and Manuscript Library, Yale University)

story. It is to that story and its origins that we must turn for the therapeutic and creative alternatives to the pathologies expressed in *The Little White Bird*.

In 1901, the Barries decided to spend their summer holiday at Black Lake Cottage in Surrey. Not coincidentally, the Llewelyn Davies family had let a farmhouse at Tilford, and the boys were able to spend their days on the shores of the lake with Barrie. Black Lake Island was turned, with little effort, into a desert island filled with pirates, redskins, and wild animals. Barrie recorded it all with his camera, and, one day, he had the idea of creating a book that would be bound to resemble an adventure story for boys. Of the two copies that were printed, only one exists today—Arthur Llewelyn Davies lost his on a train ("doubtless his own way of commenting on the whole fantastic affair," as his son Peter later put it).[32] *The Boy Castaways of Black Lake Island, being a record of the terrible adventures of the brothers Davies in the summer of 1901 faithfully set forth*

32. Birkin, *J. M. Barrie and the Lost Boys*, 88.

by Peter Llewelyn Davies was "published" in 1901 and contained no text—only sixteen chapter headings and thirty-six photographs with a legend under each. Its adventures were framed by a description of the boys' mother and by "Advice to Parents about bringing up their Children." The pictures show the boys at play, and the one and only grown-up to be found in the book's pages is a sinister-looking J. M. Barrie, also known as Captain Swarthy.

J. M. Barrie, 1901. (Beinecke Rare Book and Manuscript Library, Yale University)

The red and black cover to *The Boy Castaways* is based on a photograph of three of the boys wielding improvised weapons—spades and other gardening tools. Bows and arrows were also in use on the "island," along with knives, and by the end of the summer Jack's lip was split by an arrow from George's bow, much to the alarm of their mother, who insisted on replacing the weapons with less dangerous implements. The chapter titles take the boys from home ("Our amusing Mother—her indiscretions") through a "fearful hurricane" that culminates in the wreck of their ship, named *Anna Pink*. Marooned on the island, the boys make a hut, discover pirates, board their ship, produce a "Holocaust" of pirates, narrowly escape a tiger, enjoy the "pleasures of tobacco," and set sail for England.

Barrie became Uncle Jimmy to the boys, a droll, avuncular celebrity who not only choreographed their summer escapades on Black Lake Island but also introduced their mother to the frothy pleasures of a lavish lifestyle. In 1902, Sylvia accompanied Barrie and his wife to Paris, "living in great splendour" and celebrating what Arthur called "the huge success of Barrie's new play and new book."[33] The boys, meanwhile, were growing up, and discovering what Barrie called "the tree of knowledge": "Sometimes you swung back into the wood, as the unthinking may at a cross-road take a familiar path that no longer leads home; or you perched ostentatiously on its boughs to please me, pretending that you still belonged."[34]

33. Ibid., 96.

34. J. M. Barrie, Dedication, *Peter Pan* (New York: Oxford University Press, 1995), vii.

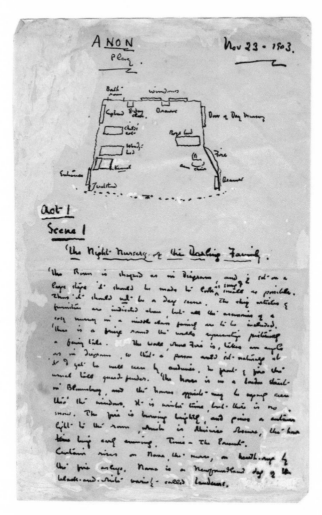

Manuscript of act 1 for the planned play *Anon*, set in the night nursery of the Darling family, 1903. (Beinecke Rare Book and Manuscript Library, Yale University)

While Sylvia Davies was pregnant with her fifth child, Barrie sat down at his desk to begin a play with the heading "ANON." He drew a detailed stage set called "The Night Nursery of the Darling Family" and began to imagine a strange little boy who slips into the nursery and takes the Darling children to a land resembling the world of *The Boy Castaways of Black Lake Island*.

Although Barrie claimed to be unable to recall writing *Peter Pan*, he had, in a sense, been writing it all his life, for the play stitched together facts and fantasies from his own childhood games and adult experiences. As a boy, he loved reading tales about desert islands and pirates, and he retained a lifelong love of *Robinson Crusoe*, which he had first read with his mother. Fascinated by Stevenson's *Treasure Island*, he was even more taken with Ballantyne's *Coral Island* and felt the urge to "stop everybody in the street & ask if they've read *The Coral Island*. Feel sorry for if not." But literary influences loomed no larger than inspiration from real life, and in the Darling household we see mirrored, faithfully at times and at times in parodic form, Arthur and Sylvia Llewelyn Davies and their children.

Just how closely Barrie modeled Mr. and Mrs. Darling on the Llewelyn Davies couple becomes evident from the description of the household economy by their son Peter Davies. He notes "the simplicity of the way the family lived: hardly a drink . . . no car or carriage, practically no restaurants to eat and drink expensively in, of course no wireless or refrigerators or other gadgets, and no

Sylvia Llewelyn Davies with Jack, Peter, and George, 1901. (Beinecke Rare Book and Manuscript Library, Yale University)

serious school bills. I think A. Ll. D. [Arthur Llewelyn Davies] always had lunch at an A.B.C. for about 6d., and I take it S. [Sylvia] made most of her own lovely clothes. . . . What emerges is that they concentrated on essentials . . . and evolved, on a small income, something as near to perfection in the way of family life as could be wished."[35]

The first draft of the stage version of *Peter Pan* was written in less than four months. The play remained a work in progress, with endless revision and recasting as Barrie reimagined a number of scenes and the ending in particular. Odd as it may seem to us today, the entire enterprise was considered a wild gamble. When Barrie read the script to his friend the actor Beerbohm Tree, the reaction was less than enthusiastic. In a mild panic, Tree sent the following message to Charles Frohman, a man who stood to lose colossal sums of money from a production of the play: "Barrie has gone out of his mind. . . . I am

35. Dunbar, *J. M. Barrie*, 128.

Nina Boucicault's costume for the first production of *Peter Pan*. Peter Pan has not always worn green, and costumes and illustrations before Disney's *Peter Pan* reveal a variety of colors ranging from red through rust to brown. (Courtesy of Great Ormond Street Hospital Children's Charity)

sorry to say it but you ought to know. . . . He's just read me a play . . . so I am warning you. I know I have not gone woozy in my mind because I have tested myself since hearing it but Barrie must be mad."[36]

Frohman did not heed the warning. He was completely enamored of the "dream child" presented to him, and only one obstacle stood in the way of production: the title had to be changed. *The Great White Father* was renamed *Peter Pan*, and rehearsals began in earnest in October 1904 at the Duke of York's Theatre in London.

With the renowned actress Nina Boucicault (daughter of the playwright Dion Boucicault) as a hauntingly enigmatic Peter Pan and the equally

36. Phyllis Robbins, *Maude Adams: An Intimate Portrait* (New York: Putnam, 1956), 90.

distinguished Gerald du Maurier as an edgy, sinister Captain Hook, the play won the hearts of the audience—mainly adult theatergoers on opening night. Frohman waited nervously in New York by the telephone and received, finally, the following message: "PETER PAN ALRIGHT. LOOKS LIKE A BIG SUCCESS."

The telegram was prophetic, and with *Peter Pan*'s success came theatrical acclaim in the most robust possible terms for J. M. Barrie. He had already established himself in professional terms, both as novelist and dramatist. Awards were now bestowed on him with astonishing frequency. And there was more money available than he could ever imagine spending, given his modest tastes and needs. (In its seven-month run in New York, *Peter Pan* made the then extraordinary sum of over half a million dollars for Barrie and Frohman.)

While *Peter Pan* was in rehearsal, Arthur and Sylvia had moved to quarters in the town of Berkhamsted to accommodate their growing family—they now had five sons in all. Barrie missed his daily encounters with the boys in

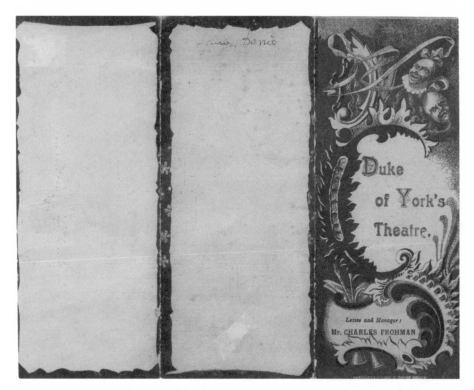

Program for the first performance of *Peter Pan*. (Beinecke Rare Book and Manuscript Library, Yale University)

Kensington Gardens. As he wrote to Peter, "Sometimes when I am walking in the Gardens with Luath [the successor to Porthos] I see a vision and cry Hurray, there's Peter, and then Luath barks joyously and we run to the vision and then it turns out to be not Peter but just another boy, and then I cry like a water cart and Luath hangs his sorrowful tail."[37] Distance did nothing to diminish Barrie's feelings for the boys and for "Jocelyn" (the pet name he used in letters to Sylvia), and early in 1906, he urged Sylvia to join him and Mary in Paris, an invitation she declined on the grounds that Michael and Nico were ill. It was in the spring of that year that Barrie brought *Peter Pan* to Berkhamsted to entertain Michael, who was still too ill to come to London for the show.

Nico Davies provides fascinating insight into how Barrie's feelings were divided up in those days. Writing in 1975, he recalls that "George and Michael were The Ones—George because he had started it all, and Michael . . . because he was the cleverest of us, the most original, the potential genius. . . . I haven't the skill to answer about J. M. B. being 'in love' with George & Michael. Roughly, yes—I would agree: he was in love with each of them: as he was in love with my mother: when you come to Mary Ansell it's a different 'feeling': . . . for myself, Peter & Jack at our different times different again—nearer to normal deep affection."[38]

In the years that followed the theatrical triumph of *Peter Pan*, Barrie was tested in ways he could never have imagined. He had always been on intimate terms with personal tragedy: the accidental death of his brother, the loss of his sister to cancer, the passing of his mother—each had required another trip up Cemetery Hill in Kirriemuir, and each had proven, in different ways, traumatic. But Barrie's professional ambition always remained strong, fortified by a deep love of hard work and by pride in literary accomplishment. Possessed of staunch Scottish determination, he was able to manage periodic bouts of depression that mystified friends when the ordinarily affable playwright wrapped himself in dour silence.

No one could have imagined on that day when *Peter Pan* was performed for Michael in Berkhamsted that Arthur and Sylvia would be gone in a matter

37. Ibid., 143.

38. Birkin, *J. M. Barrie and the Lost Boys*, 130.

of years, long before their boys had grown up. In 1906 they were both still healthy. Barrie himself was mourning the death of his agent, Arthur Addison Bright, a man who had been for many years his "most loved friend." Bright committed suicide after it was revealed that he had embezzled thousands of pounds from his clients. Barrie never paid much attention to his earnings—he would stuff checks into drawers and leave them there for months on end—and might never have noticed the missing sums had others not uncovered the fraudulent transactions. With characteristic generosity, he worried more about the corrupting influence of his high earnings than about the actual embezzlement of funds.

In early June of 1906, within days of Bright's suicide, doctors discovered that Arthur Davies had cancer. What had appeared to be nothing more than an abscess turned out to be a life-threatening tumor. Surgeons removed half of Arthur's upper jaw and palate. Even under the best of circumstances,

Letter of October 22, 1905, to Michael Davies from J. M. Barrie with letters reversed. (Beinecke Rare Book and Manuscript Library, Yale University)

Arthur's speech would be permanently impaired, his face disfigured, and his career as barrister at an end. Barrie put his financial resources at the disposal of Arthur and Sylvia. If Arthur had once found Barrie's courtship of his wife and children mildly irritating, he was now deeply grateful to Uncle Jimmy: "Barrie has been wonderful to us—we look on him as a brother."[39]

Arthur responded to the challenges of his disfiguring illness with courage, enduring agonizing pain, periodic heavy bleeding, attempts to fit him with a prosthetic device, and, finally, the news that the cancer had spread and could not be cured. Buoyed by the affectionate care of his wife and by Barrie's "unfailing kindness and tact," he lived on for several months after the operation.[40] Barrie kept vigil at Arthur's bedside on many occasions, and, shortly before his death,

39. Chaney, *Hide-and-Seek with Angels*, 253.

40. Birkin, *J. M. Barrie and the Lost Boys*, 145.

J. M. Barrie with the Llewelyn Davies boys at Scourie Lodge, 1911. George and Peter stand in the back row, with Nico and Michael in the front. (Beinecke Rare Book and Manuscript Library, Yale University)

on April 19, 1907, Arthur wrote a touching note about how much he liked to "just see" Barrie.

The Davies home in Berkhamsted was sold, and Sylvia returned to London with her boys. The family's new house, in Campden Hill Square, was not far from the Barrie residence at Leinster Corner. A second unsavory drama unfolded, far more momentous for Barrie than the embezzling episode, this time involving Barrie's own domestic circumstances. The gardener at Black Lake Cottage, filled with resentment over Mrs. Barrie's constant complaints about his work, revealed that an affair was being carried on behind Barrie's back. Confronted by her husband, Mary owned up to the affair with Gilbert Cannan, a charismatic young writer several years her junior, and she asked Barrie for a divorce. Given Barrie's cult of beautiful women and their children, who could blame Mary for moving ahead with divorce proceedings? With a husband more devoted to other women's children than to her, it must have been something of a challenge for her to remain married to a man described by H. G. Wells as a "genius" with "little virility."[41] In the Barries' social circle, there was gossip not just about Mary's infidelity but also of an unconsummated marriage.

Barrie himself apparently never had the desire to stray with adults. His adoration of the Llewelyn Davies boys and his devotion to Sylvia had always been enough to sustain him. But he was deeply hurt by Mary's infidelity and tried in vain to talk her into leaving Cannan even if she went ahead with a legal separation. He loathed the idea of seeing his name in the newspapers in connection with divorce. Henry James, H. G. Wells, and other writers appealed to the press to limit their coverage of the marital turmoil in Barrie's life: "He is a man for whom the inevitable pain of these proceedings would be greatly

Mary Ansell, 1893. (Courtesy of Great Ormond Street Hospital Children's Charity)

increased by publicity." And they hoped that the press, "as a mark of respect and gratitude to a writer of genius, will unite in abstaining from any mention of the case."[42]

The Barrie divorce was finalized in 1909, and just two days later Sylvia Davies collapsed at home. The diagnosis was cancer, and the tumor was so close to her heart and lungs that an operation was out of the question. When Sylvia died a year later, on August 27, 1910, Barrie was at her side. She was only forty-four and left behind five orphaned boys. Peter Davies described the desolate atmosphere on the day of his mother's death, when the boys were returning from a day of fishing: "It was a grey, glowering, drizzly sort of day. . . . Somehow or other the dreadful significance of [the drawn blinds]

41. William Meredith uses the phrase in a letter to Barrie's publisher. See Dunbar, *J. M. Barrie*, 180.

42. Dunbar, *J. M. Barrie*, 181.

George, Peter, and Jack Llewelyn Davies, 1899. (Courtesy of Great Ormond Street Hospital Children's Charity)

conveyed itself to my shocked understanding, and with heart in boots and unsteady knees I covered the remaining thirty or forty yards to the front door. There J.M.B. awaited me: a distraught figure, arms hanging limp, hair disheveled, wild-eyed."[43]

Sylvia had left a will, written at the farmhouse and, according to Barrie, not found until a few months after her death. Barrie wrote out the entire last testament in his own hand and described it as an "exact copy of Sylvia's will." A key sentence concerned how the five boys would be raised, and Barrie reproduced it as follows: "What I would like would be if Jimmy would come to Mary [Hodgson, the devoted nanny], and that the two together would be looking after the boys and the house and helping each other. And it would be so nice for Mary." In fact, Sylvia had written "Jenny" (Mary Hodgson's sister), and not Jimmy. "Jimmy" had managed, with just a few strokes of the pen, to become linked with their nanny, the closest he would get to de facto fatherhood. Campden Hill Square remained the boys' home, and Mary Hodgson was also still in charge of the household. Barrie himself divided his time between his own flat and their living quarters, but he called the latter home.

What was in the children's "best interests"? It is not entirely clear how the boys would have received the financial support they needed from the blood relatives on each side of the family. Many of the uncles and aunts had their own children, and none had the resources to support all five boys, whom Sylvia had wished to keep, at all costs, together. All of the boys went to Eton, save Jack. Certainly they would never have made it there without Barrie's support, although it bears noting that all but George were desperately unhappy for stretches of time there.

As for the possibility that there was something more than paternal in Barrie's interest in the boys, statements by Peter and Nico make it clear that what appears at times to be an unhealthy obsession never went beyond the bounds of appropriate affection. "I'm 200% certain there was never a desire to kiss

43. Ibid., 190.

[On black-edged paper]

11 September 1910   Chocorua
                                     New Hampshire

My dear dear Mrs du Maurier

It is by a letter from Mrs Francis Ford, my Sussex neighbour, that I am unutterably shocked and stricken to hear of the tragic fact of dear Sylvia's death. It moves me to the deepest pity and sympathy that you should have had helplessly to watch the dreadful process of her going, and to see that beautiful, that exquisite light mercilessly quenched. What you have had to go through in it all, dear Mrs du Maurier, and what you all, and what her young children, have, affects me more than I can say. She leaves with us an image of such extraordinary loveliness, nobleness and charm - ever unforgettable and touching. What a tragedy all this latter history of hers! May you yourself find strength somehow not to be shaken to pieces by such sorrows. They call out for you all my faithfullest old friendship and affection - and above all make me want to know about her children, of whose brightness and bravery and promise I have so delightful an impression. I saw her much less lately than I desired - I had so long and dismal an illness myself for so many months of this dreadful year. And since then, being somewhat better, but miserably anxious and overstrained for my last surviving, my elder and beloved brother, I helped my poor sister-in-law to bring him back to this place from England, terribly suffering, and dying in the plenitude of his great powers - so that we too are stricken and sit in darkness. He died here sixteen days ago. I stay in America a while - some months - to be near her and his children - but I shall see you as soon as possible after that - as soon as all this darkness clears a little.

Please believe, dearest Mrs du Maurier, in all the old-time intimacy of interest of your faithfullest HENRY JAMES

Typescript of Henry James's letter to Daphne du Maurier about the death of Sylvia Llewelyn Davies. (Beinecke Rare Book and Manuscript Library, Yale University)

(except upon the cheek!) though things obviously went through his mind—often producing magic—which never go through the more ordinary minds of such as myself," Nico later wrote. "All I can say for certain is that I . . . never heard one word or saw one glimmer of anything approaching homosexuality or paedophilia: had he either of these leanings in however slight a symptom I would have been aware. He was an innocent—which is why he could write *Peter Pan*."[44] Whatever desires he had were sublimated and found their expression either in his writing or through his avuncular relationship with the children.

44. Yeoman, *Now or Neverland*, 147.

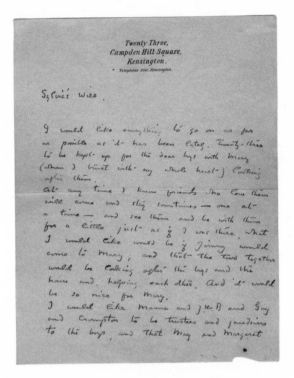

J. M. Barrie's transcription of Sylvia Llewelyn Davies's will. (Beinecke Rare Book and Manuscript Library, Yale University)

Still, who can fail to be disturbed by Barrie's flagrant misrepresentation of Sylvia's last wishes and by what later appeared to some to be deliberate efforts to cut the boys off from family friendships that had flourished while Arthur and Sylvia were still alive? The boys became Barrie's chief preoccupation, and it is hard to imagine how anyone could have been more dedicated than Barrie to their welfare and well-being. In the years following Sylvia's death, he was far less prolific an author than in the previous decade. Barrie became increasingly absorbed in the boys' lives, and, although he did "a little writing," there was a dramatic change in productivity, especially considering that literature was his game. "I have not much concern now with literature and drama, which both have flowed me by," he confessed to his old friend Arthur Quiller-Couch. "I have in a sense a larger family than you now. Five boys whose father died four years ago and now their mother last summer, and I look after them, and it is my main reason for going on. The Llewelyn Davies boys."[45]

The Llewelyn Davies brothers had, now, truly become "my boys." Barrie was a bachelor of fifty when he adopted them. Only two of the five, Nico and Michael, were still at home. George was at Eton, with plans to attend Cambridge—"the most gallant of you all," as Barrie wrote in the dedicatory preface to *Peter Pan*, and the boys themselves would not have disagreed. Peter was also at Eton, with Jack forging plans to enter the navy. Barrie prided himself on giving his boys the best possible education, and he revered British public schools, even if he did not feel entirely comfortable with their elitism. "All I am arguing," he once said in a speech to a school run by his niece, "is this, that if [the public schools] are so splendid, a way in should be found

45. Viola Meynell, ed., *Letters of J. M. Barrie* (London: Peter Davies, 1942), 22.

J. M. Barrie at the door to his study in Adelphi Terrace, 1933. (Beinecke Rare Book and Manuscript Library, Yale University)

for the boys outside."[46] The boys were given the best of everything—summer holidays, clothing, theater, and the finest restaurants. It is especially moving to learn, from Barrie's letters, about the exact contents of the many packages containing food and clothing he sent to George when the young man was facing the sanguinary horrors of combat at the western front during World War I.

Summers were spent fishing in areas so remote that, when World War I finally broke out, it took more than a day for the news to reach Argyllshire and the lodge where Barrie and the boys were staying. By early September, George and Peter had become junior officers in the army, and Jack a sublieutenant in the British navy. Although Barrie felt confident that the young men who had enlisted would be "right as rain," hopes of a quick victory were dashed as the body count mounted. "I have lost all sense I ever had of war being glorious," Barrie wrote to George, "it is just unspeakably monstrous to me now."[47] Guy du

46. Allen Wright, *J. M. Barrie: Glamour of Twilight* (Edinburgh: Ramsay Head Press, 1976), 20.

47. Birkin, *J. M. Barrie and the Lost Boys*, 243.

Peter Llewelyn Davies, 1916. (Beinecke Rare Book and Manuscript Library, Yale University)

Maurier, the boys' uncle, was serving in the Royal Fusiliers, and his letters back home included frighteningly graphic reports about rotting corpses, decomposing body parts, and the mud, blood, and stench of the trenches. "The war has done at least one big thing," Barrie wrote, in a speech entitled "Courage," delivered at St. Andrews. "It has taken Spring out of the year. And, this accomplished, our leading people are amazed to find that the other seasons are not conducting themselves as usual. The spring of the year lies buried in the fields of France."[48]

Stationed on the front in Belgium, George had entered the military with no illusions about what he would be facing. He realized that he would most likely "stop a bullet," and he went into battle in the early hours of March 15 with premonitions of death. Still, he had tried to maintain a light-hearted tone in letters to his Uncle Jim. On the day before he was killed, he urged Barrie to "keep your heart up" and to remember "how good an experience like this is for a chap who's been very idle before."[49] Promising to write frequently, he begged Barrie to keep up his "courage." Tragically, George was shot in the head while sitting with other officers taking instruction from a colonel, and he died instantly. He had "won the love of everyone," according to Alfred Lord Tennyson's son, who wrote Peter Davies that he and his comrades all believed they had lost "one of their best friends."[50]

The terrible knock at the front door of Campden Hill Square came on March 15, 1915, the very day of George's death. Mary Hodgson and Nico were asleep in the night nursery. "I heard Uncle Jim's voice," Mary later reported, "an eerie Banshee wail—'Ah-h-h! They'll all go, Mary—Jack, Peter, Michael—even

48. Wright, 27.

49. Ibid., 244.

50. Ibid.

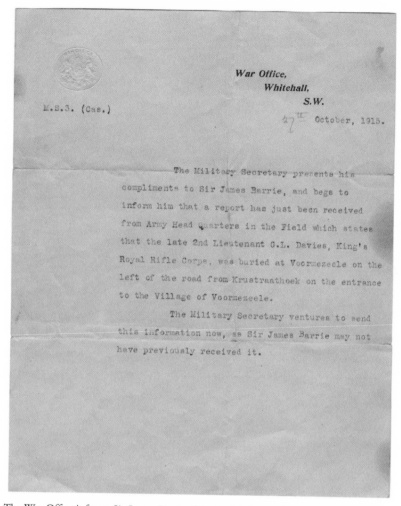

The War Office informs Sir James Barrie of the burial site for George Llewelyn Davies.
(Beinecke Rare Book and Manuscript Library, Yale University)

little Nico—This dreadful war will get them all in the end. . . . I knew that George was dead."[51] The loss of George had a devastating effect on the family, loosening bonds that had been forged over the years. "As it was circumstances were too much for J.M.B. left solitary, as well as for us," Peter wrote, "and we became gradually . . . individuals with little of the invaluable, cohesive strength of the united family."[52]

Just a few weeks later, Charles Frohman boarded a ship in New York bound

51. Ibid., 243.

52. Ibid., 245.

for Britain. Barrie had asked him to help out with the staging of his play *Rosy Rapture*, and Frohman moved his trip up to oblige Barrie. On May 7, 1915, the elegant ocean liner *Lusitania*, with Frohman aboard, sank to the bottom of the sea in perhaps the most dramatic and horrific civilian attack of World War I. Of the 1,959 passengers, 1,198 perished, among them Frohman, who had refused a place on one of the few lifeboats.

The war years inevitably witnessed dramatic changes in the household, first with the departure of Mary Hodgson, then with the hiring of Cynthia Asquith as Barrie's personal secretary. Asquith had plenty to do, for Barrie had continued with many of his old habits, including the practice of stuffing checks into a desk drawer and promptly forgetting about them. In the next two decades, Barrie finally plunged back into the game of literature, writing plays and screenplays as well as supervising productions. There were nearly fourteen screen adaptations of his work, including *Sentimental Tommy*, which was filmed by Paramount. Cynthia did more than arrange Barrie's business affairs. Married, with a family of her own, she nonetheless developed deep connections to the "impenetrable shell of sadness and preoccupation" that Barrie had become and provided personal, moral support for his remaining years.

Even Cynthia was helpless in the face of the news that came to Barrie in 1920. In the middle of the night, Barrie called her to report: "I have had the most terrible news. Michael has been drowned at Oxford." The month was May, and Barrie had left his flat in the late evening to post a letter to Michael. A reporter from a London newspaper stopped him to ask for details about "the drowning." Barrie had no idea that he was referring to the death in Sandford pool of two undergraduates, Rupert Buxton and Michael Llewelyn Davies. "All is different to me now," Barrie wrote to an old friend. "Michael was pretty much my world." Nothing seemed to matter, and, with the one "great thing" gone, other things could feel only empty and trivial.

Barrie was never quite himself after Michael's death—he was nearly as deeply affected as his mother had been by the death of David. He continued writing in his notebooks, and small pieces of work were produced, but nothing major came from his pen again. Emotionally exhausted and with nerves strained, he nonetheless remained a public figure, accepting awards and becoming rector of the University of St. Andrews, where he gave an impressive address at the end of his term in 1922. He recalled his early days in London and the "glory"

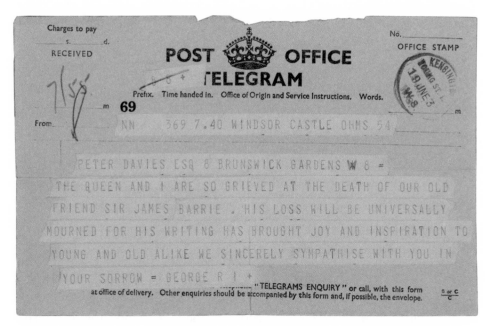

Telegram of June 19, 1937, to Peter Davies expressing King George's condolences on learning about J. M. Barrie's death. (Beinecke Rare Book and Manuscript Library, Yale University)

of being swallowed up in the city, "not knowing a soul, with no means of subsistence, and the fun of working till the stars went out."[53] "Courage" was the title of Barrie's ninety-minute speech, and courage, for Barrie, was "proof of our immortality." Thunderous applause greeted the speech, and Barrie was carried triumphantly on the shoulders of the undergraduates as they poured out of the hall to greet the crowds waiting outside.

Later, Barrie would recall the speech at St. Andrews and worry about how "monstrous" it felt to remain alive when Michael was no longer living. He had recurrent nightmares about Michael, who seemed to embody the "true meaning" of *Peter Pan*: "Desperate attempt to grow up but can't."[54] In the last two years of his life he dedicated his efforts to a play called *The Boy David*, a work that took up the biblical story of the young king but that also resonated with Barrie's life (his dead brother was named David) and with his art (the boy in *The Little White Bird* is named David). But its debut in Edinburgh was

53. Chaney, *Hide-and-Seek with Angels*, 349.

54. Beinecke Library, MS Vault BARRIE, A2/40.

marred by harsh reviews from London critics who had traveled north to see the production, and the play closed after only seven weeks.

Surrounded by friends and showered with honors but bedeviled by dark moods and poor health, Barrie remained conflicted about how to manage his life, asserting at one moment that it was a "law" of his nature to be by himself, at another that he was "alone and lonely." Cynthia Asquith remained devoted to Barrie, organizing his life and ensuring that he was supported by friends and that he became part of a tight-knit social circle that included her own husband and children. There were many highlights: Barrie was invited to become president of the Society of Authors in 1928; he became chancellor of the University of Edinburgh in 1930; he paid a festive visit to Kirriemuir and had tea with the duke and duchess of York, along with their two small daughters, Elizabeth and Margaret. Barrie described how he had a "ferocity of attachment" to his native region and how the houses and hills there had a "steadying effect" on him. These were what Cynthia Asquith referred to as the "gloom and glory" days, but, with Barrie's deteriorating health, there was far more gloom than glory. Plagued by insomnia all his life, Barrie began taking doses of prescribed heroin that produced terrible mood swings rather than the promised tranquilizing effects. After a dinner party with H. G. Wells hosted by Cynthia and her husband, Beb, Barrie became ill and was transported to a nursing home, and the end came in a matter of days.

Sir James Matthew Barrie died on June 19, 1937, with Peter and Nico at his side. Cynthia Asquith arrived from Cornwall, and Mary Cannan traveled from France to be at the bedside of the man who had once been her husband. The funeral became an occasion for national mourning, and many prominent figures walked behind the coffin on its way to Cemetery Hill in Kirriemuir. At his death Barrie was one of the most famous men of his time. When Chaplin went to London in 1921, he had been asked whom he wished to meet, and at the top of the list was J. M. Barrie.

Given his immense success as a writer and dramatist, it was hardly surprising that Barrie left a considerable fortune behind. In 1929, when asked to lead the appeal for the Great Ormond Street Hospital for Sick Children, Barrie had declined, but he generously offered the hospital the rights to *Peter Pan*, *The Little White Bird*, *Peter Pan in Kensington Gardens*, and *Peter and Wendy*. The bulk

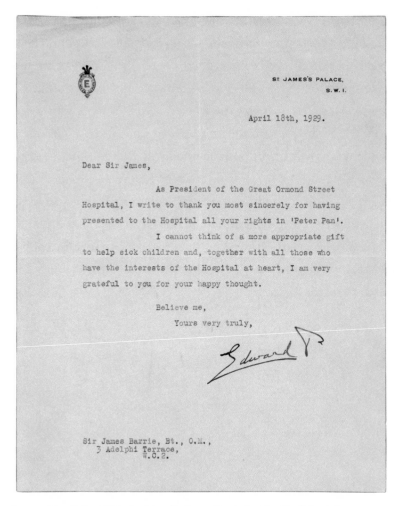

St JAMES'S PALACE,
S. W. I.

April 18th, 1929.

Dear Sir James,

     As President of the Great Ormond Street
Hospital, I write to thank you most sincerely for having
presented to the Hospital all your rights in 'Peter Pan'.

     I cannot think of a more appropriate gift
to help sick children and, together with all those who
have the interests of the Hospital at heart, I am very
grateful to you for your happy thought.

     Believe me,

     Yours very truly,

     Edward P.

Sir James Barrie, Bt., O.M.,
  3 Adelphi Terrace,
    W.C.2.

Letter of April 18, 1929, thanking Sir James Barrie for his gift of the rights to
Peter Pan to the Great Ormond Street Hospital. (Beinecke Rare Book and Manuscript
Library, Yale University)

of the estate—beyond bequests to Mary Cannan and to a few servants, friends,
and relatives—went to Cynthia Asquith. Jack Llewelyn Davies received £6,000
and Nico, £3,000, and Peter shared Barrie's furniture, letters, manuscripts, and
papers with Cynthia Asquith. The boys could not but be unhappy about the
distribution of the estate's assets (despite and perhaps also because of Barrie's
earlier generosity to them and their family). Years later, Peter's son expressed
how deeply his father resented the fact that he had virtually been cut out of the
will: "My father had mixed feelings about the whole business of Peter Pan. He
accepted that Barrie considered that he was the inspiration for Peter Pan and it

was only reasonable that my father should inherit everything from Barrie. That was my father's expectation. It would have recompensed him for the notoriety he had experienced since being linked with Peter Pan—something he hated."

That Great Ormond Street Hospital became the beneficiary of *Peter Pan* ends the story of J. M. Barrie on a powerfully magnanimous note. Barrie understood well the perils of inheritances, and he no doubt hoped that the three surviving boys would find in their work the same passion and success that he experienced. If it was not to be (although Peter and Nico had some success in the publishing business), there is full consolation in the fact that *Peter Pan* benefited thousands of children who passed through the doors of Great Ormond Street Hospital. Peter Pan may never have grown up, but the play about him enabled many children to survive illnesses, giving them a chance to grow up through the boy who refused to do so.

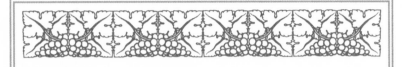

THE ANNOTATED

PETER PAN

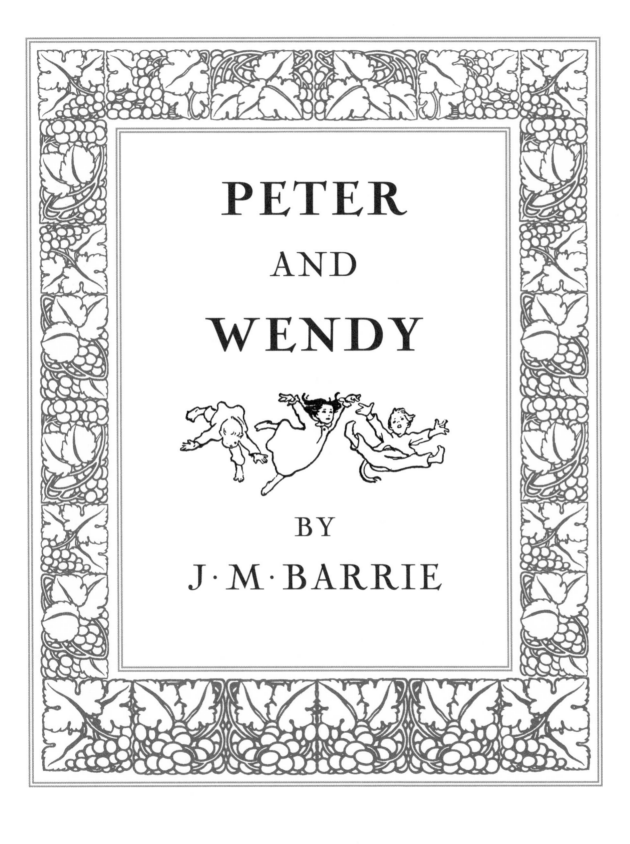

PETER
AND
WENDY

BY
J·M·BARRIE

A Note on the Text of Peter and Wendy

Barrie published his novel *Peter and Wendy* in 1911, and it was released again in 1915 as *Peter Pan and Wendy* in the form of a school edition. Both volumes had pen-and-ink illustrations by the British artist F. D. Bedford, who had made a name for himself as an illustrator for books by Charles Dickens, George MacDonald, and E. V. Lucas. Trained as an architect, Bedford placed Barrie's characters in intricately fashioned landscapes of expressive depth. In 1921, the volume was reissued again under the title *Peter Pan and Wendy*, with full-page color illustrations by Mabel Lucie Attwell, whose child-centered, appealingly sweet, pastel images were much in vogue at the time. Since then, the volume is usually published under the title *Peter Pan*. The text that follows is based on *Peter and Wendy*, published by Hodder & Stoughton in 1911. The images are from *Peter and Wendy*, published by Charles Scribner's Sons in 1911.

The Darling family takes center stage, with Mr. Darling warding off Wendy's efforts to have him take his medicine, while Mrs. Darling lavishes maternal affection on the boys. Neverland looms large in the figures of Hook and Tiger Lily, both wielding sinister weapons (hook and tomahawk), and mermaids prepare to lure the children to their underwater realm. Peter observes it all from on high with a playful benevolence.
(© 1911 Hodder Children's Books, a division of Hachette UK)

PETER FLEW IN

The Darling children sleep peacefully as Peter crosses the threshold in the glow of Tinker Bell's light and the stars above. A border of fanciful beasts and other artwork adorn the nursery walls. (© 1911 Hodder Children's Books, a division of Hachette UK)

THE BIRDS WERE FLOWN

Mr. and Mrs. Darling mourn the flight of the children, and Nana moans in sympathy. The darkness of London is pierced by what is most likely the cometlike appearance of the children on their way to Neverland. The disorder in the nursery reminds us that the children have chosen an anarchic alternative to domestic life. (© 1911 Hodder Children's Books, a division of Hachette UK)

"LET HIM KEEP WHO CAN"

The Darling children manage to preserve their strength by nipping food out of the mouths of birds. The children mingle with the birds in a euphoric fantasy alive with playful energy. (© 1911 Hodder Children's Books, a division of Hachette UK)

THE NEVER NEVER LAND

Peter Pan plays his pipes on a boulder, surrounded by creatures both feral and tame. Clusters of Indians, pirates, and mermaids appear in the middle ground, while mountains in the background form a background for the conflict between Hook and the crocodile. (© 1911 Hodder Children's Books, a division of Hachette UK)

SUMMER DAYS ON THE LAGOON

The arc of a rainbow unites water and air, while creatures of the sea and of the heavens mingle joyfully with one another. In this radiant setting, the romance of Neverland is presented with intensely detailed compositional energy. (© 1911 Hodder Children's Books, a division of Hachette UK)

PETER ON GUARD

Surrounded by dancing fairies, Peter, with sword in hand, nods off in front of the house with its chimney made from John's hat. Danger appears in the form of the wolves lurking behind a rock and running in a pack. The deciduous tree near the house forms a contrast with the palm trees in other illustrations. (© 1911 Hodder Children's Books, a division of Hachette UK)

"TO DIE WILL BE AN AWFULLY BIG ADVENTURE?"

Peter gazes at the moon in the heavens from his island perch as he contemplates death by drowning. Bedford added the question mark to what in the novel is a declaration. (© 1911 Hodder Children's Books, a division of Hachette UK)

WENDY'S STORY

No longer the center of attention, Peter seems enveloped in melancholy while Wendy tells the lost boys a story. Aboveground, the Indians eavesdrop through openings in the tree trunks. (© 1911 Hodder Children's Books, a division of Hachette UK)

9

FLUNG LIKE BALES

In a scene resembling the biblical Massacre of Innocents, the lost boys are flung from hand to hand in a "ruthless" manner. Hook ponders how to manage a horrified Wendy, who is paralyzed by the scene unfolding before her eyes. (© 1911 Hodder Children's Books, a division of Hachette UK)

HOOK OR ME THIS TIME

As comfortable on land as he is in the water or in the air, Peter is that rare creature who is not even aware when he is passing from one domain into the other. As he moves from shore to water, he plots his conquest of Hook. (© 1911 Hodder Children's Books, a division of Hachette UK)

PETER AND JANE

Wendy watches her daughter Jane delight in the sensory bliss of flight, while Peter and Wendy gaze on with delight in one case and anxiety in the other. (© 1911 Hodder Children's Books, a division of Hachette UK)

"THIS MAN IS MINE!"

Peter has two swords to defend himself in the fight with Hook, whose pugnacious strength is intensified by the oversized hook extending from one arm. With Medusa-like locks, Hook towers over his nimble opponent. The lost boys watch with trepidation and admiration; all the while the crocodile makes its way, in profile, toward the ship. (© 1911 Hodder Children's Books, a division of Hachette UK)

1. *All children, except one, grow up.* That J. M. Barrie might have been referring to himself with this opening sentence becomes evident from a 1922 notebook entry, which reveals that, late in life, he discovered the relevance of Peter Pan to his own life story: "It is as if long after writing 'P. Pan' its true meaning came to me—Desperate attempt to grow up but can't." Perhaps he is referring here to his failed marriage or to his devotion to children and childhood games, perhaps to both. Barrie may also have been alluding to his brother David, who died young. "When I became a man, he was still a boy of thirteen," he wrote, in *Margaret Ogilvy*, a biography of his mother. In *Peter Pan in Kensington Gardens*, Barrie tells us that "Peter is ever so old, but he is really always the same age, so that does not matter in the least. His age is one week, and though he was born so long ago he has never had a birthday, nor is there the slightest chance of his ever having one. The reason is that he escaped from being a human when he was seven days old; he escaped by the window and flew back to the Kensington Gardens."

The first paragraph begins with "all children," then switches from "they" to "you." First Barrie speaks as an adult, using "they" to refer to children. Then he identifies with children when he declares: "You always know after you are two." Barrie's friend the historical novelist Maurice Hewlett published a play in 1898 called *Pan and the Young Shepherd*, and it opened with the line: "Boy, boy, wilt thou be a boy for ever?" (Otherwise the play bears little resemblance to Barrie's work.)

The importance of "growing up" is emphasized through its threefold repetition (a trademark of Barrie's style) in the first paragraph: "grow up," "will grow up," and "must grow up."

2. *Wendy.* Wendy's name was coined through a collaboration between J. M. Barrie and Margaret Henley, daughter of the Victorian poet William Ernest Henley, famous for his poem "Invictus." A close friend of Barrie, he served as editor of the *Scots Observer*, published in Edinburgh from 1888 onward. Margaret evidently called Barrie her "fwendy" and thereby inspired the name Wendy, which became enormously popular in Anglo-American cultures after Barrie's play was staged. "I got the name of Wendy from her for one of my characters; it was the nearest she could reach to calling me Friend," Barrie wrote, in a collection of essays called *The Greenwood Hat* (183). Margaret Henley died at age six. "The lovely child died when she was about five," Barrie recalled, "one might call it a sudden idea that came to her in the middle of her romping." The name Wendy has also been seen as related to Gwendolyn. More importantly, it signals a unique identity and a kind of blank slate for the character who joins Peter Pan in Neverland.

3. *Mrs. Darling put her hand to her heart.* "Darling" was the term Barrie used in his correspondence with Sylvia Llewelyn Davies, whom he also addressed by her middle name, Jocelyn. "Darling J.," he would write, as well as "Dearest Jocelyn." In *Margaret Ogilvy*, Barrie described the challenges of using that particular term of endearment for anyone else, even a character in a play: "I hope I may not be disturbed, for tonight I must make my hero say 'Darling,' and it needs both privacy and concentration" (126).

4. *Wendy knew that she must grow up.* The narrator takes us inside the mind of the child. Beginning with an utterance that seeks to establish a cultural truth ("All children, except one, grow up"), the narrator channels Wendy's sudden awareness that she cannot remain two forever. It is significant that Wendy is "playing in a garden," an idyllic realm that recalls Adam and Eve's banishment from paradise. The scene evokes another mother-daughter pairing: Demeter and Persephone, who are separated when Persephone is abducted by Hades and taken to the land of the dead, the Underworld. Mrs. Darling's lament, "Oh, why can't you remain like this for ever!" captures the sorrow of loss through change, both individual and seasonal in the myth.

*

CHAPTER 1

Peter Breaks Through

All children, except one, grow up.[1] They soon know that they will grow up, and the way Wendy[2] knew was this. One day when she was two years old she was playing in a garden, and she plucked another flower and ran with it to her mother. I suppose she must have looked rather delightful, for Mrs. Darling put her hand to her heart[3] and cried, "Oh, why can't you remain like this for ever!" This was all that passed between them on the subject, but henceforth Wendy knew that she must grow up.[4] You always know after you are two. Two is the beginning of the end.[5]

Of course they lived at 14, and until Wendy came her mother was the chief one. She was a lovely lady, with a romantic mind and such a sweet mocking mouth. Her romantic mind was like the tiny boxes, one within the other, that come from the puzzling East,[6] however many you discover there is always one more; and her sweet mocking mouth had one kiss on it[7] that Wendy could never get, though there it was, perfectly conspicuous in the right-hand corner.

The way Mr. Darling won her was this: the many gentlemen who had been boys when she was a girl discovered simultaneously that they loved her, and they all ran to her house to propose to her except Mr. Darling, who took a cab and nipped

5. *You always know after you are two. Two is the beginning of the end.* Two may be the beginning of the end, but Barrie had also once extended the important years of life when he declared, "Nothing that happens after we are twelve matters very much." Age two appears to mark the advent of self-consciousness, for that is when the child suddenly becomes knowing—"you always know."

6. *the puzzling East.* Mrs. Darling, through her association with the enigmatic Orient, is positioned as mysteriously exotic, unknowable, and "other." Barrie subscribes to contemporary British stereotypes about the inscrutability of those living in non-Western cultures.

7. *one kiss on it.* Kisses will become central in the exchange between Wendy and Peter, where kisses are confused with thimbles and vice versa. The unavailable kiss will reappear in that exchange. And Peter will take one kiss with him at the end of the story, "the kiss that had been for no one else."

8. *not only loved him but respected him.* Mr. Darling, as revealed in the calculations he will make about household expenses, is something of a buffoon, even at the office. His need to tell Wendy about "her mother" and the passion and admiration she feels for him turns him into a comic figure who requires more attention and pampering than the children. Barrie's refusal to model the Darlings on the traditional Victorian family in which the father enjoyed absolute power over his wife and children has been seen as scoring a hit on Arthur Davies, who was facing challenges supporting his family as a barrister. In the play, an elaborate stage direction accompanies Mr. Darling's first appearance, turning him into a faceless clerk who depends on reassurance from those at home: "He is really a good man as breadwinners go, and it is hard luck for

in first, and so he got her. He got all of her, except the innermost box and the kiss. He never knew about the box, and in time he gave up trying for the kiss. Wendy thought Napoleon could have got it, but I can picture him trying, and then going off in a passion, slamming the door.

Mr. Darling used to boast to Wendy that her mother not only loved him but respected him.[8] He was one of those deep ones who know about stocks and shares. Of course no one really knows, but he quite seemed to know, and he often said stocks were up and shares were down in a way that would have made any woman respect him.

Mrs. Darling was married in white, and at first she kept the books perfectly, almost gleefully, as if it were a game, not so much as a brussels sprout was missing; but by and by whole cauliflowers dropped out, and instead of them there were pic-

Mabel Lucie Attwell, *Peter Pan and Wendy*, 1921. (Lucie Attwell Ltd. Courtesy of Vicki Thomas Associates)

tures of babies without faces. She drew them when she should have been totting up. They were Mrs. Darling's guesses.

Wendy came first, then John, then Michael.

For a week or two after Wendy came it was doubtful whether they would be able to keep her, as she was another mouth to feed. Mr. Darling was frightfully proud of her, but he was very honourable, and he sat on the edge of Mrs. Darling's bed, holding her hand and calculating expenses,[9] while she looked at him imploringly. She wanted to risk it, come what might, but that was not his way; his way was with a pencil and a piece of paper, and if she confused him with suggestions he had to begin at the beginning again.

"Now don't interrupt," he would beg of her. "I have one pound seventeen[10] here, and two and six at the office; I can cut off my coffee at the office, say ten shillings, making two nine and six, with your eighteen and three makes three nine seven, with five naught naught in my cheque-book makes eight nine seven,—who is that moving?—eight nine seven, dot and carry seven—don't speak, my own—and the pound you lent to that man who came to the door—quiet, child—dot and carry child—there, you've done it!—did I say nine nine seven? yes, I said nine nine seven; the question is, can we try it for a year on nine nine seven?"

"Of course we can, George,"[11] she cried. But she was prejudiced in Wendy's favour, and he was really the grander character of the two.

"Remember mumps," he warned her almost threateningly, and off he went again. "Mumps one pound, that is what I have put down, but I dare say it will be more like thirty shillings—don't speak—measles one five, German measles half a guinea, makes two fifteen six—don't waggle your finger—whooping-cough, say fifteen shillings"—and so on it went, and it added up differently each time; but at last Wendy just got through, with mumps reduced to twelve six, and the two kinds of measles treated as one.

him to be propelled into the room now, when if we had brought him in a few minutes earlier or later he might have made a fairer impression. In the city where he sits on a stool all day, as fixed as a postage stamp, he is so like all the others on stools that you recognize him not by the face but by his stool, but at home the way to gratify him is to say that he has a distinct personality. He is very conscientious, and in the days when Mrs. Darling gave up keeping the house books correctly and drew pictures instead (which he called her guesses), he did all the totting up for her, holding her hand while he calculated whether they could have Wendy or not, and coming down on the right side."

9. *calculating expenses.* Mr. Darling is consumed by anxieties about finances, and he repeatedly worries about the costs of children. The intensity of those anxieties suggests that children represent more than a financial threat. Not only do the children demand attention from Mrs. Darling, they will also grow up, displacing the older generation.

10. *"one pound seventeen."* Mr. Darling is calculating that he has one pound and seventeen shillings. "Three nine seven" is three pounds, nine shillings, and seven pence, and half a guinea equals one pound. Mr. Darling is not so much greedy or mercenary as he is anxious about family finances. He hopes to capitalize on Peter Pan's shadow: "There is money in this, my love. I shall take it to the British Museum tomorrow and have it priced." As Cecil Eby points out, Mr. Darling has "the soul of a Dickensian bookkeeper" who measures the world "with a stick calibrated in pounds and shillings" (131).

11. *"George."* The names of the male members of the Darling family are drawn from the families of Arthur Llewelyn Davies

John, Wendy, Michael, and Nana. (*Peter Pan and Wendy by J. M. Barrie, Retold for the Nursery by May Byron*. Illustrated by Kathleen Atkins)

and Sylvia Llewelyn Davies, née du Maurier. George is named after Sylvia's brother and the firstborn in the Llewelyn Davies family. (He was called Alexander in early drafts of the play.) Michael is named after the fourth son of Arthur and Sylvia. And John is named after the second son, nicknamed Jack.

12. *this nurse was a prim Newfoundland dog, called Nana.* The dog Nana as nurse introduces the twin themes of play and masquerade, with dogs in the roles of humans, and vice versa (Mr. Darling will later reverse roles with Nana and move into her house). As in the child's world, the division between humans and animals remains fluid. Barrie himself owned a St. Bernard named Porthos, and in the Disney version of *Peter Pan*, Nana is a St. Bernard. Porthos died in 1902, and Barrie's next dog was a Newfoundland named Luath, who became the model for stage Nanas. Luath was anything but prim, and he had what one Barrie biographer

There was the same excitement over John, and Michael had even a narrower squeak; but both were kept, and soon you might have seen the three of them going in a row to Miss Fulsom's Kindergarten school, accompanied by their nurse.

Mrs. Darling loved to have everything just so, and Mr. Darling had a passion for being exactly like his neighbours; so, of course, they had a nurse. As they were poor, owing to the amount of milk the children drank, this nurse was a prim Newfoundland dog, called Nana,[12] who had belonged to no one in particular until the Darlings engaged her. She had always thought children important, however, and the Darlings had become acquainted with her in Kensington Gardens,[13] where she spent most of her spare time peeping into perambulators, and was much hated by careless nursemaids, whom she followed to their homes and complained of to their mistresses. She proved to be quite a treasure of a nurse. How thorough she was at bath-time; and up at any moment of the night if one of her charges made the slightest cry. Of course her kennel was in the nursery. She had a genius for knowing when a cough is a thing to have no patience with and when it needs stocking round your throat. She believed to her last day in old-fashioned remedies like rhubarb leaf,[14] and made sounds of contempt over all this new-fangled talk about germs, and so on. It was a lesson in propriety to see her escorting the children to school, walking sedately by their side when they were well behaved, and butting them back into line if they strayed. On John's footer[15] days she never once forgot his sweater, and she usually carried an umbrella in her mouth in case of rain. There is a room in the basement of Miss Fulsom's school where the nurses wait. They sat on forms, while Nana lay on the floor, but that was the only difference. They affected to ignore her as of an inferior social status to themselves, and she despised their light talk. She resented visits to the nursery from Mrs. Darling's friends, but if they did come she first whipped off Michael's pinafore and put him into the one with blue braiding, and smoothed out Wendy and made a dash at John's hair.

No nursery could possibly have been conducted more correctly, and Mr. Darling knew it, yet he sometimes wondered uneasily whether the neighbours talked.

He had his position in the city to consider.

Nana also troubled him in another way. He had sometimes a feeling that she did not admire him.[16] "I know she admires you tremendously, George," Mrs. Darling would assure him, and then she would sign to the children to be specially nice to father. Lovely dances followed, in which the only other servant, Liza, was sometimes allowed to join. Such a midget she looked in her long skirt and maid's cap, though she had sworn, when engaged, that she would never see ten again. The gaiety of those romps! And gayest of all was Mrs. Darling, who would pirouette so wildly that all you could see of her was the kiss, and then if you had dashed at her you might have got it. There never was a simpler happier family[17] until the coming of Peter Pan.[18]

Mrs. Darling first heard of Peter when she was tidying up her children's minds.[19] It is the nightly custom of every good mother after her children are asleep to rummage in their minds and put things straight for next morning, repacking into their proper places the many articles that have wandered during the day. If you could keep awake (but of course you can't) you would see your own mother doing this, and you would find it very interesting to watch her. It is quite like tidying up drawers. You would see her on her knees, I expect, lingering humorously over some of your contents, wondering where on earth you had picked this thing up, making discoveries sweet and not so sweet, pressing this to her cheek as if it were as nice as a kitten, and hurriedly stowing that out of sight. When you wake in the morning, the naughtiness and evil passions with which you went to bed have been folded up small and placed at the bottom of your mind; and on the top,

refers to as a "passion for motoring." His name may come from the infamous forged epic poem penned by the Scottish writer James Macpherson. In that work, known as *Ossian*, Cuchullin's dog is called Luath. Luath may also have been named after a collie in Robert Burns's "The Twa Dogs." One expert on Newfoundland dogs reports that "In addition to being something of a status symbol, Newfoundlands were also employed as canine nannies and personal companions, and saw great popularity as gun dogs" (Bendure 70).

In the introduction to the play *Peter Pan*, Barrie pointed out that "at one matinee we even let him [Luath] for a moment take the place of the actor who played Nana, and I don't know that any members of the audience ever noticed the change, though he introduced some 'business' that was new to them but old to you and me."

13. *Kensington Gardens*. In Barrie's time, Kensington Gardens had a rustic quality to it, with sheep grazing on its lawns. Hyde Park and Kensington Gardens are divided by the Long Water and the Serpentine. Barrie lived at 133 Gloucester Road, just a short distance from Kensington Gardens. There he took daily walks with Porthos that led to the meeting with the Llewelyn Davies brothers, who lived at 31 Kensington Park Gardens. To honor the fame he brought to that park, Barrie was presented with a key to the gate of Kensington Gardens. Viscount Esher, secretary to His Majesty's Office of Works, made the arrangement, and Barrie, with characteristic mock gravity, vowed never to misuse his privileges.

14. *rhubarb leaf*. The rhubarb root was used to treat infant digestive problems and was also a traditional remedy for constipation and diarrhea. First grown as a market crop in England in 1810, rhubarb gained swiftly in popularity over the next cen-

Postcard of Gerard du Maurier as Mr. Darling in *Peter Pan*. Nana is played by Arthur Lupino. (Beinecke Rare Book and Manuscript Library, Yale University)

tury. Barrie no doubt meant rhubarb root rather than leaf, since rhubarb leaves contain toxic substances, including oxalic acid.

15. *footer*. In England, soccer is known as football, and sometimes referred to as "footer" or "footie."

16. *she did not admire him*. Mr. Darling's insecurities and need for respect, even from the family dog, are referred to repeatedly.

17. *There never was a simpler happier family*. The statement may possibly be an allusion to the famous first sentence of Tolstoy's *Anna Karenina*: "Happy families are all alike; every unhappy family is unhappy in its own way." Barrie refers to Tolstoy often in his essays, citing him approv-

ingly, for example, on the effects of smoking in "The Wicked Cigar."

18. *Peter Pan*. When Captain Hook asks, "Pan, who and what are thou?," Peter exuberantly replies: "I'm youth, I'm joy . . . I'm a little bird that has broken out of the egg." Barrie, when asked by Nina Boucicault (the first actress to play the role of Peter Pan) for some hints about the character, refused to tip his hand much: "Peter is a bird . . . and he is one day old" (Hanson 36). The allusion to hatching may refer to the antics of the British actor John Rich, who portrayed Harlequin hatching from an egg onstage at the beginning of his performances. Peter, like the Harlequin figure, is something of a trickster and magician and gifted in the art of masquerade and mimicry. And his surname may be inspired not just by the Greek god but also by "panto," the name commonly used to describe the extravagant theatrical pantomimes staged for children in the Victorian era. Like those pantomimes, *Peter Pan* has a Principal Boy, a Principal Girl (Wendy), a Demon King (Hook), and a Good Fairy (Tinker Bell). The original productions of *Peter Pan* followed the pantomime tradition of having villains enter from stage left while other (good) characters entered from stage right. For the first few performances in London, Columbine and Harlequin ended the play with a dance.

In *Peter Pan in Kensington Gardens*, Peter Pan is a baby boy who rides a goat and plays the syrinx (the Greek Pan's musical pipe with seven reeds). He is described as a "little half-and-half." He is neither "exactly human" nor "exactly a bird" and is designated as a "Betwixt-and-Between" (17). The older Peter is sometimes depicted with the *lagobolon*, a hook for catching small game and controlling herds (note the connection to Captain Hook).

The original Greek Pan was part goat, part god, joy and "panic" combined, and he was often depicted with the syrinx, his pipes, or a *lagobolon*. As the son of Hermes and the daughter of the shepherd Dryops, he possessed a mercurial temperament and lightning-rapid mobility. He was also associated with the rural delights beautifully aired, are spread out your prettier thoughts, ready for you to put on.

I don't know whether you have ever seen a map of a person's mind.[20] Doctors sometimes draw maps of other parts of you, and your own map can become intensely interesting, but catch them trying to draw a map of a child's mind, which is not only confused, but keeps going round all the time. There are zigzag lines on it, just like your temperature on a card, and these are probably roads in the island; for the Neverland is always more or less an island,[21] with astonishing splashes of colour here and there, and coral reefs and rakish-looking craft[22] in the offing, and savages and lonely lairs, and gnomes who are mostly tailors, and caves through which a river runs, and princes with six elder brothers, and a hut fast going to decay, and one very small old lady with a hooked nose. It would be an easy map if that were all; but there is also first day at school, religion, fathers, the round pond, needlework, murders, hangings, verbs that take the dative, chocolate pudding day, getting into braces,[23] say ninety-nine, three-pence for pulling out your tooth yourself, and so on, and either these are part of the island or they are another map showing through, and it is all rather confusing, especially as nothing will stand still.

Of course the Neverlands vary a good deal. John's, for instance, had a lagoon with flamingoes flying over it at which John was shooting, while Michael, who was very small, had a flamingo with lagoons flying over it. John lived in a boat turned upside down on the sands, Michael in a wigwam, Wendy in a house of leaves deftly sewn together. John had no friends, Michael had friends at night, Wendy had a pet wolf forsaken by its parents; but on the whole the Neverlands have a family resemblance, and if they stood still in a row you could say of them that they have each other's nose, and so forth. On these magic shores children at play are for ever beaching their coracles.[24] We too have been there;[25] we

of pastoral life. In *The Golden Bough*, the Scottish anthropologist Sir James Frazer describes Pan as a goatish demigod allied with Dionysus as well as with "Satyrs, and Silenuses" (538). Pan also displays a kinship with Icarus, Phaeton, Hermes, Narcissus, and Adonis. Hermes, in particular, is closely linked with Peter Pan, for he is at once trickster, psychopomp (leading souls to Hades), and dream maker. The mythological Pan inspires terror through his association with excess, intoxication, and licentiousness.

Barrie's hero owes something to the cultural mania about Pan in the Edwardian era. Kenneth Grahame immortalized Pan as the "Piper at the Gates of Dawn" in *The Wind in the Willows* (1908). In an essay entitled "Pan's Pipes" (1881), Robert Louis Stevenson proclaimed that "Pan is not dead." Pan is the hero of Kipling's *Puck of Pook's Hill* (1906), and Dickon in Frances Hodgson Burnett's *Secret Garden* is a Pan figure, a good-natured rural savior who communes with nature. In E. M. Forster's "Story of a Panic" (1904), the death of Pan is mourned.

Barrie eventually settled on using *Peter Pan* as his title, but he had also contemplated other possibilities, among them "Anon," "Fairy," "The Great White Father," and "The Boy Who Hated Mothers."

19. *tidying up her children's minds*. Mrs. Darling engages at night in the supremely maternal activity of tidying up her children's minds, which, as we discover, are filled with clutter collected in the course of the day. The parallels set up between housekeeping (cleaning drawers) and child rearing (tidying up minds) reinforce the notion that both are women's work. Unlike Walter Benjamin, who endorsed the revolutionary messiness of the child's mind, Mrs. Darling is a true Victorian at heart, taming and domesticating her children by concealing everything that does

not conform to her standards of innocence and sweetness. There is no evidence that Barrie knew of Freud's work, but many of his ideas seem to capture in poetic terms concepts such as repression, as developed in *The Interpretation of Dreams* (1900).

20. *a map of a person's mind.* Only a few years earlier, Freud had begun mapping the mind that Barrie describes here. Barrie's description of a "child's mind" and his inventory of what it contains modulates into an account of what Neverland looks like. Neverland is a domain of febrile activity and eternal return ("keeps going round all the time"), animation, and anarchy. Combining elements both fanciful and factual (stories and the residues of everyday experience), it contains gnomes, savages, and princes but also verbs that take the dative, fathers, and the round pond. To adults, the febrile activity and emotional overload of the child's mind make it appear alarmingly unstable. But the heterogeneous enumeration of what is in Neverland also pays tribute to the richness of the child's imagination and memory.

21. *Neverland is always more or less an island.* "Never-Never" was a term used in the nineteenth century to describe uninhabited regions of Australia. It is still used today to describe remote regions in that country. In 1904, the British actor and playwright Wilson Barrett published a work called *The Never-Never Land.* Its cover was decorated with kangaroos, and the first sentence read: "At Woolloogolonga Gully, in the Never-Never Land of Queensland, Australia, it was one hundred and twenty in the shade."

Peter Pan's island was called "Never Never Never Land" in the first draft of the play, but was soon abbreviated to "Never Never Land" in the performed version. When *Peter Pan* was first published as a play, the island became "The Never Land," and in *Peter and Wendy* it is most often referred to as "Neverland." The term has sometimes been seen as a command—never to land. As a place where lost boys sleep, it also becomes the domain of the dead, with the boys

moving almost directly from the womb to the tomb.

Neverland may be modeled on Tír na nÓg, the most prominent of the Otherworlds in Irish mythology, an island that cannot be located on a map. Mortals can reach it only by invitation from one of the fairies residing on it. A place of eternal youth and beauty, it is a utopian land of music, pleasure, happiness, and eternal life.

Sarah Gilead sees the "never" in Neverland as a form of "stark denial" in its double meaning: "on the one hand, the refusal of the self to conceive of its own end and, on the other, the absolute reality of death" (286). She points out that Neverland is a "realm of death under the cover of boyish fun and adventure." That the boys live underground in houses that resemble coffins offers further evidence of Neverland as the Underworld.

Peter and Wendy, like Daniel Defoe's *Robinson Crusoe* (1719), Johann Wyss's *Swiss Family Robinson* (translated into English in 1814), and Robert Louis Stevenson's *Treasure Island* (1883), belongs to the genre of the island fantasy. In Barrie's day, there were also countless Robinsonnades, along with parodies, prequels, and sequels to *Robinson Crusoe*, among them R. M. Ballantyne's *The Dog Crusoe* (1861) and W. Clark Russell's *The Frozen Pirate* (1887), inspired perhaps by the *Arctic Crusoe*, published in 1854.

Barrie often set his plays on islands (*The Admirable Crichton* is a prime example), and he once remarked, in a public lecture: "I should feel as if I had left off my clothing, if I were to write without an island" (Birkin 253).

22. *coral reefs and rakish-looking craft.* Barrie's Neverland is deeply literary, containing elements of adventure stories (islands, pirates, reefs, and boats) and also features of fairy tales (mermaids and fairy dust), along with streaks of poetry (the "caves through which a river runs" recall Coleridge's sacred river that winds through caverns in "Kubla Khan"). The strange mix of pirates and fairies had been kept separate in two earlier works, *The Boy Castaways of Black Lake Island* and *The Little White Bird*, but was

Peter Pan flies through at the window. (*Peter Pan and Wendy
by J. M. Barrie, Retold for the Nursery by May Byron*. Illustrated
by Kathleen Atkins)

can still hear the sound of the surf, though we shall land no
more.

Of all delectable islands the Neverland is the snuggest
and most compact;[26] not large and sprawly, you know, with
tedious distances between one adventure and another, but
nicely crammed. When you play at it by day with the chairs
and table-cloth, it is not in the least alarming, but in the two
minutes before you go to sleep it becomes very nearly real.
That is why there are night-lights.

Occasionally in her travels through her children's minds
Mrs. Darling found things she could not understand, and
of these quite the most perplexing was the word Peter. She
knew of no Peter, and yet he was here and there in John and
Michael's minds, while Wendy's began to be scrawled all over
with him. The name stood out in bolder letters than any of

preserved in *Peter and Wendy*. Stories about
pirates satisfied the desires of the older
Llewelyn Davies boys, while tales about
fairies appealed to the younger boys.

23. *getting into braces.* In contrast to its
American usage as an orthodontic appli-
ance, braces is the British term for
suspenders.

24. *coracles.* Made of waterproof material
stretched over a wicker or wood frame,
coracles are lightweight, oval-shaped boats
generally built to carry one person for the
purpose of fishing or transportation.

25. *We too have been there.* The narrator
reminds us here of his adult status and
how, as an adult, he can no longer see or
inhabit Neverland. His sole means of
access is through sound.

26. *Neverland is the snuggest and most compact.* Fictional islands each have their own
unique symbolic geography, but, as places
cut off from the rest of the world, they all
provide a site for reflecting on identity or
reinventing the self. "To be born is to be
wrecked on an island," Barrie wrote, in
the introduction to a 1913 edition of *The
Coral Island*, a novel for boys first published in 1853 by the Scotsman R. M. Ballantyne. Barrie had reveled in Ballantyne's
work, which featured three boys—Ralph
Rover, Jack Martin, and Peterkin Gay—
shipwrecked on an uninhabited Polynesian
island, where they encounter danger in the
form of pirates as well as of natives who
practice infanticide and cannibalism. Ballantyne, Barrie wrote, was "another one of
my gods, and I wrote long afterwards an
introduction . . . in which I stoutly held
that men and women should marry young
so as to have many children who could
read 'The Coral Island'" (*The Greenwood
Hat*, 81). *Coral Island* inspired not only
Barrie but also Nobel laureate William

Golding, who read the volume as a boy long before he wrote the novel *Lord of the Flies*.

the other words, and as Mrs. Darling gazed she felt that it had an oddly cocky appearance.

"Yes, he is rather cocky," Wendy admitted with regret. Her mother had been questioning her.

"But who is he, my pet?"

"He is Peter Pan, you know, mother."

At first Mrs. Darling did not know, but after thinking back into her childhood she just remembered a Peter Pan who was said to live with the fairies. There were odd stories about him; as that when children died he went part of the way with them, so that they should not be frightened. She had believed in him at the time, but now that she was married and full of sense she quite doubted whether there was any such person.

"Besides," she said to Wendy, "he would be grown up by this time."

"Oh no, he isn't grown up," Wendy assured her confidently, "and he is just my size." She meant that he was her size in both mind and body; she didn't know how she knew it, she just knew it.

Mrs. Darling consulted Mr. Darling, but he smiled pooh-pooh. "Mark my words," he said, "it is some nonsense Nana has been putting into their heads; just the sort of idea a dog would have. Leave it alone, and it will blow over."

But it would not blow over; and soon the troublesome boy gave Mrs. Darling quite a shock.

Children have the strangest adventures without being troubled by them. For instance, they may remember to mention, a week after the event happened, that when they were in the wood they met their dead father and had a game with him. It was in this casual way that Wendy one morning made a disquieting revelation. Some leaves of a tree had been found on the nursery floor, which certainly were not there when the children went to bed, and Mrs. Darling was puzzling over them when Wendy said with a tolerant smile:

"I do believe it is that Peter again!"

"Whatever do you mean, Wendy?"

"It is so naughty of him not to wipe," Wendy said, sighing. She was a tidy child.

She explained in quite a matter-of-fact way that she thought Peter sometimes came to the nursery in the night and sat on the foot of her bed and played on his pipes to her.[27] Unfortunately she never woke, so she didn't know how she knew, she just knew.

"What nonsense you talk, precious. No one can get into the house without knocking."

"I think he comes in by the window," she said.

"My love, it is three floors up."

"Were not the leaves at the foot of the window, mother?"

It was quite true; the leaves had been found very near the window.

Mrs. Darling did not know what to think, for it all seemed so natural to Wendy that you could not dismiss it by saying she had been dreaming.

"My child," the mother cried, "why did you not tell me of this before?"

"I forgot," said Wendy lightly. She was in a hurry to get her breakfast.

Oh, surely she must have been dreaming.

But, on the other hand, there were the leaves. Mrs. Darling examined them carefully; they were skeleton leaves, but she was sure they did not come from any tree that grew in England. She crawled about the floor, peering at it with a candle for marks of a strange foot. She rattled the poker up the chimney and tapped the walls. She let down a tape from the window to the pavement, and it was a sheer drop of thirty feet, without so much as a spout to climb up by.

Certainly Wendy had been dreaming.

But Wendy had not been dreaming, as the very next night showed, the night on which the extraordinary adventures of these children may be said to have begun.

27. *played on his pipes to her.* Peter's pipes enable him to imitate his earlier incarnation as a bird. "Being partly human," we are told, he needs an instrument and therefore makes a pipe of reeds. In *Peter Pan in Kensington Gardens*, Peter's heart is "so glad" that he wants to sing all day long. He fashions a pipe of reeds and sits by the shore, "practicing the sough of the wind and the ripple of the water, and catching handfuls of the shine of the moon, and he put them all in his pipe and played them so beautifully that even the birds were deceived" (46–47).

28. *sat down tranquilly by the fire to sew.* Sewing and mending are feminine activities associated with Mrs. Darling, Wendy, and Tinker Bell. Tinker Bell is so named "because she mends pots and kettles," and both Mrs. Darling and Wendy are seen sewing and darning. Smee, the most effeminate of the pirates, is seen "hemming placidly" before battle. Sewing and mending are linked to "tidying up" and the many other maternal efforts to create domestic order where there is anarchy, clutter, and disrepair. Associated with tranquillity, inwardness, and coziness, these activities stand in opposition to the world of adventure. Alfred, Lord Tennyson's poem "The Princess" set forth clearly the nineteenth-century gendered division of labor that is enacted in *Peter Pan*:

> Man for the Field and
> Woman for the Hearth:
> Man for the Sword and
> for the Needle She:
> Man with the Head and
> Woman with the Heart:
> Man to command and
> Woman to obey;
> All else confusion . . .

29. *the nursery dimly lit.* In autobiographical reminiscences, Barrie remarked on the contrast between people raised in a nursery and those from other social classes who were not. He himself had never had a nursery, nor had the "most genteel friend of his childhood ever had a nursery." "It seems to me," he added (referring to himself in the third person), "looking back, that he was riotously happy without nurseries, without even a nana (but with someone better) to kiss the place when he bumped. The children of six he had met were, if boys, helping their father to pit the potatoes, and, if girls, they were nurses (without knowing the word) to some one smaller than themselves. He came of parents who could not afford nurseries, but who could

On the night we speak of all the children were once more in bed. It happened to be Nana's evening off, and Mrs. Darling had bathed them and sung to them till one by one they had let go her hand and slid away into the land of sleep.

All were looking so safe and cosy that she smiled at her fears now and sat down tranquilly by the fire to sew.[28]

It was something for Michael, who on his birthday was getting into shirts. The fire was warm, however, and the nursery dimly lit[29] by three night-lights, and presently the sewing lay on Mrs. Darling's lap. Then her head nodded, oh, so gracefully. She was asleep. Look at the four of them, Wendy and Michael over there, John here, and Mrs. Darling by the fire. There should have been a fourth night-light.

The window flew open!

Gwynedd M. Hudson.

While she slept she had a dream. She dreamt that the Neverland had come too near and that a strange boy had broken through from it. He did not alarm her, for she thought she had seen him before in the faces of many women who have no children. Perhaps he is to be found in the faces of some mothers also. But in her dream he had rent the film that obscures the Neverland, and she saw Wendy and John and Michael peeping through the gap.

The dream by itself would have been a trifle, but while she was dreaming the window of the nursery blew open, and a boy did drop on the floor. He was accompanied by a strange light, no bigger than your fist, which darted about the room like a living thing; and I think it must have been this light that wakened Mrs. Darling.

She started up with a cry, and saw the boy, and somehow she knew at once that he was Peter Pan. If you or I or Wendy had been there we should have seen that he was very like Mrs. Darling's kiss. He was a lovely boy, clad in skeleton leaves and the juices that ooze out of trees;[30] but the most entrancing thing about him was that he had all his first teeth. When he saw she was a grown-up, he gnashed the little pearls at her.

by dint of struggle send their daughters to boarding-schools and their sons to universities" (*The Greenwood Hat*, 151). Barrie's parents valued education above all else and were willing to live modestly to ensure that their children attended the best schools. That education enabled Barrie to move with ease across class boundaries soon after his first success as an author. Upper-class friends and acquaintances invariably referred to Barrie's short stature, his ubiquitous pipe, and his melancholy disposition, only rarely taking note of his humble social origins. The combination of genius, fame, and eccentricity did much to transcend class differences.

30. *clad in skeleton leaves and the juices that ooze out of trees.* Surprisingly, Peter Pan is not clad in greenery. That he wears a costume of delicate skeleton leaves points to his ethereal, "uncivilized" qualities as well as to a connection with seasonal change and death. Skeleton leaves can be produced by separating the cellular matter filling up spaces between a leaf's veins or vascular tissue. The process is accomplished by dropping leaves in water and letting them remain in it until the fleshy matter decomposes but before the fibers begin to decay. Peter has presumably gathered skeleton leaves from the floor of the forest. Whatever their color may be, his way of dressing links him to the Green Man of Nature, a sinister figure connected with the devil. The oozing juices that hold the leaves together weld vitality to the hint of death in "skeleton" leaves.

CHAPTER 2

The Shadow

1. *a shooting star.* Lady Cynthia Asquith, Barrie's personal secretary for nearly twenty years, reports that her employer once rhapsodized about "the beauty of the word 'star,'" which he believed to be "the loveliest in the English language." By a "cursed compulsion," Cynthia felt obliged to point out that "star" spelled backwards yields "rats," the mere mention of which would drive Barrie "white-lipped" from any room.

2. *proved to be the boy's shadow.* Often seen in symbolic terms as a manifestation of the soul, shadows have played a key role in literary works ranging from Adelbert von Chamisso's *The Marvelous Story of Peter Schlemihl* and Edgar Allan Poe's "Shadow: A Parable" to Oscar Wilde's "The Fisherman and His Soul" and Hugo von Hofmannsthal's *The Woman without a Shadow*. The shadow is sometimes also a sign of the undead, who feed upon the living. In Chamisso's story, the sinister man who proposes the exchange of shadow for soul lifts up Schlemihl's shadow, folds it up, and puts it in his pocket. And in Hans Christian Andersen's "The Shadow," the scholar of the story "loses his life" to his sinister shadow-double.

Mrs. Darling screamed, and, as if in answer to a bell, the door opened, and Nana entered, returned from her evening out. She growled and sprang at the boy, who leapt lightly through the window. Again Mrs. Darling screamed, this time in distress for him, for she thought he was killed, and she ran down into the street to look for his little body, but it was not there; and she looked up, and in the black night she could see nothing but what she thought was a shooting star.[1]

She returned to the nursery, and found Nana with something in her mouth, which proved to be the boy's shadow.[2] As he leapt at the window Nana had closed it quickly, too late to catch him, but his shadow had not had time to get out; slam went the window and snapped it off.

You may be sure Mrs. Darling examined the shadow carefully, but it was quite the ordinary kind.[3]

Nana had no doubt of what was the best thing to do with this shadow. She hung it out at the window, meaning "He is sure to come back for it; let us put it where he can get it easily without disturbing the children."

But unfortunately Mrs. Darling could not leave it hanging out at the window; it looked so like the washing and lowered the whole tone of the house. She thought of showing it to Mr. Darling, but he was totting up winter greatcoats for John and Michael, with a wet towel round his head to keep his brain clear, and it seemed a shame to trouble him; besides, she knew exactly what he would say: "It all comes of having a dog for a nurse."

She decided to roll the shadow up and put it away carefully in a drawer, until a fitting opportunity came for telling her husband. Ah me!

The opportunity came a week later, on that never-to-be-forgotten Friday. Of course it was a Friday.

"I ought to have been specially careful on a Friday," she used to say afterwards to her husband, while perhaps Nana was on the other side of her, holding her hand.

"No, no," Mr. Darling always said, "I am responsible for it all. I, George Darling, did it. *Mea culpa, mea culpa.*"[4] He had had a classical education.

They sat thus night after night recalling that fatal Friday,[5] till every detail of it was stamped on their brains and came through on the other side like the faces on a bad coinage.

"If only I had not accepted that invitation to dine at 27," Mrs. Darling said.

"If only I had not poured my medicine into Nana's bowl," said Mr. Darling.

"If only I had pretended to like the medicine," was what Nana's wet eyes said.

"My liking for parties, George."

"My fatal gift of humour, dearest."

"My touchiness about trifles, dear master and mistress."[6]

Then one or more of them would break down altogether; Nana at the thought, "It's true, it's true, they ought not to have had a dog for a nurse." Many a time it was Mr. Darling who put the handkerchief to Nana's eyes.

"That fiend!" Mr. Darling would cry, and Nana's bark was the echo of it, but Mrs. Darling never upbraided Peter; there

3. *quite the ordinary kind.* The irony of the detachable shadow as "ordinary" suggests that No. 14 has its own whimsical oddities.

4. *"Mea culpa, mea culpa."* A Latin phrase meaning "It's my fault," from a traditional prayer in the Mass of the Roman Catholic Church known as *Confiteor* ("I confess"). The narrator's tongue-in-cheek allusion to Mr. Darling's classical education offers further evidence of a mildly contemptuous attitude toward the father of the children. Note Mr. Darling's childlike tendency to repeat words and phrases.

5. *They sat thus night after night recalling that fatal Friday.* The conversation between Mr. and Mrs. Darling has a retarding effect on the action, taking us to the post-Neverland period in which the two recall the "dreadful evening" on which the children are taken away by Peter Pan. In their tedious and repetitive ("night after night") grown-up fashion, they try to determine how the event might have been avoided.

6. *"My touchiness about trifles, dear master and mistress."* This is the only moment in the story when Nana appears to have the gift of language. She speaks first with her "wet eyes," but this sentence contains no qualifying statement about how she speaks, although presumably she could also continue to communicate through those eyes.

7. *"I won't go to bed," he had shouted.* Barrie captures here the desire of children to stay up and to resist the nighttime ritual of bathing, which signals bedtime. Michael's determined words open the play *Peter Pan*, and he is said to speak them in an "obstreperous" tone.

8. *playing at being herself and father.* As in Neverland, the children delight in impersonating grown-ups, and in this case the two older children take on the role of Mother and Father. Barrie's play and novel are permeated with discourses about make-believe and role playing.

was something in the right-hand corner of her mouth that wanted her not to call Peter names.

They would sit there in the empty nursery, recalling fondly every smallest detail of that dreadful evening. It had begun so uneventfully, so precisely like a hundred other evenings, with Nana putting on the water for Michael's bath and carrying him to it on her back.

"I won't go to bed," he had shouted,[7] like one who still believed that he had the last word on the subject, "I won't, I won't. Nana, it isn't six o'clock yet. Oh dear, oh dear, I shan't love you any more, Nana. I tell you I won't be bathed, I won't, I won't!"

Then Mrs. Darling had come in, wearing her white evening-gown. She had dressed early because Wendy so loved to see her in her evening-gown, with the necklace George had given her. She was wearing Wendy's bracelet on her arm; she had asked for the loan of it. Wendy so loved to lend her bracelet to her mother.

She had found her two older children playing at being herself and father[8] on the occasion of Wendy's birth, and John was saying:

"I am happy to inform you, Mrs. Darling, that you are now a mother," in just such a tone as Mr. Darling himself may have used on the real occasion.

Wendy had danced with joy, just as the real Mrs. Darling must have done.

Then John was born, with the extra pomp that he conceived due to the birth of a male, and Michael came from his bath to ask to be born also, but John said brutally that they did not want any more.

Michael had nearly cried. "Nobody wants me," he said, and of course the lady in the evening-dress could not stand that.

"I do," she said, "I so want a third child."

"Boy or girl?" asked Michael, not too hopefully.

"Boy."

Then he had leapt into her arms. Such a little thing for Mr. and Mrs. Darling and Nana to recall now, but not so little if that was to be Michael's last night in the nursery.

They go on with their recollections.

"It was then that I rushed in like a tornado, wasn't it?" Mr. Darling would say, scorning himself; and indeed he had been like a tornado.

Perhaps there was some excuse for him. He, too, had been dressing for the party, and all had gone well with him until he came to his tie. It is an astounding thing to have to tell, but this man, though he knew about stocks and shares, had no real mastery of his tie. Sometimes the thing yielded to him without a contest, but there were occasions when it would have been better for the house if he had swallowed his pride and used a made-up tie.

This was such an occasion. He came rushing into the nursery with the crumpled little brute of a tie[9] in his hand.

"Why, what is the matter, father dear?"

"Matter!" he yelled; he really yelled. "This tie, it will not tie." He became dangerously sarcastic. "Not round my neck! Round the bed-post! Oh yes, twenty times have I made it up round the bed-post, but round my neck, no! Oh dear no! begs to be excused!"

He thought Mrs. Darling was not sufficiently impressed, and he went on sternly, "I warn you of this, mother, that unless this tie is round my neck we don't go out to dinner to-night, and if I don't go out to dinner to-night, I never go to the office again, and if I don't go to the office again, you and I starve, and our children will be flung into the streets."

Even then Mrs. Darling was placid. "Let me try, dear," she said, and indeed that was what he had come to ask her to do; and with her nice cool hands she tied his tie for him, while the children stood around to see their fate decided. Some men would have resented her being able to do it so easily, but Mr. Darling was far too fine a nature for that; he thanked her care-

9. *little brute of a tie*. Mr. Darling's struggle with the tie reminds us once again that he is more like a child than an adult. He anthropomorphizes objects and endows the trivial (the tie's failure to settle into a knot) with monumental consequences ("our children will be flung into the streets").

10. *It was an opportunity.* Mrs. Darling's observation about the children's souls provides the chance not only for telling about Peter Pan but also for displaying his shadow/soul.

lessly, at once forgot his rage, and in another moment was dancing round the room with Michael on his back.

"How wildly we romped!" says Mrs. Darling now, recalling it.

"Our last romp!" Mr. Darling groaned.

"O George, do you remember Michael suddenly said to me, 'How did you get to know me, mother?'"

"I remember!"

"They were rather sweet, don't you think, George?"

"And they were ours, ours, and now they are gone."

The romp had ended with the appearance of Nana, and most unluckily Mr. Darling collided against her, covering his trousers with hairs. They were not only new trousers, but they were the first he had ever had with braid on them, and he had to bite his lip to prevent the tears coming. Of course Mrs. Darling brushed him, but he began to talk again about its being a mistake to have a dog for a nurse.

"George, Nana is a treasure."

"No doubt, but I have an uneasy feeling at times that she looks upon the children as puppies."

"Oh no, dear one, I feel sure she knows they have souls."

"I wonder," Mr. Darling said thoughtfully, "I wonder." It was an opportunity,[10] his wife felt, for telling him about the boy. At first he pooh-poohed the story, but he became thoughtful when she showed him the shadow.

"It is nobody I know," he said, examining it carefully, "but he does look a scoundrel."

"We were still discussing it, you remember," says Mr. Darling, "when Nana came in with Michael's medicine. You will never carry the bottle in your mouth again, Nana, and it is all my fault."

Strong man though he was, there is no doubt that he had behaved rather foolishly over the medicine. If he had a weakness, it was for thinking that all his life he had taken medicine boldly; and so now, when Michael dodged the spoon in Nana's mouth, he had said reprovingly, "Be a man, Michael."

"Won't; won't!" Michael cried naughtily. Mrs. Darling left the room to get a chocolate for him, and Mr. Darling thought this showed want of firmness.

"Mother, don't pamper him," he called after her. "Michael, when I was your age I took medicine without a murmur. I said 'Thank you, kind parents, for giving me bottles to make we well.'"

He really thought this was true, and Wendy, who was now in her night-gown, believed it also, and she said, to encourage Michael, "That medicine you sometimes take, father, is much nastier, isn't it?"

"Ever so much nastier," Mr. Darling said bravely, "and I would take it now as an example to you, Michael, if I hadn't lost the bottle."

He had not exactly lost it; he had climbed in the dead of night to the top of the wardrobe and hidden it there. What he did not know was that the faithful Liza had found it, and put it back on his wash-stand.

"I know where it is, father," Wendy cried, always glad to be of service. "I'll bring it," and she was off before he could stop her. Immediately his spirits sank in the strangest way.

"John," he said, shuddering, "it's most beastly stuff. It's that nasty, sticky, sweet kind."

"It will soon be over, father," John said cheerily, and then in rushed Wendy with the medicine in a glass.

"I have been as quick as I could," she panted.

"You have been wonderfully quick," her father retorted, with a vindictive politeness that was quite thrown away upon her. "Michael first," he said doggedly.

"Father first," said Michael, who was of a suspicious nature.

"I shall be sick, you know," Mr. Darling said threateningly.

"Come on, father," said John.

11. *"a cowardy custard."* The phrase is drawn from a British schoolyard taunt: "Cowardy, cowardy custard, / Eats his mother's mustard." In a holiday entertainment (*The Greedy Dwarf*) written by Barrie for the Llewelyn Davies boys, Barrie played the role of "Cowardy Custard."

"Hold your tongue, John," his father rapped out.

Wendy was quite puzzled. "I thought you took it quite easily, father."

"That is not the point," he retorted. "The point is, that there is more in my glass than in Michael's spoon." His proud heart was nearly bursting. "And it isn't fair; I would say it though it were with my last breath; it isn't fair."

"Father, I am waiting," said Michael coldly.

"It's all very well to say you are waiting; so am I waiting."

"Father's a cowardy custard."[11]

"So are you a cowardy custard."

"I'm not frightened."

"Neither am I frightened."

"Well, then, take it."

"Well, then, you take it."

Wendy had a splendid idea. "Why not both take it at the same time?"

"Certainly," said Mr. Darling. "Are you ready, Michael?"

Wendy gave the words, one, two, three, and Michael took his medicine, but Mr. Darling slipped his behind his back.

There was a yell of rage from Michael, and "O father!" Wendy exclaimed.

"What do you mean by 'O father'?" Mr. Darling demanded. "Stop that row, Michael. I meant to take mine, but I—I missed it."

It was dreadful the way all the three were looking at him, just as if they did not admire him. "Look here, all of you," he said entreatingly, as soon as Nana had gone into the bathroom. "I have just thought of a splendid joke. I shall pour my medicine into Nana's bowl, and she will drink it, thinking it is milk!"

It was the colour of milk; but the children did not have their father's sense of humour, and they looked at him reproachfully as he poured the medicine into Nana's bowl.

"What fun!" he said doubtfully, and they did not dare expose him when Mrs. Darling and Nana returned.

"Nana, good dog," he said, patting her, "I have put a little milk into your bowl, Nana."

Nana wagged her tail, ran to the medicine, and began lapping it. Then she gave Mr. Darling such a look, not an angry look: she showed him the great red tear that makes us so sorry for noble dogs, and crept into her kennel.

Mr. Darling was frightfully ashamed of himself, but he would not give in. In a horrid silence Mrs. Darling smelt the bowl. "O George," she said, "it's your medicine!"

"It was only a joke," he roared, while she comforted her boys, and Wendy hugged Nana. "Much good," he said bitterly, "my wearing myself to the bone trying to be funny in this house."

And still Wendy hugged Nana. "That's right," he shouted. "Coddle her! Nobody coddles me. Oh dear no! I am only the breadwinner, why should I be coddled, why, why, why!"

"George," Mrs. Darling entreated him, "not so loud; the servants will hear you." Somehow they had got into the way of calling Liza the servants.

"Let them!" he answered recklessly. "Bring in the whole world. But I refuse to allow that dog to lord it in my nursery for an hour longer."

The children wept, and Nana ran to him beseechingly, but he waved her back. He felt he was a strong man again. "In vain, in vain," he cried; "the proper place for you is the yard, and there you go to be tied up this instant."

"George, George," Mrs. Darling whispered, "remember what I told you about that boy."

Alas, he would not listen. He was determined to show who was master in that house, and when commands would not draw Nana from the kennel, he lured her out of it with honeyed words, and seizing her roughly, dragged her from

12. *Danger!* The narrator speaks here, inserting his own sense of excitement about the perils to come and his own vicarious participation in the children's adventures. The lack of quotation marks indicates that he has produced the word.

the nursery. He was ashamed of himself, and yet he did it. It was all owing to his too affectionate nature, which craved for admiration. When he had tied her up in the back-yard, the wretched father went and sat in the passage, with his knuckles to his eyes.

In the meantime Mrs. Darling had put the children to bed in unwonted silence and lit their night-lights. They could hear Nana barking, and John whimpered, "It is because he is chaining her up in the yard," but Wendy was wiser.

"That is not Nana's unhappy bark," she said, little guessing what was about to happen; "that is her bark when she smells danger."

Danger![12]

"Are you sure, Wendy?"

"Oh yes."

Mrs. Darling quivered and went to the window. It was securely fastened. She looked out, and the night was peppered with stars. They were crowding round the house, as if curious to see what was to take place there, but she did not notice this, nor that one or two of the smaller ones winked at her. Yet a nameless fear clutched at her heart and made her cry, "Oh, how I wish that I wasn't going to a party to-night!"

Even Michael, already half asleep, knew that she was perturbed, and he asked, "Can anything harm us, mother, after the night-lights are lit?"

"Nothing, precious," she said; "they are the eyes a mother leaves behind her to guard her children."

She went from bed to bed singing enchantments over them, and little Michael flung his arms round her. "Mother," he cried, "I'm glad of you." They were the last words she was to hear from him for a long time.

No. 27 was only a few yards distant, but there had been a slight fall of snow, and Father and Mother Darling picked their way over it deftly not to soil their shoes. They were already the only persons in the street, and all the stars were watching them.[13] Stars are beautiful, but they may not take an active part in anything, they must just look on for ever.[14] It is a punishment put on them for something they did so long ago that no star now knows what it was. So the older ones have become glassy-eyed and seldom speak (winking is the star language), but the little ones still wonder. They are not really friendly to Peter, who had a mischievous way of stealing up behind them and trying to blow them out; but they are so fond of fun that they were on his side to-night, and anxious to get the grown-ups out of the way. So as soon as the door of 27 closed on Mr. and Mrs. Darling there was a commotion in the firmament, and the smallest of all the stars in the Milky Way screamed out:

"Now, Peter!"

13. *all the stars were watching them.* No. 14 and Neverland share some features, and the two sites are not defined in pure opposition to each other. Nature is animated and magical from the vantage point of the Darling nursery, with stars invested with curiosity about human beings. Mrs. Darling sings "enchantments" to the children when they go to bed.

14. *they must just look on for ever.* The allusion to extraterrestrial beings condemned to witness and watch rather than participate resonates with Barrie's own sense that he was forever destined to be nothing more than an onlooker in life. In chapter 16, the narrator will complain about his own limited role in the lives of the Darling children: "That is all we are, lookers-on."

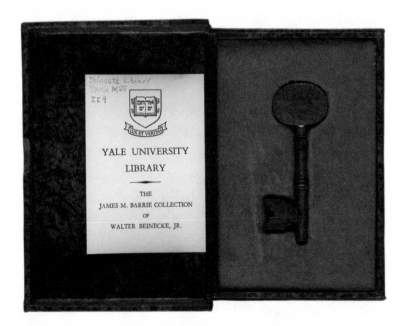

J. M. Barrie's key to Kensington Gardens. Shortly after the publication of *The Little White Bird*, Barrie was given his own key to the gardens by the Duke of Cambridge, Ranger of the Gardens. (Beinecke Rare Book and Manuscript Library, Yale University)

CHAPTER 3

Come Away, Come Away!¹

1. *Come Away, Come Away!* The title echoes W. B. Yeats's 1889 poem "The Stolen Child": "Come away, O human child! / To the waters and the wild / With a faery, hand in hand." Like the Darling children, the child of Yeats's poem is escorted by a fairy to an island far away from the ordinary world, "more full of weeping than you can understand."

2. *a thousand times brighter.* Powerful light effects are found in Neverland, and Tinker Bell is one of the creatures who provide unearthly illumination, somewhat dimmer than the "million golden arrows" that point the way to Neverland. Colorful radiance is the hallmark of many fantasy worlds in children's literature—Oz and Narnia are prime examples.

3. *you saw it was a fairy.* Barrie wrote of Tinker Bell's origins as a creature made up during the days spent with the Llewelyn Davies boys at Black Lake: "It was one evening when we climbed the wood carrying [Michael] to show him what the trail was like by twilight. As our lanterns twinkled among the leaves, he saw a twinkle

For a moment after Mr. and Mrs. Darling left the house the night-lights by the beds of the three children continued to burn clearly. They were awfully nice little night-lights, and one cannot help wishing that they could have kept awake to see Peter; but Wendy's light blinked and gave such a yawn that the other two yawned also, and before they could close their mouths all the three went out.

There was another light in the room now, a thousand times brighter² than the night-lights, and in the time we have taken to say this, it has been in all the drawers in the nursery, looking for Peter's shadow, rummaged the wardrobe and turned every pocket inside out. It was not really a light; it made this light by flashing about so quickly, but when it came to rest for a second you saw it was a fairy,³ no longer than your hand, but still growing. It was a girl called Tinker Bell⁴ exquisitely gowned in a skeleton leaf, cut low and square, through which her figure could be seen to the best advantage. She was slightly inclined to *embonpoint*.⁵

A moment after the fairy's entrance the window was blown open by the breathing of the little stars, and Peter dropped in. He had carried Tinker Bell part of the way, and his hand was still messy with the fairy dust.

stand still for a moment and he waved his foot gaily to it, thus creating Tink."

Fairyland is usually represented in folklore as a parallel universe, one that can be entered by stepping into a fairy ring or interrupting a fairy dance. By invoking fairies and introducing Tinker Bell as an inhabitant of Neverland, Barrie alludes to two different traditional stories, one about fairies as dethroned gods who spend their time fighting and feasting on a "blessed isle" (rather like the lost boys), the other about mortals who are taken away to fairyland to care for lost children (rather like Wendy). In Celtic mythology, the "blessed isle"—also known as the "Isles of the Blest," "The Fortunate Isle," "The Isle of Content," and the "Land of the Young" (the site of perpetual youth and springtime)—is also the Land of the Dead. There, eternal youth lives in a perpetual springtime. Access was often through burial mounds guarded by faery folk. Peter Pan does not grow up and remains young forever in part perhaps because he belongs to the dead.

Barrie was living in an era with a euphoric faith in fairies and elfin folk—as well as in demons who spirit children away from the human world into utopian realms where pain and suffering are banished and beauty reigns supreme. He was no doubt familiar with Goethe's poem "Erl-King," Browning's "Pied Piper of Hamelin: A Child's Story," and George MacDonald's *At the Back of the North Wind*, all of which express profound anxieties about fairies and demons with power over children.

Victorian culture was open to the sorcery of elfin people, and fairies appeared often in the art, literature, and plays of the time. *A Midsummer Night's Dream* and *The Tempest* were staged frequently and inspired the nineteenth-century rage for fairy paintings and even the fashion for fairy wallpapers designed for bedrooms and nurseries. The cult of fairy lore served both as a form of protest against the rise of industrialism and worship of material wealth and as a nostalgic gesture toward the enchantments of rural life and childhood. It had a complicated, mysterious, and sensually stirring dimension but could also slide easily into the artless and banal.

4. *a girl called Tinker Bell.* Tinker Bell was originally a fairy-tinker, a creature who mended pots and pans. In Scottish parlance, the word tinker was used to describe Gypsies who engaged in service trades such as knife sharpening and mending household items. Like the fairies in *Peter Pan*, they were perceived in Edwardian times as a flighty, nomadic folk, characterized by lawlessness and childlike behavior. The *Oxford English Dictionary* connects "tinker" with Gypsies in Scottish and Irish usages of the term. In the original manuscript to the play, Tinker Bell was called Tippy or Tippytoe.

5. embonpoint. From the French, *en bon point*, meaning "in good condition," and used in English to describe someone who is plump, chubby, or buxom.

6. *ha'pence.* A ha'pence is a small coin, or halfpenny. If Mrs. Darling tidies up the metaphorical chests of drawers that are the children's minds, Peter Pan flings the contents of the real chest of drawers in the nursery to the ground, creating disorderly clutter.

7. *he forgot that he had shut Tinker Bell up in the drawer.* Peter's forgetfulness is part of his identity as the *puer aeternus*, the boy who will never grow up. He is always forgetting things, and, once Wendy returns to No. 14 in London, he begins to lose his memory of the lost boys, Hook, Tinker Bell, and, presumably, Wendy as well.

8. *"Wendy Moira Angela Darling."* The name Moira has two competing histories, one connecting it with the Greek word for fate or destiny, the other linking it to the British Isles, where it is a variant of Mary and literally means "bitter."

"Tinker Bell," he called softly, after making sure that the children were asleep, "Tink, where are you?" She was in a jug for the moment, and liking it extremely; she had never been in a jug before.

"Oh, do come out of that jug, and tell me, do you know where they put my shadow?"

The loveliest tinkle as of golden bells answered him. It is the fairy language. You ordinary children can never hear it, but if you were to hear it you would know that you had heard it once before.

Tink said that the shadow was in the big box. She meant the chest of drawers, and Peter jumped at the drawers, scattering their contents to the floor with both hands, as kings toss ha'pence[6] to the crowd. In a moment he had recovered his shadow, and in his delight he forgot that he had shut Tinker Bell up in the drawer.[7]

If he thought at all, but I don't believe he ever thought, it was that he and his shadow, when brought near each other, would join like drops of water; and when they did not he was appalled. He tried to stick it on with soap from the bathroom, but that also failed. A shudder passed through Peter, and he sat on the floor and cried.

His sobs woke Wendy, and she sat up in bed. She was not alarmed to see a stranger crying on the nursery floor; she was only pleasantly interested.

"Boy," she said courteously, "why are you crying?"

Peter could be exceedingly polite also, having learned the grand manner at fairy ceremonies, and he rose and bowed to her beautifully. She was much pleased, and bowed beautifully to him from the bed.

"What's your name?" he asked.

"Wendy Moira Angela Darling,"[8] she replied with some satisfaction. "What is your name?"

"Peter Pan."

She was already sure that he must be Peter, but it did seem a comparatively short name.

"Is that all?"

"Yes," he said rather sharply. He felt for the first time that it was a shortish name.

"I'm so sorry," said Wendy Moira Angela.

"It doesn't matter," Peter gulped.

She asked where he lived.

"Second to the right,"[9] said Peter, "and then straight on till morning."

"What a funny address!"

Peter had a sinking. For the first time he felt that perhaps it was a funny address.

"No, it isn't," he said.

"I mean," Wendy said nicely, remembering that she was hostess, "is that what they put on the letters?"

He wished she had not mentioned letters.

"Don't get any letters," he said contemptuously.

"But your mother gets letters?"

"Don't have a mother," he said. Not only had he no mother, but he had not the slightest desire to have one. He thought them very overrated persons. Wendy, however, felt at once that she was in the presence of a tragedy.

"O Peter, no wonder you were crying," she said, and got out of bed and ran to him.

"I wasn't crying about mothers," he said rather indignantly. "I was crying because I can't get my shadow to stick on. Besides, I wasn't crying."

"It has come off?"

"Yes."

Then Wendy saw the shadow on the floor, looking so draggled,[10] and she was frightfully sorry for Peter. "How awful!" she said, but she could not help smiling when she saw that he had been trying to stick it on with soap. How exactly like a boy!

9. *"Second to the right."* When Robert Louis Stevenson invited Barrie to visit him on Upolu, one of the Samoan islands, he provided the following instructions: "You take the boat to San Francisco, and then my place is second to the left." Stevenson had written repeatedly to Barrie, encouraging him to make the journey: "We would have some grand cracks! Come, it will broaden your mind and be the making of me" (Chaney 123). Stevenson's poor health (he suffered from tuberculosis) had led to his self-imposed exile on the remote South Sea Island, and he died there in 1894. Vailima, Stevenson's estate, was, for Barrie, "the one spot on earth I had any craving to visit" (*Margaret Ogilvy*, 148), but Stevenson's death put an end to his "scheme for travel." Barrie worked hard to secure Stevenson's posthumous literary reputation and sought to erect a monument to his memory, despite some fierce local opposition to honoring the author of *The Strange Case of Dr. Jekyll and Mr. Hyde* and *The Master of Ballantrae*, in addition to *Treasure Island*. In *Margaret Ogilvy*, Barrie described how Stevenson was "the spirit of boyhood tugging at the skirts of this old world of ours and compelling it to come back and play" (146).

10. *draggled.* soiled and wet, as if dragged through the mud.

11. *housewife*. The "sewing housewife," "housewife sewing kit," or just plain "housewife" was a kit containing needles, thread, scissors, and other items related to mending. It was part of the standard issue for British soldiers until after World War II.

12. *he crowed rapturously*. Peter's narcissistic glee is expressed repeatedly through crowing. The term "cocky" used to describe him had its origins in the mid-nineteenth century and was used by Charles Kingsley in *The Water-babies* (1863): "He looked the cockiest little man of all little men." Crowing and crying are what Peter uses to express emotional extremes, and they remind us of his origins in a god with a double nature as beast and human. Peter crows to signal his return to Neverland, to mark triumphs over his enemies, and sometimes, as here, just to signal that he is "pleased" with himself.

13. *she replied with hauteur*. Wendy speaks to Peter in a condescending way, answering his cockiness with her own arrogance, or hauteur, a word derived from the French word *haut*, meaning tall.

Fortunately she knew at once what to do. "It must be sewn on," she said, just a little patronizingly.

"What's sewn?" he asked.

"You're dreadfully ignorant."

"No, I'm not."

But she was exulting in his ignorance. "I shall sew it on for you, my little man," she said, though he was tall as herself, and she got out her housewife,[11] and sewed the shadow on to Peter's foot.

"I daresay it will hurt a little," she warned him.

"Oh, I shan't cry," said Peter, who was already of the opinion that he had never cried in his life. And he clenched his teeth and did not cry; and soon his shadow was behaving properly, though still a little creased.

"Perhaps I should have ironed it," Wendy said thoughtfully; but Peter, boylike, was indifferent to appearances, and he was now jumping about in the wildest glee. Alas, he had already forgotten that he owed his bliss to Wendy. He thought he had attached the shadow himself. "How clever I am!" he crowed rapturously,[12] "oh, the cleverness of me!"

It is humiliating to have to confess that this conceit of Peter was one of his most fascinating qualities. To put it with brutal frankness, there never was a cockier boy.

But for the moment Wendy was shocked. "You conceit," she exclaimed, with frightful sarcasm; "of course I did nothing!"

"You did a little," Peter said carelessly, and continued to dance.

"A little!" she replied with hauteur;[13] "if I am no use I can at least withdraw"; and she sprang in the most dignified way into bed and covered her face with the blankets.

To induce her to look up he pretended to be going away, and when this failed he sat on the end of the bed and tapped her gently with his foot. "Wendy," he said, "don't withdraw. I can't help crowing, Wendy, when I'm pleased with myself."

Still she would not look up, though she was listening eagerly. "Wendy," he continued, in a voice that no woman has ever yet been able to resist, "Wendy, one girl is more use than twenty boys."

Now Wendy was every inch a woman, though there were not very many inches, and she peeped out of the bedclothes.

"Do you really think so, Peter?"

"Yes, I do."

"I think it's perfectly sweet of you," she declared, "and I'll get up again"; and she sat with him on the side of the bed. She also said she would give him a kiss if he liked, but Peter did not know what she meant, and he held out his hand expectantly.

"Surely you know what a kiss is?" she asked, aghast.

"I shall know when you give it to me," he replied stiffly; and not to hurt his feelings she gave him a thimble.[14]

"Now," said he, "shall I give you a kiss?" and she replied with a slight primness, "If you please." She made herself rather cheap by inclining her face toward him, but he merely dropped an acorn button into her hand; so she slowly returned her face to where it had been before, and said nicely that she would wear his kiss on the chain round her neck. It was lucky that she did put it on that chain, for it was afterwards to save her life.

When people in our set are introduced, it is customary for them to ask each other's age, and so Wendy, who always liked to do the correct thing, asked Peter how old he was. It was not really a happy question to ask him; it was like an examination paper that asks grammar, when what you want to be asked is Kings of England.

"I don't know," he replied uneasily, "but I am quite young." He really knew nothing about it; he had merely suspicions, but he said at a venture, "Wendy, I ran away the day I was born."

Wendy was quite surprised, but interested; and she indi-

14. *she gave him a thimble.* Young audiences participated in the early productions, not just by clapping their hands to save Tinker Bell but also by throwing thimbles onstage to Peter. A twelve-year-old girl describes her efforts: "I nearly shouted myself hoarse. I tried to throw a thimble onto the stage. I don't know whether it arrived, because there were such a lot of other thimbles thrown" (Gubar 200). For the remainder of the story, Peter will mistake thimbles for kisses.

15. *"its laugh broke into a thousand pieces."* In *Peter Pan in Kensington Gardens*, the narrator declares that fairies never do "anything useful." In language reminiscent of Peter's words, he describes the origins of fairies: "When the first baby laughed for the first time, his laugh broke into a million pieces, and they all went skipping about. That was the beginning of fairies. They look tremendously busy, you know, as if they had not a moment to spare, but if you were to ask them what they are doing, they could not tell you in the least."

16. *"they soon don't believe in fairies."* On several occasions, Barrie mourned the disappearance of the idyllic pastoral life of his boyhood in Kirriemuir, a place that had been sustained by faith, not only in matters religious but also in fairies and sprites. By 1922, when Sir Arthur Conan Doyle was rejoicing over the case of two girls who had reportedly seen and photographed fairies in a glade behind their home in the village of Cottingley, in West Yorkshire, he could be dismissed as a mystic and kook. The physician who had written the Sherlock Holmes stories rhapsodized about the possibility that the world could be reenchanted through "well-authenticated" cases of fairy presences: "The thought of them, even when unseen, will add a charm to every brook and valley and give romantic interest to every country walk. The recognition of their existence will jolt the material twentieth-century mind out of its heavy ruts in the mud, and will make it admit that there is a glamour and a mystery to life" (Conan Doyle 32). Barrie's secretary, Cynthia Asquith, describes Conan Doyle's visit to Barrie's summer residence and how relieved she was that the famous author did not put the question "Do you believe in fairies?" to Barrie (Asquith, *Portrait* 172). The spiritualist turn in Conan Doyle's life and his faith in the five Cottingley fairies (the photographs were

cated in the charming drawing-room manner, by a touch on her night-gown, that he could sit nearer her.

"It was because I heard father and mother," he explained in a low voice, "talking about what I was to be when I became a man." He was extraordinarily agitated now. "I don't want ever to be a man," he said with passion. "I want always to be a little boy and to have fun. So I ran away to Kensington Gardens and lived a long long time among the fairies."

She gave him a look of the most intense admiration, and he thought it was because he had run away, but it was really because he knew fairies. Wendy had lived such a home life that to know fairies struck her as quite delightful. She poured out questions about them, to his surprise, for they were rather a nuisance to him, getting in his way and so on, and indeed he sometimes had to give them a hiding. Still, he liked them on the whole, and he told her about the beginning of fairies.

"You see, Wendy, when the first baby laughed for the first time, its laugh broke into a thousand pieces,[15] and they all went skipping about, and that was the beginning of fairies."

Tedious talk this, but being a stay-at-home she liked it.

"And so," he went on good-naturedly, "there ought to be one fairy for every boy and girl."

"Ought to be? Isn't there?"

"No. You see children know such a lot now, they soon don't believe in fairies,[16] and every time a child says, 'I don't believe in fairies,' there is a fairy somewhere that falls down dead."

Really, he thought they had now talked enough about fairies, and it struck him that Tinker Bell was keeping very quiet. "I can't think where she has gone to," he said, rising, and he called Tink by name. Wendy's heart went flutter with a sudden thrill.

"Peter," she cried, clutching him, "you don't mean to tell me that there is a fairy in this room!"[17]

"She was here just now," he said a little impatiently. "You don't hear her, do you?" and they both listened.

"The only sound I hear," said Wendy, "is like a tinkle of bells."

"Well, that's Tink, that's the fairy language. I think I hear her too."

The sound came from the chest of drawers, and Peter made a merry face. No one could ever look quite so merry as Peter, and the loveliest of gurgles was his laugh. He had his first laugh still.

"Wendy," he whispered gleefully, "I do believe I shut her up in the drawer!"

He let poor Tink out of the drawer, and she flew about the nursery screaming with fury. "You shouldn't say such things," Peter retorted. "Of course I'm very sorry, but how could I know you were in the drawer?"

Wendy was not listening to him. "O Peter," she cried, "if she would only stand still and let me see her!"

"They hardly ever stand still," he said, but for one moment Wendy saw the romantic figure come to rest on the cuckoo clock. "O the lovely!" she cried, though Tink's face was still distorted with passion.

"Tink," said Peter amiably, "this lady says she wishes you were her fairy."

Tinker Bell answered insolently.

"What does she say, Peter?"

He had to translate. "She is not very polite. She says you are a great ugly girl, and that she is my fairy."

He tried to argue with Tink. "You know you can't be my fairy, Tink, because I am a gentleman and you are a lady."

To this Tink replied in these words, "You silly ass," and disappeared into the bathroom. "She is quite a common fairy," Peter explained apologetically, "she is called Tinker Bell because she mends the pots and kettles."

They were together in the armchair by this time, and Wendy plied him with more questions.

"If you don't live in Kensington Gardens now—"

revealed to be a hoax) were triggered by a deep depression following the deaths of his wife, his son, a brother, and two nephews.

17. *"you don't mean to tell me that there is a fairy in this room!"* In traditional lore, fairies are associated with the practice of stealing human children, and Peter and Tinker Bell might be seen as co-conspirators as they enter the Darling home.

18. *"the lost boys."* Peter Pan is, in some ways, a compensatory dream child for all the boys who have fallen out of perambulators. He was once a dead baby, but he is also a fantasy child, as J. M. Barrie acknowledged, in an autograph addition for the second draft of the ending of the 1908 play: "I think now—that Peter is only a sort of dead baby—he is the baby of all the people who never had one." Mrs. Darling also discerns Peter in the features of women who have never had children. In *The Little White Bird*, Peter finds two babies who have fallen unnoticed from their perambulators: one is named Phoebe, the other Walter, and both are about a year old. The term "lost" is used frequently as a euphemism for "dead," as in "he lost his father" or "she lost a child."

"Sometimes I do still."

"But where do you live mostly now?"

"With the lost boys."[18]

"Who are they?"

"They are the children who fall out of their perambulators when the nurse is looking the other way. If they are not claimed in seven days they are sent far away to the Neverland to defray expenses. I'm captain."

"What fun it must be!"

"Yes," said cunning Peter, "but we are rather lonely. You see we have no female companionship."

"Are none of the others girls?"

"Oh, no; girls, you know, are much too clever to fall out of their prams."

This flattered Wendy immensely. "I think," she said, "it is perfectly lovely the way you talk about girls; John there just despises us."

For reply Peter rose and kicked John out of bed, blankets and all; one kick. This seemed to Wendy rather forward for a first meeting, and she told him with spirit that he was not captain in her house. However, John continued to sleep so placidly on the floor that she allowed him to remain there. "And I know you meant to be kind," she said, relenting, "so you may give me a kiss."

For the moment she had forgotten his ignorance about kisses. "I thought you would want it back," he said a little bitterly, and offered to return her the thimble.

"Oh dear," said the nice Wendy, "I don't mean a kiss, I mean a thimble."

"What's that?"

"It's like this." She kissed him.

"Funny!" said Peter gravely. "Now shall I give you a thimble?"

"If you wish to," said Wendy, keeping her head erect this time.

Peter thimbled her, and almost immediately she screeched. "What is it, Wendy?"

"It was exactly as if someone were pulling my hair."

"That must have been Tink. I never knew her so naughty before."

And indeed Tink was darting about again, using offensive language.

"She says she will do that to you, Wendy, every time I give you a thimble."

"But why?"

"Why, Tink?"

Again Tink replied, "You silly ass." Peter could not understand why, but Wendy understood; and she was just slightly disappointed when he admitted that he came to the nursery window not to see her but to listen to stories.[19]

"You see, I don't know any stories. None of the lost boys knows any stories."

"How perfectly awful," Wendy said.

"Do you know," Peter asked, "why swallows build in the eaves of houses? It is to listen to the stories.[20] O Wendy, your mother was telling you such a lovely story."

"Which story was it?"

"About the prince who couldn't find the lady who wore the glass slipper."

"Peter," said Wendy excitedly, "that was Cinderella,[21] and he found her, and they lived happily ever after."[22]

Peter was so glad that he rose from the floor, where they had been sitting, and hurried to the window. "Where are you going?" she cried with misgiving.

"To tell the other boys."

"Don't go Peter," she entreated, "I know such lots of stories."

Those were her precise words, so there can be no denying that it was she who first tempted him.[23]

He came back, and there was a greedy look in his eyes now which ought to have alarmed her,[24] but did not.

19. *not to see her but to listen to stories.* Peter is drawn to the Darling nursery window because of the stories told in it, not because of a desire to take Wendy to Neverland. In Neverland, there are plenty of adventures, but no memory and therefore also no stories. Ironically, Peter becomes the main character in one of the most famous cultural stories for children, yet he is forever banished from the nursery, where that story is read and told.

20. *"It is to listen to the stories."* Barrie may have been inspired by Hans Christian Andersen's "Thumbelina," which ends by describing how a swallow flies from the "warm lands" back to Denmark to build a nest above the window of "the man who can tell you fairy tales." Andersen is one of the authors whose name appeared on the curtain designed for the 1908 revival of *Peter Pan*. The curtain displays a sampler supposedly stitched by Wendy, including the names of—besides Andersen—Charles Lamb, Robert Louis Stevenson, and Lewis Carroll. Although Barrie does not have much to say about Andersen, he most likely knew his work through his friend Andrew Lang, who produced popular anthologies of fairy tales from all over the world. Barrie must have recognized in Andersen a kindred spirit, for the Danish writer of working-class origins was also a prolific playwright, devoted to the theater, and had the same reputation for streaks of "whimsy" in his work.

21. *"Cinderella."* Barrie's play *A Kiss for Cinderella* opened in London in March 1916 and at Christmas in New York in the same year. Barrie had been "slinging off heaven knows how many short plays, once I think six in a week," and the Cinderella play was one of the few works in that period that was not designated for the war effort. In 1926 Herbert Brenon directed a silent film version of *A Kiss for Cinder-*

ella, with Betty Bronson, who had played Peter Pan in the Paramount film. Barrie's Cinderella is a saintly young woman whose good deeds fail to rescue her from a death that resembles the martyrdom of Hans Christian Andersen's Little Match Girl.

22. *"they lived happily ever after."* Stanley Green and Betty Comden, hired to write the screenplay for the 1954 musical *Peter Pan*, added some dialogue about *Hamlet*. After telling the boys that Cinderella and Sleeping Beauty both live happily ever after, Tootles asks about the end of *Hamlet*. Wendy replies: "*Hamlet*! Well, the Prince Hamlet died, and the king died, and the Queen died, and Ophelia died, and Polonius died, and Laertes died, and. . . ." "And?" the boys ask. "Well the rest of them lived happily ever after!" Wendy declares.

23. *it was she who first tempted him.* In the play *Peter Pan,* Wendy is seen as something of an intruder in the boys' world. The stage directions emphasize that she may have "bored her way in at last whether we wanted her or not." And Barrie adds that Peter simply had to give in to Wendy's insistence on going to Neverland: "It may be that even Peter did not really bring her to the Never Land of his free will, but merely to do so because she would not stay away" (84). The allusion to the biblical story of Adam and Eve shines through, with Wendy as temptress and Peter as a "greedy" Adam.

24. *there was a greedy look in his eyes now which ought to have alarmed her.* Peter seems to recognize the bonding power of stories and their capacity to serve as a lure for the lost boys. Like James Barrie himself, the narrator is a storyteller who uses tales to hold the attention of children, and he has deep insight into Peter's motives for bringing Wendy to Neverland.

"Oh, the stories I could tell to the boys!" she cried, and then Peter gripped her and began to draw her toward the window.

"Let me go!" she ordered him.

"Wendy, do come with me and tell the other boys."

Of course she was very pleased to be asked, but she said, "Oh dear, I can't. Think of mummy! Besides, I can't fly."

"I'll teach you."

"Oh, how lovely to fly."[25]

"I'll teach you how to jump on the wind's back, and then away we go."

"Oo!" she exclaimed rapturously.

"Wendy, Wendy, when you are sleeping in your silly bed you might be flying about with me saying funny things to the stars."

"Oo!"

"And, Wendy, there are mermaids."

"Mermaids! With tails?"

"Such long tails."

"Oh," cried Wendy, "to see a mermaid!"

He had become frightfully cunning. "Wendy," he said, "how we should all respect you."

She was wriggling her body in distress. It was quite as if she were trying to remain on the nursery floor.

But he had no pity for her.

"Wendy," he said, the sly one, "you could tuck us in at night."

"Oo!"

"None of us has ever been tucked in at night."

"Oo," and her arms went out to him.

"And you could darn our clothes, and make pockets for us. None of us has any pockets."

How could she resist. "Of course it's awfully fascinating!" she cried. "Peter, would you teach John and Michael to fly too?"

25. *"Oh, how lovely to fly."* The desire to fly can be traced back to the Greek myth about Daedalus and Icarus. Daedalus, a renowned architect and craftsman, attempted to escape imprisonment on Crete by fashioning wings for himself and his son, Icarus. As noted in the introduction, he warned Icarus against flying too close to the sun, but the boy, overcome by giddy curiosity, soared so high that his wings, made of wax, melted, and he plunged into the sea. In children's literature, characters are frequently airborne, and flight comes to represent liberation from adult authority and the possibility of adventure. "Where needs are unmet, desires take wing," Jerry Griswold tells us, in a moving meditation on flight in stories as varied as George MacDonald's *The Light Princess* (1864), Pamela Travers's *Mary Poppins* (1934), and Virginia Hamilton's *The People Could Fly* (1985).

Just two years before *Peter Pan* was performed, in 1902, the children in Edith Nesbit's *Five Children and It* famously wish for wings and fly up to a church tower. "Of course you all know what flying feels like," Nesbit wrote, "because everyone has dreamed about flying, and it seems so beautifully easy—only, you can never remember how you did it; and as a rule you have to do it without wings, in your dreams, which is more clever and uncommon, but not so easy to remember the rule for" (Nesbit 99). Nesbit also emphasizes how flying is "more wonderful and more like real magic than any wish the children had had yet."

Many stories for children also show characters riding through the air on sleds (Hans Christian Andersen's "The Snow Queen"), winged horses (Madeleine L'Engle's *A Wrinkle in Time*), and lions (C. S. Lewis's Chronicles of Narnia).

26. *you heard its three wicked inmates breathing angelically.* The children are described by Liza as "little angels," and we receive a first hint in this passage about how children can be both angelic and wicked, or "innocent" and "heartless," as we learn at the tale's end. The children's facial expressions also assume an "awful craftiness" even as they are presented as cheerfully innocent. As one critic starkly puts it, in a study of British childhood: "The Victorian child is a symbol of innocence, the Edwardian child of hedonism" (Wullschläger 109). If Lewis Carroll's Alice is sweet, well mannered, and innocent, J. M. Barrie's Peter Pan is, by contrast, self-centered, impertinent, and pleasure-seeking. In a sense, the idealized child of the Victorian era made it possible for adults to discover the demon in children, for the increasing investment in toys, clothes, education, and care could easily backfire when children did not live up perfectly to the expectation of innocent beauty.

"If you like," he said indifferently; and she ran to John and Michael and shook them. "Wake up," she cried, "Peter Pan has come and he is to teach us to fly."

John rubbed his eyes. "Then I shall get up," he said. Of course he was on the floor already. "Hallo," he said, "I am up!"

Michael was up by this time also, looking as sharp as a knife with six blades and a saw, but Peter suddenly signed silence. Their faces assumed the awful craftiness of children listening for sounds from the grown-up world. All was as still as salt. Then everything was right. No, stop! Everything was wrong. Nana, who had been barking distressfully all the evening, was quiet now. It was her silence they had heard.

"Out with the light! Hide! Quick!" cried John, taking command for the only time throughout the whole adventure. And thus when Liza entered, holding Nana, the nursery seemed quite its old self, very dark; and you would have sworn you heard its three wicked inmates breathing angelically[26] as they slept. They were really doing it artfully from behind the window curtains.

Liza was in a bad temper, for she was mixing the Christmas puddings in the kitchen, and had been drawn away from them, with a raisin still on her cheek, by Nana's absurd suspicions. She thought the best way of getting a little quiet was to take Nana to the nursery for a moment, but in custody of course.

"There, you suspicious brute," she said, not sorry that Nana was in disgrace, "they are perfectly safe, aren't they? Every one of the little angels sound asleep in bed. Listen to their gentle breathing."

Here Michael, encouraged by his success, breathed so loudly that they were nearly detected. Nana knew that kind of breathing, and she tried to drag herself out of Liza's clutches.

But Liza was dense. "No more of it, Nana," she said sternly, pulling her out of the room. "I warn you if you bark again I shall go straight for master and missus and bring them home from the party, and then, oh, won't master whip you, just."

She tied the unhappy dog up again, but do you think Nana ceased to bark? Bring master and missus home from the party! Why, that was just what she wanted. Do you think she cared whether she was whipped so long as her charges were safe? Unfortunately Liza returned to her puddings, and Nana, seeing that no help would come from her, strained and strained at the chain until at last she broke it. In another moment she had burst into the dining-room of 27 and flung up her paws to heaven, her most expressive way of making a communication. Mr. and Mrs. Darling knew at once that something terrible was happening in their nursery, and without a good-bye to their hostess they rushed into the street.

But it was now ten minutes since three scoundrels had been breathing behind the curtains; and Peter Pan can do a great deal in ten minutes.

We now return to the nursery.[27]

"It's all right," John announced, emerging from his hiding-place. "I say, Peter, can you really fly?"

Instead of troubling to answer him Peter flew round the room, taking the mantelpiece on the way.

"How topping!" said John and Michael.

"How sweet!" cried Wendy.

"Yes, I'm sweet, oh, I am sweet!" said Peter, forgetting his manners again.

It looked delightfully easy, and they tried it first from the floor and then from the beds, but they always went down instead of up.

"I say, how do you do it?" asked John, rubbing his knee. He was quite a practical boy.

"You just think lovely wonderful thoughts,"[28] Peter explained, "and they lift you up in the air."

He showed them again.

27. *We now return to the nursery*. The narrator, like Peter, is betwixt and between, speaking sometimes with the voice of an adult (as when he refers to the children as "three scoundrels") yet also enamored of the pleasures of learning how to fly. The narrator never lets us forget his presence.

28. *"You just think lovely wonderful thoughts."* In his dedication to the printed play, Barrie felt obliged to add a parental warning: "after the first production I had to add something to the play at the request of parents . . . about no one being able to fly until the fairy dust had been blown on him; so many children having gone home and tried it from their beds and needed surgical attention." C. S. Lewis similarly added several warnings about entering wardrobes as well as about the hazards of closing the door behind you, all in response to parental concerns about how the Pevensie children reach Narnia in *The Lion, the Witch and the Wardrobe*. Cynthia Asquith writes in her memoir of Barrie that she did not dare tell her employer that "one child had been killed because, after seeing *Peter Pan*, he 'thought beautiful thoughts,' and confident that these thoughts would enable him to fly, jumped out of the nursery window!" (Asquith, *Portrait*, 20). There is no historical evidence or documentation that this incident ever occurred.

"You're so nippy at it," John said; "couldn't you do it very slowly once?"

Peter did it both slowly and quickly. "I've got it now, Wendy!" cried John, but soon he found he had not. Not one of them could fly an inch, though even Michael was in words of two syllables, and Peter did not know A from Z.

Of course Peter had been trifling with them, for no one can fly unless the fairy dust has been blown on him. Fortunately, as we have mentioned, one of his hands was messy with it, and he blew some on each of them, with the most superb results.

"Now just wriggle your shoulders this way," he said, "and let go."

They were all on their beds, and gallant Michael let go first. He did not quite mean to let go, but he did it, and immediately he was borne across the room.

Peter and the children fly away. (*Peter Pan and Wendy by J. M. Barrie, Retold for the Nursery by May Byron.* Illustrated by Kathleen Atkins)

"I flewed!"[29] he screamed while still in mid-air.

John let go and met Wendy near the bathroom.

"Oh, lovely!"

"Oh, ripping!"

"Look at me!"

"Look at me!"

"Look at me!"

They were not nearly so elegant as Peter, they could not help kicking a little, but their heads were bobbing against the ceiling, and there is almost nothing so delicious as that. Peter gave Wendy a hand at first, but had to desist, Tink was so indignant.

Up and down they went, and round and round. Heavenly was Wendy's word.

"I say," cried John, "why shouldn't we all go out?"

Of course it was to this that Peter had been luring them.

Michael was ready: he wanted to see how long it took him to do a billion miles. But Wendy hesitated.

"Mermaids!" said Peter again.

"Oo!"

"And there are pirates."[30]

"Pirates," cried John, seizing his Sunday hat, "let us go at once."

It was just at this moment that Mr. and Mrs. Darling hurried with Nana out of 27. They ran into the middle of the street to look up at the nursery window; and, yes, it was still shut, but the room was ablaze with light, and most heart-gripping sight of all, they could see in shadow on the curtain three little figures in night attire circling round and round, not on the floor but in the air.

Not three figures, four!

In a tremble they opened the street door. Mr. Darling would have rushed upstairs, but Mrs. Darling signed to him to go softly. She even tried to make her heart go softly.

Will they reach the nursery in time?[31] If so, how delightful

29. *"I flewed!"* Michael's coinage combines the correct past tense with an additional "ed" in an effort to mimic adult speech. The term "flewed" reminds us that he is still very much a child and that he has the capacity to "believe" in flight. Yet it also points forward to his desire to become one of the grown-ups.

30. *"And there are pirates."* Tales about pirates on the high seas became popular after the publication of Daniel Defoe's *Captain Singleton* (1720), and the genre flourished in Anglo-American culture. "Pirates" was a common epithet that included both British sea-robbers and men who set sail from North Africa and became part of their own governments' revenue machinery. From the seventeenth century on, stories about Europeans captured on the high seas and enslaved by "Barbary pirates" flourished; among them can be counted Rossini's *L'italiana in Algeri* (1813). Tom Sawyer captures the romance of piracy when he observes that pirates "have just a bully time . . . and kill everybody in the ships—make 'em walk a plank" (93). Barrie's pirates are fanciful in their dress, manner, and speech, and they are based on parodic figures (Gilbert and Sullivan's *Pirates of Penzance* was on the London stage in 1880) as much as on fictional and historical models. They have a sense of adventure, and, in the preface to *Peter Pan*, Hook is linked with Captain James Cook, who was killed in 1778 by Hawaiian natives. Hook is clearly also inspired by Robert Louis Stevenson's Long John Silver, the peg-legged pirate who captures young Jim Hawkins in *Treasure Island* (1883).

Daphne du Maurier, in a memoir about her father, Gerald du Maurier, writes about Hook: "He was a tragic and rather ghastly creation who knew no peace, and whose soul was in torment; a dark shadow; a sinister dram; a bogey of fear who lives in the grey recesses of every small boy's mind. All boys had their Hooks, as Barrie knew; he was the phantom who came by night and stole his way into their murky dreams. . . . And because he had imagination and a spark of genius, Gerald made him alive" (Dunbar 141).

31. *Will they reach the nursery in time?* At times the narrator seems to be telling the story to a group of listeners. With this question, he creates the sense that he is narrating the events as they unfold and that he has no foreknowledge of how things will turn out. And yet he can still reassure readers that everything will, as in the fairy tale "Cinderella," cited earlier, "come right in the end."

32. *"Cave, Peter!"* "Cave" is from the Latin term *cavere*. The star is telling Peter to watch out and beware of danger.

33. *The birds were flown.* The children are characterized as having reverted to their earlier form as birds. In *Peter Pan in Kensington Gardens*, Barrie writes: "All children could have such recollections if they would press their hands hard to their temples for, having been birds before they were human, they are naturally a little wild during the first few weeks, and very itchy at the shoulders, where their wings used to be" (Hollindale 13). Peter has become a Pied Piper figure, seducing the children, in this case, with the promise of flight and leading them out of their homes into an enchanted retreat.

for them, and we shall all breathe a sigh of relief, but there will be no story. On the other hand, if they are not in time, I solemnly promise that it will all come right in the end.

They would have reached the nursery in time had it not been that the little stars were watching them. Once again the stars blew the window open, and that smallest star of all called out:

"Cave, Peter!"[32]

Then Peter knew that there was not a moment to lose. "Come," he cried imperiously, and soared out at once into the night, followed by John and Michael and Wendy.

Mr. and Mrs. Darling and Nana rushed into the nursery too late. The birds were flown.[33]

CHAPTER 4

The Flight

Second to the right, and straight on till morning."[1]

That, Peter had told Wendy, was the way to the Neverland; but even birds, carrying maps and consulting them at windy corners, could not have sighted it with these instructions. Peter, you see, just said anything that came into his head.

At first his companions trusted him implicitly, and so great were the delights of flying that they wasted time circling round church spires or any other tall objects on the way that took their fancy.

John and Michael raced, Michael getting a start.

They recalled with contempt that not so long ago they had thought themselves fine fellows for being able to fly round a room.

Not long ago. But how long ago? They were flying over the sea before this thought began to disturb Wendy seriously. John thought it was their second sea and their third night.

Sometimes it was dark and sometimes light, and now they were very cold and again too warm. Did they really feel hungry at times, or were they merely pretending, because Peter had such a jolly new way of feeding them? His way was to pursue birds who had food in their mouths suitable for

1. *"Second to the right, and straight on till morning."* The address for Neverland is made up by Peter on the spur of the moment, and it has been repeatedly evoked as a navigational tool for those seeking creative solutions for reaching a destination or goal. As noted earlier, Robert Louis Stevenson's instructions on how to reach Vailima, his estate in the Samoan Islands, may have inspired the wording of directions to Neverland: "You take the boat at San Francisco, and then my place is the second to the left" (*Margaret Ogilvy*, 147).

2. *the next time you fell he would let you go.* Peter's flightiness consists of a need for variety and an inability to form attachments. Lacking any understanding of death, he puts the children at constant risk, seeing everything as a mere adventure rather than a real danger. Peter's love of variety in sports reveals a lack of commitment that translates into the human sphere as well. His poor memory makes him an unreliable and capricious host.

3. *"Follow my Leader."* The game Follow my Leader was played among Native American tribes, with a leader improvising steps and movements that would be followed by others in the rhythms set by a song sung by all. "Follow my Leader where'er he goes; / What he'll do next, nobody knows" are the words in one such song made up for children playing the game.

humans and snatch it from them; then the birds would follow and snatch it back; and they would all go chasing each other gaily for miles, parting at last with mutual expressions of good-will. But Wendy noticed with gentle concern that Peter did not seem to know that this was rather an odd way of getting your bread and butter, nor even that there are other ways.

Certainly they did not pretend to be sleepy, they were sleepy; and that was a danger, for the moment they popped off, down they fell. The awful thing was that Peter thought this funny.

"There he goes again!" he would cry gleefully, as Michael suddenly dropped like a stone.

"Save him, save him!" cried Wendy, looking with horror at the cruel sea far below. Eventually Peter would dive through the air, and catch Michael just before he could strike the sea, and it was lovely the way he did it; but he always waited till the last moment, and you felt it was his cleverness that interested him and not the saving of human life. Also he was fond of variety, and the sport that engrossed him one moment would suddenly cease to engage him, so there was always the possibility that the next time you fell he would let you go.[2]

He could sleep in the air without falling, by merely lying on his back and floating, but this was, partly at least, because he was so light that if you got behind him and blew he went faster.

"Do be more polite to him," Wendy whispered to John, when they were playing "Follow my Leader."[3]

"Then tell him to stop showing off," said John.

When playing Follow my Leader, Peter would fly close to the water and touch each shark's tail in passing, just as in the street you may run your finger along an iron railing. They could not follow him in this with much success, so perhaps it was rather like showing off, especially as he kept looking behind to see how many tails they missed.

"You must be nice to him," Wendy impressed on her brothers. "What could we do if he were to leave us!"

"We could go back," Michael said.

"How could we ever find our way back without him?"

"Well, then, we could go on," said John.

"That is the awful thing, John. We should have to go on, for we don't know how to stop."

This was true; Peter had forgotten to show them how to stop.

John said that if the worst came to the worst, all they had to do was to go straight on, for the world was round, and so in time they must come back to their own window.

"And who is to get food for us, John?"

"I nipped a bit out of that eagle's mouth pretty neatly, Wendy."

"After the twentieth try," Wendy reminded him. "And even though we became good at picking up food, see how we bump against clouds and things if he is not near to give us a hand."

Indeed they were constantly bumping. They could now fly strongly, though they still kicked far too much; but if they saw a cloud in front of them, the more they tried to avoid it, the more certainly did they bump into it. If Nana had been with them, she would have had a bandage round Michael's forehead by this time.

Peter was not with them for the moment, and they felt rather lonely up there by themselves. He could go so much faster than they that he would suddenly shoot out of sight, to have some adventure in which they had no share. He would come down laughing over something fearfully funny he had been saying to a star, but he had already forgotten what it was, or he would come up with mermaid scales still sticking to him, and yet not be able to say for certain what had been happening. It was really rather irritating to children who had never seen a mermaid.

4. *he did not remember them.* That Peter has no memory and lives in an eternal present has been seen as the curse of living in Neverland. But because Neverland makes you forget everything, it also opens up worlds of possibilities and allows you to try out everything. In this sense, it begins to resemble Wonderland, for everything is new and arouses curiosity for the elated pilgrims wandering through it. Peter lives each moment to the fullest, reveling in the opportunities it offers and disregarding what was past and what the future holds. His identity remains unstable, for he can freely reinvent himself at any moment, even to the extent of turning into his own adversary.

5. *the island was out looking for them.* That Neverland can be reached only by invitation from the island makes it clear that some (in particular, adults) are banished from landing on its "magic shores."

6. *a million golden arrows.* Neverland is characterized by luminescence and beauty radiating from the sun. Its reflected glory has the power to attract and animate.

"And if he forgets them so quickly," Wendy argued, "how can we expect that he will go on remembering us?"

Indeed, sometimes when he returned he did not remember them,[4] at least not well. Wendy was sure of it. She saw recognition come into his eyes as he was about to pass them the time of day and go on; once even she had to tell him her name.

"I'm Wendy," she said agitatedly.

He was very sorry. "I say, Wendy," he whispered to her, "always if you see me forgetting you, just keep on saying 'I'm Wendy,' and then I'll remember."

Of course this was rather unsatisfactory. However, to make amends he showed them how to lie out flat on a strong wind that was going their way, and this was such a pleasant change that they tried it several times and found that they could sleep thus with security. Indeed they would have slept longer, but Peter tired quickly of sleeping, and soon he would cry in his captain voice, "We get off here." So with occasional tiffs, but on the whole rollicking, they drew near the Neverland; for after many moons they did reach it, and, what is more, they had been going pretty straight all the time, not perhaps so much owing to the guidance of Peter or Tink as because the island was out looking for them.[5] It is only thus that any one may sight those magic shores.

"There it is," said Peter calmly.

"Where, where?"

"Where all the arrows are pointing."

Indeed a million golden arrows[6] were pointing out the island to the children, all directed by their friend the sun, who wanted them to be sure of their way before leaving them for the night.

Wendy and John and Michael stood on tiptoe in the air to get their first sight of the island. Strange to say, they all recognised it at once, and until fear fell upon them they hailed it, not as something long dreamt of and seen at last, but as a familiar friend to whom they were returning home for the holidays.

"John, there's the lagoon."

"Wendy, look at the turtles burying their eggs in the sand."

"I say, John, I see your flamingo with the broken leg!"

"Look, Michael, there's your cave!"

"John, what's that in the brushwood?"

"It's a wolf with her whelps. Wendy, I do believe that's your little whelp!"

"There's my boat, John, with her sides stove in!"[7]

"No, it isn't. Why, we burned your boat."

"That's her, at any rate. I say, John, I see the smoke of the redskin camp!"[8]

"Where? Show me, and I'll tell you by the way smoke curls whether they are on the war-path."

"There, just across the Mysterious River."

"I see now. Yes, they are on the war-path right enough."

Peter was a little annoyed with them for knowing so much; but if he wanted to lord it over them his triumph was at hand, for have I not told you that anon fear fell upon them?

It came as the arrows went, leaving the island in gloom.

In the old days at home the Neverland had always begun to look a little dark and threatening by bedtime. Then unexplored patches arose in it and spread; black shadows moved about in them; the roar of the beasts of prey was quite different now, and above all, you lost the certainty that you would win. You were quite glad that the night-lights were in. You even liked Nana to say that this was just the mantelpiece over here, and that the Neverland was all make-believe.

Of course the Neverland had been make-believe in those days; but it was real now, and there were no night-lights, and it was getting darker every moment, and where was Nana?

They had been flying apart, but they huddled close to Peter now. His careless manner had gone at last, his eyes were sparkling, and a tingle went through them every time they

7. *"with her sides stove in!"* "Stove in" comes from "stave in," meaning "to smash a hole in" or "to crush."

8. *"the redskin camp!"* In Anglo-American cultures, the term "redskin" has been used from the eighteenth century onward as a pejorative way of designating Native Americans. In litigation over the trademarks used by the Washington Redskins football team, Native American activist Suzan Shown Harjo claimed that the word had its origins in "the practice of presenting bloody red skins and scalps as proof of Indian kill for bounty payments." Ives Goddard, a linguist at the Smithsonian Institute, has argued that the term did not begin as an insult. According to him, the color designations "red" and "white" were first used by Native Americans themselves to make racial distinctions. Goddard identifies the earliest example of redskin in 1769, when three Piankashaw chiefs sent statements to a military commander, using the term (later written out in a French translation of their speeches as "peaux Rouges"). The first documented public uses of redskin came in 1812, when President Madison gave a reception for an Indian delegation in Washington and addressed them, throughout his speech, as "red people," "red children," "red tribes," and "red brethren." French Crow, chief of the Wahpekute band, declared himself on that occasion to be "a red-skin," as did No Ears, one of the second chiefs of the Little Osages.

Barrie uses the term to refer to American Indians, and, oddly, creates a tribe called the Piccaninny. In the screenplay for *Peter Pan*, Barrie advised staging scenes of "real redskin warfare that will be recognized as such by all readers of Fenimore Cooper."

9. *pushing their way through hostile forces.* The journey to Neverland has been seen as a journey to the unconscious but also as a move in the direction of discovering imagination, identity, and everything that lurks hidden in the mind. That the children can only "break through" when they are fast asleep and that they discover powerful paths of resistance suggests a connection with Freudian dream worlds, but their journey seems in many ways more attuned to Jungian than Freudian developmental trajectories. In Neverland, they could be said to discover their individuality through powerful encounters with shadows, archetypes, and the anima, as Jungian critics eagerly point out.

10. *with eyes so bright.* Peter's eyes seem to be as bright as the stars. They "sparkle," and they link him to the light of the "million golden arrows" pointing the way to Neverland.

touched his body. They were now over the fearsome island, flying so low that sometimes a tree grazed their feet. Nothing horrid was visible in the air, yet their progress had become slow and laboured, exactly as if they were pushing their way through hostile forces.[9] Sometimes they hung in the air until Peter had beaten on it with his fists.

"They don't want us to land," he explained.

"Who are they?" Wendy whispered, shuddering.

But he could not or would not say. Tinker Bell had been asleep on his shoulder, but now he wakened her and sent her on in front.

Sometimes he poised himself in the air, listening intently, with his hand to his ear, and again he would stare down with eyes so bright[10] that they seemed to bore two holes to earth. Having done these things, he went on again.

His courage was almost appalling. "Do you want an adventure now," he said casually to John, "or would you like to have your tea first?"

Wendy said "tea first" quickly, and Michael pressed her hand in gratitude, but the braver John hesitated.

"What kind of adventure?" he asked cautiously.

"There's a pirate asleep in the pampas just beneath us," Peter told him. "If you like, we'll go down and kill him."

"I don't see him," John said after a long pause.

"I do."

"Suppose," John said a little huskily, "he were to wake up."

Peter spoke indignantly. "You don't think I would kill him while he was sleeping! I would wake him first, and then kill him. That's the way I always do."

"I say! Do you kill many?"

"Tons."

John said "how ripping," but decided to have tea first. He asked if there were many pirates on the island just now, and Peter said he had never known so many.

"Who is captain now?"

"Hook," answered Peter; and his face became very stern as he said that hated word.

"Jas. Hook?"[11]

"Ay."

Then indeed Michael began to cry, and even John could speak in gulps only, for they knew Hook's reputation.

"He was Blackbeard's bo'sun,"[12] John whispered huskily. "He is the worst of them all. He is the only man of whom Barbecue[13] was afraid."

"That's him," said Peter.

"What is he like? Is he big?"

"He is not so big as he was."

"How do you mean?"

"I cut off a bit of him."

"You!"

"Yes, me," said Peter sharply.

"I wasn't meaning to be disrespectful."

"Oh, all right."

"But, I say, what bit?"

"His right hand."

"Then he can't fight now?"

"Oh, can't he just!"

"Left-hander?"

"He has an iron hook instead of a right hand, and he claws with it."

"Claws!"

"I say, John," said Peter.

"Yes."

"Say, 'Ay, ay, sir.'"

"Ay, ay, sir."

"There is one thing," Peter continued, "that every boy who serves under me has to promise, and so must you."

John paled.

"It is this, if we meet Hook in open fight, you must leave him to me."

11. *"Jas. Hook?"* J. M. Barrie gave Hook his own first name, James. In early drafts of the plays, Hook was represented as a headmaster and embodied to some extent the harsh and cruel, but also pedantic, elements of institutional life. In the course of revisions, Hook became a volatile mix of aristocrat and pirate, diabolical yet also curiously addicted to good form. Barrie implies that Hook (not his "true name") attended Eton College, and, in the play, Hook's last words are "Floreat Etona" (May Eton Flourish), the motto of the college. (Four of the Llewelyn Davies boys attended Eton.)

In stage versions, the same actor often plays Mr. Darling and Hook, presumably because "all grown-ups are pirates." (Barrie had originally planned to have Dorothea Baird, the actress playing Mrs. Darling, also play Hook, but Gerald du Maurier, who played the first Hook onstage, persuaded the playwright to give him the double role.) In a speech given at Eton with the title "Captain Hook at Eton," Barrie declared the pirate to be "the handsomest man I have ever seen, though, at the same time, slightly disgusting." Barrie had invented a character known as "Captain Swarthy," a "black man" and pirate, while playing games with the Llewelyn Davies brothers. He wrote the first draft of the play without Hook, for he already had a villain: "P[eter] a demon boy (villain of the story)." Andrew Birkin writes that only the need for a "front-cloth scene" (a scene included to give the stagehands time to change the scenery) gave rise to the pirate captain. The front-cloth scene became a new set: The Pirate Ship.

In his scenario for the screen version of *Peter Pan*, Barrie emphasized that "Hook should be played absolutely seriously, and the actor must avoid all temptation to play the part as if he was conscious of its humours. There *is* such a temptation, and in the stage play the actors of the part have sometimes yielded to it, with fatal results."

While writing *Mary Rose* (a play about a dead mother who haunts her living son) in 1920, Barrie developed a severe cramp in his right hand and, from then on, wrote only with his left hand. He recounts: "About fifteen years ago a great change came over my hand-writing. I was saved by an attack of writer's cramp to which, once abhorred, I now make a reverential bow, though it is as ready as ever to pounce if thoughtlessly I take up the pen in my right hand. I had to learn to write with the left, not so irksome to me as it would be to most, for I am naturally left-handed (and still kick with the left foot). I now write as easily with this hand as once with the other, and if I take any pains the result is almost pleasing to the eye. . . . Nevertheless, there is not the same joy in writing with the left hand as with the right. One thinks down the right arm, while the left is at best an amanuensis" (Meynell vi).

Prosthetic limbs had not yet been invented in Barrie's day, and hooks were then not as unusual as they are today. One critic located a picture of local worthies in Kirriemuir, with a postman, who also worked as a mason, shown with a hook.

12. *"He was Blackbeard's bo'sun."* "Bo'sun" is an abbreviation for boatswain, an unlicensed member of a merchant ship who takes on supervisory roles. Blackbeard's real name was Edward Teach (1680–1718), and he terrorized the Caribbean Islands and western Atlantic with his attacks on ships. Captured in 1718, he was decapitated and his head displayed on the bowsprit of his captor's ship, then placed on a pike in Virginia as a warning to those who were considering taking up the life of a pirate.

13. *Barbecue*. In Robert Louis Stevenson's *Treasure Island*, Long John Silver goes by the names "Barbecue" and "the Sea-Cook."

"I promise," John said loyally.

For the moment they were feeling less eerie, because Tink was flying with them, and in her light they could distinguish each other. Unfortunately she could not fly so slowly as they, and so she had to go round and round them in a circle in which they moved as in a halo. Wendy quite liked it, until Peter pointed out the drawback.

"She tells me," he said, "that the pirates sighted us before the darkness came, and got Long Tom[14] out."

"The big gun?"

"Yes. And of course they must see her light, and if they guess we are near it they are sure to let fly."

"Wendy!"

"John!"

"Michael!"

"Tell her to go away at once, Peter," the three cried simultaneously, but he refused.

"She thinks we have lost the way," he replied stiffly, "and she is rather frightened. You don't think I would send her away all by herself when she is frightened!"

For a moment the circle of light was broken, and something gave Peter a loving little pinch.

"Then tell her," Wendy begged, "to put out her light."

"She can't put it out. That is about the only thing fairies can't do. It just goes out of itself when she falls asleep, same as the stars."

"Then tell her to sleep at once," John almost ordered.

"She can't sleep except when she's sleepy. It is the only other thing fairies can't do."

"Seems to me," growled John, "these are the only two things worth doing."

Here he got a pinch, but not a loving one.

"If only one of us had a pocket," Peter said, "we could carry her in it." However, they had set off in such a hurry that there was not a pocket between the four of them.

14. *"Long Tom."* The pirates' gun is named Long Tom, and, after it is fired at Peter and the Darling children, it reappears when Starkey uses it as a launching pad to jump into the ocean and when Peter falls asleep by it.

61

15. *"Where are they, where are they, where are they?"* Barrie's love of repetition in sets of three comes alive in this chapter, with three children, whose names are repeated in a triple sequence, and who speak simultaneously. Long Tom's triple question reveals a determination to find the three children, but it also reveals something about how Barrie combines sophisticated diction with speech mannerisms characteristic of dialogue between parents and children. Repetition is used frequently by young children (ages two to three) and also by their adult caregivers. Children most likely use it to sustain a conversation because it makes minimal processing demands and yet is a way of showing attentiveness. Caregivers have a different purpose, using repetition to acknowledge what a child has said, to avoid overloading a child's processing abilities, and to prompt a child.

He had a happy idea. John's hat!

Tink agreed to travel by hat if it was carried in the hand. John carried it, though she had hoped to be carried by Peter. Presently Wendy took the hat, because John said it struck against his knee as he flew; and this, as we shall see, led to mischief, for Tinker Bell hated to be under an obligation to Wendy.

In the black topper the light was completely hidden, and they flew on in silence. It was the stillest silence they had ever known, broken once by a distant lapping, which Peter explained was the wild beasts drinking at the ford, and again by a rasping sound that might have been the branches of trees rubbing together, but he said it was the redskins sharpening their knives.

Even these noises ceased. To Michael the loneliness was dreadful. "If only something would make a sound!" he cried.

As if in answer to his request, the air was rent by the most tremendous crash he had ever heard. The pirates had fired Long Tom at them.

The roar of it echoed through the mountains, and the echoes seemed to cry savagely, "Where are they, where are they, where are they?"[15]

Thus sharply did the terrified three learn the difference between an island of make-believe and the same island come true.

When at last the heavens were steady again, John and Michael found themselves alone in the darkness. John was treading the air mechanically, and Michael without knowing how to float was floating.

"Are you shot?" John whispered tremulously.

"I haven't tried yet," Michael whispered back.

We know now that no one had been hit. Peter, however, had been carried by the wind of the shot far out to sea, while Wendy was blown upwards with no companion but Tinker Bell.

It would have been well for Wendy if at that moment she had dropped the hat.

I don't know whether the idea came suddenly to Tink, or whether she had planned it on the way, but she at once popped out of the hat and began to lure Wendy to her destruction.

Tink was not all bad: or, rather, she was all bad just now, but, on the other hand, sometimes she was all good. Fairies have to be one thing or the other, because being so small they unfortunately have room for one feeling only at a time. They are, however, allowed to change, only it must be a complete change. At present she was full of jealousy of Wendy. What she said in her lovely tinkle Wendy could not of course understand, and I believe some of it was bad words, but it sounded kind, and she flew back and forward, plainly meaning "Follow me, and all will be well."

What else could poor Wendy do? She called to Peter and John and Michael, and got only mocking echoes in reply. She did not yet know that Tink hated her with the fierce hatred of a very woman. And so, bewildered, and now staggering in her flight, she followed Tink to her doom.

CHAPTER 5

The Island Come True

1. *woke into life.* The narrator freely admits that he identifies with Peter and the children by using a speech register closer to that of a child than an adult. Although he has a sophisticated awareness of grammar rules (as becomes evident from his reference to the "pluperfect"), he elects to use the simple past tense endorsed by Peter Pan. Here we have encapsulated the narrator's dilemma: he tries to channel childhood but is condemned to the reflective style and self-conscious condition of adulthood. In a draft for his novel *Sentimental Tommy,* Barrie wrote about the attempt to recapture childhood: "Cast your mind back into its earliest years, and thro' them you will see flitting dimly the elusive form of a child. He is yourself, as soon as you can catch him. But move a step nearer, and he is not there. Among the mists of infancy he plays hide and seek with you, until one day he trips and falls into the daylight. Now you seize him; and with that touch you two are one. It is the birth of self-consciousness" (Beinecke Library, MS Vault BARRIE, S45).

2. *things are usually quiet on the island.* Life on the island is described in the narrative present to underscore the recurrent nature

Feeling that Peter was on his way back, the Neverland had again woke into life.[1] We ought to use the pluperfect and say wakened, but woke is better and was always used by Peter.

In his absence things are usually quiet on the island.[2] The fairies take an hour longer in the morning, the beasts attend to their young, the redskins feed heavily for six days and nights, and when pirates and lost boys meet they merely bite their thumbs at each other.[3] But with the coming of Peter, who hates lethargy, they are under way again: if you put your ear to the ground now, you would hear the whole island seething with life.

On this evening the chief forces of the island were disposed as follows. The lost boys were out looking for Peter, the pirates were out looking for the lost boys, the redskins were out looking for the pirates, and the beasts were out looking for the redskins. They were going round and round the island,[4] but they did not meet because all were going at the same rate.

All wanted blood except the boys, who liked it as a rule, but to-night were out to greet their captain. The boys on the island vary, of course, in numbers, according as they get killed and so on; and when they seem to be growing up, which is against the rules, Peter thins them out; but at this time there were six of them, counting the twins as two. Let us pretend to lie here[5] among the sugar-cane and watch them as they steal by in single file, each with his hand on his dagger.

They are forbidden by Peter to look in the least like him, and they wear the skins of bears slain by themselves, in which they are so round and furry that when they fall they roll. They have therefore become very sure-footed.

The first to pass is Tootles,[6] not the least brave but the most unfortunate of all that gallant band. He had been in fewer adventures than any of them, because the big things constantly happened just when he had stepped round the corner; all would be quiet, he would take the opportunity of going off to gather a few sticks for firewood, and then when he returned the others would be sweeping up the blood. This ill-luck had given a gentle melancholy to his countenance, but instead of souring his nature had sweetened it, so that he was quite the humblest of the boys. Poor kind Tootles, there is danger in the air for you to-night. Take care lest an adventure is now offered you, which, if accepted, will plunge you in deepest woe. Tootles, the fairy Tink, who is bent on mischief this night is looking for a tool, and she thinks you the most easily tricked of the boys. 'Ware Tinker Bell.

Would that he could hear us, but we are not really on the island,[7] and he passes by, biting his knuckles.

Next comes Nibs, the gay and debonair, followed by Slightly,[8] who cuts whistles out of the trees and dances ecstatically to his own tunes. Slightly is the most conceited of the boys. He thinks he remembers the days before he was lost, with their manners and customs, and this has given his nose an offensive tilt. Curly is fourth; he is a pickle,[9] and so often has he had to deliver up his person when Peter said sternly, "Stand forth the one who did this thing," that now at the command he stands forth automatically whether he has done

of what happens. Nothing ever changes, even if there are occasional singular adventures, for everything is make-believe. "In the mythical land of immortality, time is definitely circular, archaic," Maria Nikolajeva notes, in a study that divides up children's literature according to its deep temporal structures—linear, cyclical, and carnivalesque (90). *Peter Pan*, like many of the childhood utopias with characters dwelling in a self-contained pastoral setting, invariably faces the challenge of what to do with the child reluctant to grow up.

3. *they merely bite their thumbs at each other.* The *Oxford English Dictionary* defines the phrase "bite the thumb at" as a gesture of defiance. The thumb nail is put into the mouth and made to create a noise by its snapping against the front teeth.

4. *They were going round and round the island.* When Peter absents himself from Neverland, the inhabitants seek a therapeutic alternative to adventure, avoiding conflict through circular movement. Their procession moves along in an eternal present devoid of confrontation and transformative energy.

5. *Let us pretend to lie here.* Once again, the narrator calls attention to the fact that everything he does is make-believe, even as he allows us to "watch" the boys with him.

6. *The first to pass is Tootles.* The lost boys, rather than having actual names, are called by epithets: Tootles, Curly, Nibs, Slightly, and the Twins. The lack of a Christian name and surname reduces their identity to a collective stereotype, and, in the play, they speak as a chorus rather than as individuals. Peter is the only one of them with a boy's name.

7. *but we are not really on the island.* Once again the narrator shatters the illusion,

calling attention to the fictionality of his work, this time constructing a contradiction by suggesting that he is not on the island, even as he witnesses the adventures that take place there.

8. *followed by Slightly.* In the play *Peter Pan,* Slightly explains how he received his name: ". . . my mother had wrote my name on the pinafore I was lost in. 'Slightly Soiled'; that's my name."

9. *he is a pickle.* A British colloquial term for a boy who is always causing trouble or for a mischievous child.

10. *"Avast belay, yo ho."* Pirates, redskins, boys, and parents all speak in different registers, in part for the sake of differentiation, in part to create histrionic effects. The Indians often speak in what we see today as offensive stereotypical gibberish: "Scalp um, oho, velly quick." Hook resorts to archaic language and inversion and is flamboyant in his use of bombast. And even Peter seems to emote in unexpected ways: "Dark and sinister man, have at thee."

11. *on Execution dock.* Located on the Thames in Wapping, part of the Docklands to the east of the City of London, Execution Dock was used for over four hundred years to hang criminals sentenced by the Admiralty Court. It consisted of a wooden gallows built on the low-water mark. Pirates, mutineers, and smugglers were paraded across London Bridge past the Tower of London before they were publicly executed at the dock. Their remains were often left on display for days at a time, washed over three times by the tide, as prescribed by Admiralty law, as a warning to offenders. On occasion, the corpses were tarred, bound in chains, and put inside an iron cage, suspended from a gibbet at a site of maximum visibility.

it or not. Last come the Twins, who cannot be described because we should be sure to be describing the wrong one. Peter never quite knew what twins were, and his band were not allowed to know anything he did not know, so these two were always vague about themselves, and did their best to give satisfaction by keeping close together in an apologetic sort of way.

The boys vanish in the gloom, and after a pause, but not a long pause, for things go briskly on the island, come the pirates on their track. We hear them before they are seen, and it is always the same dreadful song:

"Avast belay, yo ho, heave to,[10]
A-pirating we go,
And if we're parted by a shot
We're sure to meet below!"

A more villainous-looking lot never hung in a row on Execution dock.[11] Here, a little in advance, ever and again with his head to the ground listening, his great arms bare, pieces of eight[12] in his ears as ornaments, is the handsome Italian Cecco,[13] who cut his name in letters of blood on the back of the governor of the prison at Gao.[14] That gigantic black behind him has had many names since he dropped the one with which dusky mothers still terrify their children on the banks of the Guadjo-mo.[15] Here is Bill Jukes, every inch of him tattooed, the same Bill Jukes who got six dozen on the *Walrus* from Flint[16] before he would drop the bag of moidores; and Cookson, said to be Black Murphy's brother (but this was never proved); and Gentleman Starkey, once an usher in a public school and still dainty in his ways of killing; and Skylights (Morgan's Skylights); and the Irish bo'sun Smee,[17] an oddly genial man who stabbed, so to speak, without offence, and was the only Nonconformist in Hook's crew; and Noodler, whose hands were fixed on backwards; and

During the early years of the eighteenth century, entire crews were sent to the gallows. Captain Kidd, convicted of piracy and murder, was executed there in 1701, and his rotting corpse, its eyes pecked out by seagulls but its bones kept in place by a cage, remained on display for years after his execution, "as a great terror to all persons from committing ye like crimes" (Konstam and Kean, 181).

12. *pieces of eight.* The term designates the Spanish dollar or eight-real coin, a silver coin worth eight reales that became a world currency in the late eighteenth century. Minted after the Spanish currency reform of 1497, it was widely used in Europe, the Americas, and the Far East, and remained legal tender in the United States until 1857.

13. *the handsome Italian Cecco.* While preparing the script for *Peter Pan*, Barrie read pirate literature widely in search of names and colorful details. He reread *Treasure Island* and studied a number of other works, including Charles Johnson's *History of Pirates* (1724). Cecco has no buccaneering model, and he is most likely named after Cecco Hewlett, son of the novelist Maurice Hewlett. Cookson is most likely taken from Captain John Coxon, who plundered a town on the Spanish Main. Black Murphy was a historical pirate, as was Skylights.

14. *the prison at Gao.* Gao is sometimes emended to read "Goa" in more recent printings. Goa is a former Portuguese colony in southern India, conquered in the early sixteenth century and freed in 1961. The change from "Gao" to "Goa" is made plausible by the reference in *Treasure Island* to "the boarding of the *Viceroy of the Indies* out of Goa," witnessed by Long John Silver's parrot, and by the mention of "moidores," or Portuguese gold pieces, that follows.

15. *Guadjo-mo.* The made-up name refers to a tropical river. Barrie developed his island fantasy from historical fact and imaginative fiction, and he rarely invented geographical place names.

16. *six dozen on the* Walrus *from Flint.* Jukes received six dozen lashes on the *Walrus*, Captain Flint's ship in Robert Louis Stevenson's *Treasure Island*.

17. *the Irish bo'sun Smee.* Smee came to be Irish when Barrie, hoping to individualize the parts of Smee and Starkey, asked George Shelton, the original Smee, how to give the pirates stronger profiles. Shelton proposed making "an Irishman of mine," and Barrie shot back "Shelton, he *is* an Irishman." Oddly, he is described as a Nonconformist, one of the Protestant Christians of England and Wales who refused to conform to the practices of the Church of England.

18. *Alf Mason.* Barrie adds here a tribute to his contemporary the novelist and politician Alfred Edward Woodley Mason (1865–1948), best known for detective novels featuring the French sleuth Inspector Hanaud, and for his novel *The Four Feathers.*

19. *the only man that the Sea-Cook feared.* Sea-Cook, as noted earlier, was the nickname for Long John Silver in *Treasure Island,* which Stevenson had originally called *The Sea Cook.*

20. *blackavized.* Usually written as black-a-vised, the term was used in the nineteenth century to describe a person of dark complexion. Charlotte Brontë wrote, in *Jane Eyre*: "I would advise her black-aviced suitor to look out."

21. *a* raconteur *of repute.* Hook, unlike Peter, is no stranger to stories. That the French term for storytelling is used to describe him (he is also dubbed a "grand seigneur") emphasizes his exotic, man-of-the-world character.

22. *Charles II.* Charles II (Charles Stuart) lived from 1630 to 1685 and ruled England, Scotland, and Ireland during the Restoration period. Crowned king of England and Ireland in 1661, he had been proclaimed king of Scots in 1649. Known as the "Merrie Monarch," he was a pleasure-loving ruler, welcomed back and seen as providing relief from a decade of rule by Oliver Cromwell and the Puritans.

Robt. Mullins and Alf Mason[18] and many another ruffian long known and feared on the Spanish Main.

In the midst of them, the blackest and largest jewel in that dark setting, reclined James Hook, or as he wrote himself, Jas. Hook, of whom it is said he was the only man that the Sea-Cook feared.[19] He lay at his ease in a rough chariot drawn and propelled by his men, and instead of a right hand he had the iron hook with which ever and anon he encouraged them to increase their pace. As dogs this terrible man treated and addressed them, and as dogs they obeyed him. In person he was cadaverous and blackavized,[20] and his hair was dressed in long curls, which at a little distance looked like black candles, and gave a singularly threatening expression to his handsome countenance. His eyes were of the blue of the forget-me-not, and of a profound melancholy, save when he was plunging his hook into you, at which time two red spots appeared in them and lit them up horribly. In manner, something of the grand seigneur still clung to him, so that he even ripped you up with an air, and I have been told that he was a *raconteur* of repute.[21] He was never more sinister than when he was most polite, which is probably the truest test of breeding; and the elegance of his diction, even when he was swearing, no less than the distinction of his demeanour, showed him one of a different cast from his crew. A man of indomitable courage, it was said that the only thing he shied at was the sight of his own blood, which was thick and of an unusual colour. In dress he somewhat aped the attire associated with the name of Charles II,[22] having heard it said in some earlier period of his career that he bore a strange resemblance to the ill-fated Stuarts; and in his mouth he had a holder of his own contrivance which enabled him to smoke two cigars at once. But undoubtedly the grimmest part of him was his iron claw.

Let us now kill a pirate, to show Hook's method. Skylights will do. As they pass, Skylights lurches clumsily against him, ruffling his lace collar; the hook shoots forth, there is a tearing sound and one screech, then the body is kicked aside, and the pirates pass on. He has not even taken the cigars from his mouth.

Such is the terrible man against whom Peter Pan is pitted. Which will win?

On the trail of the pirates, stealing noiselessly down the war-path, which is not visible to inexperienced eyes, come the redskins, every one of them with his eyes peeled. They carry tomahawks and knives, and their naked bodies gleam with paint and oil. Strung around them are scalps, of boys as well as of pirates, for these are the Piccaninny tribe,[23] and not to be confused with the softer-hearted Delawares or the Hurons. In the van, on all fours, is Great Big Little Panther, a brave of so many scalps that in his present position they somewhat impede his progress. Bringing up the rear, the place of greatest danger, comes Tiger Lily,[24] proudly erect, a princess in her own right. She is the most beautiful of dusky Dianas[25] and the belle of the Piccaninnies, coquettish, cold and amorous by turns; there is not a brave who would not have the wayward thing to wife, but she staves off the altar with a hatchet. Observe how they pass over fallen twigs without making the slightest noise. The only sound to be heard is their somewhat heavy breathing. The fact is that they are all a little fat just now after the heavy gorging, but in time they will work this off. For the moment, however, it constitutes their chief danger.

The redskins disappear as they have come like shadows, and soon their place is taken by the beasts, a great and motley procession: lions, tigers, bears,[26] and the innumerable smaller savage things that flee from them, for every kind of beast, and, more particularly, all the man-eaters, live cheek by jowl on the favoured island. Their tongues are hanging out, they are hungry to-night.

When they have passed, comes the last figure of all, a gigantic crocodile. We shall see for whom she is looking presently.[27]

23. *these are the Piccaninny tribe*. The term Piccaninny derives from the Portuguese *pequenino* (boy, child), a noun based on the adjective for "very small or tiny." The word belongs to a Portuguese-based pidgin associated with the seventeenth-century slave trade on the Atlantic coasts. First used in writing to describe the children of women in Barbados, the term today can refer either to a black child of African descent or to an American Indian child. It is considered racially offensive and has led to a certain discomfort about Barrie's use of racial stereotyping in *Peter Pan*. Drawing on the adventure stories read in his youth by authors such as James Fenimore Cooper, Barrie exaggerates and so overdoes the rhetoric used to describe the natives of Neverland that—as some critics argue—he ends by undoing racial stereotyping. Still, it is difficult to defend Barrie, for the term Piccaninny, used well into the twentieth century, collapses categories of racial and national difference and is used in a manner that cannot but appear to be condescending and disparaging, particularly for child readers. Native to Neverland, the Piccaninny are constantly referred to as "savage." They are described with racial stereotypes that see native populations as naked, violent, and full of stealth and cunning.

24. *Tiger Lily*. Tiger Lily is a native princess with a name that combines a ferocious animal with a beautiful flower. She has been described as the "other woman," in both senses of the term—an exotic alternative to the domestic Wendy, who plays the "loyal housewife." In the screenplay for the silent film version of *Peter Pan*, Barrie imagined the following courtship scene: "Tiger Lily comes into view. Then we see a redskin evidently proposing to the beautiful creature, who is the Indian princess. She whips out her hatchet and fells him."

25. *dusky Dianas.* In Roman mythology, Diana is the goddess of the hunt. She is associated with wild beasts and woodlands, and is often referred to as the moon goddess. A chaste goddess, she is said to have transformed Actaeon into a stag and set his own raging hunting dogs after him. Her ire was provoked when the Theban hero observed her naked while she was bathing in the woods.

26. *lions, tigers, bears.* L. Frank Baum's novel *The Wizard of Oz* contains the famous line "Lions and tigers and bears! Oh my!" Baum's work was published in 1900, predating *Peter and Wendy*, but there is no evidence that Barrie knew the work.

27. *for whom she is looking presently.* This is the first point in the text that assigns gender to the crocodile, and some will be

The crocodile passes, but soon the boys appear again, for the procession must continue indefinitely until one of the parties stops or changes its pace. Then quickly they will be on top of each other.[28]

All are keeping a sharp look-out in front, but none suspects that the danger may be creeping up from behind. This shows how real the island was.

The first to fall out of the moving circle was the boys. They flung themselves down on the sward, close to their underground home.

"I do wish Peter would come back," every one of them said nervously, though in height and still more in breadth they were all larger than their captain.

"I am the only one who is not afraid of the pirates," Slightly said, in the tone that prevented his being a general favourite; but perhaps some distant sound disturbed him, for he added

C is the Crocodile

C is the Crocodile Creepy who ate
The right hand of Hook and covets
   its mate
He makes a loud ticking wherever he
   goes
For he swallowed a Clock (To kill time
   I suppose)

Oliver Herford's *The Peter Pan Alphabet*, published in 1907. (Beinecke Rare Book and Manuscript Library, Yale University)

hastily, "but I wish he would come back, and tell us whether he has heard anything more about Cinderella."[29]

They talked of Cinderella, and Tootles was confident that his mother must have been very like her.

It was only in Peter's absence that they could speak of mothers, the subject being forbidden by him as silly.

"All I remember about my mother," Nibs told them, "is that she often said to father, 'Oh, how I wish I had a cheque-book of my own!'[30] I don't know what a cheque-book is, but I should just love to give my mother one."

While they talked they heard a distant sound. You or I, not being wild things of the woods,[31] would have heard nothing, but they heard it, and it was the grim song:

> "Yo ho, yo ho, the pirate life,
> The flag o' skull and bones,
> A merry hour, a hempen rope,
> And hey for Davy Jones."[32]

At once the lost boys—but where are they? They are no longer there. Rabbits could not have disappeared more quickly.

I will tell you where they are. With the exception of Nibs, who has darted away to reconnoitre, they are already in their home under the ground, a very delightful residence of which we shall see a good deal presently. But how have they reached it? for there is no entrance to be seen, not so much as a pile of brushwood, which, if removed, would disclose the mouth of a cave. Look closely, however, and you may note that there are here seven large trees,[33] each having in its hollow trunk a hole as large as a boy. These are the seven entrances to the home under the ground, for which Hook has been searching in vain these many moons. Will he find it to-night?

As the pirates advanced, the quick eye of Starkey sighted

surprised to learn that Hook is pursued by a female crocodile. As the "last figure of all" in the procession, the crocodile takes on symbolic importance, representing annihilation and death, "creeping up from behind." Creatures that can exist on both land and water, crocodiles are also associated with primal powers. In ancient Egypt, the crocodile was venerated as a powerful deity, both solar and chthonic, that is, masculine and feminine.

28. *Then quickly they will be on top of each other.* Barrie suggests here that conflict and violence will erupt as soon as one of the parties (redskins, lost boys, fairies, beasts, or pirates) decides to move away from its single, fixed pace on Neverland. A similarly precarious network of relationships can be found in the Darling household, with collisions occurring whenever one person puts his foot down.

29. *"whether he has heard anything more about Cinderella."* "Cinderella" is the story that Peter Pan hears at the Darling household, and it is also the tale that Wendy tells the boys. The fairy tale, as written down by Charles Perrault in late seventeenth-century France and by the Brothers Grimm over a century later, is set in the domestic sphere and tells of persecution, romance, and marriage. It is about rites and customs ordinarily excluded from Neverland until Wendy's arrival—hence perhaps its allure for the lost boys.

30. *"a cheque-book of my own!"* The humor of Nibs's desire for a checkbook will escape children but will be understood by adults. One critic makes the brilliant point that "Barrie uses adult voices speaking childishly to create social comedy for children, and children's voices speaking in naively adult terms to create social comedy for adults" (Hollindale 2008, 314).

31. *wild things of the woods.* Was Maurice Sendak inspired by this phrase when writing *Where the Wild Things Are*? It is unlikely but nonetheless a wonderful coincidence that Barrie used the term "wild things" in *Peter Pan*.

32. *"Davy Jones."* Davy Jones is the nickname for the spirit of the sea or the sailor's devil, in some ways the male counterpart to mermaids, who lure sailors down to the depths of the sea but also warn them of their impending fate. Davy Jones's locker refers to the resting place for drowned sailors. The origins of the term, first used in Tobias Smollett's *The Adventures of Peregrine Pickle* (1751), are not known: "This same Davy Jones, according to sailors, is the fiend that presides over all the evil spirits of the deep, and is often seen in various shapes, perching among the rigging on the eve of hurricanes, shipwrecks, and other disasters to which a sea-faring life is exposed, warning the devoted wretch of death and woe" (Smollett IV, 221–22).

33. *seven large trees.* In 1873 Barrie went off to study at Dumfries Academy, in southwestern Scotland (his older brother had a post there as school inspector). At the academy, Barrie not only composed his first play, *Bandelero the Bandit*, but also played pirate games with the son of the sheriff clerk of Dumfries. The Home Underground, with its many tree-trunk entrances, may have been inspired by some of the sites in the gardens of the sheriff's home, Moat Brae. Barrie later wrote that the games played there had created "a sort of Odyssey that was long afterwards to become the play of *Peter Pan*. For our escapades in a certain Dumfries garden, which is enchanted land to me, were certainly the genesis of that nefarious work" (*Speeches* 86).

Nibs disappearing through the wood, and at once his pistol flashed out. But an iron claw gripped his shoulder.

"Captain, let go!" he cried, writhing.

Now for the first time we hear the voice of Hook. It was a black voice. "Put back that pistol first," it said threateningly.

"It was one of those boys you hate. I could have shot him dead."

"Ay, and the sound would have brought Tiger Lily's redskins upon us. Do you want to lose your scalp?"

"Shall I after him, captain," asked pathetic Smee, "and tickle him with Johnny Corkscrew?" Smee had pleasant names for everything, and his cutlass was Johnny Corkscrew, because he wriggled it in the wound. One could mention many lovable traits in Smee. For instance, after killing, it was his spectacles he wiped instead of his weapon.

"Johnny's a silent fellow," he reminded Hook.

"Not now, Smee," Hook said darkly. "He is only one, and I want to mischief all the seven. Scatter and look for them."

The pirates disappeared among the trees, and in a moment their captain and Smee were alone. Hook heaved a heavy sigh; and I know not why it was, perhaps it was because of the soft beauty of the evening, but there came over him a desire to confide to his faithful bo'sun the story of his life. He spoke long and earnestly, but what it was all about Smee, who was rather stupid, did not know in the least.

Anon he caught the word Peter.

"Most of all," Hook was saying passionately, "I want their captain, Peter Pan. 'Twas he cut off my arm." He brandished the hook threateningly. "I've waited long to shake his hand with this. Oh, I'll tear him!"

"And yet," said Smee, "I have often heard you say that hook was worth a score of hands, for combing the hair and other homely uses."

"Ay," the captain answered, "if I was a mother I would pray to have my children born with this instead of that," and he

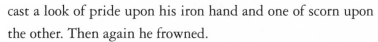
34. *"and then he'll get you."* Observe that the crocodile changes gender. The pirates describe it as a male of the species.

35. *"Odds bobs, hammer and tongs."* The expression is taken from a sea ballad in Frederick Marryat's novel *Snarleyyow; or, The Dog Friend* (1837): "Odds, bobs, hammer and tongs, long as I've been to sea, / I've fought 'gainst every odds—and I've gained the victory." Barrie was familiar with Marryat's many adventure books for boys.

cast a look of pride upon his iron hand and one of scorn upon the other. Then again he frowned.

"Peter flung my arm," he said, wincing, "to a crocodile that happened to be passing by."

"I have often," said Smee, "noticed your strange dread of crocodiles."

"Not of crocodiles," Hook corrected him, "but of that one crocodile." He lowered his voice. "It liked my arm so much, Smee, that it has followed me ever since, from sea to sea and from land to land, licking its lips for the rest of me."

"In a way," said Smee, "it's a sort of compliment."

"I want no such compliments," Hook barked petulantly. "I want Peter Pan, who first gave the brute its taste for me."

He sat down on a large mushroom, and now there was a quiver in his voice. "Smee," he said huskily, "that crocodile would have had me before this, but by a lucky chance it swallowed a clock which goes tick tick inside it, and so before it can reach me I hear the tick and bolt." He laughed, but in a hollow way.

"Some day," said Smee, "the clock will run down, and then he'll get you."[34]

Hook wetted his dry lips. "Ay," he said, "that's the fear that haunts me."

Since sitting down he had felt curiously warm. "Smee," he said, "this seat is hot." He jumped up. "Odds bobs, hammer and tongs[35] I'm burning."

They examined the mushroom, which was of a size and solidity unknown on the mainland; they tried to pull it up, and it came away at once in their hands, for it had no root. Stranger still, smoke began at once to ascend. The pirates looked at each other. "A chimney!" they both exclaimed.

They had indeed discovered the chimney of the home under the ground. It was the custom of the boys to stop it with a mushroom when enemies were in the neighbourhood.

Not only smoke came out of it. There came also children's

voices, for so safe did the boys feel in their hiding-place that they were gaily chattering. The pirates listened grimly, and then replaced the mushroom. They looked around them and noted the holes in the seven trees.

"Did you hear them say Peter Pan's from home?" Smee whispered, fidgeting with Johnny Corkscrew.

Hook nodded. He stood for a long time lost in thought, and at last a curdling smile lit up his swarthy face. Smee had been waiting for it. "Unrip your plan, captain,"[36] he cried eagerly.

"To return to the ship," Hook replied slowly through his teeth, "and cook a large rich cake of a jolly thickness with green sugar on it. There can be but one room below, for there is but one chimney. The silly moles had not the sense to see that they did not need a door apiece. That shows they have no mother.[37] We will leave the cake on the shore of the mermaids' lagoon. These boys are always swimming about there, playing with the mermaids. They will find the cake and they will gobble it up, because, having no mother, they don't know how dangerous 'tis to eat rich damp cake." He burst into laughter, not hollow laughter now, but honest laughter. "Aha, they will die."

Smee had listened with growing admiration.

"It's the wickedest, prettiest policy ever I heard of!" he cried, and in their exultation they danced and sang:

> "Avast, belay, when I appear,
>   By fear they're overtook;
> Nought's left upon your bones when you
>   Have shaken claws with Cook."[38]

They began the verse, but they never finished it, for another sound broke in and stilled them. It was at first such a tiny sound that a leaf might have fallen on it and smothered it, but as it came nearer it was more distinct.

36. *"Unrip your plan, captain."* Unrip is a now obsolete verb, meaning to disclose or make known.

37. *"That shows they have no mother."* Hook twice emphasizes that the absence of a mother puts the children at risk. His plan seems designed by a villain who, once again, thinks more like a child than like an adult. The plot he cooks up about a cake covered with green sugar may well have been invented by Barrie and the Llewelyn Davies boys during some of the pirate games at Black Lake Island.

38. *"Have shaken claws with Cook."* Cook is changed to Hook in most reissued editions of *Peter and Wendy*.

Tick tick tick tick.

Hook stood shuddering, one foot in the air.

"The crocodile," he gasped, and bounded away, followed by his bo'sun.

It was indeed the crocodile. It had passed the redskins, who were now on the trail of the other pirates. It oozed on after Hook.

Once more the boys emerged into the open; but the dangers of the night were not yet over, for presently Nibs rushed breathless into their midst, pursued by a pack of wolves. The tongues of the pursuers were hanging out; the baying of them was horrible.

"Save me, save me!" cried Nibs, falling on the ground.

"But what can we do, what can we do?"

It was a high compliment to Peter that at that dire moment their thoughts turned to him.

"What would Peter do?" they cried simultaneously.

Almost in the same breath they cried, "Peter would look at them through his legs."

And then, "Let us do what Peter would do."

It is quite the most successful way of defying wolves, and as one boy they bent and looked through their legs. The next moment is the long one, but victory came quickly, for as the boys advanced upon them in the terrible attitude, the wolves dropped their tails and fled.

Now Nibs rose from the ground, and the others thought that his staring eyes still saw the wolves. But it was not wolves he saw.

"I have seen a wonderfuller thing," he cried, as they gathered round him eagerly. "A great white bird. It is flying this way."

"What kind of a bird, do you think?"

"I don't know," Nibs said, awestruck, "but it looks so weary, and as it flies it moans, 'Poor Wendy.'"

"Poor Wendy?"

"I remember," said Slightly instantly, "there are birds called Wendies."

"See, it comes," cried Curly, pointing to Wendy in the heavens.

Wendy was now almost overhead, and they could hear her plaintive cry. But more distinct came the shrill voice of Tinker Bell. The jealous fairy had now cast off all disguise of friendship, and was darting at her victim from every direction, pinching savagely each time she touched.

"Hullo, Tink," cried the wondering boys.

Tink's reply rang out: "Peter wants you to shoot the Wendy."

It was not in their nature to question when Peter ordered. "Let us do what Peter wishes!" cried the simple boys. "Quick, bows and arrows."

All but Tootles popped down their trees. He had a bow and arrow with him, and Tink noted it, and rubbed her little hands.

"Quick, Tootles, quick," she screamed. "Peter will be so pleased."

Tootles excitedly fitted the arrow to his bow. "Out of the way, Tink," he shouted; and then he fired, and Wendy fluttered to the ground with an arrow in her breast.[39]

39. *Wendy fluttered to the ground with an arrow in her breast.* In his preface to the play *Peter Pan*, Barrie described how "we first brought Peter down" with an arrow in Kensington Gardens. He added: "I seem to remember that we believed we had killed him . . . and that after a spasm of exultation in our prowess the more soft-hearted among us wept and all of us thought of the police" (Hollindale 2008, 75). Barrie was no doubt aware of how arrows that strike but fail to kill are associated with Cupid, the god who inspires romantic love with his weapons.

CHAPTER 6

The Little House

oolish Tootles was standing like a conqueror over Wendy's body when the other boys sprang, armed, from their trees.

"You are too late," he cried proudly, "I have shot the Wendy. Peter will be so pleased with me."

Overhead Tinker Bell shouted "Silly ass!" and darted into hiding. The others did not hear her. They had crowded round Wendy, and as they looked a terrible silence fell upon the wood. If Wendy's heart had been beating they would all have heard it.

Slightly was the first to speak. "This is no bird," he said in a scared voice. "I think this must be a lady."

"A lady?" said Tootles, and fell a-trembling.

"And we have killed her," Nibs said hoarsely.

They all whipped off their caps.

"Now I see," Curly said: "Peter was bringing her to us." He threw himself sorrowfully on the ground.

"A lady to take care of us at last," said one of the twins, "and you have killed her."

They were sorry for him, but sorrier for themselves, and when he took a step nearer them they turned from him.

Tootles' face was very white, but there was a dignity about him now that had never been there before.

"I did it," he said, reflecting. "When ladies used to come to me in dreams, I said, 'Pretty mother, pretty mother.' But when at last she really came, I shot her."

He moved slowly away.

"Don't go," they called in pity.

"I must," he answered, shaking; "I am so afraid of Peter."

It was at this tragic moment that they heard a sound which made the heart of every one of them rise to his mouth. They heard Peter crow.

"Peter!" they cried, for it was always thus that he signalled his return.

"Hide her," they whispered, and gathered hastily around Wendy. But Tootles stood aloof.

Again came that ringing crow, and Peter dropped in front of them. "Greetings, boys," he cried, and mechanically they saluted, and then again was silence.

He frowned.

"I am back," he said hotly, "why do you not cheer?"

They opened their mouths, but the cheers would not come. He overlooked it in his haste to tell the glorious tidings.

"Great news, boys," he cried, "I have brought at last a mother for you all."

Still no sound, except a little thud from Tootles as he dropped on his knees.

"Have you not seen her?" asked Peter, becoming troubled. "She flew this way."

"Ah me!" one voice said, and another said, "Oh, mournful day."

Tootles rose. "Peter," he said quietly, "I will show her to you;" and when the others would still have hidden her he said, "Back, twins, let Peter see."

1. *He thought of hopping off in a comic sort of way.* Peter's reaction reveals that he does not understand death any better than he understands sexual attraction, and his response to Wendy's apparent death reminds us that Barrie invariably pairs innocence with heartlessness. Once again, we see that Peter cannot be touched (in the sense of moved emotionally) by those around him.

2. *"Oh, dastard hand."* At times Peter and the boys appear to be playacting rather than engaging in rough-and-tumble antics. The inflated rhetoric is a reminder of what Barrie loved, as a boy, about the theater and its culture. It is quite possible that the expressive intensity and histrionics of the stage enabled him, as a boy actor, to display emotions that he could otherwise not express.

3. *"She lives."* This scene of recovery anticipates Tinker Bell's survival after drinking the medicine tainted by Hook. Neverland, as the site of make-believe, allows for the possibility of revival, either through faith in fairies (as is the case for Tinker Bell) or through marvelous coincidences (as is true when the arrow is deflected by the button Peter gives to Wendy).

So they all stood back, and let him see, and after he had looked for a little time he did not know what to do next.

"She is dead," he said uncomfortably. "Perhaps she is frightened at being dead."

He thought of hopping off in a comic sort of way[1] till he was out of sight of her, and then never going near the spot any more. They would all have been glad to follow if he had done this.

But there was the arrow. He took it from her heart and faced his band.

"Whose arrow?" he demanded sternly.

"Mine, Peter," said Tootles on his knees.

"Oh, dastard hand,"[2] Peter said, and he raised the arrow to use it as a dagger.

Tootles did not flinch. He bared his breast. "Strike, Peter," he said firmly, "strike true."

Twice did Peter raise the arrow, and twice did his hand fall. "I cannot strike," he said with awe, "there is something stays my hand."

All looked at him in wonder, save Nibs, who fortunately looked at Wendy.

"It is she," he cried, "the Wendy lady; see, her arm!"

Wonderful to relate, Wendy had raised her arm. Nibs bent over her and listened reverently. "I think she said, 'Poor Tootles,'" he whispered.

"She lives,"[3] Peter said briefly.

Slightly cried instantly, "The Wendy lady lives."

Then Peter knelt beside her and found his button. You remember she had put it on a chain that she wore round her neck.

"See," he said, "the arrow struck against this. It is the kiss I gave her. It has saved her life."

"I remember kisses," Slightly interposed quickly, "let me see it. Ay, that's a kiss."

Peter did not hear him. He was begging Wendy to get

better quickly, so that he could show her the mermaids. Of course she could not answer yet, being still in a frightful faint; but from overhead came a wailing note.

"Listen to Tink," said Curly, "she is crying because the Wendy lives."

Then they had to tell Peter of Tink's crime, and almost never had they seen him look so stern.

"Listen, Tinker Bell," he cried; "I am your friend no more. Begone from me for ever."

She flew on to his shoulder and pleaded, but he brushed her off. Not until Wendy again raised her arm did he relent sufficiently to say, "Well, not for ever, but for a whole week."

Do you think Tinker Bell was grateful to Wendy for raising her arm? Oh dear no, never wanted to pinch her so much. Fairies indeed are strange, and Peter, who understood them best, often cuffed them.

But what to do with Wendy in her present delicate state of health?

"Let us carry her down into the house," Curly suggested.

"Ay," said Slightly, "that is what one does with ladies."

"No, no," Peter said, "you must not touch her. It would not be sufficiently respectful."

"That," said Slightly, "is what I was thinking."

"But if she lies there," Tootles said, "she will die."

"Ay, she will die," Slightly admitted, "but there is no way out."

"Yes, there is," cried Peter. "Let us build a little house round her."[4]

They were all delighted. "Quick," he ordered them, "bring me each of you the best of what we have. Gut our house. Be sharp."

In a moment they were as busy as tailors the night before a wedding. They skurried this way and that, down for bedding, up for firewood, and while they were at it, who should appear but John and Michael. As they dragged along the ground

4. *"Let us build a little house round her."* In *Peter Pan in Kensington Gardens*, fairies build a little house around Maimie Mannering: "The house was exactly the size of Maimie, and perfectly lovely. One of her arms was extended, and this had bothered them for a second, but they built a veranda round it, leading to the front door. The windows were the size of a coloured picture-book, and the door rather smaller, but it would be easy for her to get out by taking off the roof. The fairies, as is their custom, clapped their hands with delight over their cleverness, and they were so madly in love with the little house that they could not bear to think they had finished it. So they gave it ever so many little extra touches, and even then they added more extra touches." The "little house" was modeled on a tiny wash-house adjacent to Barrie's home in Kirriemuir. The wash-house was used as the site for the seven-year-old Barrie's theatrical productions.

5. *"Chairs and a fender first."* A fender is a metal frame plated before a fire to keep coals or wood in place.

6. *"fetch a doctor."* This incident did not appear in the first performance of the play. It was most likely inspired by a scene in Seymour Hicks's children's play *Bluebell in Fairyland*.

they fell asleep standing, stopped, woke up, moved another step and slept again.

"John, John," Michael would cry, "wake up! Where is Nana, John, and mother?"

And then John would rub his eyes and mutter, "It is true, we did fly."

You may be sure they were very relieved to find Peter.

"Hullo, Peter," they said.

"Hullo," replied Peter amicably, though he had quite forgotten them. He was very busy at the moment measuring Wendy with his feet to see how large a house she would need. Of course he meant to leave room for chairs and a table. John and Michael watched him.

"Is Wendy asleep?" they asked.

"Yes."

"John," Michael proposed, "let us wake her and get her to make supper for us"; but as he said it some of the other boys rushed on carrying branches for the building of the house. "Look at them!" he cried.

"Curly," said Peter in his most captain voice, "see that these boys help in the building of the house."

"Ay, ay, sir."

"Build a house?" exclaimed John.

"For the Wendy," said Curly.

"For Wendy?" John said, aghast. "Why, she is only a girl!"

"That," explained Curly, "is why we are her servants."

"You? Wendy's servants!"

"Yes," said Peter, "and you also. Away with them."

The astounded brothers were dragged away to hack and hew and carry. "Chairs and a fender first,"[5] Peter ordered. "Then we shall build a house round them."

"Ay," said Slightly, "that is how a house is built; it all comes back to me."

Peter thought of everything. "Slightly," he cried, "fetch a doctor."[6]

"Ay, ay," said Slightly at once, and disappeared, scratching his head. But he knew Peter must be obeyed, and he returned in a moment, wearing John's hat and looking solemn.

"Please, sir," said Peter, going to him, "are you a doctor?"

The difference between him and the other boys at such a time was that they knew it was make-believe, while to him make-believe and true were exactly the same thing.[7] This sometimes troubled them, as when they had to make-believe that they had had their dinners.

If they broke down in their make-believe he rapped them on the knuckles.

"Yes, my little man," anxiously replied Slightly, who had chapped knuckles.

"Please, sir," Peter explained, "a lady lies very ill."

She was lying at their feet, but Slightly had the sense not to see her.

"Tut, tut, tut," he said, "where does she lie?"

"In yonder glade."

"I will put a glass thing in her mouth," said Slightly; and he made-believe to do it, while Peter waited. It was an anxious moment when the glass thing was withdrawn.

"How is she?" inquired Peter.

"Tut, tut, tut," said Slightly, "this has cured her."

"I am glad!" Peter cried.

"I will call again in the evening," Slightly said; "give her beef tea[8] out of a cup with a spout to it"; but after he had returned the hat to John he blew big breaths, which was his habit on escaping from a difficulty.

In the meantime the wood had been alive with the sound of axes; almost everything needed for a cosy dwelling already lay at Wendy's feet.

"If only we knew," said one, "the kind of house she likes best."

"Peter," shouted another, "she is moving in her sleep."

"Her mouth opens," cried a third, looking respectfully into it. "Oh, lovely!"

7. *to him make-believe and true were exactly the same thing*. The inability to distinguish play from reality marks a critical difference between Peter and the other boys. Peter is, after all, the boy who will not grow up, and knowing the difference between fantasy and reality serves as a critical milestone in the process of maturation.

8. *beef tea*. This concoction was a liquid extract from beef, often served to those who were ailing or invalid. Beef tea is still used today to fend off chills and is sold commercially under the name Bovril.

9. *"I wish I had a pretty house."* Barrie included the song in order to fill up the time it took to put up Wendy's house. The full version of the song is included in John Crook's music for the play, published by W. Paxon and Co. Ltd. in 1905. "I wish I had a darling house" was the original wording of the song's first line, but Barrie excised "darling" in rehearsal and replaced it with "pretty." Crook was the composer who conducted the orchestra of the Duke of York's Theatre, where *Peter Pan* made its debut.

"Perhaps she is going to sing in her sleep," said Peter. "Wendy, sing the kind of house you would like to have."

Immediately, without opening her eyes, Wendy began to sing:

> "I wish I had a pretty house,[9]
> The littlest ever seen,
> With funny little red walls
> And roof of mossy green."

They gurgled with joy at this, for by the greatest good luck the branches they had brought were sticky with red sap, and all the ground was carpeted with moss. As they rattled up the little house they broke into song themselves:

> "We've built the little walls and roof
> And made a lovely door,
> So tell us, mother Wendy,
> What are you wanting more?"

To this she answered greedily:

> "Oh, really next I think I'll have
> Gay windows all about,
> With roses peeping in, you know,
> And babies peeping out."

With a blow of their fists they made windows, and large yellow leaves were the blinds. But roses—?

"Roses," cried Peter sternly.

Quickly they made-believe to grow the loveliest roses up the walls.

Babies?

To prevent Peter ordering babies they hurried into song again:

"We've made the roses peeping out,
  The babes are at the door,
We cannot make ourselves, you know,
  'cos we've been made before."

Peter, seeing this to be a good idea, at once pretended that it was his own. The house was quite beautiful, and no doubt Wendy was very cosy within, though, of course, they could no longer see her. Peter strode up and down, ordering finishing touches. Nothing escaped his eagle eye. Just when it seemed absolutely finished:

"There's no knocker on the door," he said.

They were very ashamed, but Tootles gave the sole of his shoe, and it made an excellent knocker.

Absolutely finished now, they thought.

Not of bit of it. "There's no chimney," Peter said; "we must have a chimney."

"It certainly does need a chimney," said John importantly. This gave Peter an idea. He snatched the hat off John's head, knocked out the bottom, and put the hat on the roof.[10] The little house was so pleased to have such a capital chimney, that, as if to say thank you, smoke immediately began to come out of the hat.

Now really and truly it was finished. Nothing remained to do but to knock.

"All look your best," Peter warned them; "first impressions are awfully important."

He was glad no one asked him what first impressions are; they were all too busy looking their best.

He knocked politely; and now the wood was as still as the children, not a sound to be heard except from Tinker Bell, who was watching from a branch and openly sneering.

What the boys were wondering was, would any one answer the knock? If a lady, what would she be like?

10. *put the hat on the roof.* Make-believe provides the foundation and building blocks for the house. Roses and babes are created through the imagination, and the building of the house functions as an exercise in improvisation, with a shoe as knocker and a hat as chimney. In Neverland, as the narrator observes, the make-believe becomes real, and it is through play that fantasies take material shape.

11. *"Lovely, darling house."* Wendy's pun (restored in the dialogue) recalls her own home and reminds us that her presence allows the boys to construct a domestic idyll in Neverland. She quickly becomes the mother that the lost boys desire.

12. *"I have no real experience."* Wendy is recruited into motherhood at a young age. Barrie's mother, as we learn in *Margaret Ogilvy*, took on maternal duties at a young age: "She was eight when her mother's death made her mistress of the house and mother to her little brother, and from that time she scrubbed and mended and baked and sewed, and argued with the flesher about the quarter pound of beef and penny bone . . . and she carried the water from the pump, and had her washing days and her ironings and a stocking always on the wire for odd moments" (*Margaret Ogilvy*, 28–29). The attention to sewing and to domestic activities throughout are a clear homage to Margaret Ogilvy, and Barrie freely conceded that his mother appeared in every work he had written. Wendy can also be seen as a Snow White figure who takes care of seven lost boys.

13. *"you naughty children."* As soon as Wendy assumes the role of mother, she becomes both scolder and storyteller, admonishing the children to come indoors and promising them a fairy tale. She slips with ease into the maternal role occupied by Mrs. Darling, and domestic order is established by the end of the chapter.

The door opened and a lady came out. It was Wendy. They all whipped off their hats.

She looked properly surprised, and this was just how they had hoped she would look.

"Where am I?" she said.

Of course Slightly was the first to get his word in. "Wendy lady," he said rapidly, "for you we built this house."

"Oh, say you're pleased," cried Nibs.

"Lovely, darling house,"[11] Wendy said, and they were the very words they had hoped she would say.

"And we are your children," cried the twins.

Then all went on their knees, and holding out their arms cried, "O Wendy lady, be our mother."

"Ought I?" Wendy said, all shining. "Of course it's frightfully fascinating, but you see I am only a little girl. I have no real experience."[12]

"That doesn't matter," said Peter, as if he were the only person present who knew all about it, though he was really the one who knew least. "What we need is just a nice motherly person."

"Oh dear!" Wendy said, "you see, I feel that is exactly what I am."

"It is, it is," they all cried; "we saw it at once."

"Very well," she said, "I will do my best. Come inside at once, you naughty children;[13] I am sure your feet are damp. And before I put you to bed I have just time to finish the story of Cinderella."

In they went; I don't know how there was room for them, but you can squeeze very tight in the Neverland. And that was the first of the many joyous evenings they had with Wendy. By and by she tucked them up in the great bed in the home under the trees, but she herself slept that night in the little house, and Peter kept watch outside with drawn sword, for the pirates could be heard carousing far away and the wolves were on the prowl. The little house looked so cosy and safe in the darkness, with a bright light showing through its blinds, and the chimney smoking beautifully, and Peter standing on guard. After a time he fell asleep, and some unsteady fairies had to climb over him on their way home from an orgy. Any of the other boys obstructing the fairy path at night they would have mischiefed,[14] but they just tweaked Peter's nose and passed on.

14. *they would have mischiefed.* "Mischief" is used here as a verb, meaning to do physical harm to or attack. After the fairies tweak Peter's nose in the play, we discover: "Fairies, you see, can touch him."

Mabel Lucie Attwell, *Peter Pan and Wendy*, 1921. (Lucie Attwell Ltd. Courtesy of Vicki Thomas Associates)

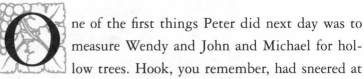

CHAPTER 7

The Home under the Ground

1. *But you simply must fit*. The narrator uses a form of address that suggests the novel's origins in an oral storytelling situation. The conversational "you"—here as elsewhere in the work—allows us to conjure up an adult speaking to a child or to a group of children, explaining exactly how "you" are fitted to a tree.

One of the first things Peter did next day was to measure Wendy and John and Michael for hollow trees. Hook, you remember, had sneered at the boys for thinking they needed a tree apiece, but this was ignorance, for unless your tree fitted you it was difficult to go up and down, and no two of the boys were quite the same size. Once you fitted, you drew in your breath at the top, and down you went at exactly the right speed, while to ascend you drew in and let out alternately, and so wriggled up. Of course, when you have mastered the action you are able to do these things without thinking of them, and nothing can be more graceful.

But you simply must fit,[1] and Peter measures you for your tree as carefully as for a suit of clothes: the only difference being that the clothes are made to fit you, while you have to be made to fit the tree. Usually it is done quite easily, as by your wearing too many garments or too few; but if you are bumpy in awkward places or the only available tree is an odd shape, Peter does some things to you, and after that you fit. Once you fit, great care must be taken to go on fitting, and this, as Wendy was to discover to her delight, keeps a whole family in perfect condition.

Wendy and Michael fitted their trees at the first try, but John had to be altered a little.

After a few days' practice they could go up and down as gaily as buckets in a well. And how ardently they grew to love their home under the ground; especially Wendy. It consisted of one large room, as all houses should do, with a floor in which you could dig if you wanted to go fishing, and in this floor grew stout mushrooms[2] of a charming colour, which were used as stools. A Never tree tried hard to grow in the centre of the room,[3] but every morning they sawed the trunk through, level with the floor. By tea-time it was always about two feet high, and then they put a door on top of it, the whole thus becoming a table; as soon as they cleared away, they sawed off the trunk again, and thus there was more room to play. There was an enormous fireplace which was in almost any part of the room where you cared to light it, and across this Wendy stretched strings, made of fibre, from which she suspended her washing. The bed was tilted against the wall by day, and let down at 6:30, when it filled nearly half the room; and all the boys except Michael slept in it, lying like sardines in a tin. There was a strict rule against turning round until one gave the signal, when all turned at once. Michael should have used it also; but Wendy would have a baby, and he was the littlest, and you know what women are, and the short and long of it is that he was hung up in a basket.

It was rough and simple, and not unlike what baby bears would have made of an underground house in the same circumstances. But there was one recess in the wall, no larger than a bird-cage, which was the private apartment of Tinker Bell. It could be shut off from the rest of the house by a tiny curtain, which Tink, who was most fastidious, always kept drawn when dressing or undressing. No woman, however large, could have had a more exquisite boudoir and bedchamber combined. The couch, as she always called it, was a genuine Queen Mab,[4] with club legs; and she varied the

2. *grew stout mushrooms*. Fairies were frequently associated with mushrooms and toadstools in Victorian England. Arthur Rackham and Richard Dadd, among other British illustrators, brought the two together, with fairies often dancing in a ring around toadstools, or a ring of mushrooms serving as a stage for the fairy dance.

3. *A Never tree tried hard to grow in the centre of the room.* Trees here are connected with individuals (each child has his own), and they are part of the island's landscape, but they also have a cosmic significance. In many mythological systems, a tree is rooted at the world's navel (*omphalos*)—at its "centre"—as the *axis mundi*. In Norse mythology Yggdrasil is the World Tree, a great ash joining different worlds and generating life.

4. *Queen Mab*. Queen Mab, the fairy ruler of European folklore, gave dreams to human beings. She was also known as a mischief maker who sometimes exchanged babies at their birth. Mercutio describes her in *Romeo and Juliet* as "the fairies' midwife, and she comes / In shape no bigger than an agate-stone." The remaining pieces of furniture have equally whimsical names, used in part to satirize the pretentiousness of antique dealers in Barrie's London.

5. *rampagious.* Usually spelled "rampageous," the term means "unruly," "boisterous," or "given to rampages."

6. *roasted breadfruit.* Mammee-apples are from the mammee tree of tropical South America and resemble mangosteens. Tappa rolls are rolls of unwoven cloth made from the paper mulberry tree in Polynesia. They are not edible. Calabashes of poe-poe are gourds containing the Hawaiian food poi, made from the corm of the taro plant. These exotic dishes do not fix Neverland's location, but they make it clear that Peter inhabits a tropical island.

7. *stodge just to feel stodgy.* "Stodge" means to gorge, and to "feel stodgy" is to have eaten one's fill.

8. *Make-believe was so real to him.* Cynthia Asquith, who carried out her secretarial duties right in Barrie's home and spent more time with him than almost any other person did, reports that her employer wandered "in some entrancing borderland between fantasy and fact. For him the frontier between these two realms was never very clearly marked. Once, when he had just told me some ostensibly autobiographical anecdote, a genuinely puzzled, even worried, expression came into his face. 'I can't remember, now, whether the actual incident ever really took place,' he said wistfully" (Asquith, *Portrait*, 76).

bedspreads according to what fruit-blossom was in season. Her mirror was a Puss-in-Boots, of which there are now only three, unchipped, known to the fairy dealers; the wash-stand was Pie-crust and reversible, the chest of drawers an authentic Charming the Sixth, and the carpet and rugs of the best (the early) period of Margery and Robin. There was a chandelier from Tiddlywinks for the look of the thing, but of course she lit the residence herself. Tink was very contemptuous of the rest of the house, as indeed was perhaps inevitable; and her chamber, though beautiful, looked rather conceited, having the appearance of a nose permanently turned up.

I suppose it was all especially entrancing to Wendy, because those rampagious[5] boys of hers gave her so much to do. Really there were whole weeks when, except perhaps with a stocking in the evening, she was never above ground. The cooking, I can tell you, kept her nose to the pot. Their chief food was roasted breadfruit,[6] yams, cocoa-nuts, baked pig, mammee-apples, tappa rolls and bananas, washed down with calabashes of poe-poe; but you never exactly knew whether there would be a real meal or just a make-believe, it all depended upon Peter's whim. He could eat, really eat, if it was part of a game, but he could not stodge just to feel stodgy,[7] which is what most children like better than anything else; the next best thing being to talk about it. Make-believe was so real to him[8] that during a meal of it you could see him getting rounder. Of course it was trying, but you simply had to follow his lead, and if you could prove to him that you were getting loose for your tree he let you stodge.

Wendy's favourite time for sewing and darning was after they had all gone to bed. Then, as she expressed it, she had a breathing time for herself; and she occupied it in making new things for them, and putting double pieces on the knees, for they were all most frightfully hard on their knees.

When she sat down to a basketful of their stockings, every heel with a hole in it, she would fling up her arms and exclaim, "Oh dear, I am sure I sometimes think spinsters are to be envied!"[9]

Her face beamed when she exclaimed this.

You remember about her pet wolf. Well, it very soon discovered that she had come to the island and it found her out, and they just ran into each other's arms. After that it followed her about everywhere.

As time wore on did she think much about the beloved parents she had left behind her? This is a difficult question, because it is quite impossible to say how time does wear on in the Neverland, where it is calculated by moons and suns, and there are ever so many more of them than on the mainland. But I am afraid that Wendy did not really worry about her father and mother; she was absolutely confident that they would always keep the window open for her to fly back by, and this gave her complete ease of mind. What did disturb her at times was that John remembered his parents vaguely only, as people he had once known, while Michael was quite willing to believe that she was really his mother. These things scared her a little, and nobly anxious to do her duty, she tried to fix the old life in their minds by setting them examination papers on it, as like as possible to the ones she used to do at school. The other boys thought this awfully interesting, and insisted on joining, and they made slates for themselves, and sat round the table, writing and thinking hard about the questions she had written on another slate and passed round. They were the most ordinary questions—"What was the colour of Mother's eyes? Which was taller, Father or Mother? Was Mother blonde or brunette? Answer all three questions if possible." "(A) Write an essay of not less than 40 words on How I spent my last Holidays, or The Characters of Father and Mother compared. Only one of these to be attempted." Or "(1) Describe Mother's laugh; (2) Describe Father's laugh; (3) Describe Mother's Party Dress; (4) Describe the Kennel and its Inmate."

9. *"Oh dear, I am sure I sometimes think spinsters are to be envied!"* Wendy appears to be following a script, quoting phrases she has heard from her own mother and mimicking her behavior.

The Home under the ground.

10. *he despised all mothers except Wendy*. The narrator inserts "despise" and "mother" into the same sentence with alarming frequency. He will later report that mothers are always willing to be buffers (or mediators) and that children resent them for it. And near the end of the novel, the narrator will, out of the blue, denounce Mrs. Darling, claiming that she has "no proper spirit."

11. *the only boy on the island who could neither write nor spell*. With no education at all, Peter is not only the boy who will not grow up but also the boy who will never read. His illiteracy can be connected with his lack of memory and inability to think beyond the present moment to the past or to the future. Growing up in a family and in a culture that understood the value of education, Barrie may have inserted this aside to show exactly how far Peter stands from culture and how closely allied he is with nature. And school is also, of course, the antithesis of Neverland.

They were just everyday questions like these, and when you could not answer them you were told to make a cross; and it was really dreadful what a number of crosses even John made. Of course the only boy who replied to every question was Slightly, and no one could have been more hopeful of coming out first, but his answers were perfectly ridiculous, and he really came out last: a melancholy thing.

Peter did not compete. For one thing he despised all mothers except Wendy,[10] and for another he was the only boy on the island who could neither write nor spell;[11] not the smallest word. He was above all that sort of thing.

By the way, the questions were all written in the past tense. What was the colour of Mother's eyes, and so on. Wendy, you see, had been forgetting too.

Adventures, of course, as we shall see, were of daily occurrence; but about this time Peter invented, with Wendy's help, a new game that fascinated him enormously, until he suddenly had no more interest in it, which, as you have been told, was what always happened with his games. It consisted in pretending not to have adventures, in doing the sort of thing John and Michael had been doing all their lives: sitting on stools flinging balls in the air, pushing each other, going out for walks and coming back without having killed so much as a grizzly. To see Peter doing nothing on a stool was a great sight; he could not help looking solemn at such times, to sit still seemed to him such a comic thing to do. He boasted that he had gone walking for the good of his health. For several suns these were the most novel of all adventures to him; and John and Michael had to pretend to be delighted also; otherwise he would have treated them severely.

He often went out alone, and when he came back you were never absolutely certain whether he had had an adventure or not. He might have forgotten it so completely that he said nothing about it; and then when you went out you found the body; and, on the other hand, he might say a great deal about it, and yet you could not find the body. Sometimes he came home with his head bandaged, and then Wendy cooed over him and bathed it in lukewarm water, while he told a dazzling tale. But she was never quite sure, you know. There were, however, many adventures which she knew to be true because she was in them herself, and there were still more that were at least partly true, for the other boys were in them and said they were wholly true. To describe them all would require a book as large as an English-Latin, Latin-English Dictionary, and the most we can do is to give one as a specimen of an average hour on the island. The difficulty is which one to choose. Should we take the brush with the redskins at Slightly Gulch? It was a sanguinary affair, and especially interesting as showing one of Peter's peculiarities, which was that in the middle of a fight he would suddenly change sides. At the Gulch, when victory was still in the balance, sometimes leaning this way and sometimes that, he called out, "I'm redskin to-day; what are you, Tootles?" And Tootles answered, "Redskin; what are you, Nibs?" and Nibs said, "Redskin; what are you Twin?" and so on; and they were all redskin; and of course this would have ended the fight had not the real redskins, fascinated by Peter's methods, agreed to be lost boys for that once, and so at it they all went again, more fiercely than ever.

The extraordinary upshot of this adventure was—but we have not decided yet[12] that this is the adventure we are to narrate. Perhaps a better one would be the night attack by the redskins on the house under the ground, when several of them stuck in the hollow trees and had to be pulled out like corks. Or we might tell how Peter saved Tiger Lily's life in the Mermaids' Lagoon, and so made her his ally.

Or we could tell of that cake the pirates cooked so that the boys might eat it and perish; and how they placed it in one cunning spot after another; but always Wendy snatched it from the hands of her children, so that in time it lost its

12. *but we have not decided yet.* The narrator produces a fictional space in which multiple outcomes are possible and in which everything remains provisional and contingent. Like Peter, the narrator is unpredictable, mercurial, and resistant to being fixed.

13. *he drew a circle round him on the ground with an arrow*. The gesture of drawing an exclusionary circle with a weapon is repeated by Hook, when he uses his "iron claw" to draw "a circle of dead water round him, from which they fled like affrighted fishes." The final combat between Peter Pan and Hook takes place when the boys form "a ring round them." Again we see how episodes in the work are inspired by boys' play, with theatrical gestures (a weapon flourished) and arrangements (combat with spectators) adding to the effect of the stage version.

succulence, and became as hard as a stone, and was used as a missile, and Hook fell over it in the dark.

Or suppose we tell of the birds that were Peter's friends, particularly of the Never bird that built in a tree overhanging the lagoon, and how the nest fell into the water, and still the bird sat on her eggs, and Peter gave orders that she was not to be disturbed. That is a pretty story, and the end shows how grateful a bird can be; but if we tell it we must also tell the whole adventure of the lagoon, which would of course be telling two adventures rather than just one. A shorter adventure, and quite as exciting, was Tinker Bell's attempt, with the help of some street fairies, to have the sleeping Wendy conveyed on a great floating leaf to the mainland. Fortunately the leaf gave way and Wendy woke, thinking it was bath-time, and swam back. Or again, we might choose Peter's defiance of the lions, when he drew a circle round him on the ground with an arrow[13] and defied them to cross it; and though he waited for hours, with the other boys and Wendy looking on breathlessly from trees, not one of them dared to accept his challenge.

Which of these adventures shall we choose? The best way will be to toss for it.

I have tossed, and the lagoon has won. This almost makes one wish that the gulch or the cake or Tink's leaf had won. Of course I could do it again, and make it best out of three; however, perhaps fairest to stick to the lagoon.

CHAPTER 8

The Mermaids' Lagoon

If you shut your eyes[1] and are a lucky one, you may see at times a shapeless pool of lovely pale colours suspended in the darkness; then if you squeeze your eyes tighter, the pool begins to take shape, and the colours become so vivid that with another squeeze they must go on fire. But just before they go on fire you see the lagoon. This is the nearest you ever get to it on the mainland, just one heavenly moment; if there could be two moments you might see the surf and hear the mermaids singing.

The children often spent long summer days on this lagoon, swimming or floating most of the time, playing the mermaid games in the water, and so forth. You must not think from this that the mermaids were on friendly terms with them; on the contrary, it was among Wendy's lasting regrets that all the time she was on the island she never had a civil word from one of them. When she stole softly to the edge of the lagoon she might see them by the score, especially on Marooners' Rock, where they loved to bask, combing out their hair in a lazy way that quite irritated her; or she might even swim, on tiptoe as it were, to within a yard of them, but then they saw her and dived, probably splashing her with their tails, not by accident, but intentionally.

1. *If you shut your eyes.* The lagoon appears to be an optical illusion, a place located in the mind's eye. Creating the colors of the lagoon and its structure seems possible for every mortal. Far harder is the talent for seeing the surf, hearing the song of the mermaids, and swimming in the lagoon, as children do. In the screenplay for the silent version of *Peter Pan*, Barrie hinted at a connection between Eden and Neverland when he described the origin of fairies: "Then the scene is a primeval wood. Adam and Eve leave their child on the ground. They go. The child laughs and kicks joyously. Then the picture is full of little splashes whirling about like falling leaves, and when they come to rest they are gay little fairies."

2. *bubbles of many colours made in rainbow water*. Barrie had a gift for understanding exactly what appeals to the imagination of children, and his invention of bubbles that serve both as balls and (in the play version) as vehicles of flight gives us the poetry of childhood objects. Children tend to be fascinated by glitter, sparkle, rainbows, fireworks, kaleidoscopes, and in general by the play of color and light. The bubbles made of rainbow water are batted about under rainbows to create a world of rare visual beauty.

3. *the mermaids immediately disappeared*. Although the narrator suggests that the mermaids are too arrogant to play with mere mortals and therefore avoid them, the fact that they disappear reminds us that they are make-believe. Barrie's mermaid lagoon may have been inspired by Hans Christian Andersen's "The Little Mermaid," which has a more fully elaborated undersea realm. Recall that Andersen's name is woven into the front stage curtain of *Peter Pan*.

They treated all the boys in the same way, except of course Peter, who chatted with them on Marooners' Rock by the hour, and sat on their tails when they got cheeky. He gave Wendy one of their combs.

The most haunting time at which to see them is at the turn of the moon, when they utter strange wailing cries; but the lagoon is dangerous for mortals then, and until the evening of which we have now to tell, Wendy had never seen the lagoon by moonlight, less from fear, for of course Peter would have accompanied her, than because she had strict rules about every one being in bed by seven. She was often at the lagoon, however, on sunny days after rain, when the mermaids come up in extraordinary numbers to play with their bubbles. The bubbles of many colours made in rainbow water[2] they treat as balls, hitting them gaily from one to another with their tails, and trying to keep them in the rainbow till they burst. The goals are at each end of the rainbow, and the keepers only are allowed to use their hands. Sometimes hundreds of mermaids will be playing in the lagoon at a time, and it is quite a pretty sight.

But the moment the children tried to join in they had to play by themselves, for the mermaids immediately disappeared.[3] Nevertheless we have proof that they secretly watched the interlopers, and were not above taking an idea from them; for John introduced a new way of hitting the bubble, with the head instead of the hand, and the mermaid goalkeepers adopted it. This is the one mark that John has left on the Neverland.

It must also have been rather pretty to see the children resting on a rock for half an hour after their midday meal. Wendy insisted on their doing this, and it had to be a real rest even though the meal was make-believe. So they lay there in the sun, and their bodies glistened in it, while she sat beside them and looked important.

It was one such day, and they were all on Marooners' Rock. The rock was not much larger than their great bed, but of course they all knew how not to take up much room, and they were dozing, or at least lying with their eyes shut, and pinching occasionally when they thought Wendy was not looking. She was very busy, stitching.

While she stitched, a change came to the lagoon. Little shivers ran over it, and the sun went away and shadows stole across the water, turning it cold. Wendy could no longer see to thread her needle, and when she looked up, the lagoon that had always hitherto been such a laughing place seemed formidable and unfriendly.

It was not, she knew, that night had come, but something as dark as night had come. No, worse than that. It had not come, but it had sent that shiver through the sea to say that it was coming. What was it?

There crowded upon her all the stories she had been told of Marooners' Rock, so called because evil captains put sailors on it and leave them there to drown. They drown when the tide rises, for then it is submerged.

Of course she should have roused the children at once; not merely because of the unknown that was stalking toward them, but because it was no longer good for them to sleep on a rock grown chilly. But she was a young mother and she did not know this; she thought you simply must stick to your rule about half an hour after the mid-day meal. So, though fear was upon her, and she longed to hear male voices, she would not waken them. Even when she heard the sound of muffled oars, though her heart was in her mouth, she did not waken them. She stood over them to let them have their sleep out. Was it not brave of Wendy?

It was well for those boys then that there was one among them who could sniff danger even in his sleep. Peter sprang erect, as wide awake at once as a dog, and with one warning cry he roused the others.

He stood motionless, one hand to his ear.

"Pirates!" he cried. The others came closer to him. A

4. *happy hunting-ground*. The Native
American afterlife is designated as a paradise where game is plentiful and hunting
unlimited.

5. *"Luff, you lubber."* To "luff" is to bring
the bow of a sailing ship into the wind. A
"lubber" is a clumsy sailor.

strange smile was playing about his face, and Wendy saw it
and shuddered. While that smile was on his face no one dared
address him; all they could do was to stand ready to obey. The
order came sharp and incisive.

"Dive!"

There was a gleam of legs, and instantly the lagoon seemed
deserted. Marooners' Rock stood alone in the forbidding
waters, as if it were itself marooned.

The boat drew nearer. It was the pirate dinghy, with three
figures in her, Smee and Starkey, and the third a captive, no
other than Tiger Lily. Her hands and ankles were tied, and she
knew what was to be her fate. She was to be left on the rock
to perish, an end to one of her race more terrible than death
by fire or torture, for is it not written in the book of the tribe
that there is no path through water to the happy hunting-
ground?[4] Yet her face was impassive; she was the daughter of
a chief, she must die as a chief's daughter, it is enough.

They had caught her boarding the pirate ship with a knife
in her mouth. No watch was kept on the ship, it being Hook's
boast that the wind of his name guarded the ship for a mile
around. Now her fate would help to guard it also. One more
wail would go the round in that wind by night.

In the gloom that they brought with them the two pirates
did not see the rock till they crashed into it.

"Luff, you lubber,"[5] cried an Irish voice that was Smee's;
"here's the rock. Now, then, what we have to do is to hoist the
redskin on to it and leave her there to drown."

It was the work of one brutal moment to land the beautiful
girl on the rock; she was too proud to offer a vain resistance.

Quite near the rock, but out of sight, two heads were bobbing up and down, Peter's and Wendy's. Wendy was crying, for it was the first tragedy she had seen. Peter had seen
many tragedies, but he had forgotten them all. He was less
sorry than Wendy for Tiger Lily: it was two against one that
angered him, and he meant to save her. An easy way would

have been to wait until the pirates had gone, but he was never one to choose the easy way.

There was almost nothing he could not do, and he now imitated the voice of Hook.[6]

"Ahoy there, you lubbers!" he called. It was a marvelous imitation.

"The captain!" said the pirates, staring at each other in surprise.

"He must be swimming out to us," Starkey said, when they had looked for him in vain.

"We are putting the redskin on the rock," Smee called out.

"Set her free," came the astonishing answer.

"Free!"

"Yes, cut her bonds and let her go."

"But, captain—"

"At once, d'ye hear," cried Peter, "or I'll plunge my hook in you."

"This is queer!" Smee gasped.

"Better do what the captain orders," said Starkey nervously.

"Ay, ay." Smee said, and he cut Tiger Lily's cords. At once like an eel she slid between Starkey's legs into the water.

Of course Wendy was very elated over Peter's cleverness; but she knew that he would be elated also and very likely crow and thus betray himself, so at once her hand went out to cover his mouth. But it was stayed even in the act, for "Boat ahoy!" rang over the lagoon in Hook's voice, and this time it was not Peter who had spoken.

Peter may have been about to crow, but his face puckered in a whistle of surprise instead.

"Boat ahoy!" again came the cry.

Now Wendy understood. The real Hook was also in the water.

He was swimming to the boat, and as his men showed a light to guide him he had soon reached them. In the light of the lantern Wendy saw his hook grip the boat's side; she

6. *he now imitated the voice of Hook.* Peter can "imitate the Captain's voice so perfectly," we read, in the stage directions to *Peter Pan*, "that even the author has a dizzy feeling that at times he was really Hook." At the end of the play, Peter appears "on the poop in Hook's hat and cigars, and with a small iron claw." And in the novel, Peter sits in Hook's cabin, cigar holder in mouth, with one hand clenched, "held threateningly aloft like a hook." The two are presented as antagonists with a shared secret core.

saw his evil swarthy face as he rose dripping from the water, and, quaking, she would have liked to swim away, but Peter would not budge. He was tingling with life and also top-heavy with conceit. "Am I not a wonder, oh, I am a wonder!" he whispered to her; and though she thought so also, she was really glad for the sake of his reputation that no one heard him except herself.

He signed to her to listen.

The two pirates were very curious to know what had brought their captain to them, but he sat with his head on his hook in a position of profound melancholy.

"Captain, is all well?" they asked timidly, but he answered with a hollow moan.

"He sighs," said Smee.

"He sighs again," said Starkey.

"And yet a third time he sighs," said Smee.

"What's up, captain?"

Then at last he spoke passionately.

"The game's up," he cried, "those boys have found a mother."

Affrighted though she was, Wendy swelled with pride.

"O evil day," cried Starkey.

"What's a mother?" asked the ignorant Smee.

Wendy was so shocked that she exclaimed. "He doesn't know!" and always after this she felt that if you could have a pet pirate Smee would be her one.

Peter pulled her beneath the water, for Hook had started up, crying, "What was that?"

"I heard nothing," said Starkey, raising the lantern over the waters, and as the pirates looked they saw a strange sight. It was the nest I have told you of, floating on the lagoon, and the Never bird was sitting on it.

"See," said Hook in answer to Smee's question, "that is a mother. What a lesson. The nest must have fallen into the water, but would the mother desert her eggs? No."

There was a break in his voice, as if for a moment he recalled innocent days when—but he brushed away this weakness with his hook.

Smee, much impressed, gazed at the bird as the nest was borne past, but the more suspicious Starkey said, "If she is a mother, perhaps she is hanging about here to help Peter."

Hook winced. "Ay," he said, "that is the fear that haunts me."

He was roused from this dejection by Smee's eager voice.

"Captain," said Smee, "could we not kidnap these boys' mother and make her our mother?"

"It is a princely scheme," cried Hook, and at once it took practical shape in his great brain. "We will seize the children and carry them to the boat: the boys we will make walk the plank, and Wendy shall be our mother."

Again Wendy forgot herself.

"Never!" she cried, and bobbed.

"What was that?"

But they could see nothing. They thought it must have been a leaf in the wind. "Do you agree, my bullies?" asked Hook.

"There is my hand on it," they both said.

"And there is my hook. Swear."

They all swore. By this time they were on the rock, and suddenly Hook remembered Tiger Lily.

"Where is the redskin?" he demanded abruptly.

He had a playful humour at moments, and they thought this was one of the moments.

"That is all right, captain," Smee answered complacently; "we let her go."

"Let her go!" cried Hook.

"'Twas your own orders," the bo'sun faltered.

"You called over the water to us to let her go," said Starkey.

"Brimstone and gall,"[7] thundered Hook, "what cozening is going on here!"[8] His face had gone black with rage, but

7. *"Brimstone and gall."* Brimstone was once the common name for sulfur, and is now rarely used except in the biblical phrase "fire and brimstone." Hook combines sulfur with bile to produce his unusual curse.

8. *"what cozening is going on here!"* "Cozen" means to "cheat" or "defraud."

101

9. *"I am James Hook."* Here, as on several other occasions, Peter becomes Hook's double. Invoked as the spirit that "haunts" the lagoon, he answers Hook's questions but also leads Hook to echo his own voice.

10. *a touch of the feminine.* Hook's curls, his dress, and his mannerisms all create the effeminate effects described here, reminding us that—despite the gendered division of labor—there is also frequent gender confusion in Neverland, with its sewing pirates and brave warrior princesses.

he saw that they believed their words, and he was startled. "Lads," he said, shaking a little, "I gave no such order."

"It is passing queer," Smee said, and they all fidgeted uncomfortably. Hook raised his voice, but there was a quiver in it.

"Spirit that haunts this dark lagoon to-night," he cried, "dost hear me?"

Of course Peter should have kept quiet, but of course he did not. He immediately answered in Hook's voice:

"Odds, bobs, hammer and tongs, I hear you."

In that supreme moment Hook did not blanch, even at the gills, but Smee and Starkey clung to each other in terror.

"Who are you, stranger, speak!" Hook demanded.

"I am James Hook,"[9] replied the voice, "captain of the *Jolly Roger*."

"You are not; you are not," Hook cried hoarsely.

"Brimstone and gall," the voice retorted, "say that again, and I'll cast anchor in you."

Hook tried a more ingratiating manner. "If you are Hook," he said almost humbly, "come tell me, who am I?"

"A codfish," replied the voice, "only a codfish."

"A codfish!" Hook echoed blankly; and it was then, but not till then, that his proud spirit broke. He saw his men draw back from him.

"Have we been captained all this time by a codfish!" they muttered. "It is lowering to our pride."

They were his dogs snapping at him, but, tragic figure though he had become, he scarcely heeded them. Against such fearful evidence it was not their belief in him that he needed, it was his own. He felt his ego slipping from him. "Don't desert me, bully," he whispered hoarsely to it.

In his dark nature there was a touch of the feminine,[10] as in all the great pirates, and it sometimes gave him intuitions. Suddenly he tried the guessing game.

"Hook," he called, "have you another voice?"

Now Peter could never resist a game,[11] and he answered blithely in his own voice, "I have."

"And another name?"

"Ay, ay."

"Vegetable?" asked Hook.

"No."

"Mineral?"

"No."

"Animal?"

"Yes."

"Man?"

"No!" This answer rang out scornfully.

"Boy?"

"Yes."

"Ordinary boy?"

"No!"

"Wonderful boy?"

To Wendy's pain the answer that rang out this time was "Yes."

"Are you in England?"

"No."

"Are you here?"

"Yes."

Hook was completely puzzled. "You ask him some questions," he said to the others, wiping his damp brow.

Smee reflected. "I can't think of a thing," he said regretfully.

"Can't guess, can't guess," crowed Peter. "Do you give it up?"

Of course in his pride he was carrying the game too far, and the miscreants saw their chance.

"Yes, yes," they answered eagerly.

"Well, then," he cried, "I am Peter Pan."

Pan!

In a moment Hook was himself again, and Smee and Starkey were his faithful henchmen.

11. *Peter could never resist a game.* For Peter, everything becomes a game: eating, playing house, and even killing. In the middle of combat, he "would change sides," in which case the fascinated redskins agree to be lost boys.

12. *"lam into the pirates."* "Lam into" is schoolboy slang and is used chiefly in reference to beating a person soundly or thrashing someone.

13. *pinked.* To "pink" is to stab or pierce with a sharp weapon.

"Now we have him," Hook shouted. "Into the water, Smee. Starkey, mind the boat. Take him dead or alive."

He leaped as he spoke, and simultaneously came the gay voice of Peter.

"Are you ready, boys?"

"Ay, ay," from various parts of the lagoon.

"Then lam into the pirates."[12]

The fight was short and sharp. First to draw blood was John, who gallantly climbed into the boat and held Starkey. There was a fierce struggle, in which the cutlass was torn from the pirate's grasp. He wriggled overboard and John leapt after him. The dinghy drifted away.

Here and there a head bobbed up in the water, and there was a flash of steel followed by a cry or a whoop. In the confusion some struck at their own side. The corkscrew of Smee got Tootles in the fourth rib, but he was himself pinked[13] in turn by Curly. Farther from the rock Starkey was pressing Slightly and the twins hard.

Where all this time was Peter? He was seeking bigger game.

The others were all brave boys, and they must not be blamed for backing from the pirate captain. His iron claw made a circle of dead water round him, from which they fled like affrighted fishes.

But there was one who did not fear him: there was one prepared to enter that circle.

Strangely, it was not in the water that they met. Hook rose to the rock to breathe, and at the same moment Peter scaled it on the opposite side. The rock was slippery as a ball, and they had to crawl rather than climb. Neither knew that the other was coming. Each feeling for a grip met the other's arm: in surprise they raised their heads; their faces were almost touching; so they met.

Some of the greatest heroes have confessed that just before they fell to they had a sinking. Had it been so with Peter at that moment I would admit it.[14] After all, he was the only man that the Sea-Cook had feared. But Peter had no sinking, he had one feeling only, gladness; and he gnashed his pretty teeth with joy. Quick as thought he snatched a knife from Hook's belt and was about to drive it home, when he saw that he was higher up the rock than his foe. It would not have been fighting fair. He gave the pirate a hand to help him up.

It was then that Hook bit him.

Not the pain of this but its unfairness was what dazed Peter. It made him quite helpless. He could only stare, horrified. Every child is affected thus the first time he is treated unfairly. All he thinks he has a right to when he comes to you to be yours is fairness. After you have been unfair to him he will love you again, but will never afterwards be quite the same boy. No one ever gets over the first unfairness; no one except Peter. He often met it, but he always forgot it. I suppose that was the real difference between him and all the rest.

So when he met it now it was like the first time; and he could just stare, helpless. Twice the iron hand clawed him.

A few moments afterwards the other boys saw Hook in the water striking wildly for the ship; no elation on the pestilent face now, only white fear, for the crocodile was in dogged pursuit of him. On ordinary occasions the boys would have swum alongside cheering; but now they were uneasy, for they had lost both Peter and Wendy, and were scouring the lagoon for them, calling them by name. They found the dinghy and went home in it, shouting "Peter, Wendy" as they went, but no answer came save mocking laughter from the mermaids. "They must be swimming back or flying," the boys concluded. They were not very anxious, they had such faith in Peter. They chuckled, boylike, because they would be late for bed; and it was all mother Wendy's fault!

When their voices died away there came cold silence over the lagoon, and then a feeble cry.

"Help, help!"

14. *Had it been so with Peter at that moment I would admit it*. On several occasions the intrusive narrator reveals that he has privileged access to Peter's thoughts and feelings. "I would admit it" is a strange turn of phrase for suggesting that he would give a fair representation of what is on his own character's mind.

Mabel Lucie Attwell, *Peter Pan and Wendy*, 1921. (Lucie Attwell Ltd. Courtesy of Vicki Thomas Associates)

Two small figures were beating against the rock; the girl had fainted and lay on the boy's arm. With a last effort Peter pulled her up the rock and then lay down beside her. Even as he also fainted he saw that the water was rising. He knew that they would soon be drowned, but he could do no more.

As they lay side by side a mermaid caught Wendy by the feet, and began pulling her softly into the water. Peter, feeling her slip from him, woke with a start, and was just in time to draw her back. But he had to tell her the truth.

"We are on the rock, Wendy," he said, "but it is growing smaller. Soon the water will be over it."

She did not understand even now.

"We must go," she said, almost brightly.

"Yes," he answered faintly.

"Shall we swim or fly, Peter?"

He had to tell her.

"Do you think you could swim or fly as far as the island, Wendy, without my help?"

She had to admit that she was too tired.

He moaned.

"What is it?" she asked, anxious about him at once.

"I can't help you, Wendy. Hook wounded me. I can neither fly nor swim."

"Do you mean we shall both be drowned?"

"Look how the water is rising."

They put their hands over their eyes to shut out the sight. They thought they would soon be no more. As they sat thus something brushed against Peter as light as a kiss, and stayed there, as if saying timidly, "Can I be of any use?"

It was the tail of a kite, which Michael had made some days before. It had torn itself out of his hand and floated away.

"Michael's kite," Peter said without interest, but next moment he had seized the tail, and was pulling the kite toward him.

"It lifted Michael off the ground," he cried; "why should it not carry you?"

"Both of us!"

"It can't lift two; Michael and Curly tried."

"Let us draw lots," Wendy said bravely.

"And you a lady; never." Already he had tied the tail round her. She clung to him; she refused to go without him; but with a "Good-bye, Wendy," he pushed her from the rock; and in a few minutes she was borne out of his sight. Peter was alone on the lagoon.

The rock was very small now; soon it would be submerged. Pale rays of light tiptoed across the waters; and by and by

15. *"To die will be an awfully big adventure."*
That the fear of death or negation of death
can turn into a death wish becomes evident from this moment in the play.

George Llewelyn Davies first uttered
the famous line that ends chapter 8
when Barrie described to him how Peter
Pan guides dead children to Neverland.
(Barrie sometimes offered small royalty
payments, with mock contracts, to the five
Llewelyn Davies brothers when he used
their phrasing in a work.) In the final stage
direction for the play, Peter's resistance
to love and domesticity receives the
following gloss: "If he could get the hang
of the thing, his cry might become 'To live
would be an awfully big adventure.'"

Readers of the Harry Potter books will
recall Dumbledore's declaration that "to
the well-organized mind, death is but
the next great adventure" (J. K. Rowling,
Harry Potter and the Sorcerer's Stone, 297).
The line was most likely inspired by Peter
Pan's words, which reveal fearlessness in
the face of death and the capacity to turn
every experience into an adventure.

As noted earlier, Charles Frohman, the
renowned theatrical entrepreneur who
had sponsored the first production of *Peter
Pan*, went down on the *Lusitania* on May
7, 1915. One of the survivors reported
that he continued smoking his cigar and
talking with his fellow passengers even
after the ship was hit. As passengers clung
to the railings and the cold waters rose,
Frohman remained calm and declared
to the others: "Why fear death? It is the
greatest adventure in life" (Hayter-Menzies
78). Frohman's remark contributed to
a discourse establishing unsettling connections linking death, adventure, and World
War I with the play *Peter Pan*. The historian
Michael C. C. Adams points out that
masculinity was framed in the war era as a
turning away from marriage and domestic
life and a desire to follow the siren song
of fearlessness in the face of death and to

there was to be heard a sound at once the most musical and
the most melancholy in the world: the mermaids calling to
the moon.

Peter was not quite like other boys; but he was afraid at
last. A tremor ran through him, like a shudder passing over
the sea; but on the sea one shudder follows another till there
are hundreds of them, and Peter felt just the one. Next
moment he was standing erect on the rock again, with that
smile on his face and a drum beating within him. It was saying, "To die will be an awfully big adventure."[15]

embrace patriotic duty and sacrifice. Theodore Roosevelt, whose son was shot down in a fighter jet in 1918, described life and death as part of the "same Great Adventure." "Therefore it is that the man who is not willing to die, and the woman who is not willing to send her man to die," he added, "in a war for a great cause, are not worthy to live" (Kavey 67).

In a few minutes she was borne out of his sight

CHAPTER 9

The Never Bird

1. *it was such a gallant piece of paper*. Like Hans Christian Andersen before him, Barrie created whimsy and humor that appealed to children by endowing inanimate objects with life. In this case, the piece of paper actually turns out to be a living being, but the effect is still there.

2. *it was the Never bird*. A pelican in the original production, the bird was driven from its nest by Peter, then repelled when it attacked him. Reviewers found the scene inappropriate, and Barrie made changes that turned the bird into an ally rather than an enemy. The term Never bird, like Never tree, suggests that the island has its own unique flora and fauna.

The last sounds Peter heard before he was quite alone were the mermaids retiring one by one to their bedchambers under the sea. He was too far away to hear their doors shut; but every door in the coral caves where they live rings a tiny bell when it opens or closes (as in all the nicest houses on the mainland), and he heard the bells.

Steadily the waters rose till they were nibbling at his feet; and to pass the time until they made their final gulp, he watched the only thing on the lagoon. He thought it was a piece of floating paper, perhaps part of the kite, and wondered idly how long it would take to drift ashore.

Presently he noticed as an odd thing that it was undoubtedly out upon the lagoon with some definite purpose, for it was fighting the tide, and sometimes winning; and when it won, Peter, always sympathetic to the weaker side, could not help clapping; it was such a gallant piece of paper.[1]

It was not really a piece of paper; it was the Never bird,[2] making desperate efforts to reach Peter on her nest. By working her wings, in a way she had learned since the nest fell into the water, she was able to some extent to guide her strange craft, but by the time Peter recognized her she was very exhausted. She had come to save him, to give him her nest, though there were eggs in it. I rather wonder at the bird, for though he had been nice to her, he had also sometimes tormented her. I can suppose only that, like Mrs. Darling and the rest of them, she was melted because he had all his first teeth.

She called out to him what she had come for, and he called out to her what was she doing there; but of course neither of them understood the other's language. In fanciful stories people can talk to the birds freely, and I wish for the moment I could pretend that this were such a story, and say that Peter replied intelligently to the Never bird; but truth is best, and I want to tell only what really happened. Well, not only could they not understand each other, but they forgot their manners.

"I—want—you—to—get—into—the—nest," the bird called, speaking as slowly and distinctly as possible, "and—then—you—can—drift—ashore, but—I—am—too—tired—to—bring—it—any—nearer—so—you—must—try—to—swim—to—it."

"What are you quacking about?" Peter answered. "Why don't you let the nest drift as usual?"

"I—want—you—" the bird said, and repeated it all over.

Then Peter tried slow and distinct.

"What—are—you—quacking—about?" and so on.

The Never bird became irritated; they have very short tempers.

"You dunderheaded little jay," she screamed, "why don't you do as I tell you?"

Peter felt that she was calling him names, and at a venture he retorted hotly:

"So are you!"

Then rather curiously they both snapped out the same remark.

"Shut up!"

"Shut up!"

3. *I forget whether I have told you.* The narrator exhibits the same symptoms of short-term memory loss felt by the children who visit Neverland. Once again, he ensures that readers will not become lost in the illusion by reminding them that London and Neverland are being created for them by a narrator who appears to be improvising a tale for a "live" audience.

4. *Peter put the eggs into this hat.* The substitution of the pirate's hat for the nest was added by Barrie after reviewers protested Peter's cavalier treatment of the bird's nest and lack of compassion for the mother and her eggs.

Nevertheless the bird was determined to save him if she could, and by one last mighty effort she propelled the nest against the rock. Then up she flew; deserting her eggs, so as to make her meaning clear.

Then at last he understood, and clutched the nest and waved his thanks to the bird as she fluttered overhead. It was not to receive his thanks, however, that she hung there in the sky; it was not even to watch him get into the nest; it was to see what he did with her eggs.

There were two large white eggs, and Peter lifted them up and reflected. The bird covered her face with her wings, so as not to see the last of her eggs; but she could not help peeping between the feathers.

I forget whether I have told you[3] that there was a stave on the rock, driven into it by some buccaneers of long ago to mark the site of buried treasure. The children had discovered the glittering hoard, and when in a mischievous mood used to fling showers of moidores, diamonds, pearls and pieces of eight to the gulls, who pounced upon them for food, and then flew away, raging at the scurvy trick that had been played upon them. The stave was still there, and on it Starkey had hung his hat, a deep tarpaulin, watertight, with a broad brim. Peter put the eggs into this hat[4] and set it on the lagoon. It floated beautifully.

The Never bird saw at once what he was up to, and screamed her admiration of him; and, alas, Peter crowed his agreement with her. Then he got into the nest, reared the stave in it as mast, and hung up his shirt for a sail. At the same moment the bird fluttered down upon the hat and once more sat snugly on her eggs. She drifted in one direction, and he was borne off in another, both cheering.

Of course when Peter landed he beached his barque in a place where the bird would easily find it; but the hat was such a great success that she abandoned the nest. It drifted about till it went to pieces, and often Starkey came to the shore of

Mabel Lucie Attwell, *Peter Pan and Wendy*, 1921. (Lucie Attwell Ltd. Courtesy of Vicki Thomas Associates)

the lagoon, and with many bitter feelings watched the bird sitting on his hat. As we shall not see her again, it may be worth mentioning here that all Never birds now build in that shape of nest, with a broad brim on which the youngsters take an airing.

Great were the rejoicings when Peter reached the home under the ground almost as soon as Wendy, who had been carried hither and thither by the kite. Every boy had adventures to tell; but perhaps the biggest adventure of all was that they were several hours late for bed. This so inflated them that they did various dodgy things to get staying up still longer, such as demanding bandages; but Wendy, though glorying in having them all home again safe and sound, was scandalised by the lateness of the hour, and cried, "To bed, to bed," in a voice that had to be obeyed. Next day, however, she was awfully tender, and gave out bandages to every one, and they played till bed-time at limping about and carrying their arms in slings.

Alice B. Woodward, *The Peter Pan Picture Book*, 1907.

CHAPTER 10

The Happy Home

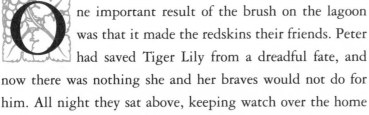ne important result of the brush on the lagoon
was that it made the redskins their friends. Peter
had saved Tiger Lily from a dreadful fate, and
now there was nothing she and her braves would not do for
him. All night they sat above, keeping watch over the home
under the ground and awaiting the big attack by the pirates
which obviously could not be much longer delayed. Even by
day they hung about, smoking the pipe of peace, and looking
almost as if they wanted tit-bits to eat.

They called Peter the Great White Father,[1] prostrating
themselves before him; and he liked this tremendously, so
that it was not really good for him.

"The great white father," he would say to them in a very
lordly manner, as they grovelled at his feet, "is glad to see the
Piccaninny warriors protecting his wigwam from the pirates."

"Me Tiger Lily," that lovely creature would reply. "Peter
Pan save me, me his velly nice friend. Me no let pirates hurt
him."

She was far too pretty to cringe in this way, but Peter
thought it his due, and he would answer condescendingly, "It
is good. Peter Pan has spoken."

Always when he said, "Peter Pan has spoken," it meant

1. *They called Peter the Great White Father.*
The Great White Father is a phrase associated with the name given by subjugated
Native Americans to the president of the
United States. It was used with both reverence and derision, sometimes with a
touch of both. Barrie may have also had
in mind the term Great White Mother,
a phrase applied to Queen Victoria, who
was known as the Grandmother of Europe
and the Mother of Peoples (she had been
buried in white with her wedding veil
in 1901). The term also plays off Barrie's
novel *The Little White Bird* and has even
been connected by imaginative critics to
Melville's great White Whale.

that they must now shut up, and they accepted it humbly in that spirit; but they were by no means so respectful to the other boys, whom they looked upon as just ordinary braves. They said "How-do?" to them, and things like that; and what annoyed the boys was that Peter seemed to think this all right.

Secretly Wendy sympathised with them a little, but she was far too loyal a housewife to listen to any complaints against father. "Father knows best," she always said, whatever her private opinion must be. Her private opinion was that the redskins should not call her a squaw.

We have now reached the evening that was to be known among them as the Night of Nights, because of its adventures and their upshot. The day, as if quietly gathering its forces,

Wendy's little house. (*Peter Pan and Wendy by J. M. Barrie, Retold for the Nursery by May Byron*. Illustrated by Kathleen Atkins)

had been almost uneventful, and now the redskins in their blankets were at their posts above, while, below, the children were having their evening meal; all except Peter, who had gone out to get the time. The way you got the time on the island was to find the crocodile, and then stay near him till the clock struck.

The meal happened to be a make-believe tea, and they sat round the board, guzzling in their greed; and really, what with their chatter and recriminations, the noise, as Wendy said, was positively deafening. To be sure, she did not mind noise, but she simply would not have them grabbing things, and then excusing themselves by saying that Tootles had pushed their elbow. There was a fixed rule that they must never hit back at meals, but should refer the matter of dispute to Wendy by raising the right arm politely and saying, "I complain of so-and-so"; but what usually happened was that they forgot to do this or did it too much.

"Silence," cried Wendy when for the twentieth time she had told them that they were not all to speak at once. "Is your calabash empty, Slightly darling?"

"Not quite empty, mummy," Slightly said, after looking into an imaginary mug.

"He hasn't even begun to drink his milk," Nibs interposed.

This was telling, and Slightly seized his chance.

"I complain of Nibs," he cried promptly.

John, however, had held up his hand first.

"Well, John?"

"May I sit in Peter's chair, as he is not here?"

"Sit in father's chair, John!" Wendy was scandalised. "Certainly not."

"He is not really our father," John answered. "He didn't even know how a father does till I showed him."

This was grumbling. "We complain of John," cried the twins.

Tootles held up his hand. He was so much the humblest of

them, indeed he was the only humble one, that Wendy was specially gentle with him.

"I don't suppose," Tootles said diffidently, "that I could be father."

"No, Tootles."

Once Tootles began, which was not very often, he had a silly way of going on.

"As I can't be father," he said heavily, "I don't suppose, Michael, you would let me be baby?"

"No, I won't," Michael rapped out. He was already in his basket.

"As I can't be baby," Tootles said, getting heavier and heavier, "do you think I could be a twin?"

"No, indeed," replied the twins; "it's awfully difficult to be a twin."

"As I can't be anything important," said Tootles, "would any of you like to see me do a trick?"

"No," they all replied.

Then at last he stopped. "I hadn't really any hope," he said.

The hateful telling broke out again.[2]

"Slightly is coughing on the table."

"The twins began with mammee-apples."

"Curly is taking both tappa rolls and yams."

"Nibs is speaking with his mouth full."

"I complain of the twins."

"I complain of Curly."

"I complain of Nibs."

"Oh dear, oh dear," cried Wendy, "I'm sure I sometimes think that children are more trouble than they are worth."

She told them to clear away, and sat down to her work-basket: a heavy load of stockings and every knee with a hole in it as usual.

"Wendy," remonstrated Michael, "I'm too big for a cradle."

"I must have somebody in a cradle," she said almost tartly,

"and you are the littlest. A cradle is such a nice homely thing to have about a house."

While she sewed they played around her;[3] such a group of happy faces and dancing limbs lit up by that romantic fire. It had become a very familiar scene this in the home under the ground, but we are looking on it for the last time.

There was a step above, and Wendy, you may be sure, was the first to recognize it.

"Children, I hear your father's step. He likes you to meet him at the door."

Above, the redskins crouched before Peter.

"Watch well, braves. I have spoken."

And then, as so often before, the gay children dragged him from his tree. As so often before, but never again.

He had brought nuts for the boys as well as the correct time for Wendy.

"Peter, you just spoil them, you know," Wendy simpered.

"Ah, old lady," said Peter, hanging up his gun.

"It was me told him mothers are called old lady," Michael whispered to Curly.

"I complain of Michael," said Curly instantly.

The first twin came to Peter. "Father, we want to dance."

"Dance away, my little man," said Peter, who was in high good humour.

"But we want you to dance."

Peter was really the best dancer among them, but he pretended to be scandalised.

"Me! My old bones would rattle!"

"And mummy too."

"What," cried Wendy, "the mother of such an armful, dance!"

"But on a Saturday night," Slightly insinuated.

It was not really Saturday night, at least it may have been, for they had long lost count of the days; but always if they

3. *While she sewed they played around her.* Like Margaret Ogilvy, Barrie's mother, Wendy becomes as a mere girl a "little mother" who carries out domestic chores—sewing, mending, and cleaning—with passionate eagerness. As noted, the drop-curtain for the revival of the play in 1909 was fashioned after a sampler—supposedly made by Wendy and signed at the bottom: "Wendy Moira Angela Darling / Her Sampler, Age 9 Years." It displayed both her storytelling skills (with characters and scenes from *Peter Pan*) and her proficiency in sewing. Sewing, storytelling, and writing are linked crafts in the sampler.

wanted to do anything special they said this was Saturday night, and then they did it.

"Of course it is Saturday night, Peter," Wendy said, relenting.

"People of our figure, Wendy."

"But it is only among our own progeny."

"True, true."

So they were told they could dance, but they must put on their nighties first.

"Ah, old lady," Peter said aside to Wendy, warming himself by the fire and looking down at her as she sat turning a heel, "there is nothing more pleasant of an evening for you and me when the day's toil is over than to rest by the fire with the little ones near by."

"It is sweet, Peter, isn't it?" Wendy said, frightfully gratified. "Peter, I think Curly has your nose."

"Michael takes after you."

She went to him and put her hand on his shoulder.

"Dear Peter," she said, "with such a large family, of course, I have now passed my best, but you don't want to change me, do you?"

"No, Wendy."

Certainly he did not want a change, but he looked at her uncomfortably; blinking, you know, like one not sure whether he was awake or asleep.

"Peter, what is it?"

"I was just thinking," he said, a little scared. "It is only make-believe, isn't it, that I am their father?"

"Oh yes," Wendy said primly.

"You see," he continued apologetically, "it would make me seem so old to be their real father."

"But they are ours, Peter, yours and mine."

"But not really, Wendy?" he asked anxiously.

"Not if you don't wish it," she replied; and she distinctly

heard his sigh of relief. "Peter," she asked, trying to speak firmly, "what are your exact feelings to me?"

"Those of a devoted son, Wendy."[4]

"I thought so," she said, and went and sat by herself at the extreme end of the room.

"You are so queer," he said, frankly puzzled, "and Tiger Lily is just the same. There is something she wants to be to me,[5] but she says it is not my mother."

"No, indeed, it is not," Wendy replied with frightful emphasis. Now we know why she was prejudiced against the redskins.

"Then what is it?"

"It isn't for a lady to tell."

"Oh, very well," Peter said, a little nettled. "Perhaps Tinker Bell will tell me."

"Oh yes, Tinker Bell will tell you," Wendy retorted scornfully. "She is an abandoned little creature."

Here Tink, who was in her boudoir, eavesdropping, squeaked out something impudent.

"She says she glories in being abandoned," Peter interpreted.

He had a sudden idea. "Perhaps Tink wants to be my mother?"

"You silly ass!" cried Tinker Bell in a passion.

She had said it so often that Wendy needed no translation.

"I almost agree with her," Wendy snapped. Fancy Wendy snapping. But she had been much tried, and she little knew what was to happen before the night was out. If she had known she would not have snapped.

None of them knew. Perhaps it was best not to know. Their ignorance gave them one more glad hour; and as it was to be their last hour on the island, let us rejoice that there were sixty glad minutes in it. They sang and danced in their nightgowns. Such a deliciously creepy song it was, in which they pretended to be frightened at their own shadows; little wit-

4. *"Those of a devoted son, Wendy."* Peter may have learned how to play "father," and he may also have picked up tips from Wendy and the boys, but his feelings for Wendy—as for Tiger Lily and Tinker Bell—remain platonic.

5. *There is something she wants to be to me.* In an early manuscript, Tiger Lily choreographs a scene that reveals her desire for Peter Pan.

TIGER LILY: Suppose Tiger Lily runs into the wood—Peter Paleface attack her—what then?
PETER: (*bewildered*) Paleface can never catch Indian girl, they run so fast.
TIGER LILY: If Peter Paleface chase Tiger Lily—she no run very fast—she tumble into a heap what then? (*Peter puzzled. She addresses Indians.*) What then?
ALL INDIANS: She him's squaw.

6. *Slightly tried to tell a story that night.* Slightly, true to his identity as a lost boy living in Neverland, compresses his story so that beginning and end are one. Living in the moment, he is unable to draw on memory to spin a narrative that recollects times past or stories once told.

7. *the story Peter hated.* Peter dislikes the story in part because of his rivalry with Mrs. Darling and in part because he himself could not return home, because the window was barred.

ting that so soon shadows would close in upon them, from whom they would shrink in real fear. So uproariously gay was the dance, and how they buffeted each other on the bed and out of it! It was a pillow fight rather than a dance, and when it was finished, the pillows insisted on one bout more, like partners who know that they may never meet again. The stories they told, before it was time for Wendy's good-night story! Even Slightly tried to tell a story that night,[6] but the beginning was so fearfully dull that it appalled not only the others but himself, and he said gloomily:

"Yes, it is a dull beginning. I say, let us pretend that it is the end."

And then at last they all got into bed for Wendy's story, the story they loved best, the story Peter hated.[7] Usually when she began to tell this story he left the room or put his hands over his ears; and possibly if he had done either of those things this time they might all still be on the island. But to-night he remained on his stool; and we shall see what happened.

CHAPTER 11

Wendy's Story

isten, then," said Wendy, settling down to her story, with Michael at her feet and seven boys in the bed. "There was once a gentleman—"

"I had rather he had been a lady," Curly said.

"I wish he had been a white rat," said Nibs.

"Quiet," their mother admonished them. "There was a lady also, and—"

"Oh, mummy," cried the first twin, "you mean that there is a lady also, don't you? She is not dead, is she?"[1]

"Oh, no."

"I am awfully glad she isn't dead," said Tootles. "Are you glad, John?"

"Of course I am."

"Are you glad, Nibs?"

"Rather."

"Are you glad, Twins?"

"We are just glad."

"Oh dear," sighed Wendy.

"Little less noise there," Peter called out, determined that she should have fair play, however beastly a story it might be in his opinion.

1. *"She is not dead, is she?"* The observation, naïve as it may seem, makes an important point about storytelling and narration. Narrative depends on the idea of the past made present, and it uses the past tense ("There once was . . .") to evoke what feels like a present moment. Hence the sentence "There was a lady also" does *not* imply that the lady is (now) dead. The twins are new to storytelling and have not yet grown accustomed to that use of the past tense. Still, the twins' question is a profound one, reminding us of how all narratives are permeated with a sense of mortality and how many take up, directly or indirectly, the theme of death.

"The gentleman's name," Wendy continued, "was Mr. Darling, and her name was Mrs. Darling."

"I knew them," John said, to annoy the others.

"I think I knew them," said Michael rather doubtfully.

"They were married, you know," explained Wendy, "and what do you think they had?"

"White rats," cried Nibs, inspired.

"No."

"It's awfully puzzling," said Tootles, who knew the story by heart.

"Quiet, Tootles. They had three descendants."

"What is descendants?"

"Well, you are one, Twin."

"Did you hear that, John? I am a descendant."

"Descendants are only children," said John.

"Oh dear, oh dear," sighed Wendy. "Now these three children had a faithful nurse called Nana; but Mr. Darling was angry with her and chained her up in the yard; and so all the children flew away."

"It's an awfully good story," said Nibs.

"They flew away," Wendy continued, "to the Neverland, where the lost children are."

"I just thought they did," Curly broke in excitedly. "I don't know how it is, but I just thought they did!"

"O Wendy," cried Tootles, "was one of the lost children called Tootles?"

"Yes, he was."

"I am in a story. Hurrah, I am in a story, Nibs."

"Hush. Now I want you to consider the feelings of the unhappy parents with all their children flown away."

"Oo!" they all moaned, though they were not really considering the feelings of the unhappy parents one jot.

"Think of the empty beds!"

"Oo!"

"It's awfully sad," the first twin said cheerfully.

Wendy. (*Peter Pan and Wendy by J. M. Barrie, Retold for the Nursery by May Byron*. Illustrated by Kathleen Atkins)

"I don't see how it can have a happy ending," said the second twin. "Do you, Nibs?"

"I'm frightfully anxious."

"If you knew how great is a mother's love," Wendy told them triumphantly, "you would have no fear." She had now come to the part that Peter hated.

"I do like a mother's love," said Tootles, hitting Nibs with a pillow. "Do you like a mother's love, Nibs?"

"I do just," said Nibs, hitting back.

"You see," Wendy said complacently, "our heroine knew that the mother would always leave the window open for her children to fly back by; so they stayed away for years and had a lovely time."

"Did they ever go back?"

"Let us now," said Wendy, bracing herself up for her finest

2. *Off we skip like the most heartless things in the world.* The narrator will close his story with words about how children are gay, innocent, and heartless. Here, the children are positioned as creatures who run off to play (forgetting the adults who love them) and return as soon as they have needs only adults can meet. The narrator uses the first person plural, identifying with children ("off *we* skip" and "*we* have an entirely selfish time"), at the same time that he produces adult judgments about children ("attractive," "selfish," "noble"). The narrator slides from one pronoun position to another and then cuts short his childlike "confidence and certainty" with "distinctly adult judgements" (Rose 71). Barrie wrote poignantly about the divide between adults and children and his dawning recognition that he no longer had a "way" with children: "I remember more vividly than most things the day I first knew it was gone. The blow was struck by a little girl, with whom I had the smallest acquaintance, but I was doing my best to entertain her when suddenly I saw upon her face the look that means, 'You are done with all this, my friend.' It is the cruelest, most candid look that ever comes into the face of a child. I had to accept it as final, though I swear I had a way with them once. That was among the most rueful days of my life" (*The Greenwood Hat*, 151–52).

effort, "take a peep into the future"; and they all gave themselves the twist that makes peeps into the future easier. "Years have rolled by; and who is this elegant lady of uncertain age alighting at London Station?"

"O Wendy, who is she?" cried Nibs, every bit as excited as if he didn't know.

"Can it be—yes—no—it is—the fair Wendy!"

"Oh!"

"And who are the two noble portly figures accompanying her, now grown to man's estate? Can they be John and Michael? They are!"

"Oh!"

" 'See, dear brothers,' says Wendy, pointing upwards, 'there is the window still standing open. Ah, now we are rewarded for our sublime faith in a mother's love.' So up they flew to their mummy and daddy, and pen cannot describe the happy scene, over which we draw a veil."

That was the story, and they were as pleased with it as the fair narrator herself. Everything just as it should be, you see. Off we skip like the most heartless things in the world,[2] which is what children are, but so attractive; and we have an entirely selfish time, and then when we have need of special attention we nobly return for it, confident that we shall be embraced instead of smacked.

So great indeed was their faith in a mother's love that they felt they could afford to be callous for a bit longer.

But there was one there who knew better; and when Wendy finished he uttered a hollow groan.

"What is it, Peter?" she cried, running to him, thinking he was ill. She felt him solicitously, lower down than his chest. "Where is it, Peter?"

"It isn't that kind of pain," Peter replied darkly.

"Then what kind is it?"

"Wendy, you are wrong about mothers."

The underground house. (*Peter Pan and Wendy by J. M. Barrie, Retold for the Nursery by May Byron*. Illustrated by Kathleen Atkins)

3. *"but the window was barred."* In Barrie's wartime play *Dear Brutus* (1917), one character tells another: "We who have made the great mistake, how differently we should all act at the second chance. But . . . there is no second chance, not for most of us. When we reach the window it is Lock-Out Time. The iron bars are up for life."

They all gathered round him in affright, so alarming was his agitation; and with a fine candour he told them what he had hitherto concealed.

"Long ago," he said, "I thought like you that my mother would always keep the window open for me; so I stayed away for moons and moons and moons, and then flew back; but the window was barred,[3] for mother had forgotten all about me, and there was another little boy sleeping in my bed."

I am not sure that this was true, but Peter thought it was true; and it scared them.

"Are you sure mothers are like that?"

"Yes."

So this was the truth about mothers. The toads!

4. *in what they called their hearts*. The narrator adds a not-so-subtle dig at "heartless" children.

5. *in half mourning*. The Victorian era is particularly known for its complex set of rituals around mourning. For Queen Victoria's own funeral, London was festooned in purple and white, since the queen herself hated black funerals. For Victorian women, there were three stages of mourning: deep or full mourning (a year and a day), second mourning (nine months), and half mourning (three to six months). The first phase required the wearing of dull black clothing without ornament and a weeping veil. In the next two phases, jewelry and other decorative touches were permitted. In the reference to Mrs. Darling's grief, we are reminded again of how a story about childhood adventures and play is filled with allusions to loss, mourning, and sorrow. Yet in the screenplay for *Peter Pan*, Barrie follows Wendy's comments about "Mother in half mourning" with a vision of Mr. and Mrs. Darling at home, "brightly practicing a new dance to a gramophone and not in mourning."

6. *Peter was killing them off*. Peter has few reservations about killing grown-ups, just as he feels no great regrets about "thinning out" the ranks of the lost boys. Magical thinking, here as elsewhere, reigns supreme, so that ordinary acts—for example, the clapping of hands, laughter, and short breaths—become endowed with the power to give life or to end it.

Still it is best to be careful; and no one knows so quickly as a child when he should give in. "Wendy, let us go home," cried John and Michael together.

"Yes," she said, clutching them.

"Not to-night?" asked the lost boys bewildered. They knew in what they called their hearts[4] that one can get on quite well without a mother, and that it is only the mothers who think you can't.

"At once," Wendy replied resolutely, for the horrible thought had come to her: "Perhaps mother is in half mourning[5] by this time."

This dread made her forgetful of what must be Peter's feelings, and she said to him rather sharply, "Peter, will you make the necessary arrangements?"

"If you wish it," he replied, as coolly as if she had asked him to pass the nuts.

Not so much as a sorry-to-lose-you between them! If she did not mind the parting, he was going to show her, was Peter, that neither did he.

But of course he cared very much; and he was so full of wrath against grown-ups, who, as usual, were spoiling everything, that as soon as he got inside his tree he breathed intentionally quick short breaths at the rate of about five to a second. He did this because there is a saying in the Neverland that, every time you breathe, a grown-up dies; and Peter was killing them off[6] vindictively as fast as possible.

Then having given the necessary instructions to the redskins he returned to the home, where an unworthy scene had been enacted in his absence. Panic-stricken at the thought of losing Wendy the lost boys had advanced upon her threateningly.

"It will be worse than before she came," they cried.

"We shan't let her go."

"Let's keep her prisoner."

"Ay, chain her up."

In her extremity an instinct told her to which of them to turn.

"Tootles," she cried, "I appeal to you."

Was it not strange? She appealed to Tootles, quite the silliest one.

Grandly, however, did Tootles respond. For that one moment he dropped his silliness and spoke with dignity.

"I am Tootles," he said, "and nobody minds me. But the first who does not behave to Wendy like an English gentleman I will blood[7] him severely."

He drew back his hanger;[8] and for that instant his sun was at noon. The others held back uneasily. Then Peter returned, and they saw at once that they would get no support from him. He would keep no girl in the Neverland against her will.

"Wendy," he said, striding up and down, "I have asked the redskins to guide you through the wood, as flying tires you so."

"Thank you, Peter."

"Then," he continued, in the short sharp voice of one accustomed to be obeyed, "Tinker Bell will take you across the sea. Wake her, Nibs."

Nibs had to knock twice before he got an answer, though Tink had really been sitting up in bed listening for some time.

"Who are you? How dare you? Go away," she cried.

"You are to get up, Tink," Nibs called, "and take Wendy on a journey."

Of course Tink had been delighted to hear that Wendy was going; but she was jolly well determined not to be her courier, and she said so in still more offensive language. Then she pretended to be asleep again.

"She says she won't," Nibs exclaimed, aghast at such insubordination, whereupon Peter went sternly toward the young lady's chamber.

"Tink," he rapped out, "if you don't get up and dress at

7. *blood*. To cause blood to flow or to wet or smear with blood.

8. *hanger*. A short sword that was usually hung from a belt.

9. *"first Thursdays."* Mrs. Darling's "at home," a set day on which she receives visitors without a formal invitation, is on the first Thursday of each month.

10. *to desert their dearest ones.* Rather than being innocents, healers, or agents of hope, children are seen as egocentric and unable to form lasting bonds. Barrie broke with Wordsworth's view of children as those who bring "hope" with their "forward-looking thoughts."

once I will open the curtains, and then we shall all see you in your *négligée*."

This made her leap to the floor. "Who said I wasn't getting up?" she cried.

In the meantime the boys were gazing very forlornly at Wendy, now equipped with John and Michael for the journey. By this time they were dejected, not merely because they were about to lose her, but also because they felt that she was going off to something nice to which they had not been invited. Novelty was beckoning to them as usual.

Crediting them with a nobler feeling Wendy melted.

"Dear ones," she said, "if you will all come with me I feel almost sure I can get my father and mother to adopt you."

The invitation was meant specially for Peter; but each of the boys was thinking exclusively of himself, and at once they jumped with joy.

"But won't they think us rather a handful?" Nibs asked in the middle of his jump.

"Oh no," said Wendy, rapidly thinking it out, "it will only mean having a few beds in the drawing-room; they can be hidden behind the screens on first Thursdays."[9]

"Peter, can we go?" they all cried imploringly. They took it for granted that if they went he would go also, but really they scarcely cared. Thus children are ever ready, when novelty knocks, to desert their dearest ones.[10]

"All right," Peter replied with a bitter smile, and immediately they rushed to get their things.

"And now, Peter," Wendy said, thinking she had put everything right, "I am going to give you your medicine before you go." She loved to give them medicine, and undoubtedly gave them too much. Of course it was only water, but it was out of a calabash, and she always shook the bottle and counted the drops, which gave it a certain medicinal quality. On this occasion, however, she did not give Peter his draught, for just as she had prepared it, she saw a look on his face that made her heart sink.

"Get your things, Peter," she cried, shaking.

"No," he answered, pretending indifference, "I am not going with you, Wendy."

"Yes, Peter."

"No."

To show that her departure would leave him unmoved, he skipped up and down the room, playing gaily on his heartless pipes. She had to run about after him, though it was rather undignified.

"To find your mother," she coaxed.

Now, if Peter had ever quite had a mother, he no longer missed her. He could do very well without one. He had thought them out, and remembered only their bad points.

"No, no," he told Wendy decisively; "perhaps she would say I was old, and I just want always to be a little boy and to have fun."

"But, Peter—"

"No."

And so the others had to be told.

"Peter isn't coming."

Peter not coming! They gazed blankly at him, their sticks over their backs, and on each stick a bundle. Their first thought was that if Peter was not going he had probably changed his mind about letting them go.

But he was far too proud for that. "If you find your mothers,"[11] he said darkly, "I hope you will like them."

The awful cynicism of this made an uncomfortable impression, and most of them began to look rather doubtful. After all, their faces said, were they not noodles to want to go?

"Now then," cried Peter, "no fuss, no blubbering; good-bye, Wendy"; and he held out his hand cheerily, quite as if they must really go now, for he had something important to do.

11. *"If you find your mothers."* Early performances of *Peter Pan* included a scene called "The Beautiful Mothers." In it, Wendy designs a series of tests to audition applicants for the position of mother for each of the lost boys. Initially there were to be twenty applicants onstage, then a mere dozen, and they were removed from the play, most likely for practical reasons— the scene was short and would have added significantly to the cast numbers.

12. *All arms were extended to him.* The chapter closes with a dramatic scene that reveals the theatrical origins of *Peter and Wendy*: sword raised, Peter is surrounded by the lost boys and the Darling children. His authority has been restored by the perils of the clash between pirates and redskins, and he is triumphant once again just at the moment when everyone is about to desert him.

She had to take his hand, and there was no indication that he would prefer a thimble.

"You will remember about changing your flannels, Peter?" she said, lingering over him. She was always so particular about their flannels.

"Yes."

"And you will take your medicine?"

"Yes."

That seemed to be everything; and an awkward pause followed. Peter, however, was not the kind that breaks down before other people. "Are you ready, Tinker Bell?" he called out.

"Ay, ay."

"Then lead the way."

Tink darted up the nearest tree; but no one followed her, for it was at this moment that the pirates made their dreadful attack upon the redskins. Above, where all had been so still, the air was rent with shrieks and the clash of steel. Below, there was dead silence. Mouths opened and remained open. Wendy fell on her knees, but her arms were extended toward Peter. All arms were extended to him,[12] as if suddenly blown in his direction; they were beseeching him mutely not to desert them. As for Peter, he seized his sword, the same he thought he had slain Barbecue with; and the lust of battle was in his eye.

CHAPTER 12

The Children
Are Carried Off

The pirate attack had been a complete surprise: a sure proof that the unscrupulous Hook had conducted it improperly, for to surprise redskins fairly is beyond the wit of the white man.

By all the unwritten laws of savage warfare[1] it is always the redskin who attacks, and with the wiliness of his race he does it just before the dawn, at which time he knows the courage of the whites to be at its lowest ebb. The white men have in the meantime made a rude stockade on the summit of yonder undulating ground, at the foot of which a stream runs; for it is destruction to be too far from water. There they await the onslaught, the inexperienced ones clutching their revolvers and treading on twigs, but the old hands sleeping tranquilly until just before the dawn. Through the long black night the savage scouts wriggle, snake-like, among the grass without stirring a blade. The brushwood closes behind them as silently as sand into which a mole has dived. Not a sound is to be heard, save when they give vent to a wonderful imitation of the lonely call of the coyote. The cry is answered by other braves; and some of them do it even better than the coyotes, who are not very good at it. So the chill hours wear on, and the long suspense is horribly trying to the paleface who has to

1. *the unwritten laws of savage warfare.* Barrie ignores here the many contemporary *written* accounts about "savage" warfare, which were recorded during centuries of conflict with Native Americans. For many European, British, and American observers, Native American warfare was ordinarily limited to raids and ambushes rather than decisive battles and conquests. Casualty rates were low, and actual warfare was ritualized and restrained rather than carried out with the intent of slaughter. The stereotype of the "wily savage" developed among white settlers as a defense against the physical superiority of Native American warriors, their knowledge of the terrain, and their strategic use of dress—with moccasins making far less noise than marching boots. Against the force of European and British weapons and arsenals, Native Americans had a chance only when they "took advantage of terrain and cover, used surprise, maneuver, sound planning, and excellent intelligence" (Deloria and Salisbury 164).

live through it for the first time; but to the trained hand those ghastly calls and still ghastlier silences are but an intimation of how the night is marching.

That this was the usual procedure was so well known to Hook that in disregarding it he cannot be excused on the plea of ignorance.

The Piccaninnies, on their part, trusted implicitly to his honour, and their whole action of the night stands out in marked contrast to his. They left nothing undone that was consistent with the reputation of their tribe. With that alertness of the senses which is at once the marvel and despair of civilised peoples, they knew that the pirates were on the island from the moment one of them trod on a dry stick; and in an incredibly short space of time the coyote cries began. Every foot of ground between the spot where Hook had landed his forces and the home under the trees was stealthily examined by braves wearing their moccasins with the heels in front. They found only one hillock with a stream at its base, so that Hook had no choice; here he must establish himself and wait for just before the dawn. Everything being thus mapped out with almost diabolical cunning, the main body of the redskins folded their blankets around them, and in the phlegmatic manner that is to them the pearl of manhood squatted above the children's home, awaiting the cold moment when they should deal pale death.

Here dreaming, though wide-awake, of the exquisite tortures to which they were to put him at break of day, those confiding savages were found by the treacherous Hook. From the accounts afterwards supplied by such of the scouts as escaped the carnage, he does not seem even to have paused at the rising ground, though it is certain that in that grey light he must have seen it: no thought of waiting to be attacked appears from first to last to have visited his subtle mind; he would not even hold off till the night was nearly spent; on he pounded with no policy but to fall to. What could the bewildered scouts do, masters as they were of every warlike artifice save this one, but trot helplessly after him, exposing themselves fatally to view, the while they gave pathetic utterance to the coyote cry.

Around the brave Tiger Lily were a dozen of her stoutest warriors, and they suddenly saw the perfidious pirates bearing down upon them. Fell from their eyes then the film through which they had looked at victory. No more would they torture at the stake. For them the happy hunting-grounds now. They knew it; but as their father's sons they acquitted themselves. Even then they had time to gather in a phalanx that would have been hard to break had they risen quickly, but this they were forbidden to do by the traditions of their race. It is written that the noble savage must never express surprise in the presence of the white. Thus terrible as the sudden appearance of the pirates must have been to them, they remained stationary for a moment, not a muscle moving; as if the foe had come by invitation. Then, indeed, the tradition gallantly upheld, they seized their weapons, and the air was torn with the war-cry; but it was now too late.

It is no part of ours to describe what was a massacre rather than a fight. Thus perished many of the flower of the Piccaninny tribe. Not all unavenged did they die, for with Lean Wolf fell Alf Mason, to disturb the Spanish Main no more; and among others who bit the dust were Geo. Scourie, Chas. Turley, and the Alsatian Foggerty.[2] Turley fell to the tomahawk of the terrible Panther, who ultimately cut a way through the pirates with Tiger Lily and a small remnant of the tribe.

To what extent Hook is to blame for his tactics on this occasion is for the historian to decide. Had he waited on the rising ground till the proper hour he and his men would probably have been butchered; and in judging him it is only fair to take this into account. What he should perhaps have done was to acquaint his opponents that he proposed to follow a

2. *Geo. Scourie, Chas. Turley, and the Alsatian Foggerty*. Geo. Scourie was named after George Ross—son of the innkeeper of Scourie Lodge, on the northwest coast of Scotland, whom the Llewelyn Davies boys befriended when they spent their holiday at Scourie Lodge in the summer of 1911. Chas. Turley is Charles Turley Smith, who wrote school stories for boys.

3. *It was Peter's cockiness*. Peter's triumphant crowing deepens Hook's sense of the boy's narcissistic vanity. When Hook encounters the sleeping Peter Pan, it is, once again, his "cockiness" that drives Hook into a homicidal frenzy. Hook's strange obsession with Peter has deep mythological roots in father/son rivalries, but here it takes an odd turn suggesting something more than a familial relationship.

new method. On the other hand, this, as destroying the element of surprise, would have made his strategy of no avail, so that the whole question is beset with difficulties. One cannot at least withhold a reluctant admiration for the wit that had conceived so bold a scheme, and the fell genius with which it was carried out.

What were his own feelings about himself at that triumphant moment? Fain would his dogs have known, as breathing heavily and wiping their cutlasses, they gathered at a discreet distance from his hook, and squinted through their ferret eyes at this extraordinary man. Elation must have been in his heart, but his face did not reflect it: ever a dark and solitary enigma, he stood aloof from his followers in spirit as in substance.

The night's work was not yet over, for it was not the redskins he had come out to destroy; they were but the bees to be smoked, so that he should get at the honey. It was Pan he wanted, Pan and Wendy and their band, but chiefly Pan.

Peter was such a small boy that one tends to wonder at the man's hatred of him. True he had flung Hook's arm to the crocodile, but even this and the increased insecurity of life to which it led, owing to the crocodile's pertinacity, hardly account for a vindictiveness so relentless and malignant. The truth is that there was a something about Peter which goaded the pirate captain to frenzy. It was not his courage, it was not his engaging appearance, it was not—. There is no beating about the bush, for we know quite well what it was, and have got to tell. It was Peter's cockiness.[3]

This had got on Hook's nerves; it made his iron claw twitch, and at night it disturbed him like an insect. While Peter lived, the tortured man felt that he was a lion in a cage into which a sparrow had come.

The question now was how to get down the trees, or how to get his dogs down? He ran his greedy eyes over them, searching for the thinnest ones. They wriggled uncomfortably, for they knew he would not scruple to ram them down with poles.

In the meantime, what of the boys? We have seen them at the first clang of weapons, turned as it were into stone figures, open-mouthed, all appealing with outstretched arms to Peter; and we return to them as their mouths close, and their arms fall to their sides. The pandemonium above has ceased almost as suddenly as it arose, passed like a fierce gust of wind; but they know that in the passing it has determined their fate.

Which side had won?

The pirates, listening avidly at the mouths of the trees, heard the question put by every boy, and alas, they also heard Peter's answer.

"If the redskins have won," he said, "they will beat the tom-tom; it is always their sign of victory."

Now Smee had found the tom-tom, and was at that moment sitting on it. "You will never hear the tom-tom again," he muttered, but inaudibly of course, for strict silence had been enjoined. To his amazement Hook signed him to beat the tom-tom; and slowly there came to Smee an understanding of the dreadful wickedness of the order. Never, probably, had this simple man admired Hook so much.

Twice Smee beat upon the instrument, and then stopped to listen gleefully.

"The tom-tom," the miscreants heard Peter cry; "an Indian victory!"

The doomed children answered with a cheer that was music to the black hearts above, and almost immediately they repeated their good-byes to Peter. This puzzled the pirates, but all their other feelings were swallowed by a base delight that the enemy were about to come up the trees. They smirked at each other and rubbed their hands. Rapidly and silently Hook gave his orders: one man to each tree, and the others to arrange themselves in a line two yards apart.

CHAPTER 13

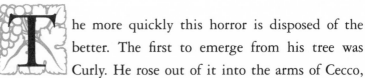

Do You Believe in Fairies?

1. *Hook entranced her*. Hook is a gentleman who minds his manners, even when staging a raid. That Wendy is fascinated by him is not surprising, given the fact that Peter and Hook shadow each other, with Peter executing a dead-on imitation of Hook. In this scene, Hook becomes something of a Svengali, the sinister fictional character in the immensely successful novel *Trilby* (1894), written by Sylvia Davies's father, George du Maurier. And Wendy's vulnerability to Hook becomes the direct cause of a "foul attempt on Peter's life."

The more quickly this horror is disposed of the better. The first to emerge from his tree was Curly. He rose out of it into the arms of Cecco, who flung him to Smee, who flung him to Starkey, who flung him to Bill Jukes, who flung him to Noodler, and so he was tossed from one to another till he fell at the feet of the black pirate. All the boys were plucked from their trees in this ruthless manner; and several of them were in the air at a time, like bales of goods flung from hand to hand.

A different treatment was accorded to Wendy, who came last. With ironical politeness Hook raised his hat to her, and, offering her his arm, escorted her to the spot where the others were being gagged. He did it with such an air, he was so frightfully *distingué* that she was too fascinated to cry out. She was only a little girl.

Perhaps it is tell-tale to divulge that for a moment Hook entranced her,[1] and we tell on her only because her slip led to strange results. Had she haughtily unhanded him (and we should have loved to write it of her), she would have been hurled through the air like the others, and then Hook would probably not have been present at the tying of the children; and had he not been at the tying he would not have discovered Slightly's secret, and without the secret he could not presently have made his foul attempt on Peter's life.

They were tied to prevent their flying away, doubled up with their knees close to their ears; and for the trussing of them the black pirate had cut a rope into nine equal pieces. All went well until Slightly's turn came, when he was found to be like those irritating parcels that use up all the string in going round and leave no tags with which to tie a knot. The pirates kicked him in their rage, just as you kick the parcel (though in fairness you should kick the string); and strange to say it was Hook who told them to belay their violence. His lip was curled with malicious triumph. While his dogs were merely sweating because every time they tried to pack the unhappy lad tight in one part he bulged out in another, Hook's master mind had gone far beneath Slightly's surface, probing not for effects but for causes; and his exultation showed that he had found them. Slightly, white to the gills, knew that Hook had surprised his secret, which was this, that no boy so blown out could use a tree wherein an average man need stick. Poor Slightly, most wretched of all the children now, for he was in a panic about Peter, bitterly regretted what he had done. Madly addicted to the drinking of water when he was hot, he had swelled in consequence to his present girth, and instead of reducing himself to fit his tree he had, unknown to the others, whittled his tree to make it fit him.

Sufficient of this Hook guessed to persuade him that Peter at last lay at his mercy; but no word of the dark design that now formed in the subterranean caverns of his mind crossed his lips; he merely signed that the captives were to be conveyed to the ship, and that he would be alone.[2]

How to convey them? Hunched up in their ropes they might indeed be rolled down hill like barrels, but most of the way lay through a morass. Again Hook's genius surmounted difficulties. He indicated that the little house must be used as a conveyance. The children were flung into it, four stout

2. *that he would be alone.* The phrase means "that he wished to be alone."

3. *periwinkle*. An evergreen known as vinca major, with violet-blue flowers. In the play, Hook's eyes are described as "blue as the forget-me-not."

pirates raised it on their shoulders, the others fell in behind, and singing the hateful pirate chorus the strange procession set off through the wood. I don't know whether any of the children were crying; if so, the singing drowned the sound; but as the little house disappeared in the forest, a brave though tiny jet of smoke issued from its chimney as if defying Hook.

Hook saw it, and it did Peter a bad service. It dried up any trickle of pity for him that may have remained in the pirate's infuriated breast.

The first thing he did on finding himself alone in the fast falling night was to tiptoe to Slightly's tree, and make sure that it provided him with a passage. Then for long he remained brooding; his hat of ill omen on the sward, so that any gentle breeze which had arisen might play refreshingly through his hair. Dark as were his thoughts his blue eyes were as soft as the periwinkle.[3] Intently he listened for any sound from the nether world, but all was as silent below as above; the house under the ground seemed to be but one more empty tenement in the void. Was that boy asleep, or did he stand waiting at the foot of Slightly's tree, with his dagger in his hand?

There was no way of knowing, save by going down. Hook let his cloak slip softly to the ground, and then biting his lips till a lewd blood stood on them, he stepped into the tree. He was a brave man; but for a moment he had to stop there and wipe his brow, which was dripping like a candle. Then, silently, he let himself go into the unknown.

He arrived unmolested at the foot of the shaft, and stood still again, biting at his breath, which had almost left him. As his eyes became accustomed to the dim light various objects in the home under the trees took shape; but the only one on which his greedy gaze rested, long sought for and found at last, was the great bed. On the bed lay Peter fast asleep.

Unaware of the tragedy being enacted above, Peter had continued, for a little time after the children left, to play gaily on his pipes: no doubt rather a forlorn attempt to prove to himself that he did not care. Then he decided not to take his medicine, so as to grieve Wendy. Then he lay down on the bed outside the coverlet, to vex her still more; for she had always tucked them inside it, because you never know that you may not grow chilly at the turn of the night. Then he nearly cried; but it struck him how indignant she would be if he laughed instead; so he laughed a haughty laugh and fell asleep in the middle of it.

Sometimes, though not often, he had dreams, and they were more painful than the dreams of other boys.[4] For hours he could not be separated from these dreams, though he wailed piteously in them. They had to do, I think, with the riddle of his existence. At such times it had been Wendy's custom to take him out of bed and sit with him on her lap, soothing him in dear ways of her own invention, and when he grew calmer to put him back to bed before he quite woke up, so that he should not know of the indignity to which she had subjected him. But on this occasion he had fallen at once into a dreamless sleep. One arm dropped over the edge of the bed, one leg was arched, and the unfinished part of his laugh was stranded on his mouth, which was open, showing the little pearls.

Thus defenceless Hook found him.[5] He stood silent at the foot of the tree looking across the chamber at his enemy. Did no feeling of compassion disturb his sombre breast? The man was not wholly evil; he loved flowers (I have been told) and sweet music (he was himself no mean performer on the harpsichord); and, let it be frankly admitted, the idyllic nature of the scene stirred him profoundly. Mastered by his better self he would have returned reluctantly up the tree, but for one thing.

What stayed him was Peter's impertinent appearance as he slept. The open mouth, the drooping arm, the arched knee:[6] they were such a personification of cockiness as, taken together, will never again, one may hope, be presented to eyes so sensitive to their offensiveness. They steeled Hook's heart.

4. *they were more painful than the dreams of other boys*. Freud's *Interpretation of Dreams*, published in 1900, placed new importance on the significance of dreams and the unconscious. Peter has just made a heroic effort to reveal that he cannot be touched and that he is immune to feelings of helplessness, even though he has just been abandoned. His defenses include playing on the pipes, rebelling against Wendy by refusing to take his medicine and lying on the coverlet, and, most importantly, laughing. And yet his dreams suggest that this second abandonment cuts deep, repeating and recalling the barred windows of home. In them, he gives in to tears rather than reining in the weeping with a "haughty laugh."

5. *Thus defenceless Hook found him*. In this scene, the entire range and play of Hook's feelings about Peter Pan are revealed. The seductive beauty of the vulnerable, sleeping child disarms Hook, and he gives in, for a moment, to his "better self."

6. *The open mouth, the drooping arm, the arched knee*. The tableau of Peter sleeping has a distinctly aesthetic and possibly erotic charge to it, with the sleeper illuminated by a lamp while his surroundings are cloaked in darkness. The beauty of the sleeping child generally evokes compassion and sympathy rather than the cold rage Hook experiences.

7. *death-dealing rings*. These are rings that contain poison.

If his rage had broken him into a hundred pieces every one of them would have disregarded the incident, and leapt at the sleeper.

Though a light from the one lamp shone dimly on the bed Hook stood in darkness himself, and at the first stealthy step forward he discovered an obstacle, the door of Slightly's tree. It did not entirely fill the aperture, and he had been looking over it. Feeling for the catch, he found to his fury that it was low down, beyond his reach. To his disordered brain it seemed then that the irritating quality in Peter's face and figure visibly increased, and he rattled the door and flung himself against it. Was his enemy to escape him after all?

But what was that? The red in his eye had caught sight of Peter's medicine standing on a ledge within easy reach. He fathomed what it was straightaway, and immediately he knew that the sleeper was in his power.

Lest he should be taken alive, Hook always carried about his person a dreadful drug, blended by himself of all the death-dealing rings[7] that had come into his possession. These he had boiled down into a yellow liquid quite unknown to science, which was probably the most virulent poison in existence.

Five drops of this he now added to Peter's cup. His hand shook, but it was in exultation rather than in shame. As he did it he avoided glancing at the sleeper, but not lest pity should unnerve him; merely to avoid spilling. Then one long gloating look he cast upon his victim, and turning, wormed his way with difficulty up the tree. As he emerged at the top he looked the very spirit of evil breaking from its hole. Donning his hat at its most rakish angle, he wound his cloak around him, holding one end in front as if to conceal his person from the night, of which it was the blackest part, and muttering strangely to himself stole away through the trees.

Peter slept on. The light guttered and went out, leaving the tenement in darkness; but still he slept. It must have been not less than ten o'clock by the crocodile, when he suddenly sat up in his bed, wakened by he knew not what. It was a soft cautious tapping on the door of his tree.

Soft and cautious, but in that stillness it was sinister. Peter felt for his dagger till his hand gripped it. Then he spoke.

"Who is that?"

For long there was no answer: then again the knock.

"Who are you?"

No answer.

He was thrilled, and he loved being thrilled. In two strides he reached the door. Unlike Slightly's door, it filled the aperture, so that he could not see beyond it, nor could the one knocking see him.

"I won't open unless you speak," Peter cried.

Then at last the visitor spoke, in a lovely bell-like voice.

"Let me in, Peter."

It was Tink, and quickly he unbarred to her. She flew in excitedly, her face flushed and her dress stained with mud.

"What is it?"

"Oh, you could never guess!" she cried, and offered him three guesses. "Out with it!" he shouted; and in one ungrammatical sentence, as long as the ribbons that conjurers pull from their mouths, she told of the capture of Wendy and the boys.

Peter's heart bobbed up and down as he listened. Wendy bound, and on the pirate ship; she who loved everything to be just so!

"I'll rescue her!" he cried, leaping at his weapons. As he leapt he thought of something he could do to please her. He could take his medicine.[8]

His hand closed on the fatal draught.

"No!" shrieked Tinker Bell, who had heard Hook muttering about his deed as he sped through the forest.

"Why not?"

"It is poisoned."

8. *He could take his medicine.* Mr. Darling's struggles with Michael over the taking of medicine ("Be a man, Michael . . . when I was your age I took medicine without a murmur") is recalled by this scene in which Peter is all too willing to swallow medicine tainted by Hook. The contrasts and similarities between Mr. Darling (a cowardly liar when it comes to the subject of medicine) and Hook (a cowardly poisoner when he sees an opportunity) are frequently invoked.

9. *His head almost filled the fourth wall of her little room.* The "fourth wall" is a term commonly used to refer to the imaginary wall that divides audience from players and action onstage. The term is also used to designate the threshold that separates readers from fictional settings. As a dramatist, Barrie would have been deeply familiar with the term, and he no doubt invokes it explicitly. Yet he applies it only to Tinker Bell's room rather than to the narrative (or play) itself, which, by appealing to its audience to save Tinker Bell, breaks down the fourth wall.

"Poisoned? Who could have poisoned it?"

"Hook."

"Don't be silly. How could Hook have got down here?"

Alas, Tinker Bell could not explain this, for even she did not know the dark secret of Slightly's tree. Nevertheless Hook's words had left no room for doubt. The cup was poisoned.

"Besides," said Peter, quite believing himself, "I never fell asleep."

He raised the cup. No time for words now; time for deeds; and with one of her lightning movements Tink got between his lips and the draught, and drained it to the dregs.

"Why, Tink, how dare you drink my medicine?"

But she did not answer. Already she was reeling in the air.

"What is the matter with you?" cried Peter, suddenly afraid.

"It was poisoned, Peter," she told him softly; "and now I am going to be dead."

"O Tink, did you drink it to save me?"

"Yes."

"But why, Tink?"

Her wings would scarcely carry her now, but in reply she alighted on his shoulder and gave his nose a loving bite. She whispered in his ear "You silly ass"; and then, tottering to her chamber, lay down on the bed.

His head almost filled the fourth wall of her little room[9] as he knelt near her in distress. Every moment her light was growing fainter; and he knew that if it went out she would be no more. She liked his tears so much that she put out her beautiful finger and let them run over it.

Her voice was so low that at first he could not make out what she said. Then he made it out. She was saying that she thought she could get well again if children believed in fairies.

Peter flung out his arms. There were no children there, and it was night-time; but he addressed all who might be dreaming of the Neverland, and who were therefore nearer to him than you think: boys and girls in their nighties, and naked papooses in their baskets hung from trees.

"Do you believe?" he cried.[10]

Tink sat up in bed almost briskly to listen to her fate.

She fancied she heard answers in the affirmative, and then again she wasn't sure.

"What do you think?" she asked Peter.

"If you believe," he shouted to them, "clap your hands; don't let Tink die."

Many clapped.

Some didn't.

A few little beasts hissed.

The clapping stopped suddenly; as if countless mothers had rushed to their nurseries to see what on earth was happening; but already Tink was saved. First her voice grew strong, then she popped out of bed; then she was flashing through the room more merry and impudent than ever. She never thought of thanking those who believed, but she would have liked to get at the ones who had hissed.

"And now to rescue Wendy."

The moon was riding in a cloudy heaven when Peter rose from his tree, begirt[11] with weapons and wearing little else, to set out upon his perilous quest. It was not such a night as he would have chosen. He had hoped to fly, keeping not far from the ground so that nothing unwonted should escape his eyes; but in that fitful light to have flown low would have meant trailing his shadow through the trees, thus disturbing birds and acquainting a watchful foe that he was astir.

He regretted now that he had given the birds of the island such strange names that they are very wild and difficult of approach.

There was no other course but to press forward in redskin fashion, at which happily he was an adept. But in what direction, for he could not be sure that the children had been taken to the ship? A light fall of snow had obliterated all foot-

10. *"Do you believe?" he cried.* When Peter utters these words in the play, he reveals—by addressing the *audience*—that the events onstage are nothing but performance and illusion. And yet, ironically, just when the theatrical apparatus is laid bare and exposed as an illusion, Peter will demand faith in the spectacle onstage by asking for palpable proof of the audience's faith in fairies. We are in the realm of what Samuel Taylor Coleridge called the willing suspension of disbelief. Barrie himself was unsure of how audiences would react, and he was pleasantly surprised by the burst of spontaneous applause on opening night. In an earlier draft of the play, Peter asked the children to wave their handkerchiefs to demonstrate their faith in fairies. Maureen Duffy sees Peter's appeal as a manipulative move on Barrie's part, "a moment when Barrie shamelessly plays on a youthful audience to bolster his own ego by demonstrating just how effective his theatrical magic is" (Duffy 308).

11. *begirt.* The word means belted.

12. *blaze.* This means cut a mark in.

13. *He was frightfully happy.* Barrie's language captures, in ingenious ways, the mental state of the child. "Frightfully happy" conveys the sense of excitement and delight children feel in situations of (make-believe) peril. Peter, we discover, is happiest when there is adventure and danger.

marks; and a deathly silence pervaded the island, as if for a space Nature stood still in horror of the recent carnage. He had taught the children something of the forest lore that he had himself learned from Tiger Lily and Tinker Bell, and knew that in their dire hour they were not likely to forget it. Slightly, if he had an opportunity, would blaze[12] the trees, for instance, Curly would drop seeds, and Wendy would leave her handkerchief at some important place. The morning was needed to search for such guidance, and he could not wait. The upper world had called him, but would give no help.

The crocodile passed him, but not another living thing, not a sound, not a movement; and yet he knew well that sudden death might be at the next tree, or stalking him from behind.

He swore this terrible oath: "Hook or me this time."

Now he crawled forward like a snake; and again, erect, he darted across a space on which the moonlight played: one finger on his lip and his dagger at the ready. He was frightfully happy.[13]

CHAPTER 14

The Pirate Ship

One green light squinting over Kidd's Creek,[1] which is near the mouth of the pirate river, marked where the brig, the *Jolly Roger* lay, low in the water; a rakish-looking craft[2] foul to the hull, every beam in her detestable, like ground strewn with mangled feathers. She was the cannibal of the seas, and scarce needed that watchful eye, for she floated immune in the horror of her name.

She was wrapped in the blanket of night, through which no sound from her could have reached the shore. There was little sound, and none agreeable save the whir of the ship's sewing machine at which Smee sat, ever industrious and obliging, the essence of the commonplace, pathetic Smee. I know not why he was so infinitely pathetic, unless it were because he was so pathetically unaware of it; but even strong men had to turn hastily from looking at him, and more than once on summer evenings he had touched the fount of Hook's tears and made it flow. Of this, as of almost everything else, Smee was quite unconscious.

A few of the pirates leant over the bulwarks, drinking in the miasma of the night; others sprawled by barrels over games of dice and cards; and the exhausted four who had carried the little house lay prone on the deck, where even in their

1. *Kidd's Creek.* William Kidd (1645–1701) was hanged at Execution Dock on May 23, 1701. One of the most famous of pirates, he was reputed to have amassed a fortune. He is immortalized in works by Edgar Allan Poe and Robert Louis Stevenson, and the pirates have named the creek at which their boat is docked after him.

2. *a rakish-looking craft.* The descriptions of the *Jolly Roger* and the everyday life of the pirates reads like a parody of parts of *Treasure Island*. In *Peter Pan*, the chief pirate is missing a hand rather than a leg, like Long John Silver.

3. *This inscrutable man.* Odd as it may seem, Captain Hook's attributes may have been inspired by Herman Melville's description of Captain Ahab. David Park Williams points out that both authors use the terms "dark," "inscrutable," and "sinister" for the two captains, who also share a "slouch (hat)" and a black brow with eyes of fire. We know that Barrie admired Melville's early work (he refers to *Typee* and *Omoo*), and it is unlikely that he would have missed reading *Moby-Dick*. See Williams 483–88.

4. *Hook was not his true name.* In 1927, Barrie gave a speech entitled "Captain Hook at Eton," in which he proved that "Hook was a good Etonian, though not a great one." He claimed that Hook had attended the most prestigious of England's schools under the name "Jacobus Hook." Barrie revealed much else in the well-received speech, including the fact that Hook had borrowed books of poetry ("mainly the Lake School") from Balliol College at Oxford. In his novel *Sentimental Tommy*, Barrie had introduced a Captain *Stroke*, who forced his enemies to walk the plank. In the scenario for the screen version of *Peter Pan*, Barrie describes Hook's cabin as being furnished like a boy's room at Eton: "It has a wicker chair and a desk with a row of books as in an Eton room. On the walls besides weapons are the colours he won at school, the ribbons, etc., arranged in the eccentric Etonian way, and the old school lists, caps, and also two pictures, which when shown in close-ups are seen to be (1) Eton College, (2) a photograph of an Eton football eleven; the central figure is Hook, as he was when a boy, but distinguishable, with a football in his hands and the prize cup between his knees."

5. *he had been at a famous public school.* Right up to opening night, Barrie had envisioned Hook ending as a schoolmaster, and

sleep they rolled skillfully to this side or that out of Hook's reach, lest he should claw them mechanically in passing.

Hook trod the deck in thought. O man unfathomable. It was his hour of triumph. Peter had been removed for ever from his path, and all the other boys were on the brig, about to walk the plank. It was his grimmest deed since the days when he had brought Barbecue to heel; and knowing as we do how vain a tabernacle is man, could we be surprised had he now paced the deck unsteadily, bellied out by the winds of his success?

But there was no elation in his gait, which kept pace with the action of his sombre mind. Hook was profoundly dejected.

He was often thus when communing with himself on board ship in the quietude of the night. It was because he was so terribly alone. This inscrutable man[3] never felt more alone than when surrounded by his dogs. They were socially inferior to him.

Hook was not his true name.[4] To reveal who he really was would even at this date set the country in a blaze; but as those who read between the lines must already have guessed, he had been at a famous public school;[5] and its traditions still clung to him like garments, with which indeed they are largely concerned. Thus it was offensive to him even now to board a ship in the same dress in which he grappled her, and he still adhered in his walk to the school's distinguished slouch. But above all he retained the passion for good form.[6]

Good form! However much he may have degenerated, he still knew that this is all that really matters.

From far within him he heard a creaking as of rusty portals, and through them came a stern tap-tap-tap, like hammering in the night when one cannot sleep. "Have you been good form to-day?" was their eternal question.

"Fame, fame, that glittering bauble, it is mine," he cried.

"Is it quite good form to be distinguished at anything?" the tap-tap from his school replied.

"I am the only man whom Barbecue feared," he urged; "and Flint himself feared Barbecue."

"Barbecue, Flint—what house?"[7] came the cutting retort.

Most disquieting reflection of all, was it not bad form to think about good form?

His vitals were tortured by this problem. It was a claw within him sharper than the iron one; and as it tore him, the perspiration dripped down his tallow countenance and streaked his doublet. Ofttimes he drew his sleeve across his face, but there was no damming that trickle.

Ah, envy not Hook.

There came to him a presentiment of his early dissolution.[8] It was as if Peter's terrible oath had boarded the ship. Hook felt a gloomy desire to make his dying speech, lest presently there should be no time for it.

"Better for Hook," he cried, "if he had had less ambition." It was in his darkest hours only that he referred to himself in the third person.

"No little children love me."[9]

Strange that he should think of this, which had never troubled him before; perhaps the sewing machine brought it to his mind. For long he muttered to himself, staring at Smee, who was hemming placidly, under the conviction that all children feared him.

Feared him! Feared Smee! There was not a child on board the brig that night who did not already love him. He had said horrid things to them and hit them with the palm of his hand because he could not hit with his fist; but they had only clung to him the more. Michael had tried on his spectacles.

To tell poor Smee that they thought him lovable! Hook itched to do it, but it seemed too brutal. Instead, he revolved this mystery in his mind: why do they find Smee lovable? He pursued the problem like the sleuth-hound that he was. If Smee was lovable, what was it that made him so? A terrible answer suddenly presented itself—"Good form?"

he was to be "dressed as a schoolmaster and carrying birch." Hook described his role in a soliloquy: "I'm a schoolmaster—to revenge myself on boys. I hook them so, and then lay on like this." He denounces Wendy for breaking the law by failing to send Peter to school and proposes catching the boys "and then I'll whack them, whack them" (Green 39). School can, of course, be the chief enemy of childhood, demanding earnestness and application in ways that play does not.

6. *passion for good form.* Hook will remain devoted, right to the end, to the idea of adhering to the codes, conventions, and values of schools for upper-class boys.

7. *"Barbecue, Flint—what house?"* Imagining Robert Louis Stevenson's pirates at Eton is even more hilarious than the idea of Hook at that educational institution.

8. *presentiment of his early dissolution.* Here we have a particularly striking example of Barrie's mock melodramatic style, which makes no concessions to child readers.

9. *"No little children love me."* Pauline Chase, the American actress who played Peter Pan from 1906 to 1913 in New York, recounted children's reactions to this line: "Stern voices in front have been heard calling out in reply, 'Serves you right!' but all are not so hard-hearted. I remember two mites being brought round, behind the scenes because they had something they wanted to say to Captain Hook, but awe fell upon them when he shook their hands (with his hook), and they could only stare at him, and say not a word. When he had gone, however, they looked very woeful, and kept repeating 'We wanted to tell him, we wanted to tell him,' and they explained to me that what they wanted to tell him was that they loved him" (Hammerton 379–80).

10. *eligible for Pop.* Pop is the name of an elite debating society and social club at Eton. The name has been given many fanciful derivations, but it most likely comes from the Latin word for tavern. In *Enemies of Promise*, the renowned critic Cyril Connolly described Pop as "an oligarchy of two dozen boys. . . . Pop were the rulers of Eton, fawned on by the masters and the helpless sixth form" (Connolly 178).

11. *they broke into a bacchanalian dance.* The bacchanalia were associated with the cult of Bacchus, Roman god of wine and intoxication. Originally held in secret and attended by women, they expanded to include men. In Barrie's day, the term was extended to drunken festivities in general. The Greek god Pan is also associated with music and dance, but in a less licentious mode.

12. *"Quiet, you scugs."* "Scug" (now obsolete) was used to designate Eton boys who, because they had received no colors in any sport, were viewed as losers.

13. *"walk the plank."* Walking the plank was a practice associated with pirates and other rogue seafarers, who made their victims—hands bound or weighed down—walk to the end of a wooden plank extended over the side of the ship. The term was first documented in 1785, and evidence of the practice can be found in many nineteenth-century accounts. It is more than likely that most pirates and mutineers preferred less elaborate means of disposing of their captives, though walking the plank erased agency and might have eased the conscience of some, since the victim was not actually pushed, fired upon, or stabbed.

Had the bo'sun good form without knowing it, which is the best form of all?

He remembered that you have to prove you don't know you have it before you are eligible for Pop.[10]

With a cry of rage he raised his iron hand over Smee's head; but he did not tear. What arrested him was this reflection:

"To claw a man because he is good form, what would that be?"

"Bad form!"

The unhappy Hook was as impotent as he was damp, and he fell forward like a cut flower.

His dogs thinking him out of the way for a time, discipline instantly relaxed; and they broke into a bacchanalian dance,[11] which brought him to his feet at once; all traces of human weakness gone, as if a bucket of water had passed over him.

"Quiet, you scugs,"[12] he cried, "or I'll cast anchor in you"; and at once the din was hushed. "Are all the children chained, so that they cannot fly away?"

"Ay, ay."

"Then hoist them up."

The wretched prisoners were dragged from the hold, all except Wendy, and ranged in line in front of him. For a time he seemed unconscious of their presence. He lolled at his ease, humming, not unmelodiously, snatches of a rude song, and fingering a pack of cards. Ever and anon the light from his cigar gave a touch of colour to his face.

"Now then, bullies," he said briskly, "six of you walk the plank[13] to-night, but I have room for two cabin boys. Which of you is it to be?"

"Don't irritate him unnecessarily," had been Wendy's instructions in the hold; so Tootles stepped forward politely. Tootles hated the idea of signing under such a man, but an instinct told him that it would be prudent to lay the responsibility on an absent person; and though a somewhat silly boy, he knew that mothers alone are always willing to be the buffer. All children know this about mothers, and despise them for it, but make constant use of it.

So Tootles explained prudently, "You see, sir, I don't think my mother would like me to be a pirate. Would your mother like you to be a pirate, Slightly?"

He winked at Slightly, who said mournfully, "I don't think so," as if he wished things had been otherwise. "Would your mother like you to be a pirate, Twin?"

"I don't think so," said the first twin, as clever as the others. "Nibs, would—"

"Stow this gab," roared Hook, and the spokesmen were dragged back. "You, boy," he said, addressing John, "you look as if you had a little pluck in you. Didst never want to be a pirate, my hearty?"

Now John had sometimes experienced this hankering at maths.[14] prep.; and he was struck by Hook's picking him out.

"I once thought of calling myself Red-handed Jack,"[15] he said diffidently.

"And a good name too. We'll call you that here, bully, if you join."

"What do you think, Michael?" asked John.

"What would you call me if I join?" Michael demanded.

"Blackbeard Joe."

Michael was naturally impressed. "What do you think, John?" He wanted John to decide, and John wanted him to decide.

"Shall we still be respectful subjects of the King?" John inquired.

Through Hook's teeth came the answer: "You would have to swear, 'Down with the King.'"

Perhaps John had not behaved very well so far, but he shone out now.

"Then I refuse," he cried, banging the barrel in front of Hook.

"And I refuse," cried Michael.

14. *maths.* Mathematics is shortened to "math" in English-speaking North America, but it is abbreviated as "maths" elsewhere.

15. *"Red-handed Jack."* A pirate with that name appears in a U.S. magazine story called "Red Handed Jack: The Terror of the Gulch" (Barnes 208). Although there is no publication date for the story, a report about it and its ill effects on youth was published in 1890 by Raymond P. Barnes in *A History of Roanoke* (Radford, VA: Commonwealth Press, 1968), 208.

16. *"Rule Britannia!"* The origins of this popular British song can be traced to a masque called *Alfred*, first performed in 1740 to commemorate George I's accession to the throne. A line in the third stanza provides a link with Neverland: "Britons never, never, never shall be slaves." Britannia was used by the Romans to refer to Great Britain (northern regions were known as Caledonia), and the area came to be personified as a goddess. Today, statues of the goddess represent the spirit of British nationalism.

17. *buffeted them in the mouth.* To "buffet" is to beat or strike with the hand, to cuff or knock about.

18. *soiled his ruff.* Hook's ruff is an article of neckwear made of muslin or linen that was worn during the reigns of Elizabeth and James I.

"Rule Britannia!"[16] squeaked Curly.

The infuriated pirates buffeted them in the mouth;[17] and Hook roared out, "That seals your doom. Bring up their mother. Get the plank ready."

They were only boys, and they went white as they saw Jukes and Cecco preparing the fatal plank. But they tried to look brave when Wendy was brought up.

No words of mine can tell you how Wendy despised those pirates. To the boys there was at least some glamour in the pirate calling; but all that she saw was that the ship had not been tidied for years. There was not a porthole on the grimy glass of which you might not have written with your finger "Dirty pig"; and she had already written it on several. But as the boys gathered round her she had no thought, of course, save for them.

"So, my beauty," said Hook, as if he spoke in syrup, "you are to see your children walk the plank."

Fine gentleman though he was, the intensity of his communings had soiled his ruff,[18] and suddenly he knew that she was gazing at it. With a hasty gesture he tried to hide it, but he was too late.

"Are they to die?" asked Wendy, with a look of such frightful contempt that he nearly fainted.

"They are," he snarled. "Silence all," he called gloatingly, "for a mother's last words to her children."

At this moment Wendy was grand. "These are my last words, dear boys," she said firmly. "I feel that I have a message to you from your real mothers, and it is this: 'We hope our sons will die like English gentlemen.'"

Even the pirates were awed; and Tootles cried out hysterically, "I am going to do what my mother hopes. What are you to do, Nibs?"

"What my mother hopes. What are you to do, Twin?"

"What my mother hopes. John, what are—?"

But Hook had found his voice again.

"Tie her up!" he shouted.

It was Smee who tied her to the mast. "See here, honey," he whispered, "I'll save you if you promise to be my mother."

But not even for Smee would she make such a promise. "I would almost rather have no children at all," she said disdainfully.

It is sad to know that not a boy was looking at her as Smee tied her to the mast; the eyes of all were on the plank: that last little walk they were about to take. They were no longer able to hope that they would walk it manfully, for the capacity to think had gone from them; they could stare and shiver only.

Hook smiled on them with his teeth closed, and took a step toward Wendy. His intention was to turn her face so that she should see the boys walking the plank one by one. But he never reached her, he never heard the cry of anguish he hoped to wring from her. He heard something else instead.

It was the terrible tick-tick of the crocodile.

They all heard it—pirates, boys, Wendy; and immediately every head was blown in one direction; not to the water whence the sound proceeded, but toward Hook. All knew that what was about to happen concerned him alone, and that from being actors they were suddenly become spectators.

Very frightful was it to see the change that came over him. It was as if he had been clipped at every joint. He fell in a little heap.

The sound came steadily nearer; and in advance of it came this ghastly thought, "The crocodile is about to board the ship!"

Even the iron claw hung inactive; as if knowing that it was no intrinsic part of what the attacking force wanted. Left so fearfully alone, any other man would have lain with his eyes shut where he fell: but the gigantic brain of Hook was still working, and under its guidance he crawled on his knees along the deck as far from the sound as he could go.

The pirates respectfully cleared a passage for him, and it was only when he brought up against the bulwarks that he spoke.

"Hide me," he cried hoarsely.

They gathered round him, all eyes averted from the thing that was coming aboard. They had no thought of fighting it. It was Fate.

Only when Hook was hidden from them did curiosity loosen the limbs of the boys so that they could rush to the ship's side to see the crocodile climbing it. Then they got the strangest surprise of the Night of Nights; for it was no crocodile that was coming to their aid. It was Peter.

He signed to them not to give vent to any cry of admiration that might rouse suspicion. Then he went on ticking.

It was PETER

CHAPTER 15

"Hook or Me This Time"

Odd things happen to all of us on our way through life without our noticing for a time that they have happened. Thus, to take an instance, we suddenly discover that we have been deaf in one ear for we don't know how long, but, say, half an hour. Now such an experience had come that night to Peter. When last we saw him he was stealing across the island with one finger to his lips and his dagger at the ready. He had seen the crocodile pass by without noticing anything peculiar about it, but by and by he remembered that it had not been ticking. At first he thought this eerie, but soon he concluded rightly that the clock had run down.

Without giving a thought to what might be the feelings of a fellow-creature thus abruptly deprived of its closest companion, Peter began to consider how he could turn the catastrophe to his own use; and he decided to tick, so that wild beasts should believe he was the crocodile and let him pass unmolested. He ticked superbly, but with one unforeseen result. The crocodile was among those who heard the sound, and it followed him, though whether with the purpose of regaining what it had lost, or merely as a friend under the belief that it was again ticking itself, will never be certainly known, for, like all slaves to a fixed idea, it was a stupid beast.

Peter reached the shore without mishap, and went straight on; his legs encountering the water as if quite unaware that they had entered a new element. Thus many animals pass from land to water, but no other human of whom I know. As he swam he had but one thought: "Hook or me this time." He had ticked so long that he now went on ticking without knowing that he was doing it. Had he known he would have stopped, for to board the brig by the help of the tick, though an ingenious idea, had not occurred to him.

On the contrary, he thought he had scaled her side as noiseless as a mouse; and he was amazed to see the pirates cowering from him, with Hook in their midst as abject as if he had heard the crocodile.

The crocodile gets Hook. (*Peter Pan and Wendy by J. M. Barrie, Retold for the Nursery by May Byron*. Illustrated by Kathleen Atkins)

The crocodile! No sooner did Peter remember it than he heard the ticking. At first he thought the sound did come from the crocodile, and he looked behind him swiftly. Then he realised that he was doing it himself, and in a flash he understood the situation. "How clever of me!" he thought at once, and signed to the boys not to burst into applause.

It was at this moment that Ed Teynte the quartermaster emerged from the forecastle and came along the deck. Now, reader, time what happened by your watch. Peter struck true and deep. John clapped his hands on the ill-fated pirate's mouth to stifle the dying groan. He fell forward. Four boys caught him to prevent the thud. Peter gave the signal, and the carrion was cast overboard. There was a splash, and then silence. How long has it taken?

"One!" (Slightly had begun to count.)

None too soon, Peter, every inch of him on tiptoe, vanished into the cabin; for more than one pirate was screwing up his courage to look round. They could hear each other's distressed breathing now, which showed them that the more terrible sound had passed.

"It's gone, captain," Smee said, wiping his spectacles. "All's still again."

Slowly Hook let his head emerge from his ruff, and listened so intently that he could have caught the echo of the tick. There was not a sound, and he drew himself up firmly to his full height.

"Then here's to Johnny Plank," he cried brazenly, hating the boys more than ever because they had seen him unbend. He broke into the villainous ditty:

> "Yo ho, yo ho, the frisky plank,
> You walks along it so,
> Till it goes down and you goes down
> To Davy Jones below!"

1. *"a touch of the cat."* The cat-o'-nine-tails was a whip with nine knotted lashes used on sailors to enforce discipline at sea. It remained until 1881 an officially authorized instrument of punishment in the British army and navy.

To terrorise the prisoners the more, though with a certain loss of dignity, he danced along an imaginary plank, grimacing at them as he sang; and when he finished he cried, "Do you want a touch of the cat[1] before you walk the plank?"

At that they fell on their knees. "No, no!" they cried so piteously that every pirate smiled.

"Fetch the cat, Jukes," said Hook; "it's in the cabin."

The cabin! Peter was in the cabin! The children gazed at each other.

"Ay, ay," said Jukes blithely, and he strode into the cabin. They followed him with their eyes; they scarce knew that Hook had resumed his song, his dogs joining in with him:

> "Yo ho, yo ho, the scratching cat,
> Its tails are nine, you know,
> And when they're writ upon your back—"

What was the last line will never be known, for of a sudden the song was stayed by a dreadful screech from the cabin. It wailed through the ship, and died away. Then was heard a crowing sound which was well understood by the boys, but to the pirates was almost more eerie than the screech.

"What was that?" cried Hook.

"Two," said Slightly solemnly.

The Italian Cecco hesitated for a moment and then swung into the cabin. He tottered out, haggard.

"What's the matter with Bill Jukes, you dog?" hissed Hook, towering over him.

"The matter wi' him is he's dead, stabbed," replied Cecco in a hollow voice.

"Bill Jukes dead!" cried the startled pirates.

"The cabin's as black as a pit," Cecco said, almost gibbering, "but there is something terrible in there: the thing you heard crowing."

The exultation of the boys, the lowering looks of the pirates, both were seen by Hook.

"Cecco," he said in his most steely voice, "go back and fetch me out that doodle-doo."[2]

Cecco, bravest of the brave, cowered before his captain, crying "No, no"; but Hook was purring to his claw.

"Did you say you would go, Cecco?" he said musingly.

Cecco went, first flinging his arms despairingly. There was no more singing, all listened now; and again came a death-screech and again a crow.

No one spoke except Slightly. "Three," he said.

Hook rallied his dogs with a gesture. "'Sdeath[3] and odds fish,"[4] he thundered, "who is to bring me that doodle-doo?"

"Wait till Cecco comes out," growled Starkey, and the others took up the cry.

"I think I heard you volunteer, Starkey," said Hook, purring again.

"No, by thunder!" Starkey cried.

"My hook thinks you did," said Hook, crossing to him. "I wonder if it would not be advisable, Starkey, to humour the hook?"

"I'll swing[5] before I go in there," replied Starkey doggedly, and again he had the support of the crew.

"Is it mutiny?" asked Hook more pleasantly than ever. "Starkey's ringleader!"

"Captain, mercy," Starkey whimpered, all of a tremble now.

"Shake hands, Starkey," said Hook, proffering his claw.

Starkey looked round for help, but all deserted him. As he backed Hook advanced, and now the red spark was in his eye. With a despairing scream the pirate leapt upon Long Tom and precipitated himself into the sea.

"Four," said Slightly.

"And now," Hook said courteously, "did any other gentleman say mutiny?" Seizing a lantern and raising his claw with

2. *"doodle-doo."* In *The Peter Pan Alphabet*, *D* stands for "Doodledoo": "D is the Dire and Dread DoodleDoo / With which Peter Daunted the Pirate crew, / And demolished a foolish old Proverb for good / By crowing before he was out of the wood."

3. *"'Sdeath."* A shortened version of the oath "God's death."

4. *"odds fish."* In *The Peter Pan Alphabet*, *O* stands for "Odds-fish," which is defined in the following way: "O's for Odds-fish— the Pirate's Oath. / To print such a word, Gentle Reader, I'm loth. / And should *You* be guilty of language so low, / I should have to stop calling you 'Gentle,' you know."

5. *"I'll swing."* I'll be hanged.

159

a menacing gesture, "I'll bring out that doodle-doo myself," he said, and sped into the cabin.

"Five." How Slightly longed to say it. He wetted his lips to be ready, but Hook came staggering out, without his lantern.

"Something blew out the light," he said a little unsteadily.

"Something!" echoed Mullins.

"What of Cecco?" demanded Noodler.

"He's as dead as Jukes," said Hook shortly.

His reluctance to return to the cabin impressed them all unfavourably, and the mutinous sounds again broke forth. All pirates are superstitious, and Cookson cried, "They do say the surest sign a ship's accurst is when there's one on board more than can be accounted for."

"I've heard," muttered Mullins, "he always boards the pirate craft last. Had he a tail, captain?"

"They say," said another, looking viciously at Hook, "that when he comes it's in the likeness of the wickedest man aboard."

"Had he a hook, captain?" asked Cookson insolently; and one after another took up the cry, "The ship's doomed." At this the children could not resist raising a cheer. Hook had well-nigh forgotten his prisoners, but as he swung round on them now his face lit up again.

"Lads," he cried to his crew, "now here's a notion. Open the cabin door and drive them in. Let them fight the doodle-doo for their lives. If they kill him, we're so much the better; if he kills them, we're none the worse."

For the last time his dogs admired Hook, and devotedly they did his bidding. The boys, pretending to struggle, were pushed into the cabin and the door was closed on them.

"Now, listen!" cried Hook, and all listened. But not one dared to face the door. Yes, one, Wendy, who all this time had been bound to the mast. It was for neither a scream nor a crow that she was watching; it was for the reappearance of Peter.

She had not long to wait. In the cabin he had found the

thing for which he had gone in search: the key that would free the children of their manacles; and now they all stole forth, armed with such weapons as they could find. First signing to them to hide, Peter cut Wendy's bonds, and then nothing could have been easier than for them all to fly off together; but one thing barred the way, an oath, "Hook or me this time." So when he had freed Wendy, he whispered for her to conceal herself with the others, and himself took her place by the mast,[6] her cloak around him so that he should pass for her. Then he took a great breath and crowed.[7]

To the pirates it was a voice crying that all the boys lay slain in the cabin; and they were panic-stricken. Hook tried to hearten them; but like the dogs he had made them they showed him their fangs, and he knew that if he took his eyes off them now they would leap at him.

"Lads," he said, ready to cajole or strike as need be, but never quailing for an instant, "I've thought it out. There's a Jonah aboard."[8]

"Ay," they snarled, "a man wi' a hook."

"No, lads, no, it's the girl. Never was luck on a pirate ship wi' a woman on board.[9] We'll right the ship when she's gone."

Some of them remembered that this had been a saying of Flint's. "It's worth trying," they said doubtfully.

"Fling the girl overboard," cried Hook; and they made a rush at the figure in the cloak.

"There's none can save you now, missy," Mullins hissed jeeringly.

"There's one," replied the figure.

"Who's that?"

"Peter Pan the avenger!" came the terrible answer; and as he spoke Peter flung off his cloak. Then they all knew who 'twas that had been undoing them in the cabin, and twice Hook essayed to speak and twice he failed. In that frightful moment I think his fierce heart broke.

6. *took her place by the mast.* This is one of many instances in which Peter uses mimicry and masquerade, impersonating another character in the play. Capricious and adept at role playing, he is able to slip out of his own identity and imitate mermaids, girls, and villains.

7. *Then he took a great breath and crowed.* Peter's crowing like a cock links him to the gods Pan and Dionysus, as does his piping. In Maurice Sendak's *In the Night Kitchen,* Mickey's shouts of "Cock-a-doodle-doo" in the nighttime may well have been inspired by Peter's crowing.

8. *"There's a Jonah aboard."* In the book of Jonah, God orders Jonah to denounce the citizens of Nineveh for their "great wickedness." Frightened and overwhelmed by the mission, Jonah flees the presence of God and sails to Tarshish. When a storm develops, the sailors blame Jonah and decide to throw him overboard, with the hope of getting their ship to shore. Miraculously, Jonah is saved when a fish swallows him. After three days and nights of prayer, Jonah is released from his underwater prison.

9. *"a woman on board."* Although seafaring men kept alive the superstition that having a woman on board was bad luck, there are many cases when wives (even of pirates) would accompany their husbands (usually the captains of ships) on voyages. Women may have been considered bad luck onboard, but as figureheads facing the sea at the bow of a ship, they were thought to protect sailors from harm. The practice of using such figures goes back to ancient times, when Pliny the Elder asserted that a bare-breasted woman could calm turbulent waters. In British countries and European lands, women were not widely used as figureheads until the nineteenth century.

10. *"Cleave him to the brisket."* In the play, Hook cries out these words, and the stage directions read: "But he has a sinking [*sic*] that this boy has no brisket." The brisket bone is the breastbone, and "cleaving to the brisket" was a phrase first used in Sir Walter Scott's novel *Rob Roy* (1817): "By the hand of my father! The first man that strikes, I'll cleave him to the brisket."

11. *buckler.* A small shield.

At last he cried, "Cleave him to the brisket,"[10] but without conviction.

"Down, boys, and at them," Peter's voice rang out; and in another moment the clash of arms was resounding through the ship. Had the pirates kept together it is certain that they would have won; but the onset came when they were still unstrung, and they ran hither and thither, striking wildly, each thinking himself the last survivor of the crew. Man to man they were the stronger; but they fought on the defensive only, which enabled the boys to hunt in pairs and choose their quarry. Some of the miscreants leapt into the sea; others hid in dark recesses, where they were found by Slightly, who did not fight, but ran about with a lantern which he flashed in their faces, so that they were half blinded and fell as an easy prey to the reeking swords of the other boys. There was little sound to be heard but the clang of weapons, an occasional screech or splash, and Slightly monotonously counting—five—six—seven—eight—nine—ten—eleven.

I think all were gone when a group of savage boys surrounded Hook, who seemed to have a charmed life, as he kept them at bay in that circle of fire. They had done for his dogs, but this man alone seemed to be a match for them all. Again and again they closed upon him, and again and again he hewed a clear space. He had lifted up one boy with his hook, and was using him as a buckler,[11] when another, who had just passed his sword through Mullins, sprang into the fray.

"Put up your swords, boys," cried the newcomer, "this man is mine."

Thus suddenly Hook found himself face to face with Peter. The others drew back and formed a ring round them.

For long the two enemies looked at one another; Hook shuddering slightly, and Peter with the strange smile upon his face.

"So, Pan," said Hook at last, "this is all your doing."

"Ay, James Hook," came the stern answer, "it is all my doing."

"Proud and insolent youth,"[12] said Hook, "prepare to meet thy doom."

"Dark and sinister man," Peter answered, "have at thee."

Without more words they fell to, and for a space there was no advantage to either blade. Peter was a superb swordsman, and parried with dazzling rapidity; ever and anon he followed up a feint with a lunge that got past his foe's defence, but his shorter reach stood him in ill stead, and he could not drive the steel home. Hook, scarcely his inferior in brilliancy, but not quite so nimble in wrist play, forced him back by the weight of his onset, hoping suddenly to end all with a favourite thrust, taught him long ago by Barbecue at Rio; but to his astonishment he found this thrust turned aside again and again. Then he sought to close and give the quietus[13] with his iron hook, which all this time had been pawing the air; but Peter doubled under it and, lunging fiercely, pierced him in the ribs. At the sight of his own blood, whose peculiar colour, you remember, was offensive to him, the sword fell from Hook's hand, and he was at Peter's mercy.

"Now!" cried all the boys, but with a magnificent gesture Peter invited his opponent to pick up his sword. Hook did so instantly, but with a tragic feeling that Peter was showing good form.

Hitherto he had thought it was some fiend fighting him, but darker suspicions assailed him now.

"Pan, who and what art thou?" he cried huskily.

"I'm youth, I'm joy," Peter answered at a venture, "I'm a little bird that has broken out of the egg."[14]

This, of course, was nonsense; but it was proof to the unhappy Hook that Peter did not know in the least who or what he was, which is the very pinnacle of good form.

"To 't again," he cried despairingly.

12. *"Proud and insolent youth."* The juxtaposition of child and adult, the one proud and insolent, the other dark and sinister, serves to emphasize the centrality of generational conflict in *Peter Pan*. In 1920, Barrie wrote about the generational divide in the aftermath of World War I: "Age & Youth the great enemies. . . . Age (wisdom) failed—Now let us see what youth (audacity) can do. . . . In short, there has arisen a new morality which seeks to go its own way agst [*sic*] the fierce protests (or despair) of the old morality. No argument can exist between the two till this is admitted. In present controversy it isn't admitted—the Old screams at the New as . . . vile [because] not Old's way—and New despises Old as played out and false sentiment. When they admit that the other has a case to state, then . . . they can argue—not before" (Yeoman 24–25).

13. *give the quietus.* Deal the death blow.

14. *"I'm a little bird that has broken out of the egg."* Peter's self-definition suggests both fragility and strength, combining the vulnerability of a newborn with the power to "break through." He refuses to categorize himself and avoids being defined by others. Like all babies, as we learn in *Peter Pan in Kensington Gardens*, he was a bird before he became a child. In a program note written for the 1908 Paris performance of *Peter Pan*, Barrie advised the audience: "[Of] Peter you must make what you will— perhaps he was a boy who died young and this is how the author perceives his subsequent adventures. Or perhaps he was a boy who was never born at all" (White and Tarr 204). In *The Little White Bird*, Barrie described children who have never had mothers (or what he also called dream children) as little white birds.

15. *sent up for good*. At Eton, a boy who was "sent up for good" was referred to the headmaster and rewarded for his good work. The custom continues today, and boys take their work to the headmaster, who signs it and gives them a prize.

16. *watching the wall-game from a famous wall*. The Eton wall game is played between the Collegers (King's Scholars) and the Oppidans (the rest of the school). The best place from which to watch it is the top of a ten-foot-high wall.

He fought now like a human flail, and every sweep of that terrible sword would have severed in twain any man or boy who obstructed it; but Peter fluttered round him as if the very wind it made blew him out of the danger zone. And again and again he darted in and pricked.

Hook was fighting now without hope. That passionate breast no longer asked for life; but for one boon it craved: to see Peter show bad form before it was cold for ever.

Abandoning the fight he rushed into the powder magazine and fired it.

"In two minutes," he cried, "the ship will be blown to pieces."

Now, now, he thought, true form will show.

But Peter issued from the powder magazine with the shell in his hands, and calmly flung it overboard.

What sort of form was Hook himself showing? Misguided man though he was, we may be glad, without sympathising with him, that in the end he was true to the traditions of his race. The other boys were flying around him now, flouting, scornful; and as he staggered about the deck striking up at them impotently, his mind was no longer with them; it was slouching in the playing fields of long ago, or being sent up for good,[15] or watching the wall-game from a famous wall.[16] And his shoes were right, and his waistcoat was right, and his tie was right, and his socks were right.

James Hook, thou not wholly unheroic figure, farewell.

For we have come to his last moment.

Seeing Peter slowly advancing upon him through the air with dagger poised, he sprang upon the bulwarks to cast himself into the sea. He did not know that the crocodile was waiting for him; for we purposely stopped the clock that this knowledge might be spared him: a little mark of respect from us at the end.

He had one last triumph, which I think we need not grudge him. As he stood on the bulwark looking over his shoulder at Peter gliding through the air, he invited him with a gesture to use his foot. It made Peter kick instead of stab.

At last Hook had got the boon for which he craved.

"Bad form," he cried jeeringly, and went content to the crocodile.

Thus perished James Hook.

"Seventeen," Slightly sang out; but he was not quite correct in his figures. Fifteen paid the penalty for their crimes that night; but two reached the shore: Starkey to be captured by the redskins, who made him nurse for all their papooses, a melancholy comedown for a pirate; and Smee, who henceforth wandered about the world in his spectacles, making a precarious living by saying he was the only man that Jas. Hook had feared.[17]

Wendy, of course, had stood by taking no part in the fight, though watching Peter with glistening eyes; but now that all was over she became prominent again. She praised them equally, and shuddered delightfully when Michael showed her the place where he had killed one; and then she took them into Hook's cabin and pointed to his watch which was hanging on a nail. It said "half-past one!"

The lateness of the hour was almost the biggest thing of all. She got them to bed in the pirates' bunks pretty quickly, you may be sure; all but Peter, who strutted up and down on the deck, until at last he fell asleep by the side of Long Tom. He had one of his dreams that night, and cried in his sleep[18] for a long time, and Wendy held him tight.

17. *he was the only man that Jas. Hook had feared.* In Stevenson's *Treasure Island*, Long John Silver is "the only man Flint feared," and the phrase becomes a leitmotif in Barrie's play.

18. *cried in his sleep.* Why Peter cries at night remains a mystery. Does he miss his mother and long to return home? Is he haunted by the specter of death (after murdering all those pirates), even though he is the boy who will never grow up? Is he distraught by the death of Hook? Despite his lack of a memory, he knows that something is missing and mourns it.

CHAPTER 16

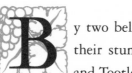

The Return Home

1. *with a rope's end in his hand.* The bo'sun's job is to keep discipline on board ship by beating disobedient or delinquent sailors with a rope's end. Tootles makes an unlikely disciplinarian, and it is hard to imagine him wielding the rope and chewing tobacco.

2. *tars before the mast.* Jack Tar was the standard name for sailors. "Before the mast" refers to the location of the sailors' quarters—here, before or in front of the mast, which was amidship.

3. *lashed himself to the wheel.* Peter has now become both captain and helmsman and, with characteristic exaggerated bravado, has lashed himself to the wheel, as if in preparation for stormy weather that might sweep him overboard.

B y two bells that morning they were all stirring their stumps; for there was a big sea running; and Tootles, the bo'sun, was among them, with a rope's end in his hand[1] and chewing tobacco. They all donned pirate clothes cut off at the knee, shaved smartly, and tumbled up, with the true nautical roll and hitching their trousers.

It need not be said who was the captain. Nibs and John were first and second mate. There was a woman aboard. The rest were tars before the mast,[2] and lived in the fo'c'sle. Peter had already lashed himself to the wheel;[3] but he piped all hands and delivered a short address to them; said he hoped they would do their duty like gallant hearties, but that he knew they were the scum of Rio and the Gold Coast, and if they snapped at him he would tear them. The bluff strident words struck the note sailors understand, and they cheered him lustily. Then a few sharp orders were given, and they turned the ship round, and nosed her for the mainland.

Captain Pan calculated, after consulting the ship's chart, that if this weather lasted they should strike the Azores about the 21st of June, after which it would save time to fly.

Some of them wanted it to be an honest ship and others were in favour of keeping it a pirate; but the captain treated them as dogs, and they dared not express their wishes to him even in a round robin.[4] Instant obedience was the only safe thing. Slightly got a dozen[5] for looking perplexed when told to take soundings.[6] The general feeling was that Peter was honest just now to lull Wendy's suspicions, but that there might be a change when the new suit was ready, which, against her will, she was making for him out of some of Hook's wickedest garments. It was afterwards whispered among them that on the first night he wore this suit[7] he sat long in the cabin with Hook's cigar-holder in his mouth and one hand clenched, all but for the forefinger, which he bent and held threateningly aloft like a hook.

Instead of watching the ship, however, we must now return to that desolate home from which three of our characters had taken heartless flight so long ago. It seems a shame to have neglected No. 14 all this time; and yet we may be sure that Mrs. Darling does not blame us. If we had returned sooner to look with sorrowful sympathy at her, she would probably have cried, "Don't be silly; what do I matter? Do go back and keep an eye on the children." So long as mothers are like this their children will take advantage of them; and they may lay to that.[8]

Even now we venture into that familiar nursery[9] only because its lawful occupants are on their way home; we are merely hurrying on in advance of them to see that their beds are properly aired and that Mr. and Mrs. Darling do not go out for the evening. We are no more than servants. Why on earth should their beds be properly aired, seeing that they left them in such a thankless hurry? Would it not serve them jolly well right if they came back and found that their parents were spending the week-end in the country? It would be the moral lesson they have been in need of ever since we met them; but if we contrived things in this way Mrs. Darling would never forgive us.

One thing I should like to do immensely, and that is to

4. *round robin*. The phrase is a term used for nautical documents of complaint, with the names of the sailors written in a circle to conceal the order in which they signed.

5. *Slightly got a dozen*. A dozen lashes.

6. *take soundings*. Soundings are taken to determine the depths of water by putting a weight on the end of a line.

7. *on the first night he wore this suit*. That Peter channels Hook by putting on his garments and pretending that he has a hook reminds us of the deep connection between boy and man, with the boy "trying on" the role of the adult.

8. *they may lay to that*. They may bet on that.

9. *Even now we venture into that familiar nursery*. We have seen how the narrator slips in and out of different roles. In this passage, he is able to make his way—like a "servant"—into the house to check on the airing of the beds. Taking on an adult judgmental role, he scolds the children for being "thankless" and calls them "brats." The chapter displays feelings of resentment toward both children and parents.

10. *in the way authors have.* Here Barrie actually refers to himself as an author of the events, thereby undermining the sense of anxiety he has built up about the return of the children. The made-up dialogue between him and Mrs. Darling that follows reveals just how much he feels marginalized by the children's mother.

11. *I despise her.* The tirade against Mrs. Darling is not completely unexpected (mothers are "despised" twice before), but it is astonishingly mean-spirited in the context of the novel's earlier sentimentalization of domestic life and of mothers. And it flagrantly contradicts the narrator's insistence that he likes Mrs. Darling "best."

12. *That is all we are, lookers-on.* Here the narrator concedes that he is perched outside the story, looking in, and can never really enter it (although he tries at various times to assume the role of adult, child, or servant). The world of family life and parenting that he has created, like Neverland, is barred to him forever. Barrie might here be reflecting on his role as outsider to the Llewelyn Davies family.

13. *jaggy things.* Prickly things or barbs.

tell her, in the way authors have,[10] that the children are coming back, that indeed they will be here on Thursday week. This would spoil so completely the surprise to which Wendy and John and Michael are looking forward. They have been planning it out on the ship: mother's rapture, father's shout of joy, Nana's leap through the air to embrace them first, when what they ought to be preparing for is a good hiding. How delicious to spoil it all by breaking the news in advance; so that when they enter grandly Mrs. Darling may not even offer Wendy her mouth, and Mr. Darling may exclaim pettishly, "Dash it all, here are those boys again." However, we should get no thanks even for this. We are beginning to know Mrs. Darling by this time, and may be sure that she would upbraid us for depriving the children of their little pleasure.

"But, my dear madam, it is ten days till Thursday week; so that by telling you what's what, we can save you ten days of unhappiness."

"Yes, but at what a cost! By depriving the children of ten minutes of delight."

"Oh, if you look at it in that way."

"What other way is there in which to look at it?"

You see, the woman had no proper spirit. I had meant to say extraordinarily nice things about her; but I despise her,[11] and not one of them will I say now. She does not really need to be told to have things ready, for they are ready. All the beds are aired, and she never leaves the house, and observe, the window is open. For all the use we are to her, we might go back to the ship. However, as we are here we may as well stay and look on. That is all we are, lookers-on.[12] Nobody really wants us. So let us watch and say jaggy things,[13] in the hope that some of them will hurt.

The only change to be seen in the night-nursery is that between nine and six the kennel is no longer there. When the children flew away, Mr. Darling felt in his bones that all the blame was his for having chained Nana up, and that from first to last she had been wiser than he. Of course, as we have seen, he was quite a simple man; indeed he might have passed for a boy again if he had been able to take his baldness off; but he had also a noble sense of justice and a lion's courage to do what seemed right to him; and having thought the matter out with anxious care after the flight of the children, he went down on all fours and crawled into the kennel. To all Mrs. Darling's dear invitations to him to come out he replied sadly but firmly:

"No, my own one, this is the place for me."

In the bitterness of his remorse he swore that he would never leave the kennel until his children came back. Of course this was a pity; but whatever Mr. Darling did he had to do in excess; otherwise he soon gave up doing it. And there never was a more humble man than the once proud George Darling, as he sat in the kennel of an evening talking with his wife of their children and all their pretty ways.

Very touching was his deference to Nana. He would not let her come into the kennel, but on all other matters he followed her wishes implicitly.

Every morning the kennel was carried with Mr. Darling in it to a cab, which conveyed him to his office, and he returned home in the same way at six. Something of the strength of character of the man will be seen if we remember how sensitive he was to the opinion of neighbours: this man whose every movement now attracted surprised attention. Inwardly he must have suffered torture; but he preserved a calm exterior even when the young criticised his little home, and he always lifted his hat courteously to any lady who looked inside.

It may have been quixotic,[14] but it was magnificent. Soon the inward meaning of it leaked out, and the great heart of the public was touched. Crowds followed the cab, cheer-

14. *It may have been quixotic*. With the term quixotic, Mr. Darling is compared to the visionary but misguided hero of Cervantes's epic work, *Don Quixote*. The comparison makes Mr. Darling's efforts appear all the more small by contrast to the deluded idealist Don Quixote.

15. *I like her best*. The narrator appears to be as flighty and capricious as Peter Pan, and now he suddenly has a change of heart, moving from "I despise her" to "I like her best."

16. *Let's*. In this one monosyllabic sentence, Barrie's narrator identifies himself with a collective "we" and becomes a spectral presence in the nursery, eerily whispering in Mrs. Darling's ear when there is no other human in the room.

ing it lustily; charming girls scaled it to get his autograph; interviews appeared in the better class of papers, and society invited him to dinner and added, "Do come in the kennel."

On that eventful Thursday week Mrs. Darling was in the night-nursery awaiting George's return home: a very sad-eyed woman. Now that we look at her closely and remember the gaiety of her in the old days, all gone now just because she has lost her babes, I find I won't be able to say nasty things about her after all. If she was too fond of her rubbishy children she couldn't help it. Look at her in her chair, where she has fallen asleep. The corner of her mouth, where one looks first, is almost withered up. Her hand moves restlessly on her breast as if she had a pain there. Some like Peter best, and some like Wendy best, but I like her best.[15] Suppose, to make her happy, we whisper to her in her sleep that the brats are coming back. They are really within two miles of the window now, and flying strong, but all we need whisper is that they are on the way. Let's.[16]

It is a pity we did it, for she has started up, calling their names; and there is no one in the room but Nana.

"O Nana, I dreamt my dear ones had come back."

Nana had filmy eyes, but all she could do was put her paw gently on her mistress's lap; and they were sitting together thus when the kennel was brought back. As Mr. Darling puts his head out to kiss his wife, we see that his face is more worn than of yore, but has a softer expression.

He gave his hat to Liza, who took it scornfully; for she had no imagination, and was quite incapable of understanding the motives of such a man. Outside, the crowd who had accompanied the cab home were still cheering, and he was naturally not unmoved.

"Listen to them," he said; "it is very gratifying."

"Lots of little boys," sneered Liza.

"There were several adults to-day," he assured her with a faint flush; but when she tossed her head he had not a word of reproof for her. Social success had not spoilt him; it had made him sweeter. For some time he sat half out of the kennel, talking with Mrs. Darling of this success, and pressing her hand reassuringly when she said she hoped his head would not be turned by it.

"But if I had been a weak man," he said. "Good heavens, if I had been a weak man!"

"And, George," she said timidly, "you are as full of remorse as ever, aren't you?"

"Full of remorse as ever, dearest! See my punishment: living in a kennel."

"But it is punishment, isn't it, George? You are sure you are not enjoying it?"

"My love!"

You may be sure she begged his pardon; and then, feeling drowsy, he curled round in the kennel.

"Won't you play me to sleep," he asked, "on the nursery piano?" and as he was crossing to the day-nursery he added thoughtlessly, "And shut that window. I feel a draught."

"O George, never ask me to do that. The window must always be left open for them, always, always."

Now it was his turn to beg her pardon; and she went into the day-nursery and played, and soon he was asleep; and while he slept, Wendy and John and Michael flew into the room.

Oh no. We have written it so, because that was the charming arrangement planned by them before we left the ship; but something must have happened since then, for it is not they who have flown in, it is Peter and Tinker Bell.

Peter's first words tell all.

"Quick, Tink," he whispered, "close the window; bar it. That's right. Now you and I must get away by the door; and when Wendy comes she will think her mother has barred her out; and she will have to go back with me."

Now I understand what had hitherto puzzled me,[17] why when Peter had exterminated the pirates he did not return to

17. *Now I understand what had hitherto puzzled me.* The improvisational quality of the narration becomes more evident in the novel's final chapters, with the narrator's emphasis on how the characters have a life of their own, with motives that are not always transparent to him.

18. *"Home, Sweet Home."* The famous song was adapted from John Howard Payne's 1823 opera *Clari, Maid of Milan* and set to music by Sir Henry Bishop, with lyrics by Payne. It begins with the words: "Mid pleasures and palaces though we may roam, / Be it ever so humble, there's no place like home." The song is used, along with "Rule, Britannia," in Sir Henry Wood's *Fantasia on British Sea Songs.* "There's no place like home" are words spoken by Dorothy in *The Wizard of Oz,* published over a decade before *Peter and Wendy.* Barrie once noted that "Scotch literature" (as he called it) was often "inspired by the domestic hearth and has treated it with a passionate understanding" (*Margaret Ogilvy,* 158).

19. *Then he unbarred the window.* With this gesture, Peter overcomes his own nature and "heartlessness." Moved by Mrs. Darling's tears, he not only feels compassion but also acts on it.

the island and leave Tink to escort the children to the mainland. This trick had been in his head all the time.

Instead of feeling that he was behaving badly he danced with glee; then he peeped into the day-nursery to see who was playing. He whispered to Tink, "It's Wendy's mother. She is a pretty lady, but not so pretty as my mother. Her mouth is full of thimbles, but not so full as my mother's was."

Of course he knew nothing whatever about his mother; but he sometimes bragged about her.

He did not know the tune, which was "Home, Sweet Home,"[18] but he knew it was saying, "Come back, Wendy, Wendy, Wendy"; and he cried exultantly, "You will never see Wendy again, lady, for the window is barred."

He peeped in again to see why the music had stopped; and now he saw that Mrs. Darling had laid her head on the box, and that two tears were sitting on her eyes.

"She wants me to unbar the window," thought Peter, "but I won't, not I."

He peeped again, and the tears were still there, or another two had taken their place.

"She's awfully fond of Wendy," he said to himself. He was angry with her now for not seeing why she could not have Wendy.

The reason was so simple: "I'm fond of her too. We can't both have her, lady."

But the lady would not make the best of it, and he was unhappy. He ceased to look at her, but even then she would not let go of him. He skipped about and made funny faces, but when he stopped it was just as if she were inside him, knocking.

"Oh, all right," he said at last, and gulped. Then he unbarred the window.[19] "Come on, Tink," he cried, with a frightful sneer at the laws of nature; "we don't want any silly mothers"; and he flew away.

Thus Wendy and John and Michael found the window

open for them after all, which of course was more than they deserved. They alighted on the floor, quite unashamed of themselves; and the youngest one had already forgotten his home.

"John," he said, looking around him doubtfully, "I think I have been here before."

"Of course you have, you silly. There is your old bed."

"So it is," Michael said, but not with much conviction.

"I say," cried John, "the kennel!" and he dashed across to look into it.

"Perhaps Nana is inside it," Wendy said.

But John whistled. "Hullo," he said, "there's a man inside it."

"It's father!" exclaimed Wendy.

"Let me see father," Michael begged eagerly, and he took a good look. "He is not so big as the pirate I killed," he said with such frank disappointment that I am glad Mr. Darling was asleep; it would have been sad if those had been the first words he heard his little Michael say.

And then he fired

Wendy and John had been taken aback somewhat at finding their father in the kennel.

"Surely," said John, like one who had lost faith in his memory, "he used not to sleep in the kennel?"

"John," Wendy said falteringly, "perhaps we don't remember the old life as well as we thought we did."

A chill fell upon them; and serve them right.

"It is very careless of mother," said that young scoundrel John, "not to be here when we come back."

It was then that Mrs. Darling began playing again.

"It's mother!" cried Wendy, peeping.

"So it is!" said John.

"Then are you not really our mother, Wendy?" asked Michael, who was surely sleepy.

"Oh dear!" exclaimed Wendy, with her first real twinge of remorse, "it was quite time we came back."

20. *just the dream hanging around her still.* Mrs. Darling herself has trouble distinguishing between dreams and reality, and the boundary between them is as fluid as that between No. 14 and Neverland.

21. *ecstasies innumerable.* The phrase has become Peter Pan's signature, indicating the euphoric quality of childhood experience. The children's joyous reunion with their parents functions as a strong contrast with whatever "ecstasies" Peter feels in Neverland. Curiously, the narrator effaces himself and asserts that Peter Pan is the only witness to this scene, suggesting perhaps that he is one with Pan. Walter Pater, the British essayist and critic whose influence on Barrie's aesthetics is profound, lauded the power of living in the moment and may well have inspired Barrie's use of the term "ecstasies": "To burn always with this hard, gem-like flame, to maintain this ecstasy, is success in life. . . . While all melts under our feet, we may well catch at any exquisite passion" (Pater 152).

"Let us creep in," John suggested, "and put our hands over her eyes."

But Wendy, who saw that they must break the joyous news more gently, had a better plan.

"Let us all slip into our beds, and be there when she comes in, just as if we had never been away."

And so when Mrs. Darling went back to the night-nursery to see if her husband was asleep, all the beds were occupied. The children waited for her cry of joy, but it did not come. She saw them, but she did not believe they were there. You see, she saw them in their beds so often in her dreams that she thought this was just the dream hanging around her still.[20]

She sat down in the chair by the fire, where in the old days she had nursed them.

They could not understand this, and a cold fear fell upon all the three of them.

"Mother!" Wendy cried.

"That's Wendy," she said, but still she was sure it was the dream.

"Mother!"

"That's John," she said.

"Mother!" cried Michael. He knew her now.

"That's Michael," she said, and she stretched out her arms for the three little selfish children they would never envelop again. Yes, they did, they went round Wendy and John and Michael, who had slipped out of bed and run to her.

"George, George," she cried when she could speak; and Mr. Darling woke to share her bliss, and Nana came rushing in. There could not have been a lovelier sight; but there was none to see it except a strange boy who was staring in at the window. He had ecstasies innumerable[21] that other children can never know; but he was looking through the window at the one joy from which he must be for ever barred.

CHAPTER 17

When Wendy Grew Up[1]

I hope you want to know what became of the other boys. They were waiting below to give Wendy time to explain about them; and when they had counted five hundred they went up. They went up by the stair, because they thought this would make a better impression. They stood in a row in front of Mrs. Darling, with their hats off, and wishing they were not wearing their pirate clothes. They said nothing, but their eyes asked her to have them. They ought to have looked at Mr. Darling also, but they forgot about him.

Of course Mrs. Darling said at once that she would have them; but Mr. Darling was curiously depressed, and they saw that he considered six a rather large number.

"I must say," he said to Wendy, "that you don't do things by halves," a grudging remark which the twins thought was pointed at them.

The first twin was the proud one, and he asked, flushing, "Do you think we should be too much of a handful, sir? Because, if so, we can go away."

"Father!" Wendy cried, shocked; but still the cloud was on him. He knew he was behaving unworthily, but he could not help it.

1. *When Wendy Grew Up*. The chapter that follows captures the essence of an epilogue that Barrie added to the production of the play. That scene, called *An Afterthought*, had a run of exactly one night, February 22, 1908, at the Duke of York's Theatre. It began with the appearance of a Baby Mermaid, who announced: "We are now going to do a new act for the first and only time on stage about what happened to Peter when Wendy grew up . . . and it will never be done again." Peter Pan returns to the nursery and is bewildered to discover that Wendy has grown up and has a daughter of her own. Peter quickly recovers from his confusion and spirits little Jane off to Neverland. Barrie stepped forward at the end of the performance (the only time he made an appearance onstage), and the scene met with a fifteen-minute round of applause.

175

2. *a cypher in his own house.* Cypher is the British term for zero. Once again, Mr. Darling sees himself as suffering from neglect and failing to receive attention and respect from his wife and children.

"We could lie doubled up," said Nibs.

"I always cut their hair myself," said Wendy.

"George!" Mrs. Darling exclaimed, pained to see her dear one showing himself in such an unfavourable light.

Then he burst into tears, and the truth came out. He was as glad to have them as she was, he said, but he thought they should have asked his consent as well as hers, instead of treating him as a cypher in his own house.[2]

"I don't think he is a cypher," Tootles cried instantly. "Do you think he is a cypher, Curly?"

"No, I don't. Do you think he is a cypher, Slightly?"

"Rather not. Twin, what do you think?"

It turned out that not one of them thought him a cypher; and he was absurdly gratified, and said he would find space for them all in the drawing-room if they fitted in.

"We'll fit in, sir," they assured him.

"Then follow the leader," he cried gaily. "Mind you, I am not sure that we have a drawing-room, but we pretend we have, and it's all the same. Hoop la!"

He went off dancing through the house, and they all cried "Hoop la!" and danced after him, searching for the drawing-room; and I forget whether they found it, but at any rate they found corners, and they all fitted in.

As for Peter, he saw Wendy once again before he flew away. He did not exactly come to the window, but he brushed against it in passing, so that she could open it if she liked and call to him. That was what she did.

"Hullo, Wendy, good-bye," he said.

"Oh dear, are you going away?"

"Yes."

"You don't feel, Peter," she said falteringly, "that you would like to say anything to my parents about a very sweet subject?"

"No."

"About me, Peter?"

"No."

Mrs. Darling came to the window, for at present she was keeping a sharp eye on Wendy. She told Peter that she had adopted all the other boys, and would like to adopt him also.

"Would you send me to school?" he inquired craftily.

"Yes."

"And then to an office?"

"I suppose so."

"Soon I should be a man?"

"Very soon."

"I don't want to go to school and learn solemn things," he told her passionately. "I don't want to be a man. O Wendy's mother, if I was to wake up and feel there was a beard!"

"Peter," said Wendy the comforter, "I should love you in a beard"; and Mrs. Darling stretched out her arms to him, but he repulsed her.

"Keep back, lady, no one is going to catch me and make me a man."

"But where are you going to live?"

"With Tink in the house we built for Wendy. The fairies are to put it high up among the tree tops where they sleep at nights."

"How lovely," cried Wendy so longingly that Mrs. Darling tightened her grip.

"I thought all the fairies were dead," Mrs. Darling said.

"There are always a lot of young ones," explained Wendy, who was now quite an authority, "because you see when a new baby laughs for the first time a new fairy is born, and as there are always new babies there are always new fairies. They live in nests on the tops of trees; and the mauve ones are boys and the white ones are girls, and the blue ones are just little sillies who are not sure what they are."[3]

"I shall have such fun," said Peter, with one eye on Wendy.

"It will be rather lonely in the evening," she said, "sitting by the fire."

3. *"little sillies who are not sure what they are."* Gender confusion manifests itself in covert ways throughout the text, and here it is articulated in clear terms for the universe of fairies.

4. to let Wendy go to him for a week every year to do his spring cleaning. As noted, Wendy can be seen as a Persephone figure who is lured away from her mother by a male mythical being associated with death. In a neat reversal of the myth, Wendy remains with her mother and returns only briefly to Neverland for spring cleaning. (In the myth, Persephone goes back *home* in the springtime.) Unlike Persephone, Wendy never becomes Peter's wife but becomes a mother herself, blending in with Mrs. Darling and becoming part of a series of mothers and daughters.

"I shall have Tink."

"Tink can't go a twentieth part of the way round," she reminded him a little tartly.

"Sneaky tell-tale!" Tink called out from somewhere round the corner.

"It doesn't matter," Peter said.

"O Peter, you know it matters."

"Well, then, come with me to the little house."

"May I, mummy?"

"Certainly not. I have got you home again, and I mean to keep you."

"But he does so need a mother."

"So do you, my love."

"Oh, all right," Peter said, as if he had asked her from politeness merely; but Mrs. Darling saw his mouth twitch, and she made this handsome offer: to let Wendy go to him for a week every year to do his spring cleaning.[4] Wendy would have preferred a more permanent arrangement; and it seemed to her that spring would be long in coming; but this promise sent Peter away quite gay again. He had no sense of time, and was so full of adventures that all I have told you about him is only a halfpenny-worth of them. I suppose it was because Wendy knew this that her last words to him were these rather plaintive ones:

"You won't forget me, Peter, will you, before spring-cleaning time comes?"

Of course Peter promised; and then he flew away. He took Mrs. Darling's kiss with him. The kiss that had been for no one else, Peter took quite easily. Funny. But she seemed satisfied.

Of course all the boys went to school; and most of them got into Class III, but Slightly was put first into Class IV and then into Class V. Class I is the top class. Before they had attended school a week they saw what goats they had been not to remain on the island; but it was too late now, and soon they settled down to being as ordinary as you or me or Jenkins minor.[5] It is sad to have to say that the power to fly gradually left them. At first Nana tied their feet to the bed-posts so that they should not fly away in the night; and one of their diversions by day was to pretend to fall off 'buses; but by and by they ceased to tug at their bonds in bed, and found that they hurt themselves when they let go of the 'bus. In time they could not even fly after their hats. Want of practice, they called it; but what it really meant was that they no longer believed.

Michael believed longer than the other boys, though they jeered at him; so he was with Wendy when Peter came for her at the end of the first year. She flew away with Peter in the frock she had woven from leaves and berries in the Neverland, and her one fear was that he might notice how short it had become; but he never noticed, he had so much to say about himself.

She had looked forward to thrilling talks with him about old times, but new adventures had crowded the old ones from his mind.

"Who is Captain Hook?" he asked with interest when she spoke of the arch enemy.

"Don't you remember," she asked, amazed, "how you killed him and saved all our lives?"

"I forget them after I kill them," he replied carelessly.[6]

When she expressed a doubtful hope that Tinker Bell would be glad to see her he said, "Who is Tinker Bell?"

"O Peter," she said, shocked; but even when she explained he could not remember.

"There are such a lot of them," he said. "I expect she is no more."

I expect he was right, for fairies don't live long, but they are so little that a short time seems a good while to them.

Wendy was pained too to find that the past year was but as yesterday to Peter; it had seemed such a long year of waiting

5. *Jenkins minor.* In English public schools, the younger or lower in standing of two boys with the same surname is called minor.

6. *"I forget them after I kill them," he replied carelessly.* Peter's amnesia is highlighted here in dramatic fashion. This scene underscores Peter's narcissism ("he had so much to say about himself"), his capriciousness ("new adventures had crowded the old ones from his mind"), and his heartlessness ("Who is Tinker Bell?").

The house in the tree tops. (*Peter Pan and Wendy by J. M. Barrie, Retold for the Nursery by May Byron.* Illustrated by Kathleen Atkins)

to her. But he was exactly as fascinating as ever, and they had a lovely spring cleaning in the little house on the tree tops.

Next year he did not come for her. She waited in a new frock because the old one simply would not meet; but he never came.

"Perhaps he is ill," Michael said.

"You know he is never ill."

Michael came close to her and whispered, with a shiver, "Perhaps there is no such person, Wendy!" and then Wendy would have cried if Michael had not been crying.

Peter came next spring cleaning; and the strange thing was that he never knew he had missed a year.

That was the last time the girl Wendy ever saw him. For a

little longer she tried for his sake not to have growing pains; and she felt she was untrue to him when she got a prize for general knowledge. But the years came and went without bringing the careless boy;[7] and when they met again Wendy was a married woman, and Peter was no more to her than a little dust in the box in which she had kept her toys. Wendy was grown up. You need not be sorry for her. She was one of the kind that likes to grow up. In the end she grew up of her own free will a day quicker than other girls.

All the boys were grown up and done for by this time; so it is scarcely worth while saying anything more about them. You may see the twins and Nibs and Curly any day going to an office, each carrying a little bag and an umbrella. Michael is an engine-driver. Slightly married a lady of title, and so he became a lord.[8] You see that judge in a wig coming out at the iron door? That used to be Tootles. The bearded man who doesn't know any story to tell his children was once John.

Wendy was married in white with a pink sash. It is strange to think that Peter did not alight in the church and forbid the banns.[9]

Years rolled on again, and Wendy had a daughter. This ought not to be written in ink but in a golden splash.[10]

She was called Jane, and always had an odd inquiring look,[11] as if from the moment she arrived on the mainland she wanted to ask questions. When she was old enough to ask them they were mostly about Peter Pan. She loved to hear of Peter, and Wendy told her all she could remember in the very nursery from which the famous flight had taken place. It was Jane's nursery now, for her father had bought it at the three per cents[12] from Wendy's father, who was no longer fond of stairs. Mrs. Darling was now dead and forgotten.[13]

There were only two beds in the nursery now, Jane's and her nurse's; and there was no kennel, for Nana also had passed away. She died of old age, and at the end she had been rather

7. *the careless boy*. The phrase captures Peter as a boy who is both uncaring and without cares. Here Barrie points readers to the consequences of failing to grow up.

8. *he became a lord*. Barrie satirizes the protocols of British aristocracy: when a woman marries a lord, she becomes a lady, but marrying a lady does not result in elevation to the status of lord. In 1913 Barrie became a baronet and henceforth became known as Sir James Barrie, a title that was often shortened to "The Bart" or changed to "the little Baronet." Michael and Nico affectionately referred to him as Sir Jazz Band Barrie or Sir Jazz. Barrie had turned down a knighthood in 1909, but he could not resist assuming this hereditary title.

9. *forbid the banns*. The banns of marriage are the public announcement in a Christian parish church declaring that a marriage will take place between two people.

10. *in a golden splash*. "A million golden arrows" point the way to Neverland, and gold becomes for Barrie the color of beauty and mystery.

11. *an odd inquiring look*. Like Lewis Carroll's Alice, Jane is curious in the double sense of the word, both "odd" (a curiosity) and "inquiring" (curious). It was Lewis Carroll's genius to recognize that children's natural curiosity was something to be promoted and fostered rather than discouraged, as it had been in earlier books for children.

12. *at the three per cents*. Once again, fathers are associated with numbers, accounting, and monetary matters.

13. *Mrs. Darling was now dead and forgotten*. It is not merely in Neverland that memory ceases to do its work. Even in London, at No. 14, memories of forebears fade more

quickly than expected. And the narrator makes a point of emphasizing the speed with which humans heal when faced with loss: "dead" *and* "forgotten." Compare those two terms with the use of "passed away" (in the next paragraph) for Nana.

14. *"What do we see now?"* The precocious Jane, described as an "artful child," recognizes that the "awful darkness" enables her and her mother to develop a form of insight described by Jonathan Swift in his *Thoughts on Various Subjects* (1711): "Vision is the art of seeing things invisible." Nighttime and darkness come to be associated with the power of imagination and storytelling, for reality gives way to a sacred and spectacular inner world, to what is described below as "the great adventure of the night."

difficult to get on with; being very firmly convinced that no one knew how to look after children except herself.

Once a week Jane's nurse had her evening off; and then it was Wendy's part to put Jane to bed. That was the time for stories. It was Jane's invention to raise the sheet over her mother's head and her own, thus making a tent, and in the awful darkness to whisper:

"What do we see now?"[14]

"I don't think I see anything to-night," says Wendy, with a feeling that if Nana were here she would object to further conversation.

"Yes, you do," says Jane, "you see when you were a little girl."

"That is a long time ago, sweetheart," says Wendy. "Ah me, how time flies!"

"Does it fly," asks the artful child, "the way you flew when you were a little girl?"

"The way I flew? Do you know, Jane, I sometimes wonder whether I ever did really fly."

"Yes, you did."

"The dear old days when I could fly!"

"Why can't you fly now, mother?"

"Because I am grown up, dearest. When people grow up they forget the way."

"Why do they forget the way?"

"Because they are no longer gay and innocent and heartless. It is only the gay and innocent and heartless who can fly."

"What is gay and innocent and heartless? I do wish I was gay and innocent and heartless."

Or perhaps Wendy admits she does see something. "I do believe," she says, "that it is this nursery."

"I do believe it is," says Jane. "Go on."

They are now embarked on the great adventure of the night when Peter flew in looking for his shadow.

"The foolish fellow," says Wendy, "tried to stick it on with soap, and when he could not he cried, and that woke me, and I sewed it on for him."

"You have missed a bit," interrupts Jane, who now knows the story better than her mother. "When you saw him sitting on the floor crying, what did you say?"

"I sat up in bed and I said, 'Boy, why are you crying?' "[15]

"Yes, that was it," says Jane, with a big breath.

"And then he flew us all away to the Neverland and the fairies and the pirates and the redskins and the mermaids' lagoon, and the home under the ground, and the little house."

"Yes! which did you like best of all?"

"I think I liked the home under the ground best of all."

"Yes, so do I. What was the last thing Peter ever said to you?"

"The last thing he ever said to me was, 'Just always be waiting for me, and then some night you will hear me crowing.' "

"Yes."

"But, alas, he forgot all about me," Wendy said it with a smile. She was as grown up as that.

"What did his crow sound like?" Jane asked one evening.

"It was like this," Wendy said, trying to imitate Peter's crow.

"No, it wasn't," Jane said gravely, "it was like this"; and she did it ever so much better than her mother.

Wendy was a little startled. "My darling, how can you know?"

"I often hear it when I am sleeping," Jane said.

"Ah yes, many girls hear it when they are sleeping, but I was the only one who heard it awake."

"Lucky you," said Jane.

And then one night came the tragedy. It was the spring of the year, and the story had been told for the night, and Jane was now asleep in her bed. Wendy was sitting on the floor, very close to the fire, so as to see to darn, for there was no other light in the nursery; and while she sat darning she

15. "'*Boy, why are you crying?*'" The end of *Peter and Wendy* takes us back to the very beginning—with an exact repetition of Wendy's query—suggesting that No. 14 may be ruled by the same cyclical time that prevails in Neverland rather than by linear time. These are the same words Jane will use when she is awakened by Peter's sobs.

heard a crow. Then the window blew open as of old, and Peter dropped on the floor.

He was exactly the same as ever, and Wendy saw at once that he still had all his first teeth.

He was a little boy, and she was grown up. She huddled by the fire not daring to move, helpless and guilty, a big woman.

"Hullo, Wendy," he said, not noticing any difference, for he was thinking chiefly of himself; and in the dim light her white dress might have been the nightgown in which he had seen her first.

"Hullo, Peter," she replied faintly, squeezing herself as small as possible. Something inside her was crying "Woman, Woman, let go of me."

"Hullo, where is John?" he asked, suddenly missing the third bed.

"John is not here now," she gasped.

"Is Michael asleep?" he asked, with a careless glance at Jane.

"Yes," she answered; and now she felt that she was untrue to Jane as well as to Peter.

"That is not Michael," she said quickly, lest a judgment should fall on her.

Peter looked. "Hullo, is it a new one?"

"Yes."

"Boy or girl?"

"Girl."

Now surely he would understand; but not a bit of it.

"Peter," she said, faltering, "are you expecting me to fly away with you?"

"Of course that is why I have come." He added a little sternly, "Have you forgotten that this is spring-cleaning time?"

She knew it was useless to say that he had let many spring-cleaning times pass.

"I can't come," she said apologetically, "I have forgotten how to fly."

"I'll soon teach you again."

"O Peter, don't waste the fairy dust on me."

She had risen; and now at last a fear assailed him. "What is it?" he cried, shrinking.

"I will turn up the light," she said, "and then you can see for yourself."

For almost the only time in his life that I know of, Peter was afraid. "Don't turn up the light," he cried.

She let her hands play in the hair of the tragic boy. She was not a little girl heart-broken about him; she was a grown woman smiling at it all, but they were wet smiles.

Then she turned up the light, and Peter saw. He gave a cry of pain; and when the tall beautiful creature stooped to lift him in her arms he drew back sharply.

"What is it?" he cried again.

She had to tell him.

"I am old, Peter. I am ever so much more than twenty. I grew up long ago."

"You promised not to!"

"I couldn't help it. I am a married woman, Peter."

"No, you're not."

"Yes, and the little girl in the bed is my baby."

"No, she's not."

But he supposed she was; and he took a step towards the sleeping child with his dagger upraised. Of course he did not strike. He sat down on the floor instead and sobbed; and Wendy did not know how to comfort him, though she could have done it so easily once. She was only a woman now, and she ran out of the room to try to think.

Peter continued to cry, and soon his sobs woke Jane. She sat up in bed, and was interested at once.

"Boy," she said, "why are you crying?"

16. *with a daughter called Margaret.* The last girl in the series is named after Barrie's mother, Margaret Ogilvy. In the biography of his mother, Barrie closes with a moving description of his mother's death and imagines the vision of her that will greet him when he dies: "And if I also live to a time when age must dim my mind and the past comes sweeping back like the shades of night over the bare road of the present it will not, I believe, be my youth I shall see here, not a boy clinging to his mother's skirts and crying, 'Wait till I'm a man, and you'll lie on feathers,' but a little girl in a magenta frock and a white pinafore, who comes toward me through the long parks, singing to herself, and carrying her father's dinner in a flagon" (207).

Peter rose and bowed to her, and she bowed to him from the bed.

"Hullo," he said.

"Hullo," said Jane.

"My name is Peter Pan," he told her.

"Yes, I know."

"I came back for my mother," he explained, "to take her to the Neverland."

"Yes, I know," Jane said, "I have been waiting for you."

When Wendy returned diffidently she found Peter sitting on the bed-post crowing gloriously, while Jane in her nighty was flying round the room in solemn ecstasy.

"She is my mother," Peter explained; and Jane descended and stood by his side, with the look in her face that he liked to see on ladies when they gazed at him.

"He does so need a mother," Jane said.

"Yes, I know," Wendy admitted rather forlornly; "no one knows it so well as I."

"Good-bye," said Peter to Wendy; and he rose in the air, and the shameless Jane rose with him; it was already her easiest way of moving about.

Wendy rushed to the window.

"No, no," she cried.

"It is just for spring-cleaning time," Jane said, "he wants me always to do his spring cleaning."

"If only I could go with you," Wendy sighed.

"You see you can't fly," said Jane.

Of course in the end Wendy let them fly away together. Our last glimpse of her shows her at the window, watching them receding into the sky until they were as small as stars.

As you look at Wendy you may see her hair becoming white, and her figure little again, for all this happened long ago. Jane is now a common grown-up, with a daughter called Margaret;[16] and every spring-cleaning time, except when he forgets, Peter comes for Margaret and takes her to the Neverland, where she tells him stories about himself, to which he listens eagerly. When Margaret grows up she will have a daughter, who is to be Peter's mother in turn; and thus it will go on, so long as children are gay and innocent and heartless.[17]

THE END

17. *gay and innocent and heartless*. With the addition of the term *heartless*, Barrie captured a change in the cultural understanding of childhood. The Victorian cult of the innocent child had done a real disservice by idealizing boys and girls, swaddling them in a serenity that denied their bright energy, their instinct for play, and their bolting curiosity. At the turn of the century, Freud was adding weight to childhood by seeing in its traumas the source of adult pathologies. Barrie, by contrast, introduced the idea of lightness and lack of gravity, uncorking the energy of children everywhere. His children can fly, and while they may be characterized by a form of flightiness and the inability to care and commit, they have finally been liberated from the pedestal on which they had been required to sit obediently still.

J. M. Barrie's
The Boy Castaways of Black Lake Island

*T*he Boy Castaways of Black Lake Island offers us the first real glimpse of Peter Pan. With its lost boys and savage pirate captain, its protective dog watching over sleeping children, and its mysterious boy described as "the sly one, the chief figure, who draws farther and farther into the wood as we advance upon him," it is the Ur–*Peter Pan,* the book that gave birth to the boy who would not grow up. Barrie writes in the preface to *Peter Pan* that the "little people" of his play all seem to emerge from the adventures recorded in a volume that he declared to be the "best and the rarest" of his works.

The Beinecke Rare Book and Manuscript Library in New Haven, Connecticut, now has the sole remaining copy of *The Boy Castaways of Black Lake Island.* Thanks to the generous cooperation of the curators and staff, all of the photographs and captions are presented here for the first time in print. These pages reveal how Peter Pan was born from the spirit of play, pantomime, and performance and show James Barrie, his dog Porthos, and three of the Llewelyn Davies boys in starring roles. In looking at illustrations that are in many ways a true curiosity, we discover how the adventures of Peter Pan and the Darling children in Neverland were a joint production, a creative collaboration joining an adult's desire to remain forever young with the child's wish to explore and experience perils in ways that only grown-ups can.

In the summer of 1901, Arthur and Sylvia Llewelyn Davies rented a cottage in Tilford, just minutes away from Black Lake Cottage, where James Barrie and his wife, Mary, were spending the summer. Barrie had spent most of June and July working on his play *Quality Street*, and he sent it off to Charles Frohman in New York just when the Davieses were settling into their cottage. Enacting a shipwreck on the "high seas" of Black Lake Island and recreating the desert island adventures described in R. M. Ballantyne's *Coral Island* with the Llewelyn Davies boys proved a therapeutic alternative for Barrie to writing. At the time, Barrie was also occasionally making mental notes for his novel *The Little White Bird*, containing the first mention of Peter Pan, and for *The Admirable Crichton*, a play about the democratizing effects of a shipwreck. But he was also immersed in the role of Captain Swarthy, a dark and sinister pirate equal to Captain Hook. George, Jack, and Peter Davies were the principal players, for Michael was still a baby and Nico had not yet been born.

For much of August, Barrie and the boys sailed on the *Anna Pink*, sharpened spears, built a hut, explored primeval forests, and killed a tiger. Eventually they sailed home for England. At the end of the summer, Barrie produced a book documenting the adventures, attributing its authorship to Peter Llewelyn Davies. He had two copies printed, one for himself and one that he gave to the boys' father, who promptly lost it on a train. Peter, as noted earlier, saw the loss of the book as his father's "way of commenting on the whole fantastic affair" and showing his disdain for the man who had become a powerful competitor for the affections of his wife and children. Barrie gave the sole remaining copy to Jack. When Arthur Llewelyn Davies was bedridden after the surgery in which his jaw was removed, he asked for the book, and it was dispatched to him at once.

The Beinecke Library at Yale University now owns this sole surviving copy of the volume. On the flyleaf, Barrie wrote a dedication: "S Ll D & A Ll D from JMB." Years later he added: "There was one other copy of this book only and it was lost in a railway train in 1901. JMB 1933."

The full title of the volume reads: *The Boy Castaways of Black Lake Island, being a record of the terrible adventures of the brothers Davies in the Summer of 1901, faithfully set forth by Peter Llewelyn Davies*. The place of publication is given as London, and "J. M. Barrie in the Gloucester Road" is listed as the publisher. In actuality, Constable in Edinburgh printed the volume. *The Boy Castaways* appears in its entirety in the pages that follow, with captioned images after a dedication, a preface, and very brief, telegram-style chapters.

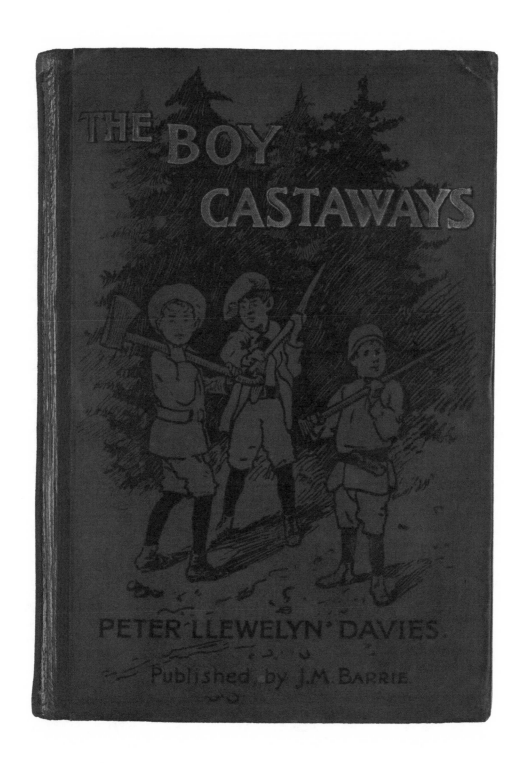

Dedication

TO OUR MOTHER
In cordial recognition
of her efforts
to elevate us
above the brutes

PREFACE

I have been requested by my brothers to write a few words of introduction to this little volume, and I comply with pleasure, though well aware that others may be better acquitted for the task.

The strange happenings here set forth with a *currente calamo* are expansions of a note-book kept by me while we were on the island, but I have thought fit, in exercise of my prerogative as general editor, to omit certain observations with regard to *flora*, *fauna*, etc., which, however valuable to myself and to others of scientific bent, would probably have but a limited interest to the lay mind. I have also in this edition excluded a chapter on *strata* as caviare to the general.

The date on which we were wrecked was this year on August 1, 1901, and I have still therefore a vivid recollection of that strange and terrible summer, when we suffered experiences such as have probably never before been experienced by three brothers. At this time the eldest, George, was eight and a month. Jack was approaching his seventh *lustrum*, and I was a good bit past four. Perhaps a few words about my companions on the island will not be deemed out of place.

George was a fine, fearless youth, and had now been a term at Wilkinson's. He was modest withal. His chief fault was wanting to do all the shooting, and carrying the arrows inside his shirt with that selfish object. Jack is also brave as a lion, but he also has many faults, and he has a weakness (perhaps pardonable) for a pretty face (bless them!). Of Peter I prefer to say nothing, hoping that the tale, as it is unwound, will show that he was a boy of deeds rather than of words, which was another of Jack's blemishes. In conclusion, I should say that the work was in the first instance compiled as a record simply, at which we could whet our memories, and that it is now published for Michael's benefit. If it teaches him by example lessons in fortitude and manly endurance, we shall consider that we were not wrecked in vain.

PETER LLEWELYN DAVIES

CONTENTS

CHAPTER I

Early Days—Our Amusing Mother—Her Indiscretions.

CHAPTER II

Schools and Schoolmasters—Mary's Bullying Ways—George teaches Wilkinson a Stern Lesson—We run away to Sea.

CHAPTER III

A Fearful Hurricane—Wreck of the *Anna Pink*—The Longboat—We go crazy from Want of Food—Proposal to eat Peter—Land ahoy!

CHAPTER IV

First Night on Black Lake Island—A Horrible Discovery— The Bread-fruit Tree—Monkeys and Cocoanuts—Turning a Turtle.

CHAPTER V

Gallant Behaviour of Jack—We make Bows and Arrows—We set about the Building of a Hut.

CHAPTER VI

Tree-cutting—Madame Bruin and her Cubs—George to the Rescue—Pig-sticking and its Dangers.

CHAPTER VII

We finish the Hut—George and Jack set off on a Voyage of Exploration round the Island—Primeval Forests—Night in the Woods—Startling Discovery that the Island is the Haunt of Captain Swarthy and his Pirate Crew.

CHAPTER VIII

Dead Men's Point—Corpsy Glen—The Valley of Rolling Stones.

CHAPTER IX

Exploration continued—We find Captain Swarthy's Dog—Suspended Animation—We are attacked by Wolves—Jack saves George's Life.

CHAPTER X

The Hut meanwhile—The Pirates set upon Peter—"Shut up"—Peter is sentenced to walk the Plank—Timely Arrival of George and Jack.

CHAPTER XI

We board the Pirate Sloop at Dawn—A Rakish Craft—George Hew-them-down and Jack of the Red Hatchet—A Holocaust of Pirates—Rescue of Peter.

CHAPTER XII

Trial of Captain Swarthy—He begs for mercy—We string him up.

CHAPTER XIII

The Rainy Season—Malarial Fever—A ship in the Offing—Disappointment nobly borne.

CHAPTER XIV

We build a boat—Narrow Escape from a Tiger—Skinning the Tiger.

CHAPTER XV

The Pleasures of Tobacco—Peter's Dream of Home—Last Night on the Island—We set sail for England, Home, and Wilkinson's.

CHAPTER XVI

Concluding Remarks—Advice to Parents about the bringing up of their Children.

We set out to be wrecked. (Beinecke Rare Book and Manuscript Library)

Michael wished us luck by waving his foot. (Beinecke Rare Book and Manuscript Library)

We were the sole survivors of the ill-fated brig *Anna Pink*. (Beinecke Rare Book and Manuscript Library)

It was a coral island glistening in the sun. (Beinecke Rare Book and Manuscript Library)

We made ourselves a rude shelter for the night. (Beinecke Rare Book and Manuscript Library)

The first night on the island fell very dark and mysterious.
(Beinecke Rare Book and Manuscript Library)

It was George waiting for the dawn with one hand upon his dagger. (Beinecke Rare Book and Manuscript Library)

George at once recognised it to be the Mango (*Mangifera Indica*) by its lancet-shaped leaves and the cucumber-shaped fruit. (Beinecke Rare Book and Manuscript Library)

It was the pirate Swarthy's dog patrolling the island. (Beinecke Rare Book and Manuscript Library)

We prepared for the pirates by making spears and other trusty weapons. (Beinecke Rare Book and Manuscript Library)

While Jack was removing the crocodiles from the stream, George shot a few parrots (*Psittacidae*) for our mid-day meal. (Beinecke Rare Book and Manuscript Library)

We begin the building of the hut. (Beinecke Rare Book and Manuscript Library)

After three weeks of incessant toil, the hut approached completion. (Beinecke Rare Book and Manuscript Library)

A last pipe before turning in. (Beinecke Rare Book and Manuscript Library)

We set off in our crazy craft for an exploration of the island. (Beinecke Rare Book and Manuscript Library)

"It is undoubtedly," said George, "the *cocos nucifera*, for observe the slender columns supporting the crown of leaves which fall with a grace that no art can imitate." (Beinecke Rare Book and Manuscript Library)

We pulled each other up the Valley of Rolling Stones. (Beinecke Rare Book and Manuscript Library)

Jack hung suspended between heaven and earth. (Beinecke Rare Book and Manuscript Library)

Deeper and deeper into those primeval forests. (Beinecke Rare Book and Manuscript Library)

The dog of a pirate had seen us. (Beinecke Rare Book and Manuscript Library)

"Surrender, or die!" (Beinecke Rare Book and Manuscript Library)

We trained the dog to watch over us while we slept. (Beinecke Rare Book and Manuscript Library)

"Truly," said George, "though the perils of these happenings are great, yet would I rejoice to endure still greater privations to be thus rewarded by such wondrous studies of nature." (Beinecke Rare Book and Manuscript Library)

We return to the hut. (Beinecke Rare Book and Manuscript Library)

They had to sit outside, because their brother was within
singing, and playing on a barbaric instrument. "The music,"
said Peter, "is rude, and to a cultivated ear discordant; but
the songs, like those of the Arab, are full of poetic imagery."
(Beinecke Rare Book and Manuscript Library)

George found himself within four paces of a tiger. (Beinecke Rare Book and Manuscript Library)

George struck at him, but missed. (Beinecke Rare Book and Manuscript Library)

We had pierced him in his vulnerable part. (Beinecke Rare Book and Manuscript Library)

We carried home the head and skin as trophies. (Beinecke Rare Book and Manuscript Library)

The pirate Swarthy came rushing upon us, armed to the teeth.
(Beinecke Rare Book and Manuscript Library)

We strung him up. (Beinecke Rare Book and Manuscript Library)

"See, brother," said Jack excitedly, "'tis the vultures swooping upon their prey." (Beinecke Rare Book and Manuscript Library)

They had picked him clean. (Beinecke Rare Book and Manuscript Library)

Last night on the island. (Beinecke Rare Book and Manuscript Library)

We set sail for England, Home, and Wilkinson's. (Beinecke Rare Book and Manuscript Library)

"To the Five, a Dedication": J. M. Barrie's Introduction to the Play *Peter Pan*

Some disquieting confessions must be made in printing at last the play of *Peter Pan*; among them this, that I have no recollection of having written it. Of that, however, anon. What I want to do first is to give Peter to the Five without whom he never would have existed. I hope, my dear sirs, that in memory of what we have been to each other you will accept this dedication with your friend's love. The play of Peter is streaky with you still, though none may see this save ourselves. A score of Acts had to be left out, and you were in them all. We first brought Peter down, didn't we, with a blunt-headed arrow in Kensington Gardens? I seem to remember that we believed we had killed him, though he was only winded, and that after a spasm of exultation in our prowess the more soft-hearted among us wept and all of us thought of the police. There was not one of you who would not have sworn as an eye-witness to this occurrence; no doubt I was abetting, but you used to provide corroboration that was never given to you by me. As for myself, I suppose I always knew that I made Peter by rubbing the five of you violently together, as savages with two sticks produce a flame. That is all he is, the spark I got from you.

We had good sport of him before we clipped him small to make him fit the boards. Some of you were not born when the story began and yet were hefty figures before we saw that the game was up. Do you remember a garden at Burpham and the initiation there of No. 4 [Michael] when he was six weeks old, and three of you grudged letting him in so young? Have you, No. 3 [Peter], forgotten the white violets at the Cistercian abbey in which we cassocked our first fairies (all little friends of St. Benedict), or your cry to the Gods, "Do I just kill one pirate all the time?" Do you remember Marooners' Hut in the haunted groves of Waverley, and the St. Bernard dog in a tiger's mask who so frequently attacked you, and the literary record of that summer, *The Boy Castaways*, which is so much the best and the rarest of this author's works? What was it that made us eventually give to the public in the thin form of a play that which had been woven for ourselves alone? Alas, I know what it was, I was losing my grip. One by one as you swung monkey-wise from branch to branch in the wood of make-believe you reached the tree of knowledge. Sometimes you swung back into the wood, as the unthinking may at a crossroad take a familiar path that no longer leads to home; or you perched ostentatiously on its boughs to please me, pretending that you still belonged; soon you knew it only as the vanished wood, for it vanishes if one needs to look for it. A time came when I saw that No. 1 [George], the most gallant of you all, ceased to believe that he was ploughing woods incarnadine, and with an apologetic eye for me derided the lingering faith of No. 2 [Jack]; when even No. 3 questioned gloomily whether he did not really spend his nights in bed. There were still two who knew no better, but their day was dawning. In these circumstances, I suppose, was begun the writing of the play of Peter. That was a quarter of a century ago, and I clutch my brows in vain to remember whether it was a last desperate throw to retain the five of you for a little longer, or merely a cold decision to turn you into bread and butter.

This brings us back to my uncomfortable admission that I have no recollection of writing the play of *Peter Pan*, now being published for the first time so long after he made his bow upon the stage. You had played it until you tired of it, and tossed it in the air and gored it and left it derelict in the mud and went on your way singing other songs; and then I stole back and sewed some of the gory fragments together with a pen-nib. That is what must have happened, but I cannot remember doing it. I remember writing the story of *Peter and Wendy* many years after the production of the play, but I might have cribbed that from some typed copy. I can haul back to mind the writing of almost every other assay of mine, however forgotten by the pretty public; but this play of Peter, no. Even my beginning as an amateur playwright, that noble mouthful, *Bandelero the Bandit*, I remember every detail of its composition in my school days at Dumfries. Not less vivid is my first little piece, produced by Mr. Toole. It was called *Ibsen's Ghost*, and was a parody of the mightiest craftsman that ever wrote for our kind friends in front. To save the management the cost of typing I wrote out the "parts," after being told what parts were, and I can still recall my first words, spoken so plaintively by a now famous actress,—"To run away from my second husband just as I ran away from my first, it feels quite like old times." On the first night a man in the pit found *Ibsen's Ghost* so diverting that he had to be removed in hysterics. After that no one seems to have thought of it at all. But what a man to carry about with one! How odd, too, that these trifles should adhere to the mind that cannot remember the long job of writing Peter. It does seem almost suspicious, especially as I have not the original MS of *Peter Pan* (except a few stray pages) with which to support my claim. I have indeed another MS, lately made, but that "proves nothing." I know not whether I lost that original MS or destroyed it or happily gave it away. I talk of dedicating the play to you, but how can I prove it is mine? How ought I to act if some other hand, who could also have made a copy, thinks it worth while to contest the cold rights? Cold they are to me now as that laughter of yours in which Peter came into being long before he was caught and written down. There is Peter still, but to me he lies sunk in the gay Black Lake.

Any one of you five brothers has a better claim to the authorship than most, and I would not fight you for it, but you should have launched your case long ago in the days when you most admired me, which were in the first year of the play, owing to a rumour's reaching you that my spoils were one-and-sixpence a night. This was untrue, but it did give me a standing among you. You watched for my next play with peeled eyes, not for entertainment but lest it contained some chance witticism of yours that could be challenged as collaboration; indeed I believe there still exists a legal document, full of the Aforesaid and Henceforward to be called Part-Author, in which for some such snatching I was tied down to pay No. 2 one halfpenny daily throughout the run of the piece.

During the rehearsals of Peter (and it is evidence in my favour that I was admitted to them) a depressed man in overalls, carrying a mug of tea or a paint-pot, used often to appear by my side in the shadowy stalls and say to me, "The gallery boys won't stand it." He then mysteriously faded away as if he were the theatre ghost. This hopelessness of his is what all dramatists are said to feel at such times, so perhaps he was the author. Again, a large number of children whom I have seen playing Peter in their homes with careless mastership, constantly putting in better words, could have thrown it off with ease. It was for such as they that after the first production I had to add something to the play at the request of parents (who thus showed that they thought me the responsible person) about no one being able to fly until the fairy dust had been blown on him; so many children having gone home and tried it from their beds and needed surgical attention.

Notwithstanding other possibilities, I think I wrote Peter, and if so it must have been in the usual inky way. Some of it, I like to think, was done in that native place which is the dearest spot on earth to me, though my last heart-beats shall be with my beloved solitary London that was so hard to reach. I must have sat at a table with that great dog waiting for me to stop, not complaining, for he knew it was thus we made our living, but giving me a look when he found he was to be in the play, with his sex changed. In after years when the actor who was Nana had to go to the wars he first taught his wife how to take his place as the dog till he came back, and I am glad that I see nothing funny in this; it seems to me to belong to the play. I offer this obtuseness on my part as my first proof that I am the author.

Some say that we are different people at different periods of our lives, changing not through effort of will, which is a brave affair, but in the easy course of nature every ten years or so. I suppose this theory might explain my present trouble, but I don't hold with it; I think one remains the same person throughout, merely passing, as it were, in these lapses of time from one room to another, but all in the same house. If we unlock the rooms of the far past we can peer in and see ourselves, busily occupied in beginning to become you and me. Thus, if I am the author in question the way he is to go should already be showing in the occupant of my first compartment, at whom I now take the liberty to peep. Here he is at the age of seven or so with his fellow-conspirator Robb, both in glengarry bonnets. They are giving an entertainment in a tiny old washing-house that still stands. The charge for admission is preens, a bool, or a peerie (I taught you a good deal of Scotch, so possibly you can follow that), and apparently the culminating Act consists in our trying to put each other into the boiler, though some say that I also addressed the spell-bound audience. This washing-house is not only the theatre of my first play, but has a still closer connection with Peter. It is the original of the little house the Lost Boys built in the Never Land for Wendy, the chief difference being that it never wore John's tall hat as a chimney. If Robb had owned a lum hat I have no doubt that it would have been placed on the washing-house.

Here is that boy again some four years older, and the reading he is munching feverishly is about desert islands; he calls them wrecked islands. He buys his sanguinary tales surreptitiously in penny numbers. I see a change coming over him; he is blanching as he reads in the high-class magazine, *Chatterbox*, a fulmination against such literature, and sees that unless his greed for islands is quenched he is for ever lost. With gloaming he steals out of the house, his library bulging beneath his palpitating waistcoat. I follow like his shadow, as indeed I am, and watch him dig a hole in a field at Pathhead farm and bury his islands in it; it was ages ago, but I could walk straight to that hole in the field now and delve for the remains. I peep into the next compartment. There he is again, ten years older, an undergraduate now and craving to be a real explorer, one of those who do things instead of prating of them, but otherwise unaltered; he might be painted at twenty on top of a mast, in his hand a spy-glass through which he rakes the horizon for an elusive strand. I go from room to room, and he is now a man, real exploration abandoned (though only because no one would have him). Soon he is even concocting other plays, and quaking a little lest some low person counts how many islands there are in them. I note that with the years the islands grow more sinister, but it is only because he has now to write with the left hand, the right having given out; evidently one thinks more darkly down the left arm. Go to the keyhole of the compartment where he and I join up, and you may see us wondering whether they would stand one more island. This journey through the house may not convince any one that I wrote Peter, but it does suggest me as a likely person. I pause to ask myself whether I read *Chatterbox* again, suffered the old agony, and buried that MS of the play in a hole in a field.

Of course this is over-charged. Perhaps we do change; except a little something in us which is no larger than a mote in the eye, and that, like it, dances in front of us beguiling us all our days. I cannot cut the hair by which it hangs.

The strongest evidence that I am the author is to be found, I think, in a now melancholy volume, the aforementioned *The Boy Castaways*; so you must excuse me for parading that work here. Officer of the Court, call *The Boy Castaways*. The witness steps forward and proves to be a book you remember well though you have not glanced at it these many years. I pulled it out of a bookcase just now not without difficulty, for its recent occupation has been to support the shelf above. I suppose, though I am uncertain, that it was I and not you who hammered it into that place of utility. It is a little battered and bent after the manner of those who shoulder burdens, and ought (to our shame) to remind us of the witnesses who sometimes get an hour off from the cells to give evidence before his Lordship. I have said that it is the rarest of my printed works, as it must be, for the only edition was limited to two copies, of which one (there was always some devilry in any matter connected with Peter) instantly lost itself in a railway carriage. This is the survivor. The idlers in court may have assumed that it is a handwritten screed, and are impressed by its bulk. It is printed by Constable's (how handsomely you did us, dear Blaikie), it contains thirty-five illustrations and is bound in cloth with a picture stamped on the cover of the three eldest of you "setting out to be wrecked." This record is supposed to be edited by the youngest of the three, and I must have granted him that honour to make up for his being so often lifted bodily out of our adventures by his nurse, who kept breaking into them for the fell purpose of giving him a mid-day rest. No. 4 rested so much at this period that he was merely an honorary member of the band, waving his foot to you for luck when you set off with bow and arrow to shoot his dinner for him; and one may rummage the book in vain for any trace of No. 5 [Nico]. Here is the title-page, except that you are numbered instead of named—

THE BOY
CASTAWAYS
OF BLACK LAKE ISLAND
Being a record of the Terrible
Adventures of Three Brothers
in the summer of 1901
faithfully set forth
by No. 3.

LONDON
Published by J. M. Barrie
in the Gloucester Road
1901

There is a long preface by No. 3 in which we gather your ages at this first flight. "No. 1 was eight and a month, No. 2 was approaching his seventh *lustrum*, and I was a good bit past four." Of his two elders, while commending their fearless dispositions, the editor complains that they wanted to do all the shooting and carried the whole equipment of arrows inside their shirts. He is attractively modest about himself, "Of No. 3 I prefer to say nothing, hoping that the tale as it is unwound will show that he was a boy of deeds rather than of words," a quality which he hints did not unduly protrude upon the brows of Nos. 1 and 2. His preface ends on a high note, "I should say that the work was in the first instance compiled as a record simply at which we could whet our memories, and that it is now published for No. 4's benefit. If it teaches him by example lessons in fortitude and manly endurance we shall consider that we were not wrecked in vain."

Published to whet your memories. Does it whet them? Do you hear once more, like some long-forgotten whistle beneath your window (Robb at dawn calling me to the fishing!) the not quite mortal blows that still echo in some of the chapter headings?—"Chapter II, No. 1 teaches Wilkinson (his master) a Stern Lesson—We Run away to Sea. Chapter III, A Fearful Hurricane—Wreck of the *Anna Pink*—We go crazy from Want of Food—Proposal to eat No. 3—Land Ahoy." Such are two chapters out of sixteen. Are these again your javelins cutting tunes in the blue haze of the pines; do you sweat as you scale the dreadful Valley of Rolling Stones, and cleanse your hands of pirate blood by scouring them carelessly in Mother Earth? Can you still make a fire (you could do it once, Mr. Seton-Thompson taught us in, surely an odd place, the Reform Club) by rubbing those sticks together? Was it the travail of hut-building that subsequently advised Peter to find a "home under the ground"? The bottle and mugs in that lurid picture, "Last night on the Island," seem to suggest that you had changed from Lost Boys into pirates, which was probably also a tendency of Peter's. Listen again to our stolen saw-mill, man's proudest invention; when he made the saw-mill he beat the birds for music in a wood.

The illustrations (full-paged) in *The Boy Castaways* are all photographs taken by myself; some of them indeed of phenomena that had to be invented afterwards, for you were always off doing the wrong things when I pressed the button. I see that we combined instruction with amusement; perhaps we had given our kingly word to that effect. How otherwise account for such wording to the pictures as these: "It is undoubtedly," says No. 1 in a fir tree that is bearing unwonted fruit, recently tied to it, "the *Cocos nucifera*, for observe the slender columns supporting the crown of leaves which fall with a grace that no art can imitate." "Truly," continues No. 1 under the same tree in another forest as he leans upon his trusty gun, "though the perils of these happenings are great, yet would I rejoice to endure still greater privations to be thus rewarded by such wondrous studies of Nature." He is soon back to the practical, however, "recognising the Mango (*Mangifera indica*) by its lancet-shaped leaves and the cucumber-shaped fruit." No. 1 was certainly the right sort of voyager to be wrecked with, though if my memory fails me not, No. 2, to whom these strutting observations were addressed, sometimes protested because none of them was given to him. No. 3 being the author is in surprisingly few of the pictures, but this, you may remember, was because the lady already darkly referred to used to pluck him from our midst for his siesta at 12 o'clock, which was the hour that best suited the camera. With a skill on which he has never been complimented the photographer sometimes got No. 3 nominally included in a wild-life picture when he was really in a humdrum house kicking on the sofa. Thus in a scene representing Nos. 1 and 2 sitting scowling outside the hut it is untruly written that they scowled because "their brother was within singing and playing on a barbaric instrument. The music," the unseen No. 3 is represented as saying (obviously forestalling No. 1), "is rude and to a cultured ear discordant, but the songs like those of the Arabs are full of poetic imagery." He was perhaps allowed to say this sulkily on the sofa.

Though *The Boy Castaways* has sixteen chapter-headings, there is no other letterpress; an absence which possible purchasers might complain of, though there are surely worse ways of writing a book than this. These headings anticipate much of the play of *Peter Pan*, but there were many incidents of our Kensington Gardens days that never got into the book, such as our Antarctic exploits when we reached the Pole in advance of our friend Captain Scott and cut our initials on it for him to find, a strange foreshadowing of what was really to happen. In *The Boy Castaways* Captain Hook has arrived but is called Captain Swarthy, and he seems from the pictures to have been a black man. This character, as you do not need to be told, is held by those in the know to be autobiographical. You had many tussles with him (though you never, I think, got his right arm) before you reached the terrible chapter (which might be taken from the play) entitled "We Board the Pirate Ship at Dawn—A Rakish Craft—No. 1 Hew-them-Down and No. 2 of the Red Hatchet—A Holocaust of Pirates—Rescue of Peter." (Hullo, Peter rescued instead of rescuing others? I know what that means and so do you, but we are not going to give away all our secrets.) The scene of the Holocaust is the Black Lake (afterwards, when we let women in, the Mermaids' Lagoon). The pirate captain's end was not in the mouth of a crocodile though we had crocodiles on the spot ("while No. 2 was removing the crocodiles from the stream No. 1 shot a few parrots, *Psittacidae*, for our evening meal"). I think our captain had divers deaths owing to unseemly competition among you, each wanting to slay him single-handed. On a special occasion, such as when No. 3 pulled out the tooth himself, you gave the deed to him, but took it from him while he rested. The only pictorial representation in the book of Swarthy's fate is in two parts. In one, called briefly "We string him up," Nos. 1 and 2, stern as Athos, are hauling him up a tree by a rope, his face snarling as if it were a grinning mask (which indeed it was), and his garments very like some of my own stuffed with bracken. The other, the same scene next day, is called "The Vultures had Picked him Clean," and tells its own tale.

The dog in *The Boy Castaways* seems never to have been called Nana but was evidently in training for that post. He originally belonged to Swarthy (or to Captain Marryat?), and the first picture of him, lean, skulking, and hunched (how did I get that effect?), "patrolling the island" in that monster's interests, gives little indication of the domestic paragon he was to become. We lured him away to the better life, and there is, later, a touching picture, a clear forecast of the Darling nursery, entitled "We trained the dog to watch over us while we slept." In this he also is sleeping, in a position that is a careful copy of his charges; indeed any trouble we had with him was because, once he knew he was in a story, he thought his safest course was to imitate you in everything you did. How anxious he was to show that he understood the game, and more generous than you, he never pretended that he was the one who killed Captain Swarthy. I must not imply that he was entirely without initiative, for it was his own idea to bark warningly a minute or two before twelve o'clock as a signal to No. 3 that his keeper was probably on her way for him (Disappearance of No. 3); and he became so used to living in the world of Pretend that when we reached the hut of a morning he was often there waiting for us, looking, it is true, rather idiotic, but with a new bark he had invented which puzzled us until we decided that he was demanding the password. He was always willing to do any extra jobs, such as becoming the tiger in mask, and when after a fierce engagement you carried home that mask in triumph, he joined in the procession proudly and never let on that the trophy had ever been part of him. Long afterwards he saw the play from a box in the theatre, and as familiar scenes were unrolled before his eyes I have never seen a dog so bothered. At one matinee we even let him for a moment take the place of the actor who played Nana, and I don't know that any members of the audience ever noticed the change, though he introduced some "business" that was new to them but old to you and me. Heigh-ho, I suspect that in this reminiscence I am mixing him up with his successor, for such a one there had to be, the loyal Newfoundland who, perhaps in the following year, applied, so to say, for the part by bringing hedgehogs to the hut in his mouth as offerings for our evening repasts. The head and coat of him were copied for the Nana of the play.

They do seem to be emerging out of our island, don't they, the little people of the play, all except that sly one, the chief figure, who draws farther and farther into the wood as we advance upon him? He so dislikes being tracked, as if there were something odd about him, that when he dies he means to get up and blow away the particle that will be his ashes.

Wendy has not yet appeared, but she has been trying to come ever since that loyal nurse cast the humorous shadow of woman upon the scene and made us feel that it might be fun to let in a disturbing element. Perhaps she would have bored her way in at last whether we wanted her or not. It may be that even Peter did not really bring her to the Never Land of his free will, but merely pretended to do so because she would not stay away. Even Tinker Bell had reached our island before we left it. It was one evening when we climbed the wood carrying No. 4 to show him what the trail was like by twilight. As our lanterns twinkled among the leaves No. 4 saw a twinkle stand still for a moment and he waved his foot gaily to it, thus creating Tink. It must not be thought, however, that there were any other sentimental passages between No. 4 and Tink; indeed, as he got to know her better he suspected her of frequenting the hut to see what we had been having for supper, and to partake of the same, and he pursued her with malignancy.

A safe but sometimes chilly way of recalling the past is to force open a crammed drawer. If you are searching for anything in particular you don't find it, but something falls out at the back that is often more interesting. It is in this way that I get my desultory reading, which includes the few stray leaves of the original MS of Peter that I have said I do possess, though even they, when returned to the drawer, are gone again, as if that touch of devilry lurked in them still. They show that in early days I hacked at and added to the play. In the drawer I find some scraps of Mr. Crook's delightful music, and other incomplete matter relating to Peter. Here is the reply of a boy whom I favoured with a seat in my box and injudiciously asked at the end what he had liked best. "What I think I liked best," he said, "was tearing up the programme and dropping the bits on people's heads." Thus am I often laid low. A copy of my favourite programme of the play is still in the drawer. In the first or second year of Peter No. 4 could not attend through illness, so we took the play to his nursery, far away in the country, an array of vehicles almost as glorious as a traveling circus; the leading parts were played by the youngest children in the London company, and No. 4, aged five, looked on solemnly at the performance from his bed and never smiled once. That was my first and only appearance on the real stage, and this copy of the programme shows I was thought so meanly of as an actor that they printed my name in smaller letters than the others.

I have said little here of Nos. 4 and 5, and it is high time I had finished. They had a long summer day, and I turn round twice and now they are off to school. On Monday, as it seems, I was escorting No. 5 to a children's party and brushing his hair in the ante-room; and by Thursday he is placing me against the wall of an underground station and saying, "Now I am going to get the tickets; don't move till I come back for you or you'll lose yourself." No. 4 jumps from being astride my shoulders fishing, I knee-deep in the stream, to becoming, while still a schoolboy, the sternest of my literary critics. Anything he shook his head over I abandoned, and conceivably the world has thus been deprived of masterpieces. There was for instance an unfortunate little tragedy which I liked until I foolishly told No. 4 its subject, when he frowned and said he had better have a look at it. He read it, and then, patting me on the back, as only he and No. 1 could touch me, said, "You know you can't do this sort of thing." End of a tragedian. Sometimes, however, No. 4 liked my efforts, and I walked in the azure that day when he returned *Dear Brutus* to me with the comment "Not so bad." In earlier days, when he was ten, I offered him the MS of my book *Margaret Ogilvy.* "Oh, thanks," he said almost immediately, and added, "Of course my desk is awfully full." I reminded him that he could take out some of its more ridiculous contents. He said, "I have read it already in the book." This I had not known, and I was secretly elated, but I said that people sometimes liked to preserve this kind of thing as a curiosity. He said "Oh" again. I said tartly that he was not compelled to take it if he didn't want it. He said, "Of course I want it, but my desk—" Then he wriggled out of the room and came back in a few minutes dragging in No. 5 and announcing triumphantly, "No. 5 will have it."

The rebuffs I have got from all of you! They were especially crushing in those early days when one by one you came out of your belief in fairies and lowered on me as the deceiver. My grandest triumph, the best thing in the play of *Peter Pan* (though it is not in it), is that long after No. 4 had ceased to believe, I brought him back to the faith for at least two minutes. We were on our way in a boat to fish the Outer Hebrides (where we caught *Mary Rose*), and though it was a journey of days he wore his fishing basket on his back all the time, so as to be able to begin at once. His one pain was the absence of Johnny Mackay, for Johnny was the loved gillie of the previous summer who had taught him everything that is worth knowing (which is a matter of flies) but could not be with us this time as he would have had to cross and re-cross Scotland to reach us. As the boat drew near the Kyle of Lochalsh pier I told Nos. 4 and 5 it was such a famous wishing pier that they had now but to wish and they should have. No. 5 believed at once and expressed a wish to meet himself (I afterwards found him on the pier searching faces confidently), but No. 4 thought it more of my untimely nonsense and doggedly declined to humour me. "Whom do you want to see most, No. 4?" "Of course I would like most to see Johnny Mackay." "Well, then, wish for him." "Oh, rot." "It can't do any harm to wish." Contemptuously he wished, and as the ropes were thrown on the pier he saw Johnny waiting for him, loaded with angling paraphernalia. I know no one less like a fairy than Johnny Mackay, but for two minutes No. 4 was quivering in another world than ours. When he came to he gave me a smile which meant that we understood each other, and thereafter neglected me for a month, being always with Johnny. As I have said, this episode is not in the play; so though I dedicate *Peter Pan* to you I keep the smile, with the few other broken fragments of immortality that have come my way.

Arthur Rackham and
Peter Pan in Kensington Gardens:
A Biography of the Artist

Arthur Rackham's illustrations for Peter Pan in Kensington Gardens *can be seen as an interpretation of Barrie's book as well as a self-contained visual narrative about adventures with fairies in London's famous park. The illustrations appear in this volume in gallery form with their original captions and with editorial commentary, along with a commentary on their relationship to the text. The text of* Peter Pan in Kensington Gardens *is readily available in print for those who seek to understand fully Peter Pan's various incarnations.*[1]

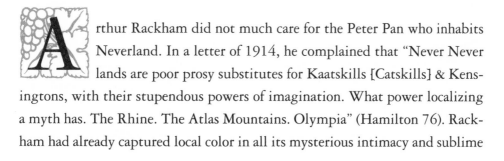rthur Rackham did not much care for the Peter Pan who inhabits Neverland. In a letter of 1914, he complained that "Never Never lands are poor prosy substitutes for Kaatskills [Catskills] & Kensingtons, with their stupendous powers of imagination. What power localizing a myth has. The Rhine. The Atlas Mountains. Olympia" (Hamilton 76). Rackham had already captured local color in all its mysterious intimacy and sublime

1. I am grateful to Adam Horn, a Harvard student in my freshman seminar on J. M. Barrie, who contributed to the essays on Rackham and assembled information about the artist and his career. As collaborator and coauthor, he helped capture the spirit of Rackham and his art.

grandeur for works by the Brothers Grimm, Jonathan Swift, and Washington Irving, and he would do the same for Shakespeare, Richard Wagner, Lewis Carroll, and Hans Christian Andersen, among many others. The expressive intensity of his illustrations for *Peter Pan in Kensington Gardens* localized Barrie's myth and animated Peter Pan and the fairies in powerful ways.

Peter Pan was invented during walks through Kensington Gardens, coming to life in conversations with children about the various sites there. Arthur Rackham reintroduced the visual element that was there from the start, drawing us into the landscape that inspired tales about what happens after Lock-out Time in the Gardens. He takes us back to a time before Neverland, when the Boy Who Wouldn't Grow Up had not yet grown up at all and was still a baby.

Born in London on September 19, 1867, seven years J. M. Barrie's junior, Rackham was the oldest surviving male in a family with twelve children. All his life he took pride in his working-class origins (though his father was a clerk in the British civil service), claiming that his artistic abilities had their roots in his ethnicity: "Cockneys are very observant of small, new, strange things" (Hamilton 20). From an early age, he demonstrated unusual talent in drawing and was known to smuggle paper and pencil into bed in order to sketch far into the night, sometimes even using a pillowcase when he had no paper. His choice of subjects as a child revealed a taste for the fantastic and imaginative, inspired perhaps by his love of Arthur Boyd Houghton's illustrations for the *Arabian Nights*.

In September 1879 Rackham began his formal education at the City of London School, where, although without special academic distinction, he was beloved by his masters and received the school prize for drawing. Prolonged illness led to a trip to Australia in early 1884, where he found ample opportunity to hone his talent for watercolor with panoramic landscapes. He returned to London in July physically renewed and determined to pursue his passion to the end. Later that year he entered the Lambeth School of Art, but financial considerations began to wear away at his ambition and determination. As he would later write to an aspiring young artist asking for guidance, drawing was a profession "to which no parent would be justified in putting a son without being able to give him a permanent income as well" (Hudson 32). Unlike Barrie, who set aside all practical considerations and traveled to London, nearly penniless, to establish himself as a journalist, Rackham showed real caution and accepted a clerkship in the Westminster Fire Office.

Rackham regularly submitted drawings to magazines—sending in everything from political cartoons to illustrated sporting events—and he left his clerkship in 1892 to become a staff illustrator with the *Westminster Budget*, a large-format magazine for which he drew many famous personages of the time. Most of this work is relatively conventional, although the mastery of line is already evident. One piece from 1893, *The Influenza Fiend*, presages Rackham's trademark style in its portrayal of a demonic disease transmitter as a wiry, deformed, goblinlike creature. With the publication of illustrations for the *Ingoldsby Legends* (1898) and *Tales from Shakespeare* (1899) Rackham reached an artistic crossroads, a phase he would later describe as the "worst time" ever in his life. His mind overflowing with images and alive with creative energy unable to express itself, he had to meet the multiple demands of the journalistic work that was putting food on the table.

At the turn of the century, Rackham revisited a childhood favorite and created ninety-nine black-and-white drawings and a color frontispiece for *Fairy Tales of the Brothers Grimm*. Greeted with immediate success, the volume was reprinted several times, and in 1909 Rackham turned forty of the original drawings into full-color illustrations. He always felt deep affection for this first commercially successful project, in part because he had produced illustrations that were less supplement and reinterpretation than creative works of their own—imaginative evocations of "once upon a time."

"His face was wizened and wrinkled like a ripe walnut," an admirer once wrote, "and as he peered short-sightedly at me out of his goggle spectacles I thought he was one of the goblins out of Grimm's Fairy Tales." Rackham was a mere thirty-three years old at the time, but he was showing signs of age, with a face deeply lined and with premature hair loss. "When he was armed with palette and paint brushes he became for me a wizard, who with one touch of his magic wand could people my universe with elves and leprechauns," that same admirer added (Hudson 50).

That romantic wizardry attracted the attention of the accomplished portrait painter Edyth Starkie, who married Rackham in 1903. In many ways the antithesis of her husband, Starkie was a spirited Irishwoman, mischievously irreverent with a keen sense of irony. Married life suited the couple, and Rackham prospered both personally and professionally. His work was exhibited widely and prominently at the Royal Academy and at the Institute of Painters of Water-Colours. *Rip Van Winkle*, published in 1905, established him as the foremost decorative illustrator of his time. The volume, with its fifty-one color plates, allowed him to display the sorcery of his style, with its landscapes of twisted undergrowth and gnarled trees haunted by curious creatures with gaunt limbs and grotesque features.

Rip Van Winkle inaugurated Rackham's longtime relationship with the venerable British publishing firm of William Heinemann, and the release of the book in limited (fully subscribed) and trade editions in multiple countries set a precedent that would be followed for years to come. The artwork itself sold well, establishing Rackham's exhibitions at the Leicester Galleries as an annual event. Thus began Rackham's twenty-year run at the top of the English illustration industry.

Hoping to capitalize further on Rackham's success, the Leicester Galleries arranged a meeting between the artist and J. M. Barrie. The success of *Peter Pan* onstage augured well for a productive collaboration. Rackham signed a contract for the gift book *Peter Pan in Kensington Gardens* (1906) at a time when *Peter and Wendy* (the novel based on the play) had not yet been conceived as a project. The fifty full-page color illustrations took Rackham nearly a year to complete, and in that time he visited Kensington Gardens frequently, where he could be seen observing and sketching. Barrie spoke concisely but accurately about his reaction to the Leicester exhibition of Rackham's work on the Peter Pan story: "It entranced me." Critics agreed for the most part, and the *Pall Mall Gazette* declared, "Rackham seems to have dropped out of some cloud in Mr. Barrie's fairyland, sent by a special providence to make pictures in tune with his whimsical genius" (Hudson 66). An enlarged version was published in 1912 and included a new color frontispiece with seven additional full-page black-and-white illustrations. *The Peter Pan Portfolio* appeared in that year as well.

Beyond its surface charm, Rackham's Peter Pan work displays a mastery of the revolutionary three-color process, color printing that was especially suited to Rackham's soft tones, and which he labored over in an attempt to achieve the right blend of colors and shades. The illustrations also reveal Rackham doing what he did best, taking a real setting—the Kensington Gardens—and infusing it with lively elements of the unreal, combining the local with the fanciful and whimsical.

Rackham's triumphs removed his financial concerns, allowing him and his wife to move into a large high-gabled red-and-brown home complete with his own studio. Success did not diminish Rackham's drive. After completing *Peter Pan in Kensington Gardens* he undertook perhaps the most daunting challenge of his career: illustrating a new edition of *Alice's Adventures in Wonderland*. John Tenniel, whose masterful drawings had appeared in the first edition of the book in 1865, was still alive at the time. His images were so closely identified with Lewis Carroll's book that many critics frowned on the notion of any competing images. Rackham's sentimental attachment to *Alice's Adventures in Wonderland*—he had read the work with his father as a child—led him to overcome any artistic inhibitions, and he completed the first half of the project. His was the most successful of the seven editions of Carroll's work to appear after the expiration of copyright in 1907, but the *Times* compared Rackham's work unfavorably with Tenniel's, dismissing the new illustrations as "forced and derivative." Discouraged, Rackham abandoned the project and decided against illustrating *Through the Looking-Glass*.

No critics grumbled over Rackham's illustrations for *A Midsummer Night's Dream* (1908). The artist's ability to blend dream and reality with mischievous suggestiveness made him an ideal illustrator for Shakespeare's work. His unique talent shone through in illustrations like "Ere the leviathan can swim a league," for which Rackham took a passing figure of speech and conceived of a hideous sea monster cresting the waves. William De Morgan, one of the founders of the Arts and Crafts movement, called this book "the most splendid illustrated work of the century, so far." Fairies were at the height of their popularity in 1909, and Rackham used his fame to speak out in favor of education focused on stimulating children's imaginations through stories and illustrations. He corresponded with children throughout his career, and the birth of his daughter, Barbara, in 1908, added to the pleasure he derived from creating books for the young.

Rackham's appeal crossed generational lines as well as cultural boundaries, and his versatility as an artist becomes evident in his illustrations for Wagner's *The Rhinegold* and *The Valkyrie* (1910) and *Siegfried and the Twilight of the Gods*

(1911). The landscapes he produced to illustrate Norse myths had a powerful impact on the young C. S. Lewis, who described the cold splendor and serenity of Rackham's landscapes in *Siegfried*: "Pure Northernness engulfed me: a vision of huge, clear spaces hanging above the Atlantic in the endless twilight of a Northern summer, remoteness, severity." Rackham's images translated sound into vision: "His pictures, which seemed to me then to be the very music made visible, plunged me a few fathoms deeper into my delight" (Hamilton 10).

With characteristic nimbleness, Rackham shifted easily from the raw, sublime beauty of Northern landscapes to images for *Aesop's Fables* (1912) and *Mother Goose* (1913). He included caricatures of himself in the Aesop volume and used his own home in Chalcot Gardens as the model for the House that Jack Built in *Mother Goose*.

Rackham enlisted in the war effort in 1914, working with the Hampstead Volunteers and digging trenches in Essex. He continued to work on his annual gift books, publishing, in the war years, *A Christmas Carol* (1915), Grimms' *Little Brother and Little Sister* (1917), and *English Fairy Tales Retold* (1918). After the war, additional fairy-tale volumes appeared, most notably *Cinderella* (1919) and *Sleeping Beauty* (1920), both of which afforded him the opportunity of developing his talent for silhouettes.

The year 1920 brought unprecedented prosperity to Rackham, with his income exceeding £7,000 (he was now closing in on J. M. Barrie's earnings), a sum amplified by his now extensive list of publications and his new American exhibitions. He purchased a country home at Houghton and a new London studio. The country home had its inconveniences—no running water, no electric lights, rats—but Rackham had already developed a distaste for modern technology, declaring that the fall of man had begun with the invention of the wheel and disapproving wholeheartedly of photography and cinema. "I would rather," he told one friend, "have a page of handwriting I couldn't read than a typewritten manuscript" (Hamilton 83).

Rackham's output remained high through the 1920s, and he illustrated a number of American classics: Nathaniel Hawthorne's *A Wonder Book* (1922), Washington Irving's *The Legend of Sleepy Hollow* (1928), and Edgar Allan Poe's *Tales of Mystery and Imagination* (1935). Fresh from a trip to the United States in 1927, where he received a warm reception and flattering attention from American publishers, he decided to try his hand at commercial art, producing advertisements for Colgate and various other companies. In 1927 Queen Mary purchased *The Holy Grail*, one of his illustrations for Mallory's *The Romance of King Arthur* (1917). The lean war years had given way to a postwar resurgence that was to mark the last real peak in Rackham's career.

Still, the market for fine books began to decline, and Rackham counted himself fortunate to receive a commission for an edition of Hans Christian Andersen's fairy tales. With his daughter, he traveled to Denmark, visiting farms and museums and absorbing local color. Hugh Walpole chose Rackham's Andersen volume as the best picture book of the year, noting that Rackham had "acquired a new tenderness and grace. His fantasy is stronger than ever" (Hudson 134). *The Arthur Rackham Fairy Book* was published in 1933, and in it, as in the illustrations for Andersen's fairy tales, the artist used a generally brighter palette.

In the summer of 1936 American publisher George Macy commissioned Rackham to illustrate James Stephen's novel *The Crock of Gold*, a strange blend of philosophy, folklore, and melodrama that contains encounters with Pan and the fairy world. In conversation, Macy casually suggested *The Wind in the Willows* as a possible next project. "Immediately a wave of emotion crossed his face," Macy recalls, "he gulped, started to say something, turned his back on me and went to the door for a few minutes" (Hudson 144). Rackham had long hoped to illustrate Grahame's work, a childhood favorite of his, and he set aside *The Crock of Gold* in order to spend the next two years on Kenneth Grahame's masterpiece.

Arthur Rackham rose to his drawing board for what would be the last time and created illustrations of heartbreaking beauty. Bedridden with cancer in 1938, he struggled to complete the illustrations and finished the last one shortly before his death, on September 6, 1939, just days after the outbreak of World War II. This last effort, like so much of his previous work, proved a beautiful localization of his personal response to a work of great imaginative power. Of all his books it best characterizes the potency of his art as described by the *Dublin Independent*: "Some of Mr. Rackham's pictures are pure poems—they set you dreaming" (Hamilton 128).

An Introduction to
Arthur Rackham's Illustrations for
Peter Pan in Kensington Gardens

GENESIS OF *PETER PAN IN KENSINGTON GARDENS*

It is not like Peter Pan to leave a trail. "He so dislikes being tracked," J. M. Barrie tells us, in his preface to *Peter Pan*, "as if there were something odd about him, that when he dies he means to get up and blow away the particles that will be his ashes" (Hollindale 2008, 84). And certainly his childlike elusiveness has always been one of his foremost charms. This is the boy who plays hide-and-seek with the stars, who slips through the arms of smitten mermaids, who can meet you and also forget you exist in a matter of moments. It is no surprise, then, that most readers would never make the effort to identify his origins. Could the boy so famous for flying really have left any footprints at all? Yes and no. Pan's literary debut in *The Little White Bird* of 1902 was not nearly as dramatic as his first appearance onstage in 1904. *The Little White Bird* also had nothing close to the impact of *Peter and Wendy*, the 1911 novelization of the play, and as a text it is in some ways as shifty as the character it introduces. Still, those who would follow Peter have one source text to which they must turn—for the path to Neverland runs directly through Kensington Gardens.

Peter Pan in Kensington Gardens (1906), the story illustrated by the renowned artist Arthur Rackham, first appeared as a six-chapter section of Barrie's *The Little White Bird* (1902). That work recounted the relationship of a bachelor (who is also the narrator) with a young boy named David, tracing the development of a friendship with obvious parallels to Barrie's own with George Llewelyn Davies, age five when the two first met in 1898 in London's Kensington Gardens. Intended for an adult readership, *The Little White Bird* met with critical acclaim, despite its unconventional style and quirky content. The book critic at the *Times* called it "one of the best things that Mr. Barrie has written." And he added: "If a book exists which contains more knowledge and more love of children, we do not know it" (Birkin 95). The book was also dedicated to "their boys (my boys)," a phrase that did not raise the eyebrows of the critic at the *Times*. It was in Kensington Gardens that Barrie had entertained the young George, the oldest of the five Llewelyn Davies boys, with stories of magic and mischief that had no morals, no lessons, and no messages whatsoever—just sheer fun, despite Barrie's later declaration that the stories contained "moral reflections."

As noted earlier in this volume, the genesis of Peter Pan recalls the origins of Lewis Carroll's *Alice's Adventures in Wonderland* and Robert Louis Stevenson's *Treasure Island*, works that were also produced in collaboration with a child, with a certain creative give-and-take as the adult cued the child and vice versa. A protagonist soon emerged, gradually inching his way to the center of the narrative. Barrie, after telling George that all children start out as birds, further assured him that his baby brother, Peter, was still able to fly, in part because his mother, Sylvia, had not weighed him at birth. Peter was able to fly to Kensington Gardens and romp with the fairies at night. But when George became skeptical of Peter's ability to fly—the infant Peter seemed to spend his nights tucked safely in bed—Barrie began to develop Peter as an independent character, a child who would soon come to dominate their stories and eventually make his way into *The Little White Bird*. Thus Peter Pan was born.

What started as one chapter soon became six, and a figure who began as a minor character quickly became central. Pan spread his dominion across the middle of the novel, acting as a force almost beyond the author's control. He had already taken over the stories Barrie told in Kensington Gardens. As Roger Lancelyn Green notes, in his *Fifty Years of Peter Pan*:

> Kensington Gardens were well peopled with fairies by the year 1901, when another character crept into being there. He came so quietly that in after years none of the children could remember how he began: he was just there, and he was so well known that of course you had always known he was there, and you didn't even think of asking why his name was Peter Pan, because of course that was his name and that was who he was. (17)

Roughly a year after the publication of *The Little White Bird*, Barrie set to work on a new play, one that sprang to life on the London stage, meeting with a level of success and admiration that even the respected author himself had never before received. The Boy Who Wouldn't Grow Up had outgrown the scenes of storytelling in Kensington Gardens and had also outgrown the pages of *The Little White Bird* to become, as Lewis Carroll put it about Alice, "large as life, and twice as natural."

The public fell in love with Peter Pan. Barrie's publishers asked him to create a narrative version of the play, and the author initially declined, apparently apprehensive about giving Peter definitive textual treatment just yet. Instead he offered to reissue the Peter Pan chapters of *The Little White Bird*, personally requesting the renowned artist Arthur Rackham as illustrator for the work. The book would be published in a sumptuous, eye-catching gift edition. London publishing house Hodder & Stoughton saw immediately the appeal of a holiday Peter Pan gift book—especially considering Charles Frohman's plans to revive *Peter Pan* annually around Christmastime. And so the idea of the chapters from *The Little White Bird* as a stand-alone novel was born.

THE BETWIXT-AND-BETWEEN APPEARS IN KENSINGTON GARDENS

Peter Pan in Kensington Gardens was a difficult, eccentric little book with beautiful illustrations, the most sought-after gift book of Christmas 1906. It opens with a map of Kensington Gardens and is, by contrast to the exotic island setting of the play *Peter Pan*, intimately tied to the gardens as a real setting grounding the stories. As Roger Lancelyn Green explains, "Kensington Gardens must always remain a special province of fairyland round which still lingers a magic of its own—or rather of Barrie's own. There certainly he not only created a new mythology, but one more definite and inevitable 'a local habitation and a name' than Olympus itself" (Green 16).

The gardens are described as a "tremendous big place" and serve as the site for miniaturized antics, from Mabel Grey's "incredible adventures, one of the least of which was that she kicked off both her boots," to Malcolm the Bold's near-drowning in St. Govor's Well. The narrative is framed as a walk through

Barrie's entry to Kensington Gardens. (Courtesy of Great Ormond Street Hospital Children's Charity)

the gardens. The narrator-guide offers only the highlights of the gardens' storied history, for if he were "to point out all the notable places as we pass up the Broad Walk, it would be time to turn back before we reach them."

The Bird's Island is one of the central locations in Kensington Gardens. On it, "all the birds are born that become baby boys and girls," and the narrator notes that Peter Pan is the only human who can land on the island, "and he is only half human." Although Peter's flying and crowing in *Peter and Wendy* suggest his kinship with birds—and in fact his being borne away by the Never bird's nest presents a strong visual metaphor to that effect—*Peter Pan in Kensington Gardens* explicitly draws that connection, telling us that Peter "escaped from being a human" by flying out his window when he was just seven days old, returning to the gardens completely unaware that he is anything other than a bird, perplexed that his attempts to draw in water through his nose and to perch on tree branches are not successful. Mystified and distraught, the little boy is left alone in the Gardens:

Poor little Peter Pan, he sat down and cried, and even then he did not know that, for a bird, he was sitting on his wrong part. It is a blessing that he did not know, for otherwise he would have lost faith in his power to fly, and the moment you doubt whether you can fly, you cease for ever to be able to do it. The reason birds can fly and we can't is simply that they have perfect faith, for to have faith is to have wings.

Flying and faith are linked here with Barrie's trademark tender sentimentality.

THE PIPER AT THE GATES OF KENSINGTON GARDENS

Peter flies to Bird's Island, which no one can reach except by flying, in order to put his case before old Solomon Caw, a crow who serves as a wizened chieftain among the birds of the island. Solomon tactfully informs the unsuspecting Peter that he is not in fact a bird, stripping Peter of his faith and therefore of his ability to fly. Trapped on the island, Peter learns that he may never again return to Kensington Gardens. In a phrase that captures the tragedy of Peter Pan perhaps more forcefully than anything in *Peter and Wendy* itself, Solomon declares: "Poor little half-and half!" before dubbing him "Betwixt-and-Between." This is the great tragedy of Peter Pan. He never really has a home, never really has a mother, and belongs neither to the world of birds nor to the world of humans. The gift of eternal youth turns him into a homeless wanderer.

Peter lives among the birds, learning their ways—including how to have a "glad heart"—from Solomon. In his time on the island he feels compelled to "sing all day long, just as the birds sing for joy, but, being partly human, he needed an instrument, so he made a pipe of reeds." Barrie's description of Pan's pipe playing is one of the most moving passages in the book:

He used to sit by the shore of the island of an evening, practicing the sough of the wind and the ripple of the water, and catching handfuls of the shine of the moon, and he put them all in his pipe and played them so beautifully that even the birds were deceived, and they would say to each other, "Was that a fish leaping in the water or was it Peter playing leaping fish on his pipe?" And sometimes he played the birth of birds, and then the mothers would turn round in their nests to see whether they had laid an egg.

Pan's pipe playing links him with the mythical Pan, but this passage in particular casts his pipe playing as a form of creativity, a form of artistry so real that it pulsates with procreative energy. The passage anticipates Peter's declaration to Hook in their final battle: "I'm youth, I'm joy . . . I'm a little bird that has broken out of the egg." Peter is distinctly linked to the ecstasies of procreation and creativity, yet he is also destined never to mature and become an adult.

Although he lingers happily with the birds, Peter longs to return to the gardens, "to play as other children play, and of course there is no such lovely place to play in as the Gardens." He has his chance at freedom when Solomon gives him a banknote from Shelley, turned by the poet into a paper boat and sent drifting up the Serpentine to Bird's Island. Peter uses the note to bribe the thrushes, who construct a nest to carry him across the Serpentine and back to the gardens. Thus finally Peter returns to the gardens, borne across with "exultation in his little breast that drove out fear." When he arrives, it is past Lock-out Time, and mortals are gone, but the fairies are there and they have come out to play.

"DO YOU BELIEVE IN FAIRIES?"

Peter Pan in Kensington Gardens introduces us to the romance of the fairy world in ways that no other work by Barrie does. The fairies' chief traits—bouncing energy, radiant beauty, and moral carelessness—tell us exactly why the creatures were so appealing to a man who devoted his afternoon walks in the park to small boys. Fairies are wee folk—miniaturized humanlike figures—who behave like children. A volatile, unpredictable lot, they can turn, in a heartbeat, from friend to foe, and vice versa. When Peter Pan arrives in their domain, they plan to "slay" him until the fairy women discover that he is a mere child, a baby using his nightgown as a sail. As nocturnal creatures, the fairies hold late-night balls to which humans are not welcome. Like Tinker Bell, they are vain and mischievous and so small that they have room "for one feeling only at a time." In the daytime they generally remain underground, in hiding, but "if you look, and they fear there is no time to hide, they stand quite still pretending to be flowers."

Both *Peter Pan in Kensington Gardens* and *Peter and Wendy* recount the origins of fairies. As Peter himself explains: "When the first baby laughed for the first time, its laugh broke into a thousand pieces, and they all went skipping about, and that was the beginning of fairies." Favoring youth, they always appoint the youngest among them as schoolmistress so that nothing will ever be taught: "they all go out for a walk and never come back." The head of the family is also always the youngest. The behavioral kinship with babies becomes evident in the narrator's explanation for the tantrums of "your baby sister": "Her fits of passion, which are awful to behold, and are usually called teething, are no such thing; they are her natural exasperation, because we don't understand her, though she is talking an intelligible language. She is talking fairy."

Barrie remains faithful to traditional British depictions of fairies as "a middle order between men and angels" or as "spiritual animals" (Briggs 11). But his fairies also differ from the folkloric norm in their desire for autonomy and their general lack of concern for human affairs. Still, they adhere to the hierarchies of the human world and mimic in many ways the culture and customs of those above ground. Maimie, the girl who stays past Lock-out Time in Kensington Gardens, discovers in the fairy world both dazzling beauty (the canopy made by the glowworms for the fairy ring) and aggressive cruelty ("Slay her!" the fairies shout when they discover her in their midst).

YOU CAN'T GO HOME AGAIN

"Of course, he had no mother—at least, what use was she to him?" The narrator of *Peter Pan in Kensington Gardens* reveals himself to be a prevaricator, at times as flighty and unreliable as the fairies. Peter Pan has a mother, and the sad fact of the matter is that Peter is no longer of use to her. As a newcomer to Kensington Gardens, he traded his music with the fairies for two "little" wishes. Holding one wish in reserve, he asks for the power to fly. Enraptured by his newfound abilities, he goes back home to seek out his mother and finds her fast asleep. From the window he admires her and is of "two minds" about whether to stay or go back. Sensing his presence, his mother awakens and whispers his name "as if it were the most lovely word in the language." At the foot of her bed, Peter plays a lullaby on his pipes, having "made it up to himself out of the way she said 'Peter.'" He leaves with the plan to return after saying his good-byes to Solomon. But months go by before he makes use of his second wish, and he returns to find the window "closed and barred," with his mother "sleeping peacefully with her arm around another little boy." The narrator explains: "There is no second chance, not for most of us. When we reach the window it is Lock-out Time. The iron bars are up for life."

For Peter, as for Barrie and the rest of us, leaving home means entering a phase in which it is impossible to return to the untroubled dyad of mother and child. This time, the iron bars are not around Kensington Gardens but around home, an idyllic haven where the child remains safe, enclosed in a domestic space. But the bars at the window suggest that home can also be a prison, a place of limited mobility and magic, too confined and narrow to contain the expansive desires of children as they grow up. The tragedy of growing up is tempered by the rainbow promise of what Kenneth Grahame called the Wide World and the Wild Wood, places that, unlike Kensington Gardens, have no limits and no Lock-out Time.

MAIMIE: THE GIRL BEFORE WENDY

Maimie Mannering is the girl who would not leave at Lock-out Time. Hiding from her nurse, who is unaware that she has not left Kensington Gardens with her brother, the four-year-old Maimie, desperate for the chance to witness a fairy ball, takes advantage of confusion about Lock-out Time and conceals herself in St. Govor's Well. The trees warn her about fairies: "They will mischief you—stab you to death, or compel you to nurse their children, or turn you into something tedious, like an evergreen oak." Following the ribbons stretched out about the gardens, the paths of the fairies, Maimie encounters Brownie, who is on her way to Queen Mab's ball, where the Duke of Christmas Daisies is hoping to find a wife. Brownie wins the duke's heart and asks the fairies to spare the life of Maimie, who is in mortal danger for eavesdropping on the fairies.

Once the fairies become aware of Maimie's help in engineering the union of Brownie and the duke, they resolve to thank her, building a beautiful house, "exactly the size of Maimie," around her to keep her warm. When Maimie awakens, she hits her head on the roof, opening it "like the lid of a box" in a scene that recalls *Alice's Adventures in Wonderland*. When she steps outside to admire the beautiful little house, it shrinks and disappears. But she is not alone. "Don't cry, pretty human, don't cry," a voice calls out. Peter Pan, a "beautiful little naked boy," stands before her, looking at her "wistfully."

It is in Kensington Gardens that Peter is first offered a kiss and given a thimble, in the belief that thimbles are kisses. "Poor little boy! he quite believed her, and to this day he wears it on his finger, though there can be scarcely any one who needs thimbles so little." And it is also in Kensington Gardens that Maimie and Peter exchange thimbles, or real kisses, and that Peter proposes to Maimie. A "delightful" idea comes into his head and he asks Maimie: "Will you marry me?"

Maimie very nearly goes away with Peter, balking only when he suggests that her mother might not always leave the window open for her. "The door will always, always be open, and mother will always be waiting at it for me," she insists. When the gates to the gardens open in the morning, Maimie promises to return, but fearing that she might linger too long with "her dear Betwixt-and-Between," she dutifully obeys her ayah. Peter's brush with love—the exchange of kisses and the proposal—may seem startling to readers of *Peter and Wendy*. Peter is "touched" by Maimie in ways that he is never really moved by Wendy. But in both encounters, Peter remains "the tragic boy," flirting with romance yet also destined to remain forever barred from human pleasures and ecstasies: "For long he hoped that some night she would come back to him; often he thought he saw her waiting for him by the shore of the Serpentine as his bark drew to land, but Maimie never went back."

Maimie returns at Easter with her mother to bring Peter a gift, the made-up goat that she uses to frighten her brother at night. Standing within a fairy ring, mother and daughter devise an incantation for the fairies, and they turn the goat into a real creature. Peter Pan is now more closely aligned with the god Pan than ever, but he remains more emphatically than ever an eternal youth, joyous and tragic at once.

PETER PAN: GUARDIAN OF THE DEAD

Peter Pan in Kensington Gardens closes with another variation on the theme of Lock-out Time, of unavoidable and abrupt endings. We learn that Peter is unable to rescue some of the children who wander into the gardens at night—precursors of the lost boys, we might say. He buries the children with his paddle-spade, erecting tombstones marked with their initials. The narrator describes two little "tombstones" erected for a boy and a girl, both about a year old, who fell "unnoticed" from their perambulators. Those stones do in fact exist in Kensington Gardens, but as parish boundary markers. The narrator tells us: "David sometimes places white flowers on these two innocent graves," and adds: "But how strange for parents, when they hurry into the Gardens at the opening of the gates looking for their lost one, to find the sweetest little tombstone instead. I do hope that Peter is not too ready with his spade. It is all rather sad."

The somber undercurrent in *Peter and Wendy* surfaces more explicitly in *Peter Pan in Kensington Gardens*. Peter's connection with river crossings, shadows, tombstones, and burials creates a narrative with a tragic turn. The joyful boy in the gardens may ride his goat and frolic with the fairies, but at Lock-out Time he is also obliged to serve as gravedigger, burying the children who perish of "cold and dark" in Kensington Gardens. The Boy Who Would Not Grow Up could just as aptly be described as the Boy Who Could Not Grow Up.

Peter Pan in Kensington Gardens has not aged particularly well, and modern readers find it something of a challenge to warm up to its eccentric style and fanciful content. The lack of clarity about the narrator's relationship to David leaves many readers mystified, disoriented, and uncomfortable. Arthur Rackham kept the book from falling into oblivion, creating a set of images that switches Barrie's prose on to maximum wattage.

This edition reproduces Rackham's illustrations rather than Barrie's text, and Barrie himself might not have objected. After all, he considered *The Boy Castaways of Black Lake Island*, a book designed for the Llewellyn Davies family, to be "so much the best and rarest of this author's works," and it consisted of nothing but captioned photographs (Hollindale 2008, 75). Readers will no doubt find Rackham's work as important to an understanding of Peter Pan as did Rackham's nephew Walter Starkie, who wrote:

> Peter Pan became the consecration of my childhood, for I had watched my Uncle's sensitive and agile paint-brushes people those trees with dwarfs and gnomes. . . . Although we children went again and again to the theatre to see the play, it was through the Rackham illustrations to Kensington Gardens and the Serpentine that Peter Pan still lived in our memories (Hudson 68).

May Peter Pan live on in our memories, not vaguely as some stock hero or cartoon character but as a fully realized, tragic, wonderful little boy who flew away from home when he was seven days old and never found his way back.

Arthur Rackham's Illustrations for
Peter Pan in Kensington Gardens

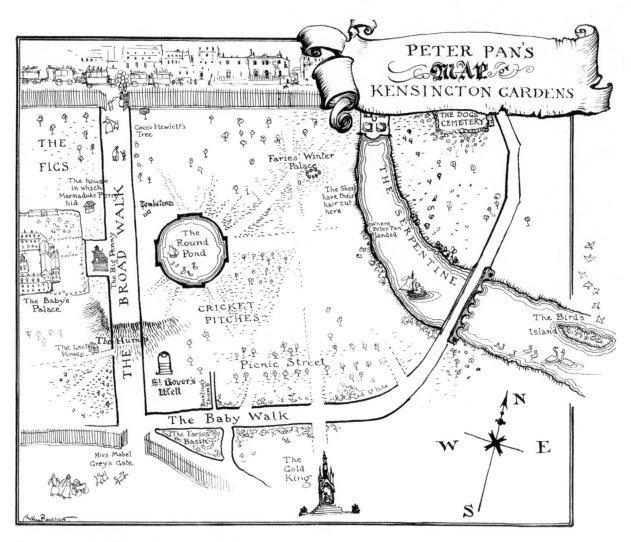

Figure 1: Peter Pan's Map of Kensington Gardens
Real bodies of water (the Round Pond and the Serpentine River) and paths (The Broad Walk) are marked out for the reader along with fanciful names such as Cecco Hewlett's Tree and the Fairies' Winter Palace. This is, after all, Peter Pan's map.

Figure 2: "The Kensington Gardens are in London, where the King lives."

Sprites and fairies lurk in the roots of trees and peer out from hiding places as a formally attired figure strolls through the Gardens. Even trees and vines are animated by the visitor, who seems oblivious to the fairy world hidden below, around, and above him (a world with its own kings and queens). The identity of the figure is not clear: he could be the King, but he might also be Pilkington, the schoolmaster mentioned in *The Little White Bird* who leads his boys through the Gardens, "glamoured to [his] crafty hook." He sends the fairies into hiding by day.

Figure 3: "The lady with the balloons, who sits just outside."

The former street vendor at the gate to Kensington Gardens is lifted into the air by her balloons. "David was very sorry for the old one, but as she did let go, he wished he had been there to see." Nothing is ever taken seriously in Kensington Gardens, which remains a safe space for whimsy precisely because the laws of gravity are defied. There is a tragicomic element to David's reaction, for it reminds us of the ease with which children can let go of benevolent adults in their lives.

Figure 4: "In the Broad Walk you meet all the people who are worth knowing."
The people "worth knowing," as Barrie put it tongue in cheek, are all well-dressed children, young and old. They are shown walking dogs, carrying balloons, skipping rope, climbing fences and taking sailboats to the Long Pond. Rackham gives us a tame Edwardian version of Pieter Brueghel's celebrated painting *Children's Games* (1560).

Figure 5: "The Hump, which is the part of the Broad Walk where all the big races are run."
The Hump is the place in Kensington Gardens where "you stop when you have run about half-way down it, and then you are lost." Here we have the first hint at the recurrent theme of lost children in Barrie's stories.

Figure 6: "There is almost nothing that has such a keen sense of fun as a fallen leaf."
Falling leaves and fairies perform a graceful minuet in an image that evokes the pleasures of flying, floating, and being wafted through the air. The clothing of the fairies closely resembles the leaves in the air, reminding us of how Peter is dressed in skeleton leaves when we first encounter him.

Figure 7: "The Serpentine begins near here. It is a lovely lake, and there is a drowned forest at the bottom of it. If you peer over the edge you can see the trees all growing upside down, and they say that at night there are also drowned stars in it."
Barrie told Rackham that he liked this illustration best of all. Stars illuminate the skies and are reflected in the lake's surface, while fairies dance in the foreground, illuminated by the reflected glory of the stars. Signs of human life appear in the bridge, the fence, and the points of artificial light.

Figure 8: "The fairies of the Serpentine." The "drowned" stars of the Serpentine form a backdrop for fairy revelry. Not reflected in the waters, the fairies clearly occupy imaginative space and cannot be mirrored or immersed in the waters of time. Like Peter Pan, they are immortals with the power of flight. Butterflies and dragonflies reveal themselves as kindred spirits.

Figure 9: "The island on which all the birds are born that become baby boys and girls." It is daytime in Kensington Gardens, and the park seems disenchanted and deprived of fairies. Children gather in small groups at the shoreline, mingling with birds attracted to them by the promise of food. Winged creatures fly above Bird's Island, which, cordoned off and mysterious, appears as a world unto itself. This scene could also be the final tableau of Hans Christian Andersen's "Ugly Duckling," which Rackham illustrated in 1932.

Figure 10: "Old Mr. Salford was a crab-apple of an old gentleman who wandered all day in the Gardens."
Mr. Salford has his name from his birthplace, Salford, a town he is eager to discuss with anyone he happens to meet in Kensington Gardens. The Albert Memorial is shown in the background, a monument to the Prince Consort (who died of typhoid in 1861) that includes a statue of Albert, a frieze of Parnassus (with 169 painters, composers, poets, architects, and sculptors depicted), and allegorical sculptures of four continents and four industrial activities. Goblins, birds, and fairies play around Mr. Salford's head, occupying a space between the monument to the Prince Consort and the dignified old gentleman.

Figure 11: "Away he flew, right over the houses to the Gardens."
Barrie was captivated by Rackham's image of Peter Pan flying away from home when he is seven days old. The serene infant floats across the space between the clouds above and the smokestacks below. Kensington Gardens was especially appealing as a destination, for it formed a utopian contrast to the smoky grime of London

Figure 12: "The fairies have their tiffs with the birds."
The fairies "usually give a civil answer to a civil question," but they flee from Peter, who labors under the delusion that he is a boy rather than a bird. Here, two fairies appear in proud profile near four birds perched on a branch. Peter belongs, yet also still does not quite belong, to the world of birds and fairies.

Figure 13: "When he heard Peter's voice he popped in alarm behind a tulip."
A fairy drops the postage stamp he has been reading to conceal himself, his anxious expression betraying fear of discovery. By contrast with the lightness of being found in many of Kensington Gardens' fairies, this unkempt figure, costumed in found objects, seems earthy and earthbound, and the feather on his head is purely decorative.

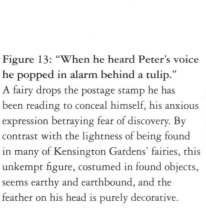

Figure 14: "A band of workmen, who were sawing down a toadstool, rushed away, leaving their tools behind them." Peter Pan throws the workers into a panic, since they perceive him as a human who has stayed in Kensington Gardens past Lock-out Time.

Figure 15: "Peter put his strange case before old Solomon Caw." Barrie loved this illustration almost as much as that of the Serpentine. Peter is perched in birdlike fashion on a branch, but Solomon slowly breaks it to him that he is no longer a bird. Peter loses faith in his ability to fly and for a time he is stranded on the island. Solomon describes him as a "poor little half-and-half" and famously dubs him a "Betwixt-and-Between." At the foot of the tree, mice busy themselves polishing shoes.

Figure 16: "Peter screamed out 'Do it again!' and with great good-nature they did it several times."
Frightened at first by a "wonderful white thing" on Bird Island, Peter comes to love the kite and even sleeps with it, "because it had belonged to a real boy." He delights in its flight, but forgets to thank the birds for demonstrating its powers, showing that "even now he had not quite forgotten what it was to be a boy." Mimicking the movements of the kite, he seeks to rise up in the air with it.

Figure 17: "A hundred flew off with the string, and Peter clung to the tail."
Peter begs the birds to fly him over Kensington Gardens. With their help, he is carried aloft by the kite but returns to earth when the kite breaks to pieces in the air.

Figure 18: "After this the birds said that they would help him no more in his mad enterprise."
Two "indignant" swans rescue Peter from the waters, and the other birds declare that they will no longer take him for joy rides. With hair wet and matted from the Serpentine, a chastened Peter untangles the remains of the kite.

Figure 19: "'Preposterous!' cried Solomon in a rage."
Solomon, responsible for sending birds to mothers who have sent him requests via the Serpentine, can make nothing of the five-pound banknote drifting his way in the form of a boat launched by the poet Shelley. The two thoughtful mouse assistants—one bespectacled—ponder the note and are equally perplexed. Solomon gives Peter the note as a plaything. From his seven days as a boy, Peter learned the value of banknotes and plans to use the one found by Solomon to facilitate his return to Kensington Gardens.

Figure 20: "For years he had been quietly filling his stocking."
Solomon Caw has no intention of remaining in office forever, and he stocks up on various oddities, ranging from crumbs to bootlaces, hoping eventually to "retire on a competency." Barrie structures the world of Kensington Gardens in ways that parody Edwardian social conventions and cultural values.

Figure 21: "When you meet grown-up people in the Gardens who puff and blow as if they thought themselves bigger than they are."
Using a broader palette, Rackham returns us to reality with a satiric look at men and women born in the "Sparrow's Year," a time when Solomon is obliged, owing to a critical shortage of thrushes, to send sparrows to ladies who have requested thrushes. The babies born that year turn into adults who "puff and blow" to make themselves look as if they started out as thrushes rather than as sparrows.

Figure 22: "He passed under the bridge and came, to his great rejoicing, within full sight of the delectable Gardens."
Using his white nightgown as a sail, Peter flies across the water just as he once flew through the air with the help of a kite. Both sail and kite harness the power of the wind to help Peter (he is nearly as white as the nightgown) reach Kensington Gardens. The Gardens appear in the background, but the focus is on the hardy infant, manning the sails.

Figure 23: "There now arose a mighty storm, and he was tossed this way and that."
Peter sails from an island in the Serpentine to Kensington Gardens in a thrush's nest (one that resembles the Never bird's nest in *Peter and Wendy*). Poised as an adventurer, he is nearly drowned, like "English mariners who have sailed westward to meet the Unknown." His nightshirt twice saves him, first when he hoists it up as a sail, then when the lady fairies "straightaway" love Peter Pan for his "baby's nightgown." Even the fish in the ocean side with the storm-tossed child, who joins the class of mythic castaways on the waters.

Figure 24: "Fairies are all more or less in hiding until dusk."

Rackham gives us another glimpse of the fairy world, which resembles a miniaturized version of domestic life in the human world. Although unable to see the gnarled roots underground, the young girl has a conspiratorial look on her face and seems to be aware of a presence below. Because fairies hide in the daytime, they never witness children's games and cannot instruct Peter on what to do with hoops.

Figure 25: "When they think you are not looking they skip along pretty lively."

The beautiful is mingled with the grotesque as fairies dance and cavort with creatures of nature. The toddler, riding on a gnome's back, shares the kinetic energy of their games.

Figure 26: "But if you look, and they fear there is no time to hide, they stand quite still pretending to be flowers."
When they meet humans, fairies use camouflage, masquerading as flowers to avoid recognition. They then rush home to tell their mothers about their "adventures." The woodland creatures respond to encounters with children in much the way children react to encounters with fairies—with wonder, astonishment, and some trepidation and terror. Fairies may pose as lilies, bluebells, crocuses, or hyacinths. Their houses are hidden because they are "the colour of the night," and their palace, "entirely built of many-coloured glasses," is the "loveliest" of all royal residences.

Figure 27: "The fairies are exquisite dancers."
The fairies' dance on a tightrope spun by a spider is accompanied by music from string and wind instruments. A spider web serves as safety net.

Figure 29: "Linkmen running in front carrying winter cherries."
Linkmen are attendants hired to carry torches for pedestrians, and these fairies are described as jolly fellows, eager to carry the winter cherries that are "fairy-lanterns."

Figure 28: "These tricky fairies sometimes slyly change the board on a ball night."
The fairies' mischievous side—along with their skillful teamwork—is illustrated clearly in this scene. When the fairies hold a ball, the closing time for Kensington Gardens is surreptitiously changed to enable preparations to begin in a timely fashion.

Figure 31: "The fairies sit round on mushrooms, and at first they are well behaved."
The fairies are able to play at being well behaved for a limited period of time. Like children, they prove unable to remain dignified and before long they "stick their fingers into butter" or "crawl over the tablecloth chasing sugar." In the midst of the pomp and pageantry of their ball, we see an aesthetic that divides the charmingly attractive women from their grotesque male counterparts.

Figure 30: "When her Majesty wants to know the time."
When Queen Mab consults her Lord Chamberlain for the time of day, he responds by blowing on a dandelion, revealing that even temporality takes a whimsical turn in the fairy world.

Figure 32: "Butter is got from the roots of old trees." A gnarled tree in a spooky forest setting has at its roots a cozy domestic scene, with fairies making cakes from the butter provided by the tree. Fairies coexist peacefully with nature.

Figure 33: "Wallflower juice is good for reviving dancers who fall to the ground in a fit."
A mouse hastens to bring wallflower juice for exhausted fairy dancers. An unusually dashing male fairy cares for the fallen dancers, for whom Peter Pan provides the music. "They bruise very easily," we are told, "and when Peter plays faster and faster they foot it till they fall down in fits."

Figure 35: "They all tickled him on the shoulder"
Gravity is lifted when the fairies tickle Peter on the shoulder, giving him the power to fly. Still hovering in the air, he is about to be propelled forward for the flight home: "I wish now to go back to mother for ever and always."

Figure 34: "Peter Pan is the fairies' orchestra."
Peter Pan plays his pipes, seated on toadstools that are aglow with his aura. His song is so beautiful that the Queen offers him "the wish of his heart." Peter decides to make two small wishes, and the first offers him the opportunity to fly back home through the window.

Figure 36: "One day they were overheard by a fairy."
Maimie Mannering listens intently while her brother boasts about his plan to sail in Peter Pan's boat. A camouflaged fairy at the base of the tree eavesdrops and turns Tony into a "marked boy," the target of constant fairy mischief. Tony sports a hat that is the color and shape of what George Llewelyn Davies wore on outings to Kensington Gardens.

Figure 37: "The little people weave their summer curtains from skeleton leaves."
Barrie described this illustration as "the gayest thing," and it displays Rackham's gift for creating a densely packed mix of delicate charm and melancholy gloom. The fairies sew summer curtains from skeleton leaves at the base of a tree, with a toadstool serving as a table for a sewing kit.

Figure 38: "An afternoon when the Gardens were white with snow."
Maimie decides to stay in the Gardens past Lock-out Time. Nature is animated through the games of children in the snow, and when they depart the trees will begin to speak, the flowers will set out on walks, and the fairies will come out of hiding.

Figure 39: "She ran to St. Govor's Well and hid."
Maimie's brother does not have the courage to stay past Lock-out Time, and she huddles in the well while visitors to the Gardens hasten to the exit. Maimie opens her eyes and feels something very cold run up her legs and arms and drop "into her heart"—"It was the stillness of the Gardens."

Figure 40: "An elderberry hobbled across the walk, and stood chatting with some young quinces."
The trees in Kensington Gardens all walk with crutches, "the sticks that are tied to young trees and shrubs," and Maimie finally learns about their actual use. The contrast between the fairies' lightness of being and the gnarled appearance of the trees is nowhere more striking than in this illustration.

Figure 41: "A chrysanthemum heard her, and said so pointedly, 'Hoity-toity, what is this?'"
The chrysanthemum exhibits distinctly adultlike behavior. Maimie is obliged to justify her presence to "the whole vegetable kingdom," and she wins over the trees, shrubs, and flowers by offering to take them for walks, inviting them to lean on her.

Figure 42: "They warned her."
The trees warn Maimie about the menace posed by the fairies: "They will mischief you—stab you to death, or compel you to nurse their children, or turn you into something tedious like an evergreen oak." Maimie, depicted in loving profile, forms a strong contrast to the fiercely gnarled trees. Safely contained by the trunks and branches yet also imprisoned by them, Maimie decides to ignore their advice.

Figure 43: "Queen Mab, who rules in the Gardens."
Queen Mab famously appears as the "fairies' midwife" in Mercutio's speech (*Romeo and Juliet*) and brings dreams of wish fulfillment. Flanked by younger fairies, she wears a robe with flowers that evoke her connection to nature. Her confident expression reflects faith in the ability of fairy girls to "bewitch" the Duke of Christmas Daisies.

Figure 45: "Fairies never say, 'We feel happy': what they say is, 'We feel *dancey*.'"
The fairies cannot dance so long as the Duke remains without wife, for "they forget all the steps when they are sad." Here, the fairies are shown in happier times, performing their nimble footwork on Christmas daisies

Figure 44: "Shook his bald head and murmured, 'Cold, quite cold.'"
A physician examines the Duke's heart, which no one has been able to warm up. The Duke of Christmas Daisies' slight stature, heavy mustache, and sallow complexion create a strong resemblance to J. M. Barrie himself.

Figure 47: "'My Lord Duke,' said the physician elatedly, 'I have the honor to inform your excellency that your grace is in love.'"

The physician's unctuous manner (he uses three honorific titles in a single sentence) and the oddity of declaring his patient to be "in love" makes the pronouncement somewhat suspect, but the words work magic on the crowd, and lead to multiple marriages among the fairy folk.

Figure 46: "Looking very undancey indeed."

The morose fairy may be Brownie, who is about to warm up the heart of the Duke of Christmas Daisies. Brownie bears a certain resemblance to Sylvia Llewelyn Davies, mother of the boys adopted by J. M. Barrie, though it seems unlikely that Rackham would have modeled Brownie on Sylvia.

Figure 48: "Building the house for Maimie."
The fairies build a house around Maimie, much like the
house built for Wendy after she is struck by Tootles' arrow.
Maimie's house shrinks and disappears as soon as she wakes
up and walks out of it.

Figure 49: "If the bad ones among the fairies happen to be out."
Malicious in appearance and in their behavior toward humans, these fairies are
goblinlike, woodland creatures that seem very much at home at the base of trees.
Oddly, Rackham illustrates the sideshow rather than the main event, giving us
vignettes about the fairies rather than representing the climax of the book—the
encounter between Peter and Maimie.

Figure 51: "I think that quite the most touching sight in the Gardens is the two tombstones of Walter Stephen Matthews and Phoebe Phelps."
The tombstones, although actually parish boundary markers, communicate the whiff of the tragic that permeates *Peter Pan in Kensington Gardens*. Children play in the Gardens, but it is there that they also can perish. The double tombstones that mark the burial site for a boy and a girl are a sobering reminder to the two couples strolling through the Gardens of their common destiny. Small wonder that one of the women casts an anxious glance at the tombstones. Like all mortals, she too will one day face the onset of Lock-out Time: "It is all rather sad."

Figure 50: "They will certainly mischief you."
Having lingered past Lock-out Time, the girl is in real danger, and we are told that Peter "has been too late several times" to save children from the fairies. Left in the cold and the dark, the children can perish in Kensington Gardens, and Peter then uses his paddle to dig a grave for them.

J. M. Barrie's Scenario for a Proposed Film of *Peter Pan*

INTRODUCTION TO BARRIE'S *PETER PAN* SCREENPLAY

Barrie was fascinated by the medium of film, and in 1915 he made a parody of *Macbeth*, called *The Real Thing at Last*. The film ran for thirty minutes and included a cast of Peter Pan veterans. In 1918 he was offered £20,000 for the film rights to *Peter Pan*. Although he refused the offer, he decided to try his hand at a reimagining of the play for the silent screen. After much negotiation, Barrie finally signed a contract with Paramount and sent them his screenplay, complete with subtitles, a profusion of new visual details, and descriptive

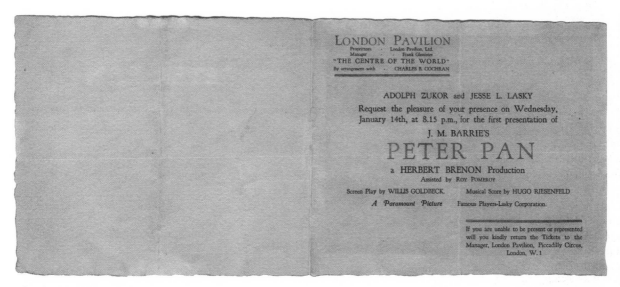

Ticket for the premiere of Paramount's film *Peter Pan*.

embellishments. From the scenario, it becomes clear that Barrie hoped for a film that would catch the wonders of Neverland. Here is a description of the mermaid lagoon: "The mermaid pictures should be a beautiful series of considerable length." And here is another of Peter at a fairy wedding: "This should be an elaborate and beautiful picture of some length, one of the prettiest in the film." And the final picture, Barrie declared, should be "the most beautiful": "Now there are only lights from moon and stars, and Peter is seen in silhouette alone, playing his pipes."

SCENARIO FOR A PROPOSED FILM OF *PETER PAN*

by J. M. Barrie

NOTE.—*The music of the acted play, as specially written for it, should accompany the pictures. Thus there is the music which always heralds Peter's appearances—the Tinker Bell music—the pirate music—the redskin music— the crocodile music, etc., all of which have a dramatic significance as well as helping in the telling of the story. Other special music should be written so that all the music accompanying the play becomes really part of it. The subtitles, i.e. the words flung on the screen, are here {in italics}. The aim has been to have as few words as possible. There are very few words in the last half hour or more of this film, and there are also about fifteen minutes of the lagoon scene without any words. Many of the chief scenes, especially those calling for novel cinema treatment, are of course not in the acted play, but where they are in it they should be acted in the same way, and to that extent the play should be a guide to the film. This scenario is very condensed: here we give only the bones of the story. The details of how to get the humours etc. must come later. The technical matters are obviously of huge importance and difficulty, and it remains to be seen whether the cinema experts can solve them.*

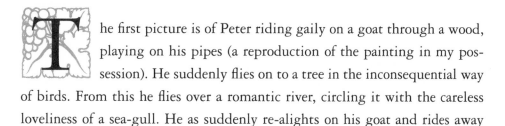

The first picture is of Peter riding gaily on a goat through a wood, playing on his pipes (a reproduction of the painting in my possession). He suddenly flies on to a tree in the inconsequential way of birds. From this he flies over a romantic river, circling it with the careless loveliness of a sea-gull. He as suddenly re-alights on his goat and rides away

From *Fifty Years of Peter Pan* by Roger Lancelyn Green (London: Peter Davies, 1954).

playing his pipes, his legs sticking out cockily. Vast practice and rehearsal will be needed to get the flying beautiful and really like a bird's. The flying must be far better and more elaborate than in the acted play, and should cover of course a far wider expanse. This incident should show at once that the film can do things for *Peter Pan* which the ordinary stage cannot do. It should strike a note of wonder in the first picture, and whet the appetite for marvels.

There was once a poor London clerk and his wife, called Mr and Mrs Darling; but what do you think they had?

Mr and Mrs Darling, who should be very tall, so as to make the children smaller, are sitting on each side of fireplace in a humble, but pleasant London sitting-room. The furniture should be of the simplest kind. There should not in this room, or any room shown in the play, be any of the massive carved furniture in heavy oak with spiral legs, etc., that is often shown in films. These are people of refined taste, but with very small means. Mr Darling is only a clerk in an office, and the humbleness of their social position should always be emphasized. She is sewing a childish garment. After a moment there come running to them one at a time their three children.

Wendy, John, and Michael.

It is a happy domestic picture, all very loving. The children romp away and the parents are there without them. They have been boisterous and Mrs Darling is tired and overworked. Mr Darling kindly tries to take the sewing from her, but she shakes her head. Liza, their little maid, comes in with the evening paper to Mr Darling. It should be a London paper, not an American one. Liza should be played by a child of about eight years of age, but with her hair up and a long skirt. She departs primly. Mr Darling points out an advertisement in the paper to Mrs Darling. It is shown in a close-up: "For nurses and nursery maids, apply Mrs S. 22 Green Street." Evidently this is what they are in need of, but they compare money and indicate that they are too poor. Then he shows her another advertisement in close-up: "Newfoundland dog for sale, cheap. *Very fond of children.* Apply Dogs' Home." He points to the underlined words in particular. She is evidently afraid, but he sees an idea in it.

Then there is a picture of Mr Darling leading a Newfoundland dog through a London street. The dog is coming willingly.

The next picture shows the result of the previous ones. We see the night nursery with three beds as in the opening of the acted play. It should be an English nursery. The Newfoundland dog, Nana, is seen going about the work of a nurse in a very practical way. We see Nana preparing the bath, bathing Michael in the bathroom very realistically, and herding the three to bed, tucking them in, etc. A long, continuous amusing picture, reproducing this incident from the play, but more fully than is possible there.

When Nana thinks they are all asleep she retires into her kennel which is in the nursery, and we see her go to sleep there with her head just out of the kennel. The naughty children are not really asleep. They jump up. Wendy makes sure that Nana is asleep, then she signs to the others, and they creep into her bed. She begins to tell them a story, while they sit up eagerly listening. It is rather dark.

(NOTE about Nana.—She should be generally played by a human being in a skin exactly like that of some real Newfoundland dog which is available, so that in certain scenes—as in the street scenes—this dog can be substituted for the actor.)

Next we have a vision of Cinderella with her broom asleep by fire in kitchen, to show that this is the story Wendy is telling.

Do you know why swallows build in the eaves of houses? It is to listen to the stories.

We see Wendy telling this to her brothers. Michael goes on tiptoe to the window to "shoo" the swallows away. Then we have an outside view of the window, with several swallows sitting on the sill, listening. Michael suddenly appears at the window, opens curtains and "shoos" them away. He returns, grinning, to Wendy's bed, thinking himself a very clever lad.

Unknown to Wendy, there was sometimes another listener to the stories.

From outside we see Peter listening at the window. Then we have alternate scenes of Wendy telling tales and Peter listening eagerly. (We should not see that Peter has flown here yet.)

One night Nana nearly caught him, and he only escaped by leaving his shadow behind.

Peter comes, stealthily, in by window to hear the story better. He crawls along the floor and listens delightedly. Nana wakes up and runs at him. He leaps out at window, but she brings down the sash so quickly that his shadow is left behind. Excitement of the children, who sit up. Mrs Darling rushes in, followed by Mr Darling. Nana has the shadow in her mouth. Mr Darling unfolds the shadow and examines it. He evidently thinks it a very naughty shadow. Mrs Darling rolls it up and puts it away in a drawer. They look out at the window, but no one can be seen. The pictures here show us that the nursery is at the top of a house in a poor, but respectable, London street. The mystery makes them uneasy. Then Mrs Darling evidently thinks Michael is looking too excited. She looks at his tongue, puts a thermometer in his mouth and produces a bottle, which we see, in a close-up, is labelled "Castor Oil." She pours some in a spoon and puts the handle into Nana's mouth.

Michael is in his own bed, with the others around. Nana crosses to him with the medicine spoon in her mouth. He is naughty and won't take it, etc., as in the play, which should be consulted here for the humours of the scene.

"Be a man, my son. I would take my *medicine now, as an example to you, if I hadn't lost the bottle."*

Mr Darling is saying this in his superior way.

"I know where you put it, father."

Wendy says this, thinking she is pleasing him. She runs off. Anguish of Mr Darling, which is increased when she returns with the bottle, which we have seen her in another picture getting from the top of a cupboard in his bedroom, where he had, doubtless, hidden it. It should be a very humble bedroom. She pours some of his medicine into a glass, and gives it to him. He glares. John chuckles at his father's predicament. Wendy gives the signal: one, two, three, for them to drink simultaneously. Humours of Michael and his father in this situation as in play.

Michael drinks his medicine, but Mr Darling ignobly conceals his glass behind his back. Michael sees this and cries. All are ashamed of Mr Darling, as they peep behind his back and see the glass. Nana sticks out her tail and struts contemptuously out of the room. He is annoyed at her. Then he indicates that he has a funny idea. He gets a milk bottle (which we see to be milk in a close-up) and pours a little milk on top of his medicine and then pours the white mixture into Nana's drinking bowl.

The others don't like this, but he points to it when Nana returns. She is grateful and begins to lap it up, then looks at him reproachfully and sneaks into her kennel. The children weep, and he is testy over the ill success of his joke. He orders Nana to come out, but she shrinks. Then, as in the play, he tries blandishment and lures her out, then suddenly seizes her and drags her away out at the door, to the grief of the children.

He foolishly ties Nana up in the yard, instead of leaving her in the nursery to guard his children.

In the next picture we see him tying Nana up in the yard below.

That night Mrs Darling had to go with her husband to a party.

First we see her in a bedroom tying her husband's tie, and we see him inking seams in his coat, and also inking his tall hat, which shows how poor they are. Then we see her in her party frock going from bed to bed kissing the children, etc. Then lighting a night-light at the head of each bedside. She has a last maternal look at them from the door, all as in play, with the accompanying music. Then we see Mr and Mrs Darling going out, and passing the yard, where Mr Darling won't let Mrs Darling fondle Nana. Nana weeps. The two pass up the street under an umbrella, as it is snowing. The house to which they go is not far away. It is in the same street, but on the opposite side. They walk. (There are no automobiles or telephones in this play.)

Next we see the outside of the window with two or three swallows on the window-sill.

Now Nana is seen fretting in the yard, as if she smelt danger. Then the nursery again. Children asleep. The night-lights blink and go out one by one in an eerie way to the music of the play, suggesting that something strange is to happen. There should be an awful creepiness here, which the music greatly helps.

The fairy, Tinker Bell.

Now we have the outside of the window, with swallows still there. The fairy music comes now. The fairy, Tink, flies on and alights on the window-sill. The swallows remain. She should be about five inches in height and, if the effect can be got, this should be one of the quaintest pictures of the film, the appearance of a real fairy. She is a vain little thing, and arranges her clothes to her satisfaction. She also keeps shoving the birds about so as to get the best place for herself. There should never be any close-up pictures of Tink or other fairies; we should always just see them as not more than five inches high. Finally she shoves the swallows off the sill. Then she pops through the window. We see her flying about the nursery, alighting on each bed, etc. Next we see Nana below looking at the sky and barking. Then we see Peter flying towards us. At first he is a mere speck in the distance. Then he comes closer and reaches the window. Now the inside of the nursery, with the children still asleep. It is rather dark now. Tink is not visible. Peter comes in through window. He has come for his shadow. He makes sure they are asleep. It should all be very dramatic here—like an attempted burglary, and the music helps. He rummages in the drawers for his shadow, finds it, sits on the floor trying to stick it on his foot with soap, which he gets from the bathroom. It won't stick on. He sobs. Wendy hears him and sits up in bed.

"Boy, why are you crying?"

She is asking this. He rises and, standing at foot of her bed, bows politely to her. She is gratified and bows from the bed in the quaint manner of the play, in which this is a popular incident.

"Girl, what is your name?"
"Wendy. What is your name?"
"Peter Pan."
"Where is your mother, Peter?"
"Don't have a mother, Wendy."
"Oh!"

As the result of this conversation Wendy springs out of bed, runs to him, puts arm round him and mothers him. It should be seen that she has at once taken the mother's place. He holds up his shadow to show that this is what is worrying him. She lifts the soap and in a close-up we see that it is marked "Soap." She is astonished at his ignorance, puts him on a chair, and proceeds to sew the shadow on to his foot in her old-fashioned, motherly way, with the business of the play, in which he suffers agonies, but is very brave. When he finds that all is well he struts about conceitedly, showing off his shadow. He dances gaily to his shadow, and brushes her aside as of no consequence, but this annoys Wendy.

"If I am no use I can at least withdraw."

We see Wendy saying this. She then haughtily leaps into bed and covers her body and face with the blankets, all in one action which is another popular incident of the play.

Peter is now sorry. First he pretends to go away, but hides. Then he leaps on to the rail at foot of the bed, sits on it and pokes her in a wheedling way with his foot.

"Wendy, don't withdraw. One girl is more use than twenty boys."

He is saying this. She peeps at him smiling and forgivingly, jumps up and sits on the side of her bed and signs to him to join her. He does so. They are a very friendly pair.

When Wendy said she would give him a kiss he held out his hand for it. He didn't know what a kiss was; and, so as not to hurt his feelings, she gave him a thimble.

We see this incident as in the play.

"Now shall I give you a kiss?"

Peter is saying this to Wendy. She nods. He gravely pulls a button off his clothes and gives it to her. We see it is a button in a close-up. She pretends pleasure, but privately makes a face.

"I ran away from home, Wendy, soon after I was born. I heard my father saying I would soon be a man: and I want always to be a little boy, and to have fun."

He tells her this. Then we see Peter's mother lying in bed and the father coming in. She holds up the baby proudly. (It must be a real baby just old enough to crawl.) The father sits on a chair talking to the mother. Now comes another realistic picture. We have visions of what the father is telling the mother, viz., of how the baby will rapidly grow up. Without the background seeming to alter we see the baby changing to a tiny boy, then to an older boy, then, through various changes to a youth and a man with a moustache, sitting like a clerk on a stool at a desk. The clothes, socks, etc. of him at one period should seem to drop off him and be replaced by others as he grows older, and we should actually see his legs growing longer, and so on. It will be worth while to devote much attention to this picture to get the right effect. The idea is to apply to the growth of a child from babyhood to manhood the same sort of cinema treatment that is sometimes given to illustrate the growth of flowers and plants. The real baby is much alarmed by all this pictorial prediction of his future. While the parents talk he creeps unseen by them out of bed and under it; emerges from under it, and crawls along floor out of the door. We see him crawling through an anteroom in which a nurse is asleep. Then he is seen crawling downstairs. Then we might get the effect of him crawling across a street full of traffic. He crawls into Kensington Gardens. There, two great birds come to his help and, sustaining him between them, fly away with him. His night-gown is now much torn.

Peter tells Wendy about his friends, the fairies. "When the first baby laughed for the first time, its laugh broke into a thousand pieces, and they all went skipping about: and that was the beginning of fairies."

He tells her this. Then the scene is a primeval wood. Adam and Eve leave their child on the ground. They go. The child laughs and kicks joyously. Then the picture is full of little splashes whirling about like falling leaves, and when they come to rest they are gay little fairies. The tinkling of bells comes here also to indicate their chatter, and we also have the fairy music.

Every time a child says "I don't believe in fairies" there is a fairy somewhere who falls down dead.

Peter is telling this to the enraptured Wendy. Then we see another nursery, with an unpleasant boy making this remark to his nurse.

Then the scene changes to a tree, on a branch of which several fairies are sitting chattering happily. They are all small like Tink. Suddenly one of them claps her hand to her heart, reels and falls to the ground. The others descend and sadly carry her remains away.

Wendy sees her first fairy.

We see Peter and Wendy chasing Tink about. Tink alights on the clock. Wendy admires her ecstatically.

But Tink loves Peter, and when she sees Wendy giving him a real kiss (now called a thimble) she misbehaves.

Peter and Wendy are now together on an armchair. She gives him a real kiss, and he likes it, beams, and solemnly gives her one. Then Tink rushes at her and pulls her hair, etc. Wendy screams. Peter threatens. The unseen bells which represent the fairy language ring agitatedly.

"She says she will do that every time I give you a thimble. But why, Tink?"

Peter is asking. The reply comes in a different kind of tinkle that should remain in the audience's memory.

She said: "You silly ass!"

Peter says this to Wendy. He chases Tink away, out of the window.

"I live in the Never, Never Land with the Lost Boys. Come with me, Wendy, and I'll teach you to fly, and you can be our mother. We do so need a mother."

Picture of Peter urging her to do this. They are now sprawling on the floor. Peter works his way along the floor to her—another comic effect in the play. Then a vision of the lost boys all perched on a branch of a tree asleep, huddled together in a row and sitting exactly like sleeping birds. They are in very ragged clothes and should look very small. Peter, himself, is one of them.

"Of course it's awfully fascinating!"

Wendy is saying this to Peter, and is screwed up in rapture as she says it.

Next a picture of little Liza asleep in the kitchen on a chair, a half-washed dish in her hands.

Then one of Nana in the yard, being annoyed by Tink, who is behaving impudently to her, teasing her, drinking from her bowl, etc. Nana makes rushes at her, but the mischievous Tink always flies out of reach.

"John, Michael, wake up. There is a boy here who is to teach us to fly and take us to the Never, Never Land. He says there are pirates and mermaids and redskins."

"I say, let's go at once."

Wendy is waking up Michael while Peter wafts John out of bed with his foot. Wendy is telling the great news, and John's is the enthusiastic reply. John puts on his long hat. John is in pyjamas, Michael in "combinations" and Wendy in a white cotton night-gown.

A *lesson in flying*

We should now have a fine series of film pictures without words. First we see Peter in the nursery showing the others how to fly, while they watch him eagerly from their beds. Then Nana in the yard tearing at her chain, and looking up at the nursery window which is the only one lit up.

Then little Liza still asleep in her chair in the kitchen—in a different position.

Then a view of Peter and the others through the window on whose sill Tink is sitting.

Then Mr Darling, Mrs Darling with others at a dinner-party.

Then the nursery again. The children are trying to fly by jumping about and falling.

"Just think lovely, wonderful thoughts, and they lift you up in the air."

Peter is saying this to them, and shows them how to do it, but still they can't. Then Nana is seen breaking her chain and rushing off down the street. She should be a real dog now.

"Wait till I blow the fairy dust on you."

Peter blows fairy dust on the children. They are boastful because, as the result of this, they can fly a yard or so now, but they are still very bad at it.

Nana is next seen bursting a door open, and rushing up a stair into a room where the dining-party is. She tells in barks of the goings-on at home. The people dining rush to the window and pull the curtains slightly open. They don't pull them open to anything like their full extent. About eighteen inches will be ample, and that only in the middle of the curtains, not the whole length. Through an aperture of about eighteen inches wide and deep the whole of the nursery window, about 80 yards away, will be seen. It is the only lighted window, and on it we can see the *shadows* of the children moving alarmingly on the nursery blind. Mr and Mrs Darling are much agitated, and rush with Nana out of the dining-room and down the stair.

Then we see the children flying in the nursery. They are clumsy compared to Peter, but are now able to revolve triumphantly round the nursery. They are in ecstasy. Then Mr and Mrs Darling hurrying with Nana along the snowy street. They point agitatedly to the window, against which the shadows of the children can be seen now flying round and round.

A close-up of this awful sight.

Then inside the nursery. All are going round in a mad delirium of delight: and then comes the flight of Peter and his companions through the window.

The parents and Nana burst into nursery just in time to see them disappear.

From the window they watch the children flying away over the house-tops.

The flight to the Never, Never Land has now begun. We see the truants flying over the Thames and the Houses of Parliament. Then an ordinary sitting of the House of Commons, faithfully reproduced. A policeman rushes in to the august Chamber and interrupts proceedings with startling news of what is happening in the air. All rush out to see, the Speaker, who is easily identified by his wig, being first. They get to the Terrace of the House and excitedly watch the flying group disappear.

Then the children flying over the Atlantic. The moon comes out. Wendy tires, Peter supports her.

Then they near New York. The Statue of Liberty becomes prominent. They are so tired that they all alight on it. It is slippery, and they can't find a resting-place. At first we should think it a real statue. Then we should get the effect of the statue mothering them by coming to life, to the extent of making them comfortable in her arms for the night.

This should be one of the most striking pictures.

Next we see them resume their journey. They cross America, with Niagara seen.

Then they are over the Pacific, where the Never, Never Land is.

The Never, Never Land.

We see the island all glorious and peaceful in a warm sun. We see the whole of it as in a map, not a modern map but the old-fashioned pictorial kind with quaintly exaggerated details. I have a map of the Never, Never Land, in this style which should be reproduced.

Then we see the sun go down and the island become dark and threatening.

Wolves are seen chasing one of the Lost Boys.

Then wild animals drinking at the ford by moonlight.

Then redskins, in the Fenimore Cooper story manner, torturing a prisoner who is tied to a tree. He is a pirate.

Tiger Lily: "Every brave would have had her to wife, but she received their advances coldly."

First Tiger Lily comes into view. Then we see a redskin evidently proposing to the beautiful creature, who is the Indian princess. She whips out her hatchet and fells him. She and all the redskins should be very tall in contrast with the children.

Then Peter is seen in the air, pointing out the distant pirate ship to Wendy. Then the dreadful ship comes into view, flying the Jolly Roger. We should have a fine, wicked pirate ship of the days when they attacked the Spanish galleons—a reproduction of some notorious ship, black and sinister, with an enormous hull which Peter is to climb presently. By and by we are to be shown various parts of the ship in detail. It is at anchor just now, and its sails are not showing. We don't see the sails until Peter gives an order much later in the play.

Jas. Hook, the Pirate Captain (Eton and Balliol).

We have here a picture of Hook dressed as he is in the play, with an iron hook instead of a right hand—a double cigar in mouth, etc. He should be very tall.

(NOTE.—About the playing of this part. Hook should be played absolutely seriously, and the actor must avoid all temptation to play the part as if he was conscious of its humours. There *is* such a temptation, and in the stage play the actors of the part have sometimes yielded to it, with fatal results. He is a blood-thirsty villain, all the more so because he is an educated man. The other pirates are rough scoundrels, but he can be horribly polite when he is most wicked. He should have the manners of a beau. But above all the part should be played with absolute seriousness and avoidance of trying to be funny. This should be insisted on throughout, and especially later in the pirate-ship scene. This same warning applies to all the pirates.)

Pathetic Smee, the Nonconformist Pirate.

Smee is in spectacles, and is the hopeless loveable-looking ruffian of the play. He is sitting on the floor in a corner of the ship. By his side are tea-pot, cup and saucer, etc. He is drinking his tea out of the saucer.

Every one of them a name of Terror on the Spanish Main.

We see the dreadful crew—about twenty in all. Starkey, Cecco, etc. Some should be dressed as in the play. The others copied from the books about buccaneers.

A pirate points out the flying children.

Then Peter in the air is giving the warning to Wendy and the others.

Then we see Long Tom, the great gun, being got ready on deck. All the pirates must be very tall. It is fired, by Hook's command.

We see Peter and his companions blown away in different directions, but evidently not damaged otherwise. They roll about in the air and then fly on. They are now separated.

The Lost Boys awaiting Peter's return.

The scene is the wood of the play with big trees that have hollow trunks. All trees should be very large to make children seem smaller. From a chimney in ground smoke is coming.

We see the children emerging above ground from their trees as in the play. First comes Slightly.

Slightly Soiled. He was so called because that was the name marked on the clothes he had been lost in.

Slightly comes, he is the comic figure among the Boys.

Tootles—Nibs—Curly—The Twins.

They come up, all differentiated as in the play. All are looking in the sky for Peter.

"Yo, ho, yo ho, the pirate life,
The flag of skull and bones.
A merry life, a hempen rope,
And hey for Davy Jones!"

Now the music of this pirate song is heard, but not the words. The Lost Boys quake for they know it means that the pirates are coming.

The boys all dart down their trees out of sight, except Nibs who steals off to reconnoitre, one of them first putting a mushroom over the chimney to hide the tell-tale smoke. The pirates are punting rafts upon a romantic river.

On one raft with cushions raising him high sits Hook regally. Several pictures of them on river. Then Hook gets off. All are looking for the boys. He signals to them to scout in different directions. They move off stealthily. Two or three of them are gigantic negroes. They are evidently villains of every race.

"'Twas Peter Pan cut off my arm and flung it to a crocodile that happened to be passing by. That crocodile liked my arm so much, Smee, that it has followed me about ever since from sea to sea and from land to land licking its lips for the rest of me."
"In a way, Captain, it's a sort of compliment."

Hook is saying this to Smee horribly, near the underground house of whose existence they don't know yet. One boy's head is out of a tree-trunk listening. He withdraws it, horrified. The whole scene is now shown in vision of Peter fighting Hook, cutting off his arm and flinging it to the crocodile.

The whack with which the arm is cut off should be so terrific that we see Hook "seeing stars," but it is not "stars" he sees; it is the trees around him all moving just for a few seconds. The same sort of curious effect as was got in my private film of *Macbeth*, when the trees were seen chasing Macbeth.

This should be in strange and dreadful scenery, quite unlike that of the island. Then we see the dogged pursuit of Hook by the crocodile on a great globe of the world. We see an actual globe. Wherever the ship goes the crocodile is swimming after it. If Hook takes to land it still follows. Thus they go over the globe, which slowly revolves for our benefit, the figures being small, but discernible and much larger than they could really be.

"One day, Smee, that crocodile swallowed a clock, which goes tick-tick inside him, and so before he can reach me I hear the tick and bolt."

Hook is telling this triumphantly. He is sitting on a large mushroom at this time, the one that conceals the chimney. Then, in a vision, we see the incident happening. Hook appears in another woodland scene near a river, but again different kind of scenery. All these scenes should be different from each other and very picturesque. He has something concealed under his cloak. He is very cunning and criminal in manner. It is a clock which he winds up. It now ticks, and we hear the ticking. He places it on the ground and hides. The crocodile comes, shoves clock about curiously and eventually swallows clock. It continues ticking, but in a more muffled way. The crocodile turns his head, trying to look at his body and goes away puzzled. Hook emerges triumphant and exits in the opposite direction villainously.

Then we see Hook and Smee again. Hook rises, evidently feeling hot. They lift the big mushroom on which he has been sitting, and discover that it conceals a chimney from which smoke now comes. They point to the holes in the trees and indicate triumphantly that they have discovered the boys' secret home. They draw their pistols and cutlasses and are about to descend the trees.

A boy has been watching again. He descends and tells the other boys. We now see the underground home, which will be described later. The boys there are all in terror, but they seize weapons.

Then, above ground again, Hook and Smee are about to descend trees when they hear an alarming sound, which we hear also. It is the tick-tick of the crocodile. They rush away. Crocodile music. The crocodile appears and plods after them. He is a sort of Nemesis, ever plodding after Hook. It will be found best sometimes to have a real crocodile of huge size, and sometimes a theatrical property.

Now boys' heads peep out at tree-trunks, watching. They disappear down trees as the redskins appear on the warpath following the pirates in single file. This is slow and creepy, to the redskin music. The redskins go off dramatically, as in the play. When they have passed the boys emerge. Nibs comes running to them excitedly pointing upwards. We now see Wendy flying alone and with difficulty. First she is seen over another part of the wood—then over the boys. Tink is also in air, dashing about.

The jealous Tink calls "Shoot the Wendy Bird!"

The bells tinkle. Tootles gets bow and arrow and shoots Wendy. We see the arrow in her. The bells ring "You silly ass!" Wendy falls to the ground. The boys gather round her.

"This is no bird. I think it must be a lady. Let me see, I remember ladies. Ay, that's a lady."

Slightly, in his conceited way, shoves the others aside and makes this disturbing announcement. All take off their caps. Tootles is scared: suddenly all look up. Peter is seen flying alone. First they are delighted. Then all gather round Wendy to hide her. Peter comes flying down.

"Boys, great news! I have brought at last a mother for us all!"

They are woebegone. Tootles nobly makes them stand aside and let Peter see Wendy.

Peter is dramatic. He goes on his knees beside her and pulls out the arrow. Tootles, baring his chest, indicates that he is the guilty one. Peter raises the arrow to use it as a dagger on Tootles. Wendy's arm rises, and a Twin points this phenomenon out to Peter who examines Wendy again. Suspense of boys.

"She lives! This is the kiss I gave her. The arrow struck against it. It has saved her life."

Peter holds up the button from her chest.
There is a close-up picture of button.

"I remember kisses. Let me see. Ay, that's a kiss."

Slightly is shown the button and gives his confident opinion. Then a picture of Tink on a tree, and Peter sternly ordering her away. She flies away crying: "You silly ass!"

John and Michael are now seen first flying and then tottering down. They are so tired that they fall asleep at once against a tree.

Then the children try to carry Wendy down a tree-trunk. They cannot get her down. Peter confides to them a grand idea, which they proceed to put into execution. It is to build a house round her.

We now see them building a house round Wendy in the elaborate manner of the play, just about the size of herself, John and Michael being waked up to join in. The house should not be a make-believe affair built of canvas as it has to be in the acted play. Here it should be a real house, though comic. We should see the boys felling trees, carpentering, etc., actually building the house with miraculous speed, much as described in *Peter Pan in Kensington Gardens*. We see them knocking in the posts, making doors, windows, etc., with lightning rapidity, and all this to music. When the little house is finished it is a beautiful little house of wood and moss, lop-sided and all wrong, but fascinating.

They survey the completed house. Peter evidently sees there is one thing wanting. He indicates that it is a chimney. He knocks the top out of John's tall hat (which John has been wearing since he left home) and puts it on roof as a chimney. Immediately smoke comes out of the hat.

Wendy consents to be their mother.

They are gathered round the little house expectantly. Peter knocks at the door. Wendy comes out in a daze. Then the scene of the play, with its business. They go on their knees, arms outstretched, asking her to be their mother. She consents. Glee. Wendy is at once maternal in manner. They dance round the house. All romp inside except Peter, who remains outside on guard with drawn sword. It gets dark. The little house is lighted up inside. The shadows of wild beasts pass in background. Peter drives away wolves. The last one is a baby wolf, so small and young, that it does not know how to run away. He lifts it up in his arms and carries it to its mother, who goes off thankfully with it. Then Peter falls asleep by the door of the little house.

Tink comes cautiously. She hops on to his knee, then on to his shoulder, kisses him. She remains there. Peter sleeps on.

One day soon after her arrival Peter took Wendy to the lagoon to see the Mermaids.

A gay procession is seen setting forth through romantic scenery. First Tootles, Nibs, Slightly, Twins, and Curly on foot gaily rollicking, leap-frogging, etc. Their clothes are now carefully darned, etc. Then Wendy, sitting on a rough little home-made sledge which is pulled by a kite string, the kite being high in the air. Then John and Michael on foot and very gay. Then last Peter riding on his goat. A peculiar effect should be tried for here, which may be got by the same mechanical means as the trees moving in earlier scene when Peter cut off Hook's arm. The effect wanted is that, as Peter passes along a sort of path, flowers come moving after him in a long procession.

"Look at those beastly flowers following me again!"

Peter is looking behind him and saying this indignantly. He signs to the flowers authoritatively to stop it, and they now stand still. He goes on, and as soon as he has disappeared they begin to follow again. He has only been hiding and now pops round the corner and catches them following. Again they stop—he waves to them to go back, and then we see them all go back till there are none left. They behave precisely like a dog following its master and ordered home. Peter now rides forward.

(NOTE.—We have now about twenty minutes of pictures without words.)

The next incident is that the kite string breaks because John tries to sit on sledge—thus showing that the kite can't pull two. Wendy tumbles out of the sledge, and the kite disappears in the air. The sledge is abandoned. Peter gallantly dismounts to let Wendy ride the goat, and on they go. Then Peter signs caution, Wendy dismounts, and they proceed stealthily on tip-toe to take the mermaids by surprise. They hide among long grass and peer at the beautiful mermaids' lagoon which now comes into view. It should be a lovely romantic lagoon in a coral island; coral reefs and Pacific vegetation. There are no mermaids at present. Peter points out objects of interest to Wendy, the chief one being a rock in the water called Marooners' Rock, of which we are to see more presently.

Then they are excited over an incident that takes place. A branch of a tree on which is a great nest breaks off and falls into the water. The mother bird is on the nest and continues to sit on it as it floats away from the branch into the lagoon. Wendy kisses her hand to it in praise of its maternal behaviour.

Next we see the mermaids. The children watch from their hiding-place. The mermaid pictures should be a beautiful series of considerable length. First the mermaids are far away, scores of them basking lazily by the shores of the lagoon, some in the water, some out of it. They should mostly be at a distance as in this way the illusion will carry best. We may see one nearer on a rock combing her hair if this can be done without the tail being unnatural. Excitement of Wendy,

Peter signs caution. All the children dive stealthily into the water, Peter leading, with the object of catching a mermaid. Alternative pictures of mermaids, and then the children swimming craftily toward them. They jump up to catch the one combing hair, but she slips through their fingers. Peter takes a flying leap through the air and alights on her back. He is wildly gay. No one else can be so gay as Peter, nor so serious, nor so gallant, nor so cocky.

Next, at another part of the lagoon we see Tiger Lily picturesquely poised by the shore with an arrow in her bow for Smee, who is coming along in a boat. From behind tree Starkey leaps on her, and Smee wades ashore to help him. Starkey is about to knife her when Smee proposes something more dreadful. It is shown us in a vision. We see Marooners' Rock in the vision with Tiger Lily lying bound on it. The tide rises till the rock and she are submerged. Starkey likes this vision, and in the next picture they have put her bound on the rock. They are in the boat now beside the rock, and we have two pictures, one of Hook swimming out to them, and one of Peter stealing to the rock to rescue Tiger Lily. Peter, unseen by the pirates, cuts her bonds and she slips into the water. Hook arrives and gets into the boat. They proudly point to the rock, and then, to their dismay, see that Tiger Lily has vanished. Hook threatens, and they go on their knees to him. He is looking everywhere for the possible foe, and Peter cannot resist rising in the water and jeering at him. At last, Hook thinks, he has got Peter. He and Smee dive and Starkey guards the boat.

The fight in the water begins. Mermaids and fishes are seen rushing away in fear. John and Starkey fight in the boat and go over in each other's embrace. The great fight is on the rock between Hook and Peter, which should be much as in the play. It ends with Peter rolling off the rock into the water, unfairly gashed by Hook, who triumphantly dives. Then we see Hook swimming to land and stealing off. Then, after Hook has disappeared, the crocodile is seen landing and pursuing him. Hook is ignorant on these occasions that the crocodile is following.

Next, the other boys gather round the drifting boat and get into it. They call and look everywhere for Peter and Wendy. The boat drifts away till it is lost sight of. Now no one is to be seen on the lagoon, which now looks cold and cruel.

Then we see the mermaids in their romantic cave. Wendy is their prisoner. They examine her curiously. They laugh derisively at her feet, so that she has to sit on her feet. They put their fingers in her eyes and swish her with their tails, which is evidently their way of hurting people. Then they sleep. She sits there staring with affrighted eyes. Peter comes and, stepping stealthily over the mermaids, rescues her and goes off. He is evidently wounded, and so is she. A mermaid wakes up and follows them, looking wicked.

Next Peter, drags Wendy on to Marooners' Rock, and both lie there in a faint. The cruel mermaid comes swimming to the rock and is pulling Wendy inch by inch into the water when Peter sits up and saves her. This should be very dramatic. The mermaid disappears. We see the two children sitting there, a touching pair, to the music of the scene. Peter points to how the water is rising, but they are too exhausted to do anything.

We see that the rock is being submerged.

Then the kite comes again into view drifting in the air. First we see it over another part of the lagoon. Then nearer the rock. Peter has an idea; he grips the tail and pulls the kite toward him.

Peter nobly ties the tail round Wendy, indicating that it can't carry two. They embrace. Then she is carried over the lagoon by the kite. Peter waves to her till she is lost to sight. He shudders as he realises his situation. We see him next alone. Then we see Wendy being carried over the island by the kite.

"To die will be an awfully big adventure."

Peter is now standing, proudly erect. The rock is sinking. It is now moonlight. Then we see another part of the lagoon with the mother-bird still drifting on her nest.

Then Peter on the rock. He is now up to his knees in water, but still brave. Then the nest drifts toward him. He sees it. The bird quacks and flies away. Peter has an inspiration. He pulls the nest toward him and takes two big eggs out of it. At first he doesn't know what to do with them. Then he lifts Starkey's hat. On Marooners' Rock is a post on which Starkey has left his hat. Peter puts the eggs into the hat and the hat in the water. The hat drifts away. He then gets into the nest and drifts in the same direction. He makes a sail of his shirt and now he goes in another direction. He is very solemn and intense, with gleaming eyes.

Several pictures of Peter in the nest. Next we see the hat alone on the lagoon. The bird flies back and sits on it.

Then we see the nest drawing near shore. Wendy wades out to meet it and they are triumphant. Peter is painfully cocky again. Last we see the hat stationary among reeds in the water. The mother bird gets off it and waddles ashore. She is presently followed by two baby birds.

In the house under the trees they lived very like baby bears.

First we see baby bears in a cave playing around their mother. She is motherly to them, but also punishes. She brings food and they gather round it greedily. They trot about after her. They curl up on the ground against her and sleep.

Then we see the boys behaving in exactly the same way with Wendy as mother. The feeding is also very like the bears. They also trot about after Wendy. They also curl up on floor against her and sleep.

When one of them wanted to turn in bed Wendy gave the signal, and they all turned simultaneously.

Wendy is giving Curly a good washing at a basin. He is dripping, etc. Michael as the baby is in a sort of bassinette, swung from roof. All the other boys are pulling down from the wall the big bed of the play. Peter is one of them. They are in night-gowns. Curly joins the others and all get into bed, lying like sardines, some heads at top of bed and some heads at foot.

After some horse-play they lie quiet. Then one holds up his hand. Wendy, who has sat down by fire to darn, gives the signal, and all turn simultaneously.

In the Neverland the Seasons succeed each other more rapidly than at home.

In illustration of this we see a new scene. It is a romantic little glade in which one fruit tree and a tiny stream of water are the chief objects. At one point the water is trickling down, and Peter comes with a home-made wooden bucket which he places beneath this trickle and sits waiting for bucket to fill slowly. The time is summer and the fruit tree is heavy with ripe fruit. Gradually the scene changes to winter. The fruit disappears, the leaves fall off and the tree is bare. The ground becomes white with snow. The stream is frozen, an icicle hangs where the water had been trickling into bucket. Peter breaks icicle. He is cold, pulls his clothes tighter round him. Then in same way the scene changes to a sunny day in spring. The tree becomes beautiful with blossom and leaves. The ground is a rich green. Peter is so warm that he has to undo his jacket. The trickle is running free again. The bucket is now full, and he departs with it quite unaware that anything out of the ordinary has happened. The whole point of this picture is that the changes should be gradual—not sudden jump from one season to another—i.e. the actual process should be seen.

Tink, of course, had an apartment of her own.

We see Tink's exquisite tiny bedroom, with her brushing hair, etc. It opens off the big room and should be shown much more beautifully than is possible in the play.

At first the newcomers had to be pulled out of their trees like a cork, but Peter altered them, and soon they fitted.

We see John and Wendy being ignominiously pulled up by the hair of the head. They had stuck in their trees. Then John is being held down, while Peter flattens him out with a rolling-pin. He is flattened out too much. He is flattened out on the ground till he covers quite a large extent—as if a 100 barrels had rolled over him. Wendy is indignant. Then Peter and the boys roll him up like a stretch of carpet and Peter works on him till he is of a correct shape and bulk. He now runs up and down the tree gaily. Wendy is then subjected to alteration. Their object is to make her shorter, so she is laid down and Peter pushes her feet and Slightly her head with the result that she is telescoped. This scene takes place beside water. Wendy runs to see her reflection in the water. We see it also. She is now very short and stout. She is in distress. The boys don't know what to do. She lies down again and Peter operates on her with the rolling-pin—successfully. Again she looks at her reflection in the water. Now she is delighted. She runs gaily up and down her tree. General happiness.

When you wanted to know the time you waited beside the crocodile till the clock struck.

Peter is sitting beside the crocodile waiting. The clock strikes 4. We should hear it also. Peter skips away.

The next picture shows Wendy as a schoolmistress. It is the underground scene, and she has a cane in her hand. On a board she has chalked in a childish hand:

"Rite down all you can remember about your adoredable parents."

All the boys, except First Twin, are in a row on their toadstools with slates, trying to write, but looking puzzled. Peter, indeed, has fallen asleep with a broken slate at his feet. First Twin is on a high stool in corner in disgrace with a fool's cap on his head. Then we are shown three of their slates in a close-up. Tootles had made an *0* on his. On Nibs's slate is written: "All I remembers about my mother is that she useder to say: 'Oh, how I wish I had a chek book of my own.'" On Michael's is written: "Are you not our mother, Wendy?" She is troubled by this. It is painful to her that they have forgotten so much.

Wendy was one of those mothers who like their offspring to have a good romp before bed-time.

First of all the boys, including Peter, in their ordinary clothes, flying about over the tree-tops, engaged in a game of football. They have a home-made football and are arranged in sides and manage to keep ball in air. They have also absurd goal-posts, which they have tied to trees, standing out higher than the trees. It is a moonlight evening.

They had many a night of joyous revelry.

We see them in their night-gowns, underground, and they are engaged in the pillow dance just as it is done in the play, except that Peter is chief dancer in place of First Twin. Wendy is sitting on a stool darning their stockings and occasionally smiling at them in a motherly way. The dance ends with a pillow fight.

Tink and her friends were sometimes a nuisance; they got into everything.

Peter is seen in underground room putting on his long boots. Evidently something is in one of them that ought not to be there. He holds it upside down and Tink drops out. Peter is so used to this kind of thing that he expresses no surprise. He just continues to put on his boots.

Then in the same room Wendy is cutting Slightly's hair like a barber. There is a pot on fire—it moves agitatedly. She lifts pot off fire and takes off lid. Tink jumps out of pot wet and indignant.

Then the same room with the bed prepared for night. Peter is sharpening a weapon. One of the pillows on bed rocks about in an odd way. Wendy is there and points this out to Peter. He seizes pillow, opens it at top and holds pillow upside down. A hundred fairies drop from pillow on to floor. Peter sweeps them away with a broom. Then they are seen above ground flying away out of the tree-trunks.

Peter loved Wendy as a son, but she wanted him to love her as something else. He could not think what it was.

She is saying this lovingly to him in the underground house, but when he is puzzled she stamps her foot, then sits forlornly.

"What can it be, Tink?"

He is asking this above ground of Tink, who replies in her bell language: "You silly ass!"

"What can it be, Tiger Lily?"

He is asking the same question of Tiger Lily. She prostrates herself before him in adoration, etc., but he can't understand. She goes away sadly. He remains hopelessly puzzled. Then he skips away indifferently.

For many moons Hook cogitated over his revenge.

We see him sitting in the crow's-nest of the ship, a perilous but romantic situation. There is a map of the island in his hands, and in a close-up we see quaint details with writing that mark places, such as "Underground Home." Little flags are stuck over map as in a war-map and he is busy using these. The moon is seen first as a quarter moon, then half and so on to full moon, then it reverses the process to indicate passing of time. He also spies on the island through a telescope.

Then we see Peter in silhouette standing motionless on a promontory watching the pirate ship in the distance. He looks very cocky.

What maddened Hook beyond endurance was Peter's cockiness. In the night-time it disturbed him like an insect.

We see Hook's cabin with no one in it at first. This cabin is largely furnished like a boy's room at Eton. It has a wicker chair and a desk with a row of books as in an Eton room. On the walls besides weapons are the colours he won at school, the ribbons, etc., arranged in the eccentric Etonian way, and the old school lists, caps, and also two pictures, which when shown in close-ups are seen to be (1) Eton College, (2) a photograph of an Eton football eleven; the central figure is Hook, as he was when a boy, but distinguishable, with a football in his hands and the prize cup between his knees. He and the other boys must wear correct colours. The cat-o'-nine-tails also hangs up prominently.

Hook comes in and begins to undress. There has probably never before been much attention given to how a buccaneer retires to bed. We endeavour to supply this want. He winds up his watch, and hangs it up, etc. Presently we see him in a nightgown. He gets into bed and finds the sheets cold. He lies in bed smoking and reading the *Eton Chronicle* (of which a real copy must be used). He lays down the cigar-holder and blows out his candle. Then we see him having a nightmare about Peter, brandishing his hook and scratching as if tortured by an insect. Peter is seen in a vision mocking him.

Months passed, and at last Hook unripped his plot.

We have now a series of pictures.

First we see the pirates, picturesque but horrible, climbing out of their ship into their two rowing-boats. They are armed to the teeth. We have a grim vision of the side of the wicked ship, old and dirty.

Next we see the redskins sitting in a circle round a fire in the open. A pipe is passed from one to another. Their wigwams are seen near by.

Then the two boats being pulled across the lagoon—Hook standing erect in one of them—Smee in the other.

Then all the children, except Peter, in the underground home. They are in their ordinary clothes, and are having a merry evening at leap-frog, etc. Wendy is sitting by the fire smiling at them and sewing as usual. Stockings and other garments hang drying on a string by the fire. Then we see the pirates landing and stealing off into the forest.

Peter was away from home that night, attending a fairy wedding.

Peter is seen at the fairy wedding. This should be an elaborate and beautiful picture of some length, one of the prettiest in the film. Peter is sitting against a tree playing his pipes, and fairies emerge from under big leaves into a fairy circle and go through a fairy wedding; an idea of what this should be like can be got from my book *Peter Pan in Kensington Gardens*. The music (which will have to be new) of this fairy scene should come from bells.

Then we see the crocodile asleep in a lonely glade beside a stream.

So preternaturally quick of hearing are all savage things that, when Smee trod on a dry twig, the sound woke the whole island into life.

We see the pirates proceeding cautiously through the wood. In a close-up we see Smee tread on a twig. Evidently the others all hear it. In a sudden stoppage of the music we should hear it also. They gape at him startled, then fling themselves among the long grass to hide. Smee is conscience-stricken. Then a series of pictures which, to have the best effect, should be short and sharp, changing quickly. They indicate the effect in different parts of the island of hearing the twig snap.

First it is heard by the children in their leap-frog games. They suddenly stop in the middle of the play, and gather, scared, round Wendy. Then the redskins hear it, leap up, seize their weapons and are at once terrible scalp-hunters on the war-path. Then the fairy wedding is interrupted by Peter hearing it, and starting to his feet. The fairies suddenly disappear. Some of them are on his knee, shoulders, etc. He brushes them off like bread-crumbs. He goes off excitedly and stealthily, with Tink.

Then the crocodile starts from his sleep on hearing it, and pounds off through the forest, dogged of purpose, on his never-ending quest.

These pictures should all be short to represent the effect of Smee's blunder, and before each one we should have repeated briefly for a second or two only the picture of Smee treading on the twig.

Tiger Lily and her braves guard the home of The Great White Father.

We see her and her redskins above the children's home, guarding it, and lying in their blankets, etc. Then Peter comes toward them through the forest, and they prostrate themselves before him. He accepts their homage as the natural thing. No one could be more cocky. He is like a king to his subjects. He descends his tree.

Then we see a pirate on top of a tree, signaling what he observes to the pirates below. They move forward furtively.

Peter found Wendy telling a story to the boys.

The children are seen, clustered in bed in their night-gowns, listening eagerly to Wendy who sits near them with Michael between her knees. Peter is sitting on a toadstool at the other end of the underground room, whittling a stick and evidently disliking the story, putting his hands over his ears, etc. Up above, as in the play, we at times see the redskins. We now have a series of visions (reproduced from the nursery scenes) illustrating Wendy's story, which is really the tale of how Wendy, John, and Michael were spirited away to the Never, Never Land. First we see the three in their nursery being put to bed by Nana. Then the mother saying good-night to them and going off with the father to the party. Then Peter enters at window. Then he teaches them how to fly. Then they fly out at window, the parents and Nana coming just too late to catch them. These, being reproductions, are brief.

Between these varied pictures we see two of Wendy telling them the story, and the children misbehaving and whacking each other as they do in the play. Peter's uneasiness increases.

"But their adoredable mother always kept the window open for them, and when at last they flew back to her, pen cannot describe the happy scene."

Wendy is saying this as in the play, and we have a vision of Mr and Mrs Darling welcoming the return of the children with joy. (It should not be the picture afterwards seen at end of play.) Peter starts up with a cry, which draws all attention to him.

"Wendy, you are wrong about Mothers. Long ago I flew back but the window was barred, and there was another little boy sleeping in my bed."

We see Peter telling this. Then we have a vision of Peter looking through the window of his old nursery, and there is a baby in the bassinette. The window is iron barred. He beats on the window in vain and is furious.

Then we see John and Michael cross to Wendy in terror.

"Perhaps Mother is in half mourning by this time."

Wendy says it, alarmed: and, in a vision, we have a picture of Mr and Mrs Darling at home brightly practising a new dance to a gramophone, and not in mourning.

"We must go back at once. You can all come with me. I am sure father and mother will adopt you."

"Won't they think us rather a handful, Wendy?"

"Oh no, it will only mean having a few beds in the drawing-room; they can be hidden behind screens on first Thursdays."

Wendy is saying it. Then, in a vision, we see the little drawing-room first as an ordinary, but quite humble, room, and then the same room with many little beds in it, and one of the lost children in each. Then we see the boys delightedly getting their bundles to accompany Wendy, and all now dressed as in this scene in the play. All are jolly except Peter, who stands with arms folded. Wendy entreats him to get ready like the others.

"Nobody is going to make me a man: I want always to be a little boy and to have fun."

He is saying this. He skips about, pretending heartlessness and playing his pipes. Wendy is in woe. She appeals to him in vain.

"You will remember about changing your flannels, Peter? and to take your medicine? I'll pour it out for you."

He nods sullenly. We see her pouring out his medicine and leaving it on a ledge at the back in a glass.

"What are your exact feelings for me, Peter?"

"Those of an adoredable son, Wendy."

She asks him lovingly, but his reply makes her stamp her foot. They are about to ascend their trees when a sudden turmoil above terrifies them. This scene has been underground only—nothing above shown.

Now the scene changes to above ground. The pirate music is heard. The redskins start up into fighting positions, and at the same moment the pirates are upon them. Now takes place the great fight between pirates and redskins, which should be a much more realistic and grim affair than in the play. There it has to be more pretence, but here we should see real redskin warfare that will be recognised as such by all readers of Fenimore Cooper, etc. Alternated with it we should see the children below listening for the result in agony. Peter has seized a sword and wants to rush up to join in the fight, but Wendy holds him back and the terrified Michael clings to his knees. Some pirates are killed, but more redskins and the remaining redskins, including Tiger Lily, are put to flight. The bodies are removed. Then the pirates gather together and listen at the trees.

"If the redskins have won they will beat the tom-tom: it is always their sign of victory."

Peter is saying it. All the children listen eagerly. At the same time we see the scene above. Hook, listening at tree has heard Peter's remark. He sees how to deceive the children. He seizes the tom-tom and wickedly beats it.

"An Indian victory! You are quite safe now, Wendy. Goodbye. Tink, lead the way."

Peter says it. All rejoice. Peter pulls the curtain of Tink's room. Tink darts about—then disappears up a tree. Peter and Wendy have an affecting farewell. Peter is breaking down and the other boys look on inquisitively. He stamps and they turn their faces away in fear of him. When he is sure they are not looking he embraces Wendy, but like a child, not like a lover. Then all but Peter disappear in tree-trunks.

Above ground we see the pirates waiting devilishly at the trees to seize the children as they come up. Tink darts up and escapes them. She flutters around and is lost sight of. Then up their trees come the doomed children, one by one, to be immediately seized before they utter a cry. They are tossed like bales of cotton from one pirate to another, and this should be a quaint effect if exactly carried out. They should probably be on wires to get it right, but there must be no burlesquing of it. All should seem natural. The last is Wendy, to whom Hook gives his arm with horrible courtesy. She takes it in a dazed way. He gives the signal and all go except himself. He stands there, a dreadful figure in his cloak.

Next a brief picture of the surviving redskins in panic, striking their tents. The squaws carry babies in the Indian way.

Then we see the underground home again. Peter thinks they have all got safely away. We see him barring the doors of the trees.

Who was Peter Pan? No one really knows. Perhaps he was just somebody's boy who never was born.

We have a picture of Peter sitting, a sad, solitary figure on the side of the bed. Then up above we see Hook listening. He produces from his pocket a bottle, and a close-up picture shows the word "Poison" on it. Scowling horribly he begins to descend a tree.

Then, below, we see Peter now lying on the bed. He has gone miserably to sleep. Hook's head appears very devilishly above the door of the tree. He can't reach the bar of the door to get in. He is foiled. Then he sees the medicine, which is within reach. He pours some poison into it. Then, with horrid triumph, he withdraws. We see him reappear at top, and now he is suddenly attacked by Tink, who flies at his face. She evidently stings him badly, but he drives her away, wraps his cloak around him and goes off villainously.

Again we see Peter on bed. Tink flies in and wakes him.

She rings excitedly, and for some time. He understands the terrible news she is telling him and seizes his dagger. He vows vengeance. He sharpens the dagger on his grindstone.

"My medicine poisoned? Rot. I promised Wendy to take it, and I will."

He is saying this to Tink, who is excitedly hopping around the glass. He takes the medicine in his hand.

She bravely drinks it.

When he sees she has done this he is amazed.

She begins to flutter about, and makes the bell-sounds.

"What? It was poisoned, and you drank it to save my life?"

Tink is fluttering about weakly. Peter is in distress.

"Tink, why did you do it?"

He asks despairingly. She tinkles back "You silly ass!" She flutters into her bedroom on to bed. Peter is in agony outside her room, looking in. Close-up picture of Tink writhing on bed. Peter's head is peering into room and will be nearly as large as the room.

"She says she thinks she could get well again if children believed in fairies. Oh, say that you believe: Wave your handkerchiefs! Don't let Tink die!"

Peter is addressing the audience. He, as it were, comes outside the scene to do so. We hope that, as in the play, the audience demonstrate. The light in the little room, which has been palpitating, grows stronger. Peter is triumphant: he thanks audience.

And now to rescue Wendy.

In a close-up we see Tink gaily dancing on her bed.

(From this point for a long time there are no words flung on screen.)

We now see Peter in pursuit of the pirates.

First he emerges from the tree. He looks for signs of which way they have gone. In a close-up we see their footmarks. He follows these. Then we see the pirates brutally leading the chained prisoners through the wood.

Then a brief picture of the redskins departing hurriedly in their Indian canoes for some new hunting-ground.

Then Hook alone triumphantly proceeding through the wood.

Then the crocodile alone (unknown to Hook) doggedly plodding after him.

Then Peter still following the trail by the footmarks.

There should be a feeling of danger in the air. It is dusk. We see the shadows of prowling wild animals. We don't see the animals themselves, only their shadows, which should make the scene more creepy.

Then the two rowing boats. The children are tossed in, again like bales of cotton.

Hook comes. The boats put off. We see them drawing near the pirate ship. Hook boards first. He hauls up the children by his hook.

We see Peter arrive at the water's edge. He is looking about him when in a sudden lull of the music he hears (and we hear) the crocodile's clock striking twice, to imply that it is half-past some hour of the evening. He searches and finds the crocodile, who was invisible when his clock struck. It is the striking of the clock that makes Peter know that the crocodile must be near by. We see Peter and the crocodile together by the water's edge. Peter explains what he wants and the crocodile signifies assent. They then enter the water together.

Then we see the hold of the pirate ship with the children lying bound.

Then Hook in his cabin sitting on his bed smiling to himself. He is in great and horrible glee. We have a picture of what this desperado is chuckling over. It is a vision of Peter underground, drinking the medicine and then writhing in death throes on the floor. Then the deck of the ship with the pirates dancing to a fiddle. Smee is sitting working at a sewing-machine. Hook appears threateningly at the door of his cabin, which opens off the deck, and all stop dancing in fear of him. They shrink back. He paces the deck gloomily, a dark spirit. He is a sort of Hamlet figure in the "To be or not to be" soliloquy. Smee is still at his sewing-machine.

A strange mood of depression comes over Hook, as if he fears his coming dissolution. Scenes of his innocent days pass before him. He sees himself again at Eton answering at "Absence" and on the football field and in "pop"—Pictures of these visions (which will be given in detail later). Then again we see him on deck brooding. Smee tears a cloth as in the play and Hook thinks an accident has happened to his trousers. He calls Starkey privately to examine him. Then Smee quite innocently does it again. Hook realises the truth this time, and threatens Smee. All the business of the play here.

Hook sits beside a barrel, on which there are playing cards.

He gives an order and pirates descend into the hold and hoist up the manacled children. We see them first in the hold, and then being brutally hoisted up. Smee ties Wendy to the mast; he is ingratiating to her, but she scorns him. All stare at Hook, who goes on playing cards without seeming to notice them. Next we see Peter and the crocodile swimming side by side. Then the deck again. Hook suddenly turns on the children threateningly. They are frightened. He raises his hat and bows with fiendish politeness to Wendy, who replies with a look of contempt. He goes from one to another clawing at them, then gives an order, and, in response, the pirates get the plank ready and extend it over the water. In a close-up the terrified children are shown graphically what is meant by the phrase "walking the plank." To the music of the pirate song Hook shows them what is to be their fate, by walking an imaginary plank.

> "Yo ho, yo ho, the frisky Plank
> You walks along it so,
> Till it goes down, and you goes down
> To Davy Jones below."

We don't hear the words, but his actions give the idea, and we hear the music. The pirates at the plank at the same time show how it works. All this should be much more graphic and realistic than in the play.

Next we see Peter and the crocodile reach the side of the ship. Peter indicates to crocodile to swim round and round the ship. Peter himself then begins his heroic ascent of the vessel, dagger in mouth. He does wonderful deeds of climbing not only up the huge hulk but among the rigging.

Next we see the crocodile in the water beside the ship and we hear its clock begin to strike the hour of 12. When it has struck 3 the scene changes to the deck of the ship, but the striking of the clock still goes on. It strikes 12 altogether. Hook hears it and is unmanned. He crouches at the side of the deck and some pirates gather round him to conceal him, while others look over the vessel's side for the crocodile. While this is going on Peter arrives on deck to the delight of the children. He does not come in the simple way followed in the play. He leaps from rope to rope, crawls along perilous masts and comes down the rigging with extraordinary courage and agility. He does not carry a clock as in play, as this is not now needed. He signs caution. A pirate comes from the back and is neatly knifed and flung overboard. Always when anyone goes overboard we should have the effect of the splash. Peter steals into Hook's cabin. The pirates peering overboard indicate to Hook that the danger is past. Hook swaggers again. He sees Slightly jeering at him, seizes him and is about to make him walk the plank at once when he has an idea. We have a vision of this idea. The vision is of the cat-o'-nine-tails hanging up in his cabin. We have a close-up picture of it.

"Fetch the cat, Jukes; it's in the cabin."

Then we see him order the pirate, Jukes, into the cabin, obviously to fetch the cat. Jukes goes. Then the music of the pirate song. Hook and pirates sing another verse which evidently, from the action, is about the cat, but before they reach the end of the verse they stop and the music itself stops abruptly. The sudden silence should be among the most impressive moments in the ship scene. This pause is because of a dreadful long-drawn-out cry from the cabin, which we need not hear. Evidently the pirates have heard something dreadful. The sudden silence should be very dramatic. After a pause Cecco goes cautiously to the cabin door and looks in. In the semi-darkness we don't see Peter, but we see his shadow standing silent against a wall, a figure of fate. Jukes is seen lying dead on the floor. Hook sees the children looking pleased, and threateningly he orders Cecco into the cabin. Cecco pleads for mercy, then shuddering goes, as dramatically as in the play. All listen intently.

There is no more dancing. Then they are again evidently startled by an awful cry. The children delightedly know that Peter must be dealing out death. Then when Hook threatens they dissemble. Starkey, quaking, peeps in at the cabin door, and we now see Cecco's body lying across that of Jukes. Peter's shadow is again seen motionless. Then another picture of the cabin, with now five bodies lying across each other, the topmost a negro. Peter's terrible shadow is still seen.

Next Hook orders Starkey into cabin, but rather than obey Starkey leaps overboard as in the play. All this scene should be very intense. Hook wants to pick out another victim, but the superstitious pirates gather together mutinously. He indicates that he will go in himself. He lifts a musket, then casts it down, and clawing with his hook (his best weapon) he goes into the cabin.

There is a moment's awful silence, and then he staggers out in a daze. Evidently from his action of clutching his brow someone has struck him a dreadful blow on the head. The pirates talk together mutinously, and while they are doing so Peter, unseen by them, emerges from the cabin. He is carrying cutlasses. He gives them to the boys who begin to cut their bonds.

Then another picture of all in same positions as before. Peter comes out: but we see that the boys' bonds are now cut. Wendy seems to be standing against the mast as before, but though the audience (or such of them as don't know the play) are meant to think that this is Wendy, it is really Peter in her cloak with face hidden. The actual Wendy is unseen. The mutinous crew now advance threateningly on Hook.

"Never was luck on a pirate ship wi' a woman aboard. Into the water with her, bullies."

He indicates Wendy as the Jonah, and that she should be flung overboard. The pirates think it is a good idea. All advance on the supposed Wendy, when suddenly the cloak is flung off, and the figure is revealed as Peter Pan, the Avenger. This should be as much a surprise to the audience as to the pirates who shrink back for a moment from the terrible boy. Wendy now puts her head out of a barrel, which lets us see where she has been hidden.

Now the fight takes place, and instead of, as in the play, its being all on deck and trivial, it should take place in various parts of the ship, and be a real stern conflict. There are individual contests in which the pirates are killed by Nibs, say, or Tootles, or John. Some pirates leap overboard—and sometimes the boys seem to be the losers, though only wounded. We don't see Peter or Hook just now. Then we see two of the boys pursued up the hatchway by Hook. They are being hard pressed by him.

Suddenly Peter appears and strikes up the swords. He and Hook stand gazing at each other. Their swords describe a circuit, and then the points reach the ground at the same time. Peter is now like a figure of fate. What he has said to the boys is "Put up your swords, boys; this man is mine."

"Rash and presumptuous youth, prepare to meet thy doom."
"Dark and sinister man, have at thee."

It should be a very real fight now between Hook and Peter, and both must be good fencers. First the one is beaten to his knees, then the other. At one point Wendy tries to save Peter. He flings her across his shoulder and fights with her thus. He knocks Hook's sword from his hand. Hook is at his mercy, but Peter chivalrously presents the sword to him. Wendy is no longer on Peter's shoulder. Now Peter seems to be lost. He loses his sword. Suddenly he runs up a rope hanging from above (as First Twin does in the acted play). Then as suddenly he lets himself fall plop on Hook who is flattened out.

"'Tis some fiend fighting me. Pan, who and what art thou?"
"I'm youth, I'm joy, I'm a little bird that has broken out of the egg."

The fight is resumed. Peter drives Hook back, up the ladder on to the poop, where the plank is. Here they wrestle together, and Peter seems to be getting the worst of it. Suddenly by a piece of ju-jitsu work he flings Hook over him and Hook comes down with a smash. Hook is now hopeless. Peter indicates sternly to him that he must walk the plank.

"Jas. Hook, thou not wholly unheroic figure, farewell."

Hook shrinks back, and won't obey the order. He shows his teeth. Peter gives an order to a boy who rushes down to cabin and brings Peter the cat-o'-nine-tails. Peter indicates that it will be his painful duty to use the cat if Hook does not at once walk the plank. Thus threatened Hook pulls himself together, and in his last moment is as brave a figure as any Sydney Carton on the scaffold.

Doubtless the "something" that is said to be part of an Eton education and that can be got nowhere else comes to his help in this unpleasant moment. He has a vision which we see, of the "Wall game," the most characteristic game of Eton College, and then he sets forth with dignity upon his impressive but brief walk along the plank. Just before the plank goes down the crocodile rears his head in the water below, the great mouth opens wide, and Hook dives straight into it, swallowed in one memorable mouthful. The crocodile waggles its head to get the legs down. They, too, disappear.

Floreat Etona.

We see the crocodile crawling ashore. He shakes out of his mouth the wooden arm with hook of the late captain. He leaves it lying on the shore and plods away, like one who has lived his great hour and can afford to take the rest of his life more leisurely.

Then we see the deck again with the boys (and Wendy) all more or less wounded and bandaged, gazing in awe at Peter who is off his head with pride in himself and is strutting up and down. He strikes Napoleonic attitudes, but is not dressed as Napoleon.

Next we see Wendy, Nibs, and Tootles in the hold opening a seaman's chest and bringing clothes out of it, pirate's clothing. Evidently the boys want to wear these clothes. We see Wendy cutting a pair of pirate trousers with scissors so as to shorten the legs for a boy. Then we see Slightly in the cook's pantry of the ship gloating over its attractive contents. He finds a big bottle marked "Plums" and begins to eat them greedily. Then we see Michael in the hold trying to shave himself with pirate razor. His face is lathered. Then Slightly again now in stomach pains, but still eating plums. Wendy finds him and destroys plums. Then she finds Michael, and cleans the lather off his face.

Then we see all the boys on deck (except Peter) in pirate clothes, all looking like pirates and liking it. The clothes don't fit them but have been roughly made smaller. Then Peter emerges from the captain's cabin and swaggers about. He is dressed in a suit of Hook's cut down but still too big, and is looking as like him as he can. He is drunk with cockiness, and all fear him. He holds a hook in his right hand, and threatens Slightly with it. He is smoking Hook's double cigar. He gives an order. Very smartly the boys obey his order, flying to the rigging instead of climbing. Up to now no sails have been set. All sail is set by them now, and the great pirate ship veering round as the sails belly out, with Peter at the wheel, should make a stirring picture.

Poor Peter is now, however, feeling squeamish as the result of his smoking. He puts away the cigars, and clutches his head. The other boys to his annoyance gather round him to see what will be the unheroic result of this misadventure. Wendy (who is still in the clothes in which she was brought aboard) appears and sees to what catastrophe the incident is tending. She orders the other boys away and then conducts Peter to the side of the vessel, over which he leans and is sick in privacy though we just guess it. Wendy stands near him solicitously but not too near, for she knows that there are moments in heroes' lives when they would prefer to be alone. He is now a little relieved, and she tries to induce him to go to Hook's cabin, of which he has become the tenant, but he won't desert the wheel and he nobly ties himself to it. She gazes at him admiringly and goes away. If possible the ship should be rocking as if in a heavy sea. It is now moving in a narrow channel between rocks that separate it from the open sea. The night is now dark.

Next we see Slightly again in the pantry. He is now eating sardines greedily, though obviously in great pain. Then the deck scene again with Peter at wheel. Wendy appears with something she is concealing in a cloth behind her back. She doesn't want Peter to see it. We wonder what it is. She sneaks into Peter's cabin with it and now we see it. It is a hot-water bottle, which she places carefully in the bed. She notices in cabin, as we do, a touching sight, viz. on the floor a little pile of the clothes Peter has taken off and left lying there after the manner of children. She folds them carefully on a chair and goes out. When she has gone, Tink pops out of a jug and hops about.

Then we have a picture of the fo'c's'le in which a number of pirates have evidently slept, for here are their bunks. It is a dark, evil-looking place, with horrible pirate weapons still hanging on its discoloured walls. In the bunks lie all the boys except Peter, all asleep though Slightly is having bad dreams, as the result of his greediness. Wendy is sitting on a stool by an oil-stove, darning away as usual. The new conditions don't bother her; she is still a mother.

Alternated with this picture we have one again of Peter still lashed to the wheel, spray splashing on him, and the ship heading out of the channel into an open and angry sea. It can be black-dark if this will help the rolling of the vessel; but if it rolls above on deck we must get a similar effect in the fo'c's'le.

After many days the gay and innocent and heartless things reach home.

We have a picture of Westminster and the Thames again with a suggestion of the pirate ship there.

Then we see the outside of the Darlings' home once more. Nana goes in at the door carrying a basket in her mouth. Then inside the house and we see Mrs Darling sitting sadly at the open nursery window. She stretches her arms out to window. Nana comes and sits sympathetically with her. She shares Mrs Darling's handkerchief with her, but it should be touching, not comic. Mr Darling is sitting dejectedly by the nursery fire. He takes from the mantelpiece a portrait. We see in a close-up that it is of the three children. He is sorrowful. Evidently he is cold, he shivers, and rises and closes the window, but Mrs Darling opens it at once indicating sweetly that it must always be kept open for them. She goes sadly into another room.

Nana is going miserably to her kennel in the nursery, but Mr Darling indicates to her that his armchair is the proper place for her, and that, as a punishment he, himself, must go into the kennel. Nana curls up on chair. Mr Darling goes into the kennel to sleep.

Then we see Mrs Darling in the other room, which is the day nursery. There is a picture of Wendy in it, over which she leans unhappily.

Then we see Peter fly in by nursery window. Nana is not there now. Peter is in his familiar garments again. He is excited and quickly bars the window to keep Wendy out. Here is repeated the vision of Peter arriving at his own nursery window and finding it barred and another child sleeping in his bed.

Then we see from nursery Wendy arriving at the window, and her terror on finding it barred. Peter is hiding and gloating over her discomfiture. She disappears. Peter is grinning and triumphantly going out by the door when we hear "Home, Sweet Home" being played on a piano in the day nursery. He steals to the door by which Mrs Darling had gone out and peeps in. The room being the day nursery is furnished as such. We see Mrs Darling at piano playing sadly. We see Peter at the door watching her, but she doesn't see him. He knows what she is sad about, but for a time he is defiant. Soon she breaks down. The picture of Wendy is in her hands and she kisses it. She is crying. He tries to be defiant still. She is now sobbing on the piano stool. He begins to cry, too, in the night nursery sitting against John's bed. At last he nobly flings the window open and goes away in a "What care I!" manner.

Again we see Mrs Darling, her shoulders heaving as she leans against the piano.

Now we see Wendy fly in, and then Michael on John's shoulders. They are in their familiar clothes. They are gleeful as they point out their old beds, etc. Michael peeps into the kennel and calls the others. They all peep at their father asleep there. They just grin. Then the piano is heard again.

They gaily peep at Mrs Darling from the door. They feel ashamed as they watch her grief.

Then Wendy has a bright idea which she explains to them in dumb-show.

They get merrily into their beds and lie beneath the blankets, covering their heads.

Mrs Darling comes to the door. She has heard nothing.

Mrs Darling looks from one bed to another, but does not believe she really sees them.

"So often in my dreams their silver voices call me that I seem still to hear them when I am awake, my little children, that I shall see no more."

The last of her words are from a chair. She stretches out her arms, thinking they are again to fall empty by her side, but the three creep to her and the arms fall on them. Rapture comes as she realizes what has happened.

Mr Darling comes out of the kennel and Nana and Liza rush in at door. There is a scene of riotous happiness, with Peter looking on from the window, a lonely figure.

Wendy indicates that she has a surprise for her parents. She opens the door, and all the other boys come in sheepishly, one at a time. They are in their pirate garments, now very soiled and torn, and are a ragged, dirty, woeful-looking lot. They are afraid of how they are to be received, and the Darlings are at first staggered, but then embrace them. General joy. Peter is again at window. Wendy runs to him and hugs him.

"Hands off, lady. No one is going to catch me and teach me solemn things. I want always to be a little boy and to have fun."

He is saying this when Mrs Darling goes towards him.

Then he flies away.

Then on an evening we see Peter in the street looking up at the nursery window. Wendy opens the window and beckons him lovingly to come up. He heartlessly flouts her entreaties and skips about playing his pipes. She flings him a letter. He runs up a tall London lamp-post to read it. It is shown on the screen in Wendy's handwriting:

"Darling Peter, Mother says she will let you come for me once a year to take me to the Never, Never Land for a week to do your spring-cleaning. Your adoredable Wendy."

At the foot of the page instead of crosses are several thimbles. Peter and she wave to each other and he flies off.

Next we see a picture of Wendy, John, and Michael going into a school in London with school satchels, etc. The old humdrum life has begun again.

Then we see Peter and Wendy flying together, through the air but without scenery. Wendy is warmly clad this time. They are evidently off to the spring-cleaning, for Peter is carrying a broom and she carries a shovel.

Very soon they all grew up except one.

It is a business street in the city. A close-up of a doorway shows these names printed on it:

3rd Floor.
Messrs Twins and Tootles, Kew Cement Co.

2nd Floor.
Messrs Curly Nibs & Co., Commissioners of Oaths.

1st Floor.
Sir S. Slightly, Financier.

Ground Floor.
Darling Bros., Solicitors.

Then we have a brief peep into each of these rooms.

First we see Tootles and the twins all on high stools at separate desks writing in ledgers.

Next Curly and Nibs in their office, also on stools busy over legal documents.

Then Slightly in a finer office. He is standing by the fire with legs outstretched, smoking a large cigar, and drinking out of a tumbler. In a close-up we see printed on tumbler the words "Brandy and Soda." Slightly is evidently rather proud of being able to drink this.

Then John and Michael. Michael is dictating to a lady typist. John is putting on an overcoat and silk hat and goes out very professionally with a roll of papers. As soon as he has gone Michael ceases to dictate but looks lovingly at typist instead. Her typing stops, she turns and looks self-consciously at him. That is all, but we guess that it is the old story. They are all now grown up young men, some of them quite tall and stout with moustaches or spectacles but all must be easily recognizable. Their hair is of course short. The effect of height can be got by making the furniture smaller than usual. All are in correct office dress, black coats, etc., Slightly being a bit of a dandy.

Peter who is just as usual, is seen looking through the window of each office and grinning cynically at them, evidently thinking that they made the grand mistake in growing up. But they are all too occupied with their own affairs to see him.

Then we have a picture of Wendy, now a sweet young woman in her wedding-gown and looking her loveliest. Presently she goes to the window which is open, and gazes out with arms outstretched. Memories of the Never, Never Land come to her, and we see them in a vision. What we see are some of the scenes that have become familiar to us—the home under the ground, the lagoon, the forest, and all those scenes are as real as ever. But the figures are only ghosts, done in the manner which is so effective on the films, i.e. they are pale ghosts of Peter, Wendy, the other boys, Hook and Tiger Lily that we see—some dancing gaily in their night-gowns, others flitting through the wood, etc. The last scene is Hook's arm lying among grass. In the hollow made by the hook a little bird has built a nest with eggs in it. This is shown in a close-up.

Then Wendy again in her wedding-gown is seen as before at window. She cries a little, then bravely pulls down window as a sign that the days of make-believe are ended. She smiles at herself.

Then we see a new nursery with one small bed in it. This bed is in much the same position as Wendy's bed in the old nursery, and in it is sleeping Jane, Wendy's daughter. We just see there is a child sleeping in it, but we don't see her face. There is another larger bed in room evidently the nurse's, but it is not occupied. Wendy is standing at foot of bed gazing lovingly at Jane, patting her, etc. She is in a semi-evening dress very simple. She goes over to fender on which some childish garments are hanging, and rearranges them. At this point Peter peeps through the window curtains at her and is bewildered and unhappy at seeing her so grown-up. When she has arranged garments on fender she goes quietly out on tiptoe, with a last loving look at child.

She is never aware of Peter's presence. She also must be as tall as possible but in her case it can't be done with making furniture smaller as this would increase size of Peter and child. It must be done artificially by high shoes, long frock, etc. As she goes out Peter comes after her with arms outstretched to her, but she doesn't see him. When she has gone he is a rather tragic lonely figure. He lies on floor and sobs precisely as he did on the occasion when he came back for his shadow. What happened then is now repeated. Jane is wakened by his sobbing and sits up in bed. Here there should be a surprise for the audience, for though the picture seems to be continuous, Jane is played by the same actress who plays Wendy. She should make herself a little different from Wendy as by a different arrangement or even colour of hair and wear a coloured woollen night-gown instead of Wendy's white cotton one. But of course they should still be very much alike.

"Boy, why are you crying?"

Peter, in answer to her question, rises, comes to foot of bed and bows as he did to Wendy. Jane replies by bowing as Wendy did.

"Girl, what is your name?"
"Jane Wendy. What is your name?"
"Peter Pan."
"Where is your mother, Peter?"
"Don't have a mother, Jane."
"Oh!"

The result of this conversation is that Jane does precisely as Wendy did. She jumps out of bed, runs to him, and puts her arms round him. She has evidently taken the mother's place.

Then a picture of Peter and Jane flying through the air carrying broom and shovel, just as we have seen Peter and Wendy doing it. They are very gay,

Jane is in the woolen night-gown; so that we see clearly that it is Jane and not Wendy.

Then the scene is again the Never, Never Land, a lovely part of the wood near a pool and waterfall. It is a sunny summer day, and first we see Jane doing Peter's washing in a tub on ground, then flying with it up to a rope that is hung high between branches. On this she hangs the garments. She is now dressed in the familiar Wendy garments, but tucked up, etc. in a businesslike way. Tink appears and pulls her hair. While the washing is going on Peter appears on his goat. The flowers are following him just as on the day when they went to the lagoon, and in the same way he orders them to go back. Then he relents and lets them come. He tethers his goat. He sits on a mossy bank playing his pipes. For a little time we see Peter and Jane thus engaged. Another vague figure appears and watches them from behind a tree unseen by them. It is the ghost of the grown-up Wendy in long dress, who has somehow got here to see that her child is safe. She is just a shadow. She watches the two sweetly, but being grown-up, she cannot join in the adventure. Tink, however, discovers her and pulls her hair. Wendy goes away sadly. The crocodile comes and tries to dance to Peter's pipes—so do bears and other friendly animals. Soon the pool and waterfall are alive with mermaids who play games, splash each other, etc. Peter continues playing his pipes and Jane attending to his washing.

Then we have the final picture, which should also be the most beautiful. It is the last moment of the acted play, but much can be done with it that is impossible in the play. The time is now sunset. We see the Tree Tops with the Little House now perched high among them. All around are tiny fairy houses (not nests as in the play, but absurd little houses of thatch and moss, each with a window and a chimney). The exact nature of these fairy houses is for future consideration. As moonlight comes, these houses light up, and at the doors, and flying about among the trees and tree-tops, are innumerable fairies, gossiping, quarrelling, and playing about. The music of this should all be as it is in the play, where it is excellent, and mixed up with it should be the bells to indicate much chatter among the fairies.

The scene goes on with changes of lighting, etc. After the Little House lights up it is sometimes in one place, sometimes in another, sometimes near, sometimes far away—once it is sailing on the lagoon, and the mermaids are pulling it about in fun—then the fairies capture it and take it back to the tree-tops. We see Peter and Jane at the door waving their handkerchiefs to us. Finally there is no girl, and he is alone. There are no animals. The fairies have gone to their houses; their lights go out (not simultaneously, but fitfully). Now there are only lights from moon and stars, and Peter is seen in silhouette alone, playing his pipes.

Peter Pan On-Screen:
A Cinematic Survey

At a meeting with Barrie in 1921, Charlie Chaplin told the author that *Peter Pan* "has even greater possibilities as a film than a play." Barrie believed that "film can do things for *Peter Pan* that the ordinary stage cannot do," and he hoped that it could "strike a note of wonder . . . and whet the appetite for marvels" (Green 169). He composed scenes for a film version (reproduced in this volume), including a soccer game played high up in the trees, but they were never used. Instead, Paramount Pictures, authorized contractually to adapt *Peter Pan* for the screen, hired Herbert Brenon to direct a film based on the play. Brenon decided against using Barrie's screenplay, and hired Willis Goldbeck to write the script.

To Lady Cynthia Asquith, Barrie wrote about his fascination with a film version of *Peter Pan* and its endless possibilities. As he worked on the screenplay, he imagined that "one could go on doing this until doom cracks, and then put in the crack." Barrie's elaborate scenario contains not just subtitles but also rich visual descriptions of each sequence, with many fantastic flourishes that would have been a challenge to film. For the first sequence, for example, Barrie wanted to show Peter riding a goat through the woods, flying up to a tree and then over a "romantic river," and finally realighting on the goat. Barrie's high-voltage demands on the new medium may have led to Paramount's decision to put the play on-screen as a filmed performance.

Below I discuss a number of screen versions of the Peter Pan story, along with Steven Spielberg's *Hook* and Marc Forster's biopic *Finding Neverland*. These adaptations mark important milestones in the reception of Barrie's work, each time reminding us of how the story has moved from the literary to the mythical, with each generation creating its own Peter Pan.

Bruce K. Hanson's *The Peter Pan Chronicles: The Nearly One-Hundred-Year History of the Boy Who Wouldn't Grow Up* documents the theatrical history of *Peter Pan*, with chapters on the many actresses who played Peter Pan: Nina Boucicault, Cecelia Loftus, and Pauline Chase in London and Maude Adams, Eva Le Gallienne, Jean Arthur, and Mary Martin in New York. He includes cast lists for productions in both cities and offers a wealth of information about the staging of *Peter Pan*. A new, updated edition of Hanson's book, *Peter Pan on Stage and Screen, 1904–2009*, is scheduled for publication in 2011.

Peter Pan, dir. Herbert Brenon, 1924

It took Hollywood nearly two decades to persuade J. M. Barrie to sign over the film rights to *Peter Pan*. Paramount, attracted by both the plot and the

Mary Brian plays Wendy Darling to Betty Bronson's Peter Pan. In the nursery of Paramount's *Peter Pan* (1924), a fascinated Wendy sews the shadow back on the feet of an animated Peter. (By permission of Paramount Pictures, Photofest)

possibilities of aerial action, finally won out, with a contract that gave Barrie the final say on casting. When the author saw Betty Bronson's tests, he cabled her immediately—not the studio—to let her know that she would be the next Peter Pan. With stunning cinematography by James Wong Howe (*The Thin Man*) and powerful performances by Betty Bronson as Peter Pan and Ernest Torrence as Captain Hook, Brenon's film—the only silent version of *Peter Pan*—has a fresh, glowing spirit even nearly a century after it was produced. It contains a range of impressive special effects, in particular the close-ups of Tinker Bell, the scenes of flying, and a sequence in which the lost boys magically gather around Wendy. The film was introduced with a note from J. M. Barrie:

> The difference between a fairy play and a realistic one is that in the former all the characters are really children with a child's outlook on life. This applies to the so-called adults of the story as well as the young people. Pull the beard off the fairy king, and you will find the face of a child.
>
> This then is the spirit of the play. And it is necessary that all of you—no matter what age you may have individually attained—should be children. PETER PAN will laughingly blow the fairy dust in your eyes and presto! You'll all be back in the nursery, and once more you'll believe in fairies, and the play moves on.

Brenon's silent film, restored from the original nitrate print and tinted, is visually stunning. Peter Pan is very real in this version of the story, and in the early part of the film, both Mr. and Mrs. Darling inspect the shadow he has left behind. Placing emphasis on Wendy's failure to persuade Peter to become something more than a "son" to her, the film ends with Mrs. Darling's agreement to allow Peter to return each year and fetch Wendy for spring housecleaning. Young romantic love has been defeated, but the Darling family proves resilient and expansive, embracing the lost boys.

The film may be set in Neverland, but the Darlings live in the United States rather than in England, and there are numerous moments of patriotic fervor and sentimental zeal in the film. The Stars and Stripes are hoisted on the mast, replacing the Skull and Bones. Michael warns the lost boys to treat Wendy as if they were "American gentlemen." Wendy tells the lost boys and her brothers that their mothers hope they "will die as American gentlemen," at which point

In a nursery modeled on F. D. Bedford's illustrations for *Peter and Wendy*, the Darling children prepare for flight through the window in the background. (By permission of Paramount Pictures, Photofest)

all the boys break out into a rendition of "My country 'tis of thee, sweet land of liberty." And Peter himself decides to return to Neverland, refusing to become the president of the United States. Mrs. Darling sings "Home, Sweet Home" right before the children return, and we see the sheet music on-screen as she accompanies herself on the piano. Perhaps the patriotic pride of the postwar generation led to the conversion of the British characters into American children.

Despite the many allusions to the American flag, American gentlemen, and the sacredness of the American hearth, the film ends with Peter's refusal to shift allegiance from Neverland to the United States, from Tinker Bell to Wendy, and from adventures to domestic bliss. Clearly outnumbered by the Darlings, Nana, and the lost boys, he stands alone in his resolve to return to mermaids and redskins (the pirates have been defeated).

The last remaining copy of the film was located by James Card, who learned of its existence while working after World War II for the Eastman Kodak Company in Rochester, New York. Considered today one of the great heroes in the field of film preservation, he learned about the famous vault containing prints

Anna May Wong plays Tiger Lily in Herbert Brenon's *Peter Pan*. No one found it odd at the time that an Asian American was cast as a Native American, nor that the "redskins" have slain a beast of the jungle. The tribe triumphantly holds weapons in the air—bows and arrows, tomahawks, and knives—as the dead lion lies at their feet. (By permission of Paramount Pictures, Photofest)

of *Peter Pan*, *Dr. Jekyll and Mr. Hyde*, and other treasures. He persuaded Iris Barry, the film preservationist at the Museum of Modern Art, to help restore the film from the original nitrate print, which had been decomposing in a Kodak vault, and he tells the full story in his book *Seductive Cinema: The Art of Silent Film*.

Peter Pan, Disney Studios, dir. Clyde Geronimi, Wilfred Jackson, and Hamilton Luske, 1953

Walt Disney was convinced that film was the best medium for *Peter Pan*: "I don't believe that what James M. Barrie actually intended ever came out on the stage. If you read the play carefully, following the author's suggestion on interpretation and staging, I think you'll agree. It's almost a perfect vehicle for

Peter and Tinker Bell lead the way to Neverland as the Darling children soar over the rooftops of London. (By permission of RKO Radio Pictures, Inc., Photofest)

cartooning. In fact, one might think that Barrie wrote the play with cartoons in mind. I don't think he was ever happy with the stage version. Live actors are limited, but with cartoons we can give free rein to the imagination."

Disney began negotiating the film rights to *Peter Pan* in 1935 and finally came to an arrangement with Great Ormond Street Hospital four years later. The project was put on hold during the war years and did not move forward with story line and character development until well after the war. The Disney version adheres closely to the play (the original plan had Nana traveling to Never Land with the children) and deviates from its terms mainly through elaboration and embellishment. Technological innovations that included the use of a multiplane camera added liveliness to the flying sequence, with the children soaring over the rooftops of London and around Big Ben.

Peter Pan was the film that created a recognizable Disney style. As a critic for the *New York Times* pointed out: "The well-bred Wendy is a virtual duplicate of the prim Snow White; the pirate, Smee, is the same as the dwarf, Happy, and Baby Michael is a Dopey who talks. Captain Hook, the horrendous villain, is J. Worthington Foulfellow in plumes and Peter himself is reminiscent of some

Peter dons a headdress and smokes a peace pipe just before the Indians break into song, asking: "What Makes the Red Man Red?" The lost boys and the Indians revel in the music and dance, while Wendy, who is ordered to fetch firewood, leaves in a huff. (By permission of RKO Radio Pictures, Inc., Photofest)

Disney's John and Michael may not have real weapons, but the lost boys, in a manner self-consciously aggressive and both cocky and kooky, march steadily forward, ready to do battle. (By permission of RKO Radio Pictures, Inc., Photofest)

Wendy threads a needle and prepares to sew Peter's shadow back on his feet. Peter's shadow stands against the wall, detached in both senses of the term, while Peter himself is absorbed in his pipes. (By permission of RKO Radio Pictures, Inc., Photofest)

of the boys in 'Pinocchio.' As for the famous Barrie fairy, the crystalline and luminous Tinker Bell, she is as nubile and coquettish as the maiden centaurs in *Fantasia* (Crowther).

The film begins with a voice-over pointing to the cyclical nature of the events depicted: "All of this has happened before and it will all happen again." It takes the children from their home in Bloomsbury to a Never Land populated by redskins and pirates. Particularly controversial is a musical number answering the question "What Makes the Red Man Red?" by tracing skin color to the blush of an "Injun prince" when he kissed a "maid" for the first time. The song begins with one of the boys noting how "enlightening" it would be to have that explanation. Indian language is reduced to a series of monosyllabic terms ("How?" and "Ugh!"), along with broken English phrases, in sharp contrast to the sophisticated language of the lost boys and the Darling children. Yet the sequence also shows the boys striving to mimic the life of the "savage" and "cunning" redskins even as Wendy rebels against the constraints of becoming a "squaw."

Disney's film keeps the focus on Wendy as well as Peter, and on how Wendy grows up, abandoning the dreams of youthful imagination. At the end of the film, she declares herself ready to grow up, and the ship that returned the children home slowly fades away. Surprisingly, the Disney film emphasizes that Never Land exists only in the imagination, and it never invites its audience to affirm its faith in fairies by applauding.

The sequel *Return to Never Land* (2002) begins when Wendy has grown up, and follows the adventures of her daughter, Jane, in Never Land. Set in World War II London during the Blitz, the film charts Jane's renewed belief in "faith, trust, and pixie dust" as she navigates Never Land in search of a way back home. In 2008, the Disney fairies franchise released a prequel called *Tinker Bell*, giving audiences the backstory to the character of the film's title.

Peter Pan, dir. Jerome Robbins, 1954

The 1954 American musical version of *Peter Pan* featured Mary Martin (the consummate Broadway star who had charmed U.S. audiences in *Annie Get Your Gun* and *South Pacific*) as Peter Pan and Cyril Ritchard as Captain Hook. After 152 performances at the Winter Garden Theatre in New York, NBC broadcast the musical live and in color on *Producers' Showcase*. "The mail has never stopped coming in asking that we do it again," Mary Martin stated, and the original cast was gathered for an encore television performance in 1956. The show attracted a record numbers of viewers. It was revived on Broadway in 1979, with Sandy Duncan in the lead role, and again in 1990 with Cathy Rigby as Peter. The music and lyrics, by Moose Charlap and Carolyn Leigh, includes "I'm Flying," "Pirate Song," "Hook's Tango," "Never Never Land," "I Gotta Crow," and, most famously, "I Won't Grow Up."

Mary Martin reported that her "honest desire" was to be part of a production that would "stand up so it can be put on year after year, all over the country with lots of people playing Peter Pan, like the English pantomimes, because generation after generation have never seen Peter Pan" (Hanson 173). Leonard Bernstein was briefly involved in the production, but his desire to incorporate an earlier score, combined with heavy commitments to other projects, prevented him from collaborating.

The musical opened to awestruck enthusiasm, with expressively eloquent

Mary Martin as Peter Pan teaches the Darling children how to fly. (By permission of NBC, Photofest)

Cathy Rigby crosses swords with Captain Hook in a 1990 Broadway revival of *Peter Pan*. Pirates, Indians, and children form a tableau of breathless witnesses to the contest between boy and man. (By permission of Photofest)

reviews. "Miss Martin is a smashing Peter Pan, boyish, eager, touching. . . . She swings through the air with a pleased grin . . . and at times and under all conditions may be put down in theatre history as one of the truly great Peter Pans of all time," the *Morning Telegraph* reported (Hanson 211). The *New York Times* described the show as "bountiful" and "good-natured" (Hanson 213). Despite a flying accident ("I nearly killed myself," Mary Martin reported), the play continued with 152 performances after its opening night, on October 20, 1954.

A listing of Broadway performances, with cast members, is available at www .broadwaymusicalhome.com/shows/peter pan.htm.

Sandy Duncan plays Peter Pan in the 1979 Broadway revival. (By permission of Photofest)

The Lost Boys, dir. Rodney Bennett, 1978

With a script by Andrew Birkin, author of *J. M. Barrie and the Lost Boys*, this award-winning docudrama was a miniseries produced by the BBC. Using voice-overs that bring in quotations from Barrie's correspondence and also provide imaginative re-creations of conversations and letters, the biopic takes us inside Barrie's mind even as it shows us the outer circumstances of his life. The script brilliantly suggests how events and relationships in Barrie's life inspired the words he put on the printed page.

Producer Louis Marks provides, in the link below, a lively account of how the docudrama came into being. "Andrew's problem," he reports, "was that he had hit a goldmine. During that winter he had been introduced, through his co-researcher Sharon Goode, to the last surviving Llewelyn Davies son, Nico, then in his seventies. At first suspicious of anyone who might want to capitalize on his family's tragic story or in any way misrepresent 'Uncle Jim,' Nico soon warmed to the project and made available a wealth of material: diaries, hundreds of letters, photographs, his late brother Peter's unpublished memoirs, and, not least, his own memories. Some of this had been used before in biographies of Barrie, but most had not. And Andrew soon discovered that much of what had been used had often been misunderstood or even mistranscribed."

With Ian Holm playing J. M. Barrie to perfection, *The Lost Boys* debuted in 1978 to highly favorable reviews. Janet Dunbar, Barrie's biographer, praised the work as "the definitive recreation of J. M. Barrie in dramatic terms." *Punch* described it, quite accurately, as a drama that advances "from competence to brilliance to deep compassion and mastery of touch, and which, for intensity of characterization and economy of writing, was a masterpiece of the televisual form." Brilliant, haunting, lovely, and disturbing: these were the terms repeatedly used to describe this televised masterpiece.

The film begins in Kensington Gardens, when J. M. Barrie meets the two oldest Llewelyn Davies boys and entertains them with his dog and games. We see the balloon lady in Arthur Rackham's illustration for *Peter Pan in Kensington Gardens* come to life on-screen. With sensitivity and tact, the film moves us through the years, from the death of the boys' parents and Barrie's painful divorce to the death of George in World War I and Michael's presumed suicide at Cambridge. A complement to Birkin's biography of Barrie, *The Lost Boys* is a finely calibrated portrayal of the writer and his relationship to the five boys he adopted. The script is available online at http://www.jmbarrie.co.uk/abpage/TLB%20SCRIPTS/TLB.htm.

Hook, dir. Steven Spielberg, 1991

Years after *Peter Pan* had been performed at the Duke of York's Theatre in London, Barrie toyed with the idea of writing *The Man Who Couldn't Grow up or The Old Age of Peter Pan*. What Barrie never executed, Steven Spielberg carried out, with a slightly different twist, in his film *Hook*, which brilliantly dramatizes what happens to Peter Pan when he falls in love and leaves Neverland. Peter Pan has turned into Peter Banning, a successful corporate lawyer with children of his own—he has crossed over to the dark side and become a pirate. With his wife, Moira, and children, Jack and Maggie (the names are tributes to Wendy, to Jack Llewelyn Davies, and to Barrie's mother, Margaret), Peter Banning returns to London for a charity event honoring Wendy Darling, Moira's grandmother and the woman who arranged Peter's adoption. Hook spirits Jack and Maggie off to Neverland, and Peter must recover his youthful verve, lost identity, and inner child to rescue the children and become a real father, a man who will keep the promises he makes to his children.

Spielberg once declared, "I have always felt like Peter Pan," and his films are filled with allusions to flying (*Catch Me If You Can*) and to the story of Peter Pan (*E.T.: The Extraterrestrial*). He had considered making a musical version of Peter Pan with Michael Jackson and instead turned his attention to a live-action film. The film's ending mimics the close of Disney's *Peter Pan* and shows the Banning family on the balcony, watching Tootles fly over London with the precious marbles he had lost as a child and finally recovered. The family has been reconstituted and strengthened now that Peter

Advertisement for Steven Spielberg's *Hook*, with Robin Williams as a grown-up Peter Pan who must find his childhood mojo and rescue his children from Captain Hook, played by Dustin Hoffman. (By permission of Tristar Pictures, Photofest)

Banning cheerfully proclaims: "To live will be an awfully big adventure."

Although the film came under some critical fire for its theme-park-world sets and its failure to explore more fully the relationship between parents and children, many scenes stand out for their power to reimagine the tale for a twentieth-century audience. The recognition scene, in particular—Peter Banning's recollection of who he once was—reminds viewers of what it takes to relate to children. Banning kneels down, bringing himself to the level of the child, removes his glasses, pulls in his stomach, and breaks into a smile, exhibiting a magical joie de vivre that is often lost in adulthood. This is "When

Peter Grew Up," but presented with the compensatory joys of raising and protecting children, becoming a father rather than remaining a child.

Peter Pan, 2003, dir. P. J. Hogan

The screenplay for this *Peter Pan*, written by Michael Goldenberg and P. J. Hogan, adheres closely to Barrie's play and novel, borrowing much of its language from the two. The film was licensed by Great Ormond Street Hospital for Children, which found it "in keeping with the original work whilst communicating to an audience with modern sensibilities." P. J. Hogan emphasized Peter's noble qualities: "This is *Peter Pan* as J. M. Barrie originally intended—a heroic, magical, real boy who fights pirates, saves children and never grows up." This *Peter Pan* is also a love story, a coming-of-age tale that begins with plans to ban Wendy from the nursery and ends with a romantic kiss from Wendy that brings Peter back to life. The sleeping Wendy first encounters Peter when he is hovering over her bed (drawing that scene at school gets her in hot water), and she wakens a sleeping Peter from Hook's deathblow with her

Felled by an arrow shot by Tootles, Wendy appears to be dead, and an anxious Peter Pan fears for her life. (By permission of Universal Pictures, Photofest)

The lost boys are picture perfect in the tropical setting. Their costumes of skins and furs have been carefully designed for maximum aesthetic effect. (By permission of Universal Pictures, Photofest)

"thimble." Still, Peter chooses not to grow up, and Wendy returns home with her brothers and with the lost boys.

Played by a boy, Peter Pan is less spritely youngster than teenage heartthrob who flirts with Wendy in the bedroom and who shares a romantic "fairy dance" with her while Hook looks on. Wendy's infatuation with Peter and Peter's seductive charms are emphasized in ways that are unusual for cinematic, musical, and theatrical adaptations, most of which move briskly along rather than lingering on enraptured facial features. Jeremy Sumpter was thirteen when he was cast as Peter Pan, and, since he—like other members of the cast—grew several inches during the filming, the height of the nursery window had to be increased twice. Both he and Wendy are presented as children on the brink of adulthood, fascinated by the discovery of unfamiliar desires and hesitatingly eager to explore them.

Roger Ebert's review of the film shrewdly notes that the movie is not "overtly sexual," but emphasizes that the "sensuality is there and the other versions have pretended that it was not." The scenes in the nursery introduce a new character, Aunt Millicent, who starts all the trouble by insisting that Wendy must grow up and have her own room. Wendy's main mission is to turn Peter into a grown-up, to move him toward an adulthood that allows the expression of romance. The two clasp hands and gaze into each other's eyes during a protracted fairy dance reminiscent of a moonlit prom night. "There's so much more," Wendy tells Peter, after urging him to return home and grow up.

Hogan had planned to film *Peter Pan* in London, Tahiti, and New Zealand but ended up shooting the film on sound stages in Australia. The lavish special effects aimed to create scenes that Scott Farrar, supervisor of visual effects, called "painterly, like something from a storybook, with gorgeous saturated colors." The children soar through the air with extraordinary ease, fight brilliantly choreographed battles, and are touched by pixie dust particles animated to look like sunlight coming through a window.

Finding Neverland, 2004, dir. Marc Forster

Based on Allan Knee's play *The Man Who Was Peter Pan*, *Finding Neverland* dramatizes Barrie's relationship with Sylvia Llewelyn Davies and her sons. Although Sylvia's husband, Arthur, was still alive when Barrie met the boys, he is deceased when the film begins and conveniently out of the way for the chaste romantic relationship that develops between Barrie and Sylvia. The five boys are reduced to four in the film, and many other liberties are taken with Barrie's life and with the theatrical history of *Peter Pan*. The production of *Peter Pan* staged at the Llewelyn Davies home was actually put on for the five-year-old Michael (illness prevented him from attending the performance at the Duke of York's Theatre), not for Sylvia, who did not become ill until several years later.

Finding Neverland focuses on how Sylvia and the boys inspired Barrie's literary creation, weaving in and out between adventures with the boys, scenes of inspiration and composition, and flashes of Barrie's own desire to hold on to his youth and imagination. We grow to admire Barrie, the man who dances with dogs in the park and balances spoons on his nose; we cheer for Peter Pan when he urges us to clap our hands and demonstrate our faith in fairies; and we weep with Peter Llewelyn Davies, who is struggling to cope with the death of his parents. Forster demonstrates real ingenuity by placing Peter Pan as a spectral

George, Michael, Jack, and Peter play pirate games with J. M. Barrie in *Finding Neverland*. Their mother, Sylvia Llewelyn Davies, clad in a simple, cream-colored dress, forms a contrast to the motley crew, with their brightly colored, outlandish costumes. (By permission of Miramax Films, Film Colony, Photofest)

Jeremy Sumpter plays a seductively beautiful Peter Pan opposite an illuminated Tinker Bell. This Peter Pan is no woman, and, although still very much a child, he has the facial hair of an adolescent. P. J. Hogan's *Peter Pan* takes a more romantic turn than most versions of the work. (By permission of ILM and Photofest)

The Llewelyn Davies boys are dressed like their mother, in white with a touch of scarlet, as they escort her to Neverland, toward the production of *Peter Pan* staged at their home and to the Land of the Dead. Julie Christie plays Sylvia's mother, Emma du Maurier, and Johnny Depp plays James Barrie at the height of his theatrical success and at a nadir in his personal life. (By permission of Miramax Films, Film Colony, Photofest)

Johnny Depp as James Barrie dances with Porthos in Kensington Gardens. (By permission of Miramax Films, Film Colony, Photofest)

presence in the London inhabited by Barrie and the boys. At night, after a romp on the beds, the tired boys are observed from outside, through the bars of their bedroom window. The camera gives us the point of view of Peter Pan, ready to "break through." In a later scene, the boys fly a kite, and the camera is positioned up in the air, with the kite, along with the same beams and bells that customarily announce Tinker Bell's presence.

Peter Pan: Adaptations, Prequels, Sequels, and Spin-Offs

Adair, G. *Peter Pan and the Only Children*. London and Basingstoke: Macmillan Children's Books, 1987.

Barry, Dave, and Ridley Pearson. *Peter and the Starcatchers*. New York: Puffin, 1994.

———. *Escape from the Carnivale*. New York: Disney Editions / Hyperion Books, 2006.

———. *Cave of the Dark Wind*. New York: Disney Editions / Hyperion Books, 2007.

———. *Peter and the Secret of Rundoon*. New York: Disney Editions / Hyperion Books, 2007.

———. *Peter and the Shadow Thieves*. New York: Disney Editions / Hyperion Books, 2007.

———. *Blood Tide*. New York: Disney Editions / Hyperion Books, 2008.

———. *Peter and the Sword of Mercy*. New York: Disney Editions / Hyperion Books, 2009.

Brady, Joan. *Death Comes for Peter Pan*. London: Secker & Warburg, 1996.

Brooks, Terry. *Hook*. New York: Ballantine, 1991.

Byron, May. *J. M. Barrie's Peter Pan & Wendy, Retold by May Byron for Boys and Girls, with the Approval of the Author*. Illus. Mabel Lucie Attwell. London: Hodder & Stoughton, 1926.

———. *J. M. Barrie's Peter Pan & Wendy, Retold by May Bryon for Little People with the Approval of the Author*. Illus. Mabel Lucie Attwell. London: Hodder & Stoughton, 1926.

———. *J. M. Barrie's Peter Pan in Kensington Gardens, Retold by May Byron for Little*

People with the Permission of the Author. Illus. Arthur Rackham. London: Hodder & Stoughton, 1929.

David, Peter. *Tigerheart.* New York: Del Rey, 2009.

Drennan, G. D. *Peter Pan, His Book, His Pictures, His Career, His Friends.* London: Mills and Boon, 1909.

Dubowski, Cathy East, adapt. *Peter Pan.* New York: Random House, 1994.

Egan, Kate. *Welcome to Neverland.* New York: HarperFestival, 2003.

Fox, Laurie. *The Lost Girls.* New York: Simon & Schuster, 2004.

Fresán, Rodrigo. *Kensington Gardens: A Novel.* Trans. Natasha Wimmer. New York: Farrar, Straus and Giroux, 2006.

Frye, Charles. *The Peter Pan Chronicles.* Charlottesville: University of Virginia Press, 1989.

Herford, Oliver. *The Peter Pan Alphabet.* New York: Charles Scribner's Sons, 1907.

McCaughrean, Geraldine. *Peter Pan in Scarlet.* New York: Simon & Schuster, 2006.

Moore, Bob, adapt. *Walt Disney's Peter Pan and the Pirates.* New York: Simon & Schuster, 1952.

O'Connor, D. S., ed. *Peter Pan Keepsake, the Story of Peter Pan Retold from Mr. Barrie's Dramatic Fantasy.* London: Chatto & Windus, 1907.

———. *The Story of Peter Pan.* London: Bell, 1912.

O'Connor, D. S., and Alice B. Woodward. *The Peter Pan Picture Book.* London: G. Bell, 1907.

O'Roarke, Jocelyn. *Who Dropped Peter Pan?* New York: Penguin, 1996.

Perkins, Frederick Orville. *Peter Pan: The Boy Who Would Never Grow Up to Be a Man.* Boston: Silver, Burdett, 1916.

Press, Jenny. *Peter Pan: A Storyteller Book.* New York: Smithmark, 1995.

Shalant, Phyllis. *When Pirates Came to Brooklyn.* New York: Dutton, 2002.

Somma, Emily. *After the Rain: A New Adventure for Peter Pan.* West Hamilton, Ontario: Daisy, 2004.

Yolen, Jane. "Lost Girls." *Sister Emily's Lightship and Other Stories.* New York: Tor, 2000.

FILMOGRAPHY

Peter Pan. Dir. Clyde Geronimi, Wilfred Jackson, and Hamilton Luske. Disney Studios, 1953.

The Lost Boys. Dir. Joel Schumacher. Warner Bros., 1987.

Hook. Dir. Steven Spielberg. Columbia/Tristar, 1991.

Return to Never Land. Dir. Donovan Cook and Robin Budd. Walt Disney, 2002.

Peter Pan. Dir. P. J. Hogan. Universal Studios, 2003.

The Lost Boys of Sudan. Dir. Jon Shenk and Megan Mylan. New Video Group, 2004.

Finding Neverland. Dir. Marc Forster. Miramax, 2004.

Tinker Bell. Walt Disney Studios, 2008.

TELEVISION PRODUCTIONS

Peter Pan. NBC. With Mary Martin. 1955.

Peter Pan. NBC. With Mia Farrow. 1976.

Peter Pan. A&E. With Cathy Rigby. 2000.

VIDEO GAMES

Disney Junior Games: Peter Pan Neverland Treasure Quest. PC. Disney Interactive. San Mateo, CA: Sony, 2002.

Fox's Peter Pan and the Pirates. Nintendo Entertainment System. THQ. Redmond, WA: Nintendo of America, 1991.

Kingdom Hearts: Chain of Memories. Game Boy Advance Prod. Square Enix. Los Angeles: Square Enix, 2002.

Peter Pan. Game Boy Advance. Prod. Atari. New York: Atari, 2003.

Peter Pan: Return to Neverland. Game Boy Advance. Prod. Disney Interactive. Burbank, CA: Disney Interactive, 2002.

A Montage of Friends, Fans, and Foes:
J. M. Barrie and Peter Pan in the World

The boy and the man who would not grow up have touched the lives of many readers, spectators, and onlookers. In the course of writing this book, I encountered a range of lively reactions and eloquent responses to the play and novel as well as to Peter Pan and his author. Rather than paraphrasing those views and incorporating them into the annotations (on a few occasions I succumbed to the temptation to place them there, too), I decided to let enthusiasts and skeptics speak for themselves. Their voices will sound full chords for those who have lost themselves in the pages of *Peter Pan* or in performances of the play. This section begins with Charlie Chaplin's reminiscence of meeting the distinguished playwright in London and ends with fellow dramatist George Bernard Shaw's recollections of his Adelphi Terrace neighbor James Barrie. In between, the voices of renowned theater critics like Alexander Woollcott mingle with the words of the very young, and we hear from actresses who have played Peter Pan as well as those who aspired to fly when they were young. Following those responses comes the reaction of adults (many of them writers) to their encounters with Peter Pan. Even in an era of stubborn cynicism, it is not easy to find naysayers when it comes to Peter Pan, but the few I did locate were given an opportunity to speak in these pages as well.

Charlie Chaplin. *"I Meet the Immortals." My Trip Abroad.* New York: Harper & Brothers, 1922. Pp. 85–89.

There is Barrie. He is pointed out to me just about the time I recognize him myself. This is my primary reason for coming. To meet Barrie. He is a small man, with a dark mustache and a deeply marked, sad face, with heavily shadowed eyes. But I detect lines of humor lurking around his mouth. Cynical? Not exactly.

I catch his eye and make motions for us to sit together, and then find that the party has been planned that way anyhow. . . .

But everyone seems jovial except Barrie. His eyes look sad and tired. But he brightens as though all along there had been that hidden smile behind the mask. I wonder if they are all friendly toward me, or if I am just the curiosity of the moment. . . .

What should I say to Barrie? Why hadn't I given it some thought? . . .

Barrie tells me that he is looking for someone to play Peter Pan and says he wants me to play it. He bowls me over completely. To think that I was avoiding and afraid to meet such a man! But I am afraid to discuss it with him seriously, am on my guard because he may decide that I know nothing about it and change his mind.

Just imagine, Barrie has asked me to play Peter Pan. It is too big and grand to risk spoiling it by some witless observation, so I change the subject and let this golden opportunity pass. I have failed completely in my first skirmish with Barrie. . . .

Barrie is speaking again about moving pictures. I must understand. I summon all of my scattered faculties to bear upon what he is saying. What a peculiarly shaped head he has.

He is speaking of *The Kid*, and I feel that he is trying to flatter me. But how he does it! He is criticizing the picture.

He is very severe. He declares that the "heaven" scene was entirely unnecessary, and why did I give it so much attention? . . . All of these things he is discussing analytically and profoundly, so much so that I find my feeling of self-consciousness is rapidly leaving me. . . .

I am thrilled at his interest and appreciation and it is borne in upon me that by discussing dramatic construction with me he is paying a very gracious and subtle compliment. It is sweet of him. It relieves me of the last vestige of my embarrassment.

"But, Sir James," I am saying. "I cannot agree with you—." Imagine the metamorphosis. And our discussion continues easily and pleasantly. I am aware of his age as he talks and I get more of his spirit of whimsicality. . . . I am wondering if Barrie resents age, he who is so youthful in spirit.

Barrie is whispering, "Let's go to my apartment for a drink and a quiet talk." And I begin to feel that things are most worth while. Knobloch and I walk with him to Adelphia [*sic*] Terrace, where his apartment overlooks the Thames Embankment.

Somehow this apartment seems just like him, but I cannot convey the resemblance in a description of it. The first thing you see is a writing desk in a huge room beautifully furnished, and with dark-wood paneling. Simplicity and comfort are written everywhere. There is a large Dutch fireplace in the right side of the room, but the outstanding piece of furniture is a tiny kitchen stove in one corner. It is polished to such a point that it takes the aspect of the ornamental rather than the useful. He explains that on this he makes his tea when servants are away. Such a touch, perhaps, just the touch to suggest Barrie.

Our talk drifts to the movies and Barrie tells me of the plans for filming *Peter Pan*. We are on very friendly ground in this discussion and I find myself giving Barrie ideas for plays while he is giving me ideas for movies, many of them suggestions that I can use in comedies. It is a great chatfest.

There is a knock at the door. Gerald du Maurier is calling. He is one of England's greatest actors and the son of the man who wrote *Trilby*. Our party lasts far into the night, until about three in the morning. I notice that Barrie looks rather tired and worn, so we leave, walking with Du Maurier up the Strand. He tells us that Barrie is not himself since his nephew was drowned, and that he has aged considerably.

Alexander Woollcott. *Shouts and Murmurs: Echoes of a Thousand and One First Nights.* New York: Century Co., 1922. Pp. 190–91.

"Barrie has gone out of his mind, Frohman," Tree said. "I am sorry to say it; but you ought to know it. He's just read me a play. He is going to read it to you, so I am warning you. I know I have not gone woozy in my mind, because I have tested myself since hearing the play; but Barrie must be mad. He has written four acts all about fairies, children, and Indians running through the most incoherent story you ever listened to; and what do you suppose? The last act is to be set on top of trees."

Rupert Brooke. *Friends and Apostles: The Correspondence of Rupert Brooke and James Strachey, 1905–1914.* Ed. Keith Hale. New Haven, CT: Yale Univ. Press, 1998. P. 25.

I suppose you know a play called *Peter Pan?* I saw it last year & fell so much in love with it that I am going up to see its revival again in a few days. I found it enchanting, adorable, and entirely beautiful. In reality, no doubt, it is very ridiculous. I am very aged & this mania for children's plays is a token of advanced senility. . . .

I have gone about as one in a dream, quoting to myself all the gorgeous fragments of *Peter Pan* I can remember. As I stroll through Cambridge, Trinity Street fades and I find myself walking by the shore of the Mermaid Lagoon, King's Chapel often shrinks before my eyes, and rises, and is suddenly the House in the Tree-tops.

"Letter to Mr. Barrie," review of *Peter Pan* in *The King*, January 14, 1904.

My advice to everyone who has children is to take them to the Duke of York's Theatre without delay. Those who have no children should immediately borrow some for the afternoon. They will find that they get a rare pleasure out of watching their little companions enjoy your quaint inventions, and there will be something wrong with them if they do not enjoy the piece on their own account as well.

Oscar Parker. "The London Stage." *The English Illustrated Magazine* 40 (1906): 40.

Peter Pan is, as I write, rapidly mounting up the score in its third "century." I was curious to see whether first impressions of this very original and daring experiment would persist upon a second hearing, a year later than the first, and accordingly I have just spent three hours with Peter and Wendy and the lost boys of "Never-never-never-land." That curiosity was all the stronger because recently I read an American critic's opinion of the play on its production this winter in New York, and the American critic's remarks were acid. He found the play "mystifyingly unsatisfactory"—"the sort of fairy story that renders a key unnecessary"—"far-fetched and complicated," and, to his mind, Peter Pan did nothing "that awoke that juvenile appreciation latent in most grown-ups." I am sorry for that critic; sorry that life has deposited so many stony strata of hard facts in his mind that the volatile essence of his childhood imagination has no chance to struggle through into memory. . . . Why should adult audiences fill the theatre here and in New York—for it is equally a success in both cities—day after day, but that Mr. Barrie plays upon an almost universal chord of sympathy with this attempt to recall—not the actual visions of childhood, but the whole mental life of the child, when reality and dreams merge into one another.

Louise Boynton. *The Century Magazine*, December 1906.

New York needed *Peter Pan*. The play came at one of those discouraged moments when the public mind was occupied to an almost morbid degree with huge and vexing problems and with things that were going wrong. Legalized evil-doing was rampant in business and politics, the exposure of fraud was the principal business of those who were not committing it. Cynicism was the dominant note in literature and dramatic art, a cheerful, clever twentieth-century cynicism, but a bitter and depressing influence for all that. At such a moment came *Peter Pan*, created in the mind of a man of insight and gentleness, embodied by a woman beautiful in life and thought, with the soul of an artist, and the heart of a child. . . .

Playing Peter Pan is not acting a role. It is embodying a living thought. It is expressing the life-force in the simplest, most beautiful way by teaching us to look at life from the child's point of view. . . . Realities that seemed formidable are found not to be real at all, and all sorts of lovely illusions are dreams that may come true.

Virginia Woolf. *A Passionate Apprentice: The Early Journals 1897–1909 of Virginia Woolf.* Ed. Mitchell A. Leaska. San Diego: Harcourt Brace Jovanovich, 1990. Pp. 227–28.

We went with Gerald to *Peter Pan*, Barries [*sic*] play—imaginative & witty like all of his, but just too sentimental.—However it was a great treat.

Max Beerbohm. *"Peter Pan* Revisited." In *Last Theatres: 1904–1910.* New York: Taplinger, 1970. P. 336.

Of course these books are not read, or are read without pleasure, by children: it is the adults who devour them, while the children satisfy their own romantic cravings with tit-bits of information purveyed by the popular press, opening wide their eyes and thrilling at the thought that if all the pins that are daily dropped in the streets within the four-mile radius were joined together lengthwise they would reach from London to Milan.

Anonymous. "Life and Letters." *Poet Lore* 17 (Spring 1906): 121.

The popular hit of the hour is J. W. [*sic*] Barrie's *Peter Pan*, yet those who manage to retain their individual power of judgment against the obsession of the multitude will find the impression made upon them by the play not so altogether satisfactory and inspiring as they had been led to suppose it would be. There is a strange mixture in it of charm and something that is not charm. . . .

If we imagine the play written by a child there are sophistications in it which could not possibly enter the mind of a child. If we imagine it written by a grown person there are childish naivetés which would be innocent enough if the childlike point of view were steadily maintained, but which, under the circumstances, become innuendoes that do not strike an absolutely pure note. This mixing up of two points of view is more a flaw in artistic construction than a flaw *per se* in the ethics of the play. . . .

An irascible idiot for a father and an amiable idiot for a mother, and anything but a refined and peaceful scene in the nursery strikes so unpleasant a note in the start that the charming scene following in which the children learn from Peter Pan how to fly hardly blots out the impression.

Alexander Woollcott. *Shouts and Murmurs: Echoes of a Thousand and One First Nights.* New York: Century Co, 1922. Pp. 198–200 and 186–89.

And the children love it. There will have to be a chapter about the *Peter Pan* audiences, and you have never really seen the play if you have not attended a matinee. You must see the miniature playgoers straining in their seats, breaking the nurse's leash and swarming incontinently down the aisles. You must see them in the boxes, looking in the perfection of their faith, as if at any moment they might attempt to fly out across the auditorium. You must hear their often embarrassingly premature rally to the defense of *Tinker Bell* and hear the shout that occasionally threatens to break up the proceedings, as when a passionately interested *Michael* on the wrong side of the footlights cries out in friendly warning: "Watch out, Peter, watch out! The old parrot's poisoned your medicine."

The historian must tell of the little folks waiting gravely at the stage-door to ask for thimbles, and maybe he will have access to the countless letters to *Peter* that have come in, heavy with pennies sent trustfully to buy a pinch of fairy dust, which is so necessary if you have forgotten how to fly.

But the dearest friends of *Peter Pan* are among the oldest living inhabitants. Austere jurists, battered rounders, famous editors and famous playwrights, slightly delirious poets and outwardly forbidding corporation presidents, these are in the ranks of the devoted. You simply cannot recognize a Peter Pantheist at sight, but when you find him reappearing at each engagement you can begin to guess his heart is in the right place.

It would be idle to pretend that everybody likes the play, but its own public is large and so shamelessly addicted to it that a dozen visits to the theater are as nothing. There are some of us who cannot hear the opening strains of the music, who cannot witness the first inordinately solemn appearance of the responsible *Liza*, without feeling an absurd desire to laugh and weep at the same time, who cannot watch *Peter* take his silent stand on guard outside the house they built for *Wendy* without a sense of exaltation that warms the heart and sends us fair uplifted to our homes.

It was on the night of November 6, 1905, that *Peter Pan* was played for the first time in New York. It had been produced triumphantly in London the year before, and quite a fever of expectancy awaited its coming to America. The arrest poster with its "Do you believe in fairies?" bedecked the bill-boards of Manhattan, and sleepy little messenger boys curled up in the corner of the Empire lobby waiting all night for the beginning of the box-office sale. But the news from the road was disheartening. Washington evidently did *not* believe in fairies, and Buffalo was cold to *Peter Pan*. On the opening night in New York, a polite and baffled audience laughed and applauded loyally—but at disconcertingly wrong moments.

The author of "The Legend of *Peter Pan*"—with whatever of reluctance or malice may color his disposition—must write one inexorable chapter devoted to the collapse of the New York reviewers. Some there were who responded gaily to the appeal of the play, but there were others who did not respond at all. Now listen to this oracle:

> Mr. Barrie, in the excess of his facetiousness, has seen fit once more to mystify his audience, and if *Peter Pan* fails to be a prolonged success

here, the blame must be laid entirely at his door. It is not only a mystery but a great disappointment . . . a conglomeration of balderdash, cheap melodrama and third-rate extravaganza. From the beginning of its second act, it invariably challenges comparison with plays like *The Wizard of Oz* and *Babes in Toyland*, and it fails to show either the sense of fun of childhood which made both pieces a delight to children of all ages. . . . For an artist of Maude Adams's standing, this play seems like a waste of time. And incidentally, if *Peter Pan* is a play at all, it is a very bad one.

. . . But the severest rebuke that was administered to the playwright appeared in "a morning newspaper" and contained these bitter reflections:

> *Peter Pan* is a riddle to which there is no answer; it baffled a large and typical Maude Adams house last night. . . . His [Barrie's] ideas of childlike simplicity are ludicrous. They seem to be the fancies of a disordered stomach. . . . It was a pity to see Miss Adams, with her delightful gifts, wasting herself on such drivel.

Well, the third-rate extravaganza celebrated its tenth anniversary with no signs of mortality; the fancies of a disordered stomach have rejoiced more than a thousand audiences in America. The *Smee*, the *Jukes*, and the *Captain Hook* among the unbelievers have been pushed into the sea, and on its tenth anniversary was it fancy that the sound the wind brought from the Empire was the crowing of *Peter* triumphant?

Nina Boucicault. In Bruce K. Hanson, *The Peter Pan Chronicles: The Nearly One-Hundred-Year History of the Boy Who Wouldn't Grow Up*. New York: Birch Lane Press, 1993. P. 31.

To me *Peter Pan* has always been much more than a fairy play for children. The fairy trappings are only a setting for the development of a serious idea. From beginning to end the story is a rather wistful commentary on human nature, taking as its theme the supreme selfishness of man and the supreme unselfishness of woman.

Peter Pan's Post Bag: Letters to Pauline Chase. London: William Heinemann, 1908. Pp. 13, 22–23, and 32–33.

My dear Peter Pan

I loved you so much that Mother said I was crying in bed for you. I wish you could come here and I would show you my puppies and things. Will you come and see us if you ever come to Bexhill. We live four miles from there in the country. We all want to see you again. Will you teach me and Baby to fly. I am sending you my sixpence. The smallest little girl in the photo is me—

With love and a hug from
Marjorie

My dear Peter Pan,

I hope you are very well.

I was at the theatre yesterday (the 8th). I think it must be very nice to fly, can you come to Grove Park, to teach me how to fly if you have not time will you ask Wendy to come.

I think it must be very tireing work for you all to have to be there afternoon and night.

I have a brother and a sister our sister goes to boarding school but she comes home every week.

Please will you write to me if you have time.

With very much love from
Charles William Eric.
P.S.—I am 8 years old.

My dear Peter & Wendy,

I did like the play SO much on Wednesday Do you remember me? I was sitting in the stage-box & I was waving to you & Wendy in the last scene in the tree-tops.

Captain Hook I HATE because he tried to kill you, he did look SO horrid when a green light was put on his face when you were asleep. He put his horrid hand right over poor wendy's mouth so that she could not speak. . . .

I wish you would teach ME to fly.

Give Wendy my love when she comes for spring-cleaning. . . .

Yours trully,

Barbara

Anonymous. *Saturday Review*, January 7, 1905.

Peter Pan; or, adds Mr. Barrie, *The Boy Who Wouldn't Grow Up.* And he himself is that boy. That child, rather; for he halted earlier than most of the men who never come to maturity—halted before the age when soldiers and steam-engines begin to dominate the soul. To remain, like Mr. Kipling, a boy, is not at all uncommon. But I know not anyone who remains, like Mr. Barrie, a child. It is this unparalleled achievement that informs so much of Mr. Barrie's later work, making it unique. This, too, surely it is that makes Mr. Barrie the most fashionable playwright of his time.

Hesketh Pearson. *Bernard Shaw: His Life and Personality.* London: Methuen, 1961. P. 282.

Agreeing with Max Beerbohm's view that *Peter Pan* was an artificial freak which missed its mark completely, and was foisted on children by the grown-ups, [George Bernard] Shaw confessed, "I wrote *Androcles and the Lion* partly to show Barrie how a play for children should be handled." Doubtless the children would have thoroughly enjoyed it, but unfortunately the grown-ups . . . considered the play blasphemous, and instead of foisting it on their offspring forbade them to see it.

Anonymous. *New York Times*, December 3, 1911.

It is enough that Mr. Barrie has put Peter into a book for fear a play would not hold him long enough. Only curmudgeons can fail to bless Mr. Barrie for doing it.

Isaac Frederick Marcosson and Daniel Frohman. *Charles Frohman: Manager and Man.* New York: Harper & Brothers, 1916. Pp. 169 and 257.

When Frohman first read *Peter Pan* he was so entranced that he could not resist telling all his friends about it. He would stop them in the street and act out the scenes. Yet it required the most stupendous courage and confidence to put on a play that, from the manuscript, sounded like a combination of circus and extravaganza; a play in which children flew in and out of rooms, crocodiles swallowed alarm-clocks, a man exchanged places with his dog in its kennel, and various other seemingly absurd and ridiculous things happened.

No one will be surprised to know that in connection with *Peter Pan* is one of the most sweetly gracious acts in Frohman's life. The original of *Peter* was sick in bed at his home when the play was produced in London. The little lad was heartsick because he could not see it. When Frohman came to London, Barrie told him about it.

"If the boy can't come to the play, we will take the play to the boy," he said.

Frohman sent his company out to the boy's home with as many "props" as could be jammed into the sick-room. While the delighted and excited child sat propped up in bed the wonders of the fairy play were unfolded before him. It is probably the only instance where a play was done before a child in his home.

Charles Frohman. *Harper's Weekly*, April 1906.

Life in the big cities where huge buildings shut off from the child all contemplation of the open sky, and where dull grey streets have replaced green fields, where the lesson of the day is "getting on in the world" rather than being a child and enjoying the dream-while of pirates, fairies, and Indians—all these are pointed out as tendencies towards early self-consciousness and the stagnation of the imagination. . . . It has fallen to Barrie to evolve what, in all my experience, the

American stage has only now accorded—namely an entertainment creative of pure fancy in the city-bred child, and quickening to the imagination of the little people whose natural Fairyland we grown-ups have possessed—an illusion of a night during which the mother or father and child find abundant delights in common and realize new joys in being complete chums.

Daphne du Maurier. *Gerald: A Portrait*. Garden City, New York: Doubleday, Doran & Co., 1935. Pp. 104–5.

When Hook first paced his quarter-deck in the year 1904, children were carried screaming from the stalls, and even big boys of twelve were known to reach for their mother's hand in the friendly shelter of the boxes. How he was hated, with his flourish, his poses, his dreaded diabolical smile! That ashen face, those blood-red lips, the long, dank, greasy curls; the sardonic laugh, the maniacal scream, the appalling courtesy of his gestures; and that above all most terrible of moments when he descended the stairs and with slow, most merciless cunning poured the poison into Peter's glass. There was no peace in those days until the monster was destroyed, and the fight upon the pirate ship was a fight to the death. Gerald *was* Hook; he was no dummy dressed from Simmons in a Clarkson wig, ranting and roaring about the stage, a grotesque figure whom the modern child finds a little comic. He was a tragic and rather ghastly creation who knew no peace, and whose soul was in torment; a dark shadow; a sinister dream; a bogey of fear who lives perpetually in the grey recesses of every small boy's mind. All boys had their Hooks, as Barrie knew; he was the phantom who came by night and stole his way into their murky dreams. He was the spirit of Stevenson and of Dumas, and he was the Father-but-for-the-grace-of-God; a lonely spirit that was terror and inspiration in one. And because he had imagination and a spark of genius, Gerald made him alive.

Pauline Chase. "Behind the Footlights: My Reminiscences of *Peter Pan.*" *The Strand*, February 1913. Pp. 73–74.

And now let me tell you about some of my behind-the-scenes reminiscences of this hardy and ever-youthful annual. First of all, I would point out that all sorts of things happen in *Peter Pan* which never happen in any other play. Thus every December a terrifying ceremony takes place, and this is the measuring of the children who play in it. They are all measured to see whether they have grown too tall, and they can all squeeze down into about two inches less than they really are; but this does not deceive the management, who have grown frightfully knowing, and sometimes they frown horribly at you and say, sternly, "We shall pass you this year, but take care, madam, take care!" And sometimes you are told, "It won't do, my lad; you've grown out of knowledge. We are sorry for you, but—farewell!" Yes, measuring day is one of the tragedies of *Peter Pan*.

Maude Adams. In Phyllis Robbins, *Maude Adams: An Intimate Portrait*. New York: G. P. Putnam's, 1956. P. 94.

Of all the plays that were trusted to my care, I loved *Chantecler* best, and then came *Peter Pan*. It was not only that *Peter* was the most delightful of all the plays, but it opened a new world to me, the beautiful world of children. My childhood and girlhood had been spent with older people, and children had always been rather terrifying to me. When one met the eyes of the little things, it was like facing the Day of Judgment. Children remained an enigma to me until, when I was a woman grown, Peter gave me open sesame; for whether I understood children or not, they understood Peter.

"J. M. Barrie in His Most Fantastic Mood—Maude Adams in Perfect Sympathy with Its Gladsome Text." *New York Times*, November 12, 1905.

Of all the gladsome Barrie fantasies, none has seemed so truly satisfying, so fully wholesome, so tenderly appealing as *Peter Pan*. He knows the heart of mankind, he understands its workings, and burrows deep in the mentalities of his subjects. No man could write a *Peter Pan* who in himself was lacking in the qualities which make the heart of a child such a wondrously beautiful thing.

Mark Twain. "Letter to Maude Adams." In Phyllis Robbins, *Maude Adams: An Intimate Portrait.* New York: G. P. Putnam's Sons, 1956. P. 92.

It is my belief that *Peter Pan* is a great and refining and uplifting benefaction to this sordid and money-mad age; and that the next best play on the board is a long way behind it as long as you play Peter.

Mark Twain. "Samuel Clemens Interviews the Famous Humorist Mark Twain." *Seattle Star*, November 30, 1905.

"[*Peter Pan*] breaks all the rules of real life drama but preserves intact all the rules of fairyland, and the result is altogether contenting to the spirit."

George Orwell. "Such, Such Were the Joys . . ." *A Collection of Essays.* New York: Houghton Mifflin Harcourt, 1970. P. 33.

There never was, I suppose, in the history of the world a time when the sheer vulgar fatness of wealth, without any kind of aristocratic elegance to redeem it, was so obtrusive as in those years before 1914. It was the age . . . of *The Merry Widow*, Saki's novels, *Peter Pan* and *Where the Rainbow Ends*, the age when people talked about chocs and cigs and ripping and topping and heavenly. . . . From the whole decade before 1914, there seems to breathe forth a smell of the more vulgar, un-grown-up kinds of luxury, a smell of brilliantine and crème de menthe and soft-centred chocolates—an atmosphere, as it were, of eating everlasting strawberry ices on green lawns to the tune of the Eton Boating Song.

Matthew White Jr. "Stage-Door Worship for Maude Adams." *The Scrap Book,* March 3, 1907: 473.

I heard the other day of a New York seamstress who has seen the play forty-seven times, and who would leave any up-town engagement in the evening at half past ten and go down to the Empire Theater, merely to see Miss Adams walk across the pavement to her carriage. On one happy occasion the actress threw some flowers to the eager admirers . . . and the seamstress was fortunate enough to catch them. Palpitating with joy, she pressed forward to the window in the carriage. In the brief moment before the horses started, she found time to express her thanks, to tell Miss Adams how many times she had seen *Peter Pan*, and to give her address.

A day or two later the seamstress received an autographed picture from her idol. After that all her spare moments were spent in haunting Miss Adams' residence, when not making part of the stage-door crowd. Among the latter she became acquainted with the little daughter of a cook. The child had seen *Peter Pan* on one never-to-be-forgotten occasion, and was saving every penny to go again.

The seamstress next made a gorgeous pin-cushion, and, watching her chance, one afternoon sprang forward and presented it to Miss Adams just before she entered her home. The actress remembered her, invited her in, and on the ensuing conversation learned about the cook's child. Before her caller left, Miss Adams gave her a pass for two, in order that she might take the little girl to the theater. But on the way home, the seamstress said to herself: "There's the cook, the child's mother. She has never seen *Peter Pan*, and I have seen it nearly fifty times. I'll give the other ticket to her!"

Which she did.

Robert Louis Stevenson. In *J. M. Barrie: Glamour of Twilight.* Edinburgh: Ramsay Head Press, 1976. P. 9.

Letter to Henry James: "Barrie is a beauty. *The Little Minister* and *The Window in Thrums*, eh? Stuff in that young man; but he must see and not to be too funny. Genius in him, but there's a journalist at his elbow—there's the risk."

Letter to J. M. Barrie: "I have no such glamour of twilight in my pen. I am a capable artist; but it begins to look like you are a genius."

Pamela Maude. *Worlds Away.* London: John Baker, 1964. Pp. 137 and 144.

He was a tiny man, and he had a pale face and large eyes with shadows around them. . . . Our parents called him "Jimmy." He was unlike anyone we had ever met, or would meet in the future. He looked fragile, but he was strong when he wrestled with Porthos, his St. Bernard dog. . . . In the evening, when the strange morning light had begun to change, Mr. Barrie held out a hand to each of us in silence, and we slipped our own into his and walked, still silently, into the beechwood. We shuffled our feet through leaves and listened, with Mr. Barrie, for sudden sound, made by birds and rabbits. One evening we saw a pea-pod lying in the hollow of a great tree-trunk, and we brought it to Mr. Barrie. . . . There, inside, was a tiny letter, folded inside the pod, that a fairy had written. Mr. Barrie said he could read fairy writing and read it to us. We received several more, in pea-pods, before the end of our visit.

E. V. Lucas. *Reading, Writing and Remembering: A Literary Record.* New York: Harper & Brothers, 1932. P. 185.

Barrie is at his best with children; in fact, he becomes a child himself, bringing to that role endless resources of fantasy, inventiveness and fun. His letters to children are a delight, and should they have been preserved—as I hope, but as he, if he really holds that all correspondence should be destroyed (a point of view in which I intensely disagree with him), is far from wishing—an entrancing book would result.

Anonymous. *Times Literary Supplement*, June 26, 1937, pp. 469–70.

It means that Barrie had the power which is much greater than that of story-telling of compelling successive generations to invent his story afresh, to tell it to themselves and in their own terms—that is to say, he was able not merely to instruct or entertain but to impregnate the collective mind of his audience. And if he did, indeed, possess this power, which is precisely the power of the great fairy-tales, criticism may as well throw its pen away, for then he is immortal by election and there is no more to be said about it.

Jack Gould. "Television Neverland." *New York Times*, March 8, 1955.

Surely there must have been a trace of fairy dust from coast to coast this morning. Last night's television presentation of Mary Martin as *Peter Pan* was a joy. Who could say whether the TV premiere was more wondrous than the Broadway opening? It is unimportant . . . for in millions of homes entire families were transported to Neverland in the happiest of circumstances.

Mary Martin. *My Heart Belongs*. New York: Quill, 1984. Pp. 11 and 202.

Of all the exciting shows, the marvelous moments, the happy memories of what now seems a long, long life, Peter and Never Land loom largest in my mind. Partly because I love Peter so, partly because everyone else in the world loves Peter so. Mostly, I think, because Never Land is the way I would like real life to be: timeless, free, mischievous, filled with gaiety, tenderness and magic. . . .

I cannot even remember a day when I didn't want to be Peter. When I was a child I was sure I could fly. In my dreams I often did, and it was always the same: I ran, raised my arms like a great bird, soared into the sky, flew.

J. R. R. Tolkien. "On Fairy-Stories." *The Tolkien Reader.* New York: Ballantine Books, 1966. Pp. 44–45.

The process of growing older is not necessarily allied to growing wickeder, though the two do often happen together. Children are meant to grow up, and not to become Peter Pans. Not to lose innocence and wonder, but to proceed on the appointed journey: that journey upon which it is certainly not better to travel hopefully than to arrive, though we must travel hopefully if we are to arrive. But it is one of the lessons of fairie-stories (if we can speak of the lessons of things that do not lecture) that on callow, lumpish, and selfish youth peril, sorrow, and the shadow of death can bestow dignity, and even sometimes wisdom.

Susanne K. Langer. *Feeling and Form: A Theory of Art.* New York: Charles Scribner's Sons, 1952. P. 318.

I, too, remember vividly to this day the terrible shock of such a recall to actuality: as a young child I saw Maude Adams in *Peter Pan*. It was my first visit to the theater, and the illusion was absolute and overwhelming, like something supernatural. At the highest point of the action (Tinker Bell had drunk Peter's poisoned medicine to save him from doing so, and was dying) Peter turned to the spectators and asked them to attest their belief in fairies. Instantly the illusion was gone; there were hundreds of children, sitting in rows, clapping and even calling, while Miss Adams, dressed up as Peter Pan, spoke to us like a teacher coaching us in a play in which she herself was taking the title role. I did not understand, of course, what had happened; but an acute misery obliterated the rest of the scene, and was not entirely dispelled until the curtain rose on a new set.

Patrick Braybrook. *J. M. Barrie: A Study in Fairies and Mortals.* New York: Haskell House, 1971. P. 122.

I do not think that most children really understand the true significance of *Peter Pan*, they look upon it as a delightful fairy story, about a boy who refuses to grow up and has delightful adventures and hair-breadth escapes. It is for the older folk to see the symbolism and philosophy that lies behind, the pathos of Peter, the utter sadness of the Never, Never Land. . . . And so every Christmas in the heart of London, the children of a West End theatre clap to proclaim that they believe in fairies. And perhaps almost unconsciously some of their parents clap also. It is the secret of the charm of *Peter Pan*, the beautiful child's world of the fairy, so far removed from the cold, commercial and bitter world that has long lost fairyland because it has long lost its childlike innocence.

Dan Kiley. *The Peter Pan Syndrome: Men Who Have Never Grown Up*. New York: Dodd, Mead, 1983. Pp. 22–24.

We all remember the compelling story of happy-go-lucky Peter Pan, right? . . . When we allow Peter Pan to touch our heart, our soul is nourished by the fountain of youth.

But how many people realize that there is another side to the classic character created by J. M. Barrie? . . . A careful and thoughtful reading of Barrie's original play opened my eyes to a chilling reality. As much as I want to believe the contrary, Peter Pan was a very sad young man. . . . For all his gaiety, he was a deeply troubled boy living in an even more troubling time. He was caught in the abyss between the man he didn't want to become and the boy he could no longer be. . . . With increasing frequency, the little-known side of the famous Pan has captured the heart and soul of a significant segment of our children. If they're not freed, they will endure endless emotional and social turmoil. I feel certain that Peter wouldn't mind if I use his story to help others. In fact, I'm not sure he would even care.

Beryl Bainbridge. *An Awfully Big Adventure*. London: Duckworth, 1989. P. 99.

"There are numerous books on the meaning behind this particular play," Meredith said. "I've read most of them and am of the opinion that they do the author a disservice. I'm not qualified to judge whether the grief his mother felt on the death of his elder brother had an adverse effect on Mr. Barrie's emotional development, nor do I care one way or the other. We all have our crosses to bear. Sufficient to say that I regard the play as pure make-believe. I don't want any truck with symbolic interpretations."

Dan Simmons. *The Fall of Hyperion.* New York: Random House, 1991. P. 205.

When Brawne Lamnia had been a child, her father a senator and their home relocated, however briefly, from Lusus to the wooded wonders of Tau Ceti Center's Administrative Residential Complex, she had seen the ancient flatfilm Walt Disney animation of *Peter Pan.* After seeing the animation, she had read the book, and both had captured her heart.

For months, the five-standard-year-old girl had waited for *Peter Pan* to arrive one night and take her away. She had left notes pointing the way to her bedroom under the shingled dormer. She had left the house while her parents slept and lain on the soft grass of the Deer Park lawns . . . and dreaming of the boy from Neverland who would some night soon take her away with him, flying toward the second star to the right, straight on till morning. She would be his companion, the mother to the lost boys, fellow nemesis to the evil Hook, and most of all, Peter's new Wendy . . . the new child-friend to the child who would not grow old.

Kay Redfield Jamison. *An Unquiet Mind: A Memoir of Moods and Madness.* New York: Vintage, 1997. P. 95.

In rare instances, lithium causes problems of visual accommodation, which can, in turn, lead to a form of blurred vision. It can also impair concentration and attention span and affect memory. Reading, which had been at the heart of my intellectual and emotional existence, was suddenly beyond my grasp. . . . I found that children's books, which, in addition to being shorter than books written for adults, also had larger print, were relatively accessible to me, and I read over and over again the classics of childhood—*Peter Pan*, *Mary Poppins*, *Charlotte's Web*, *Huckleberry Finn*, the Oz books, *Doctor Dolittle*—that had once opened up such unforgettable worlds to me. Now they gave me a second chance, a second win of pleasure and beauty.

Fanny Howe. "Fairies." In *Mirror, Mirror on the Wall: Women Writers Explore Their Favorite Fairy Tales*. Ed. Kate Bernheimer. New York: Random House, Anchor Books, 1998. P. 184.

The mad applause for Tinker Bell in the middle of the performance of *Peter Pan* is like a reenactment of the storming of the Winter Palace. It's a protection of children's rights to believe in something other than what oppressive reason allows. And that is bewilderment. A society for the protection of fairies would really be a society for the protection of bewilderment.

Mary Gaitskill. *Two Girls Fat and Thin*. New York: Simon & Schuster, 1998. P. 81.

At night on Sunday, she would read me books like *My Father's Dragon*, *Little Witch*, and *Peter Pan*. When she read *Peter Pan*, I stopped drawing pictures of heaven and began drawing Never-Never land. Never-Never Land was pink and blue and green, it had trees with homes inside them, cubby holes and hiding places, tiny women in gauze robes and flying children with rapiers in their elegant hands. Its very name made me feel a sadness like a big beautiful blanket I could wrap around myself. I tried to believe that Peter Pan might really come one night and fly me away; I was too old to believe this and I knew it, but I forced the bright polka-dotted canopy of this belief over my unhappy knowledge. And I tried to conform the suburban world around me to the world of Victorian London described in the book—which resulted in a jarring sensation each time I was forced to look at my true surroundings.

Rosemarie Skaine. *The Cuban Family: Custom and Change in an Era of Hardship.* Jefferson, NC: McFarland, 2003. P. 102.

> Operation Pedro Pan was conceived when Miami relatives could not support 15 year old Pedro Menendez. A benefactor took Pedro to the Catholic Welfare Bureau (CWB), later renamed Catholic Charities. . . . Mr. James Baker and members of the American Chamber of Commerce of Havana . . . wanted to provide shelter and education for children who did not have relatives or friends in the United States. . . . Over 14,000 young people of Cuba migrated to the United States in the early 1960s as a part of "Operation Pedro Pan." Some children never saw their families again.

L. T. Stanley. "The Spirit of Pantomime." *Queen*, November 13, 1956.

> Should you find yourself at *Peter Pan* this Christmas, the unanimous affirmative to "Do you believe in fairies?" will show you how the children are entering into the spirit of entertainment. . . . It is refreshing to capture for an hour or so our damaged sense of wonder. Of all the comforts that nature can offer, one of the loveliest and most comforting is the unrestrained laughter of children.

The Fugitive. Dir. Andrew Davis, 1993.

> COSMO RENFRO: What happened? Where'd he go?
> DEPUTY MARSHAL SAMUEL GERARD: The guy did a Peter Pan right off of this dam, right here.
> COSMO RENFRO: What?
> DEPUTY MARSHAL SAMUEL GERARD: Yeah. BOOM!

Susan Pawick, *Flying in Place.* New York: Tor Books, 2005. P. 71.

> "It sounds scary," Ginny said, "I don't remember that one. Mom didn't read me scary stories."

"You're kidding! *Peter Pan's* not scary, with Hook and the crocodile and nasty little Tinkerbell trying to get Wendy shot down like a bird?"

Ginny shook her head again. "No. I always knew it would come out all right in the end. Mom told me so the first time she read it to me."

"She never told *me* that. Just let me be terrified through the whole thing."

Douglas E. Winter. *Clive Barker: The Dark Fantastic.* New York: HarperCollins, 2001. Pp.15–16.

Although Clive adored Joan's riverbank tales, his first and true love among the books she read to him was *Peter Pan.* ("It's the book I want to be buried with," he once told me.)

Although he was entertained by other classic children's books, none seemed to connect with him. . . . "*Nothing* could compare with Peter. Because he was just everything I wanted to be. He could fly. He didn't belong to anybody. He was his own boy. And as a child I think you want that so much. All children want to be their own person, right? . . . I wanted to open the nursery windows and be gone. And the price Peter pays for that freedom didn't seem to me to be too bad a price at the age of eight. But I would always cry at the end of the book. I was acutely aware of how sad the book was. And I never quite worked that out.

Anne McCaffrey. Introduction. *Peter Pan.* New York: Modern Library, 2004. Pp. xiii–xv.

It was more than seventy years ago that my mother read *Peter Pan* aloud to my two brothers and me. I still remember two things from that first reading: the directions to the Neverland, which never allowed me to get there ("Second to the right, and then straight on till morning" was a curious way to give directions, I thought at the time), and the magical possibility of reviving a fairy (Live, Tinker Bell!). . . . the directions to the Neverland have stayed with me all my life. . . even before I became a practicing science fiction writer, I had doubts about the usefulness of such ambivalent directions. However, on close examination, if one were facing north in London, right would be east. And straight on till morning . . . depending on when you took off—and I presume that the Darling children were put to bed about seven—you'd run into morning over India or the Micronesian sea, which has ever so many lovely untouched islands where pirates might still anchor, and coves and lagoons and the tropical vegetation that F. D. Bedford captured so enchantingly in his illustrations. So, whimsical as it may seem, "straight on till morning" is valid. Barrie never suggests that the Neverland is not on earth somewhere. Using fairy dust as an early antigravity spray and conjuring happy thoughts do speed one up on good days.

Rodrigo Fresán. *Peter Pan in Kensington Gardens: A Novel.* New York: Farrar, Straus and Giroux, 2006. P. 192.

The need to get away from the house. Maybe forever. I remember feeling that and thinking that maybe I'd climb a tree in the forest of Sad Songs and never come down. I walk with my hands in my pockets, and I come to the summerhouse, where the Victorians sometimes rehearse, and I go in, and—mystery of mysteries—on the floor there's a book, and the book is called *Peter Pan.*

I open it.

I enter it.

I read:

All children, except one, grow up.

And all books, except one, grow up. *Peter Pan*—unlike all the other books we read in childhood and reread as adults; like the author of *Peter Pan*, like the reader of *Peter Pan*—doesn't grow up, will never grow up. *Peter Pan* is like Peter Pan.

I enter *Peter Pan*, never to emerge from it again.

The character is the writer.

The writer of children's literature.

Adam Gopnik. *Through the Children's Gate.* New York: Random House, 2007. Pp. 97–98.

On an airplane over middle America, I sit down to read *Peter Pan*, which we saw once but I have never really read. Maybe, I think, I can find some secret flight formula buried in the Original Text. I read with pleasure, if not with illumination. *Peter Pan*, I see, is about escape, outward motion, the flight beyond Neverland. For J. M. Barrie, the townhouse, very much like those we envy on Halloween, represented the thing to fly away from, the little prison of bourgeois bedtimes. It wasn't that Barrie didn't like the houses he knew; he tried to build one like the one in his book for the real boys who inspired the story. It was that he took the fifth-floor window for granted, as part of the bourgeois entitlement. . . .

But to us, the house in *Peter Pan* looks like an unobtainable idyll of domestic pleasure, a place to fly *to*, just as Cherry Tree Lane is the place you want your children to be, not the one you need the magic nanny to lead them out of. The Edwardian-Georgian London, which sits just before and just after the great warning disaster of liberalism, the Great War, nonetheless casts its spell as a place for children's books to come out of.

There is an untieable knot at the heart of child raising: We want both a safe house with a garden and a nursery, and the world beyond, stars and redskins and even a plank to (harmlessly) walk. . . .

"Steven Spielberg on Peter Pan." Andrew M. Gordon. *Empire of Dreams: The Science Fiction and Fantasy Films of Steven Spielberg.* Lanham, UK: Roman & Littlefield, 2008. Pp. 189, 191–92.

I have always felt like Peter Pan. I still feel like Peter Pan. It has been very hard for me to grow up. . . . I'm a victim of the Peter Pan Syndrome.

My first memory of anybody flying is in *Peter Pan*. . . . I am absolutely fascinated and terrified by flying. It is a big deal in my movies. All my movies have airplanes in them. . . . To me, flying is synonymous with freedom and unlimited imagination, but, interestingly enough, I'm afraid to fly.

Patti Smith. *Just Kids.* New York: HarperCollins, 2010. P. 10.

> "Patricia," my mother scolded, "put a shirt on!"
>
> "It's too hot," I moaned. "No one else has one on."
>
> "Hot or not, it's time you started wearing a shirt. You're about to become a young lady." I protested vehemently and announced that I was never going to become anything but myself, that I was of the clan of Peter Pan, and we did not grow up.

David Sedaris. *When You Are Engulfed in Flames.* Boston: Little, Brown and Co., 2008. P. 237.

> After Paris came London, and a bedroom on the sixth floor with windows looking onto neat rows of Edwardian chimney tops. A friend characterized it as a "Peter Pan view," and now I can't see it any other way. I lie awake thinking of someone with a hook for a hand, and then, inevitably, of youth, and whether I have wasted it.

Brom. *The Child Thief: A Novel.* New York: HarperCollins, 2009. Pp. 477–78.

> Like so many before me, I am fascinated by the tale of Peter Pan, the romantic idea of an endless childhood amongst the magical playground of Neverland. But, like so many, my mind's image of Peter Pan had always been that of an endearing, puckish prankster, the undue influence of too many Disney films and peanut-butter commercials.
>
> That is, until I read the original *Peter Pan*, not the watered-down version you'll find in children's bookshops these days, but James Barrie's original—and politically uncorrected—version, and then I began to see the dark undertones and to appreciate just what a wonderfully blood-thirsty, dangerous, and at times cruel character Peter Pan truly is.
>
> Foremost, the idea of an immortal boy hanging about nursery win-

dows and seducing children away from their families for the sake of his ego and to fight his enemies is at the very least disturbing.

A. S. Byatt. *The Children's Book.* New York: Random House, 2009. P. 669.

The penultimate scene was the testing of the Beautiful Mothers, by Wendy. The Nursery filled with a bevy of fashionably dressed women, who were allowed to claim the Lost Boys if they responded sensitively to a flushed face, or a hurt wrist, or kissed the long-lost child gently, and not too loudly. Wendy dismissed several of these fine ladies, in a queenly manner. . . . Steyning spoke to Olive behind his hand. "This will have to go." Olive smiled discreetly and nodded. Steyning said "It's part pantomime, part play. It's the play that is original, not the pantomime." "Hush," said the fashionable lady in front of him, intent on the marshalling of the Beautiful Mothers.

After the wild applause, and the buzz of discussion, Olive said to Tom: "Did you enjoy that?"

"No," said Tom, who was in a kind of agony.

"Why not?"

Tom muttered something in which the only audible word was "cardboard." Then he said "He doesn't know *anything* about boys, or making things up."

August Steyning said "You are saying it's a play for grown-ups who don't want to grow up?"

"Am I?" said Tom. He said "It's make-believe make-believe make-believe. Anyone can see all those boys are girls."

His body squirmed inside his respectable suit. Tom said "It's not like *Alice in Wonderland*. That's a real other place. This is just wires and strings and disguises."

"You have a Puritan soul," said Steyning. "I think you will find, that whilst everything you say is true, this piece will have a long life and people will suspend their disbelief, very happily."

George Bernard Shaw. In Hesketh Pearson, *George Bernard Shaw: His Life and Personality.* London: Methuen, 1961. P. 307.

I was always on affectionate terms with Barrie, like everyone else who knew him; but though I lived for many years opposite him in the Adelphi and should, one would suppose, have met him nearly every day, we met not oftener than three times in five years in the street. It was impossible to make him happy on a visit unless he could smoke like a chimney (mere cigarettes left him quite unsatisfied); and as this made our flat uninhabitable for weeks all the visiting was on our side, and was very infrequent.

I fancy Barrie was rather conscious of the fact that writers have no history and consequently no biography, not being men of action.

His wife's elopement, and the deaths of some of his adopted children in the war, were the only events in his life I knew of. Though he seemed the most taciturn of men he could talk like Niagara when he let himself go, as he did once with Granville Barker and myself on a day which we spent walking in Wiltshire when he told us about his boyhood. He said that he had bacon twice a year, and beyond this treat had to content himself with porridge. He left me under the impression that his father was a minister; but this was probably a flight of my own imagination. I believe he was a weaver.

He had a frightfully gloomy mind, which he unfortunately could not afford to express in his plays. Only in child's play could he make other people happy.

You will have a bit of a job to make a full-sized biography for him; but I daresay you will manage it if anybody can. I really knew very little about him; and yet I suspect that I knew all that there was to be known about him from the official point of view. Anyhow I liked him.

J. M. Barrie's Legacy:
Peter Pan and Great Ormond Street Hospital for Children

by Christine De Poortere

The Hospital for Sick Children at Great Ormond Street opened its doors on St. Valentine's Day in 1852 with just ten beds. It was the first children's hospital in Great Britain and quickly acquired the patronage of Queen Victoria, along with widespread public interest. Dr. Charles West founded the hospital at a time when mortality rates for children were shockingly high and when many hospitals refused to admit children because they were believed to carry infection. He was a driven, pioneering figure and worked hard to transform his vision of a children's hospital in London into reality.

When the hospital opened its doors, the first patient admitted was Eliza Armstrong, three and a half years old. She was suffering from consumption, a then common and often fatal disease. Like all hospital patients at this time, Eliza came from a family too poor to pay for medical treatment. The hospital itself was funded by charitable donations, and financing its operations was a constant challenge from the outset. It was at this point that Charles Dickens stepped in to promote the hospital. Just six weeks after it opened, he published "Drooping Buds" in his popular periodical, *Household Words*. The essay was not just an impassioned plea for the hospital but also a declaration of its absolute necessity for children. He made a compelling case for addressing the high mortality rates for children in London. Just a few weeks after the appearance of

The nursery scene is staged for patients and staff in 1929, the year Barrie donated the rights to *Peter Pan*. (Courtesy Great Ormond Street Hospital Children's Charity)

Margaret Lockwood plays Peter Pan at the hospital in 1950. (Courtesy Great Ormond Street Hospital Children's Charity)

Peggy Cummins plays Peter Pan at the hospital in 1955. (Courtesy Great Ormond Street Hospital Children's Charity)

Dickens's article, and quite possibly as a direct consequence of it, Queen Victoria made a donation to the hospital and became its official patron. With royal endorsement, the Hospital for Sick Children could now be confident of being able to move forward with its motto, "The Child First and Always."

Great Ormond Street Hospital's association with major literary figures began with Charles Dickens and has continued ever since. After all, the hospital is situated in Bloomsbury, for many years the hub of London's literary world. Figures such as Oscar Wilde, A. A. Milne, Lewis Carroll, J. B. Priestley, and Monica Dickens, to name but a few, have all supported the hospital in one way or another.

Many have given but few so generously as J. M. Barrie. And the question naturally arises, Why did J. M. Barrie give *Peter Pan* to the hospital? Until Great Ormond Street Hospital became part of the National Health Service (NHS) in 1948, it had always had to rely on private donations and assistance from the public. J. M. Barrie was known to be a generous man and was familiar with the hospital, having lived just around the corner from it during his first years in London. His name first appeared in the hospital's records when he attended a fund-raising party on New Year's Eve in 1901, and his first recorded donation was in 1908. A Peter Pan Playground was opened in Catford, South East London, in 1922, and Barrie asked that the proceeds go directly to the hospital. Since his personal secretary, Lady Cynthia Asquith, was the daughter of the Earl of Wemyss, who was then chairman of the management board of the hospital, Barrie would have been well acquainted with the hospital's work.

In February 1929, the hospital wanted to buy the site vacated by the Foundling Hospital in neighboring Coram's Field, and the governors invited Barrie to help with the fund-raising campaign. He declined but replied, "At some future time I might find a way of helping. . . . I have been through the hospital several times and wish complete success to the project." Two months later, he stunned the board—and the world—when he announced his plan to give the hospital the copyright to *Peter Pan*. In the words of hospital secretary James McKay, this was truly a "munificent gift," and the hospital's president, the Prince of Wales (later to become HM King Edward VIII), wrote to thank him personally.

The following December, at Barrie's suggestion, the nursery scene from *Peter Pan* was performed in one of the wards by a cast that included Sir Gerald

The Peter Pan statue by Diarmuid Byron-O'Connor at the entrance of Great Ormond Street Hospital. (Courtesy Great Ormond Street Hospital Children's Charity)

du Maurier and Jean Forbes-Robertson. It was watched by a delighted crowd of patients, nurses, doctors, and Barrie himself, hiding in the background. It became traditional for the cast of the London production of *Peter Pan* to perform at the hospital and visit the wards. The performances still take place today, and the actors always find it moving to understand directly just what Barrie's legacy means for children.

In 1930, the hospital founded the Peter Pan League, a club for children to whom the author A. A. Milne and E. H. Shepard, the illustrator of *Winnie-the-Pooh*, appealed "to help the Hospital to help other children when they are ill and want comforting." That same year Barrie chaired a fund-raising dinner for the hospital reconstruction and in his speech stated that "at one time Peter Pan was an invalid in the Hospital for Sick Children, and it was he who put me up to the little thing I did for the hospital." At his death in 1937, the gift was confirmed in his will. A Peter Pan Ward, a Tinker Bell play area, a statue at the entrance of the hospital, and a memorial tablet to Sir James Barrie in the hospital chapel record the institution's gratitude. Barrie's name—and that of the Boy Who Would Not Grow Up—will always hold a special place in the hearts of patients and their families, as well as everyone who works at the hospital.

Over the years, the hospital had become so closely associated with the street that in the 1990s it was officially renamed Great Ormond Street Hospital for Children. Today, it is one of the world's leading children's hospitals, with the broadest range of dedicated children's healthcare specialists under one roof in Great Britain, providing free medical care for all National Health Service

Detail of the Peter Pan statue at the hospital, showing Tinker Bell. (Courtesy Great Ormond Street Hospital Children's Charity)

patients. The hospital's pioneering research and treatment give hope to children who are suffering from the rarest, most complex, and often life-threatening conditions, from across the country and abroad. While the NHS meets the day-to-day costs of running the hospital, the fund-raising income provided by Great Ormond Street Hospital Children's Charity allows the hospital to remain at the forefront of child healthcare. J. M. Barrie's inspired legacy contributes toward the hospital's redevelopment, research, and new equipment and has been helping children to grow up for over eighty years.

Christine De Poortere
Peter Pan Director
Great Ormond Street Hospital Children's Charity

Bibliography

WORKS BY J. M. BARRIE

A. Collected Editions

Kirriemuir Edition of the Works of J. M. Barrie. 10 vols. London: Hodder & Stoughton, 1913.

The Definitive Edition of the Plays of J. M. Barrie. Ed. A. E. Wilson. London: Hodder & Stoughton, 1942.

B. Individual Works

Better Dead. London: Swann, Sonnenschein, Lowrey, 1888.

Auld Licht Idylls. London: Hodder & Stoughton, 1888.

When a Man's Single. London: Hodder & Stoughton, 1888.

An Edinburgh Eleven. London: Office of the "British Weekly," 1889.

A Window in Thrums. London: Hodder & Stoughton, 1889.

My Lady Nicotine. London: Hodder & Stoughton, 1890.

Richard Savage. London: privately printed, 1891.

The Little Minister. London: Cassell, 1891.

Margaret Ogilvy, by Her Son, J. M. Barrie. London: Hodder & Stoughton, 1896.

Sentimental Tommy. London: Cassell, 1896.

Tommy and Grizel. London: Cassell, 1900.

The Wedding Guest. Hodder & Stoughton, 1900.

The Boy Castaways of Black Lake Island. London: J. M. Barrie in the Gloucester Road, 1901.

The *Little White Bird; or, Adventures in Kensington Gardens*. London: Hodder & Stoughton, 1902.

Peter Pan in Kensington Gardens. London: Hodder & Stoughton, 1906.

Walker, London. New York & London: S. French, 1907.

Peter and Wendy. London: Hodder & Stoughton, 1911.

Quality Street. London: Hodder & Stoughton, 1913.

The Admirable Crichton. London: Hodder & Stoughton, 1914.

Half Hours. London: Hodder & Stoughton, 1914.

"Der Tag"; or, The Tragic Man. London: Hodder & Stoughton, 1914.

Alice-Sit-by-the-Fire. London: Hodder & Stoughton, 1918.

Echoes of the War. London: Hodder & Stoughton, 1918.

Mary Rose. London: Hodder & Stoughton, 1918.

Courage. London: Hodder & Stoughton, 1922.

Dear Brutus. London: Hodder & Stoughton, 1922.

"Neil and Tintinnabulum." In *The Flying Carpet*. Ed. Cynthia Asquith. London: Partridge, 1925. Pp. 65–95.

"The Blot on Peter Pan." *The Treasure Ship: A Book of Prose and Verse*. Ed. Cynthia Asquith. London: S. W. Partridge, 1926. Pp. 82–100.

Peter Pan, or The Boy Who Would Not Grow Up. London: Hodder & Stoughton, 1928.

Shall We Join the Ladies? London: Hodder & Stoughton, 1929.

The Greenwood Hat. Edinburgh: Constable, 1930.

Farewell Miss Julie Logan. London: Hodder & Stoughton, 1932.

The Boy David. London: Peter Davies, 1938.

M'Connachie & J. M. B. London: Peter Davies, 1938.

The Letters of J. M. Barrie. Ed. Viola Meynell. London: Peter Davies, 1942.

When Wendy Grew Up: An Afterthought. Foreword by Sydney Blow. Edinburgh: Thomas Nelson, 1957.

Ibsen's Ghost; or, Toole Up-to-Date. London: Cecil Woolf, 1975.

SECONDARY LITERATURE

Allen, David Rayvern. *Peter Pan & Cricket*. London: Constable, 1988.

Aller, Susan Bivin. *J. M. Barrie: The Magic behind Peter Pan*. Minneapolis: Lerner, 1994.

Alton, Anne Hiebert. *Peter Pan*. Peterborough, Ontario: Broadview Press, 2011.

Anon. "*Peter Pan*, at the Duke of York's. *Illustrated London News*, January 7, 1905.

Ansell, Mary. *Dogs and Men*. London: Duckworth, 1924.

Asquith, Cynthia. *Portrait of Barrie*. London: James Barrie, 1954.

———. *Diaries: 1915–1918*. London: Hutchinson, 1968.

Atzmon, Leslie. "Arthur Rackham's Phrenological Landscape: In-betweens, Goblins, and Femmes Fatales." *Design Issues* 18 (2002): 64–83.

Avery, Gillian. "The Cult of Peter Pan." *Word & Image* 2 (1986): 173–85.

Babbitt, Natalie. "Fantasy and the Classic Hero." In *Innocence and Experience: Essays and Conversations on Children's Literature*. Ed. B. Harrison and G. Maguire. New York: Lothrop, Lee & Shepard, 1987.

Barker, H. Granville. "J. M. Barrie as Dramatist." *The Bookman* 39 (1910): 13–21.

Baum, Rob K. "Travesty, Peterhood and the Flight of a Lost Girl." *New England Theatre Journal* 9 (1998): 71–97.

Bell, Elizabeth. "Do You Believe in Fairies? Peter Pan, Walt Disney and Me." *Women's Studies in Communication* 19 (1996): 103–26.

Bendure, Joan C. *The Newfoundland Dog: Companion Dog—Water Dog*. New York: Macmillan, 1994.

Billone, Amy. "The Boy Who Lived: From Carroll's Alice and Barrie's Peter Pan to Rowling's Harry Potter." *Children's Literature* 32 (2004): 178–202.

Birkin, Andrew. *J. M. Barrie and the Lost Boys: The Love Story That Gave Birth to Peter Pan*. New York: Clarkson N. Potter, 1979.

———. Introduction. *Peter Pan, or the Boy Who Wouldn't Grow Up*. London: The Folio Society, 1992.

———. *J. M. Barrie and the Lost Boys*. New Haven, CT: Yale University Press, 2003.

———. "Introduction." *Peter Pan in Kensington Gardens*. By J. M. Barrie. London: The Folio Society, 2004.

Blackburn, William. "Mirror in the Sea: *Treasure Island* and the Internalization of Juvenile Romance." *Children's Literature Association Quarterly* 8 (1983): 7–12.

———. "*Peter Pan* and the Contemporary Adolescent Novel." *Proceedings of the Ninth Annual Conference of the Children's Literature Association*. Boston: Northeastern University, 1983.

Blake, George. *Barrie and the Kailyard School*. London: Arthur Barker, 1951.

Blake, Kathleen. "The Sea-Dream: *Peter Pan* and *Treasure Island*." *Children's Literature* 6 (1977): 165–81.

Braybrooke, Patrick. *J. M. Barrie: A Study in Fairies and Mortals*. Philadelphia: Lippincott, 1924.

Briggs, K. M. *The Fairies in English Tradition and Literature*. Chicago: University of Chicago Press, 1967.

Bristow, Joseph. *Empire Boys: Adventures in a Man's World*. London: HarperCollins, 1991.

Brophy, Brigid, Michael Levey, and Charles Osborne. "Peter Pan." *Fifty Works of English Literature We Could Do Without*. London: Rapp & Carroll, 1967. Pp. 109–12.

Buckingham, David. *After the Death of Childhood: Growing Up in the Age of Electronic Media*. Cambridge, MA: Polity, 2000.

Byrd, M. Lynn. "Somewhere Outside the Forest: Ecological Ambivalence in Neverland from *The Little White Bird* to *Hook*." In *Wild Things: Children's Culture and Ecocriticism*. Ed. Sidney I. Dobrin and Kenneth B. Kidd. Detroit: Wayne State University Press, 2004. Pp. 48–70.

Card, James. "Rescuing Peter Pan." In *Seductive Cinema: The Art of Silent Film*. New York: Alfred A. Knopf, 1994. Pp. 81–98.

Carpenter, Humphrey. *Secret Gardens: A Study of the Golden Age of Children's Literature*. Sydney: Allen & Unwin, 1987.

Chalmers, Patrick. *The Barrie Inspiration*. London: Peter Davies, 1938.

Chase, Pauline. *Peter Pan's Postbag: Letters to Pauline Chase*. London: Heinemann, 1909.

Chassagnol, Monique. "Representing Masculinity in James Barrie's *Peter Pan*." In *Ways of Being Male: Representing Masculinities in Children's Literature and Film*. Ed. John Stephens. New York: Routledge, 2002. Pp. 200–15.

Coats, Karen. *Looking Glasses and Neverlands: Lacan, Desire and Subjectivity in Children's Literature*. Iowa City: University of Iowa Press, 2004.

Colley, Linda. *Captives: Britain, Empire, and the World, 1600–1850*. New York: Random House/Anchor Books, 2004.

Connolly, Cyril. *Enemies of Promise*. New York: Macmillan, 1948.

Coveney, Peter. *The Image of Childhood*. Baltimore: Penguin, 1967.

Crafton, Donald. "The Last Night in the Nursery: Walt Disney's *Peter Pan*." *The Velvet Light Trap*, 24 (1989): 33–52.

Crowther, Bosley. "The Screen: Disney's 'Peter Pan' Bows." *New York Times*, February 12, 1953.

Cutler, B. D. *Sir James M. Barrie: A Bibliography*. New York: Greenberg, 1931.

Daiches, David. "The Sexless Sentimentalist." *The Listener* 63 (1960): 841–43.

Darlington, William Aubrey. *J. M. Barrie*. London: Blackie & Son, 1938.

Darton, F. J. Harvey. *J. M. Barrie*. London: Nisbet, 1929.

Davis, Tracy C. "'Do You Believe in Fairies?': The Hiss of Dramatic License." *Theatre Journal* 57 (2005): 57–81.

Deloria, Philip, and Neal Salisbury. *A Companion to American Indian History*. London: Wiley Blackwell, 2004.

Doyle, Sir Arthur Conan. *The Coming of the Fairies*. 1922. London: Pavilion, 1997.

Dunbar, Janet. *J. M. Barrie: The Man Behind the Image*. New York: Houghton Mifflin, 1970.

Eby, Cecil Degrotte. *The Road to Armageddon: The Martial Spirit in English Popular Literature, 1870–1914*. Durham, NC: Duke University Press, 1987.

Egan, Michael. "The Neverland of Id: Barrie, Peter Pan, and Freud." *Children's Literature* 10 (1982): 37–55.

Elder, Michael. *The Young James Barrie*. Illus. Susan Gibson. London: Macdonald, 1968.

Fiedler, Leslie. "The Eye of Innocence." In *Salinger: A Critical and Personal Portrait*. Ed. Henry Anatole Grunwald. New York: Harper & Row. Pp. 218–45.

Fields, Armond. *Maude Adams: Idol of American Theater, 1872–1953*. Jefferson, NC: McFarland, 2004.

Fox, Paul. "Other Maps Showing Through: The Liminal Identities of Neverland." *Children's Literature Association Quarterly* 32 (2007): 252–69.

Franz, Marie-Louise von. *The Problem of the Puer Aeternus*. Toronto: Inner City Books, 2000.

Galbraith, Gretchen R. *Reading Lives: Reconstructing Childhood, Books, and Schools in Britain, 1870–1920*. London: Macmillan, 1997.

Garber, Marjorie. *Vested Interests: Cross-Dressing and Cultural Anxiety*. London: Penguin, 1992.

Garland, Herbert. *A Bibliography of the Writings of Sir James Matthew Barrie Bart., O.M.* London: Bookman's Journal, 1928.

Geduld, Harry M. *Sir James Barrie*. New York: Twayne, 1971.

Gibson, Lois Rauch. "Beyond the Apron: Archetypes, Stereotypes, and Alternative Portrayals of Mothers in Children's Literature." *Children's Literature Association Quarterly* 13 (1988): 177–81.

Gilead, Sarah. "Magic Abjured: Closure in Children's Fantasy Fiction." *Literature for Children: Contemporary Criticism*. Ed. Peter Hunt. London: Routledge, 1992. Pp. 80–109.

Goddard, Ives. "'I Am a Red-Skin': The Adoption of a Native American Expression (1769–1826)." *Native American Studies* 19 (2005): 1–20.

Golstein, Vladimir. "Anna Karenina's Peter Pan Syndrome." *Tolstoy Studies Journal* 10 (1998): 29–41.

Green, Martin. "The Charm of Peter Pan." *Children's Literature: Annual of the Modern Language Association Division on Children's Literature and the Children's Literature Association* 1981 (9): 19–27.

Green, Roger Lancelyn. *Fifty Years of Peter Pan*. London: Peter Davies, 1954.

———. *J. M. Barrie*. New York: Henry Z. Walck, 1961.

Greenham, Robert. *It Might Have Been Raining: The Remarkable Story of J. M. Barrie's Housekeeper at Black Lake Cottage*. Maidstone, Kent, UK: Elijah, 2005.

Griffith, John. "Making Wishes Innocent: Peter Pan." *The Lion and the Unicorn* 3 (1979): 28–37.

Gubar, Marah. *Artful Dodgers: Reconceiving the Golden Age of Children's Literature.* Oxford: Oxford University Press, 2009.

Hammerton, John Alexander. *J. M. Barrie and His Books: Biographical and Critical Studies.* London: Horace Marshall & Son, 1900.

———. *Barrie: The Story of a Genius.* New York: Dodd, Mead & Co., 1929.

———. *Barrieland: A Thrums Pilgrimage.* London: Sampson Low & Co., 1929.

Hanson, Bruce K. *The Peter Pan Chronicles: The Nearly One-Hundred-Year History of "The Boy Who Wouldn't Grow Up."* New York: Birch Lane Press, 1993.

Hayter-Menzies, Grant. *Mrs. Ziegfeld: The Public and Private Lives of Billie Burke.* Jefferson, NC: McFarland, 2009.

Hearn, Michael Patrick. "Introduction to J. M. Barrie's *Peter and Wendy*." *Peter Pan: The Complete Book.* Montreal: Tundra Books, 1988.

Hollindale, Peter. Introduction. *Peter Pan in Kensington Gardens and Peter and Wendy.* Oxford: Oxford University Press, 1991. Pp. vii–xxviii.

———. "Peter Pan, Captain Hook and the Book of the Video." *Signal* 72 (1993): 152–75.

———. "Peter Pan: The Text and the Myth." *Children's Literature in Education* 24 (1993): 19–30.

———, ed. *J. M. Barrie: Peter Pan and Other Plays.* Oxford: Oxford University Press, 2008.

Hudson, Derek. *Arthur Rackham, His Life and Work.* London: Heinemann, 1960.

Jack, R. D. S. "The Manuscript of *Peter Pan*." *Children's Literature* 18 (1990): 101–13.

———. *The Road to the Never Land: A Reassessment of J. M. Barrie's Dramatic Art.* Aberdeen, Scotland: Aberdeen University Press, 1991.

John, Judith Gero. "The Legacy of Peter Pan and Wendy: Images of Lost Innocence and Social Consequences in *Harriet the Spy*." In *The Image of the Child: Proceedings of the 1991 International Conference of The Children's Literature Association.* Battle Creek, MI: Children's Literature Association, 1991. Pp. 168–73.

Karpe, M. "The Origins of Peter Pan," *Psychoanalytic Review* 43 (1956): 104–10.

Kavey, Allison B., and Lester D. Friedman. *Second Star to the Right: Peter Pan in the Popular Imagination.* New Brunswick, NJ: Rutgers University Press, 2009.

Kelley-Lainé, Kathleen. *Peter Pan: The Story of a Lost Childhood.* Trans. Nissim Marshall. Rockport, MA: Element Books, 1997.

Kennedy, John. *Thrums and Barrie Country.* London: Heath Cranton, 1930.

Kiley, Dan. *The Peter Pan Syndrome: Men Who Have Never Grown Up.* New York: Dodd, Mead, 1983.

———. *The Wendy Dilemma: When Women Stop Mothering Their Men.* Westminster, MD: Arbor House, 1984.

Kincaid, James. *Child-Loving: The Erotic Child and Victorian Culture.* New York: Routledge, 1992.

Kissel, Susan. S. "'But When at Last She Really Came, I Shot Her': Peter Pan and the Drama of Gender." *Children's Literature in Education* 19 (1988): 32–41.

Knoepflmacher, U. C. *Ventures into Childland: Victorians, Fairy-Tales and Femininity.* Chicago: University of Chicago Press, 1998.

Konstam, Angus, and Roger Michael Kean. *Pirates—Predators of the Seas: An Illustrated History.* New York: Skyhorse, 2007.

Kutzer, M. Daphne. *Empire's Children: Empire and Imperialism in Classic British Children's Books.* New York: Garland, 2000.

Lane, Anthony. "Lost Boys: Why J. M. Barrie Created Peter Pan." *The New Yorker,* November 22, 2004. Pp. 98–103.

Le Gallienne, Eva. *With a Quiet Heart: An Autobiography of Eva Le Gallienne.* New York: Viking, 1953.

Lewis, Naomi. "J. M. Barrie." In *Twentieth Century Children's Writers.* Ed. Daniel Kirkpatrick. New York: Macmillan, 1978.

Linetski, Vadim. "The Promise of Expression to the 'Inexpressible Child': Deleuze, Derrida and the Impossibility of Adult's Literature." *Other Voices: The e-Journal of Cultural Criticism* 1 (January 1999).

Lundquist, Lynne. "Living Dolls: Images of Immortality in Children's Literature." In *Immortal Engines: Life Extension and Immortality in Science Fiction and Fantasy.* Ed. George Slusser, Gary Westfahl, and Eric S. Rabkin. Athens: University of Georgia Press, 1996. Pp. 201–10.

Lurie, Alison. "The Boy Who Couldn't Grow Up." *The New York Review of Books,* February 1975. Pp. 11–15.

———. *Don't Tell the Grown-Ups: The Subversive Power of Children's Literature.* Boston: Little, Brown, 1990.

Lynch, Catherine M. "Winnie Foster and Peter Pan: Facing the Dilemma of Growth." *Children's Literature Association Quarterly* 7 (1982): 107–11.

Mackail, Denis. *Barrie: The Story of J. M. B.* London: Peter Davies, 1941.

Marcosson, Isaac F., and Daniel Frohman. *Charles Frohman: Manager and Man.* New York: Harper & Brothers, 1916.

Markgraf, Carl. *J. M. Barrie: An Annotated Secondary Bibliography.* Greensboro, NC: ELT Press, 1989.

McQuade, Brett. "Peter Pan: Disney's Adaptation of J. M. Barrie's Original Work." *Mythlore* 75 (1995): 5–9.

Merivale, Patricia. *Pan the Goat-God: His Myth in Modern Times.* Cambridge, MA: Harvard University Press, 1969.

Miller, Laura. "The Lost Boy." *New York Times Book Review,* December 14, 2003. P. 35.

Morgan, Adrian. *Toads and Toadstools: The Natural History, Folklore, and Cultural Oddities of a Strange Association.* Berkeley, CA: Celestial Arts, 1995.

Morley, Sheridan. "The First *Peter Pan.*" *Theatre's Strangest Acts: Extraordinary But True Tales from Theatre's Colourful History.* London: Robson, 2006. Pp. 44–48.

Moult, Thomas. *Barrie.* London: Jonathan Cape, 1928.

Nash, Andrew. "Ghostly Endings: The Evolution of J. M. Barrie's *Farewell Miss Julie Logan.*" *Studies in Scottish Literature* 33 (2004): 124–37.

Nelson, Claudia. *Boys Will Be Girls: The Feminine Ethic and British Children's Fiction, 1857–1917.* New Brunswick, NJ: Rutgers University Press, 1991.

Nesbit, E. *Five Children and It.* New York: Random House, 2010.

Nikolajeva, Maria. *From Mythic to Linear: Time in Children's Literature.* Lanham, MD: Children's Literature Association and Scarecrow Press, 2000.

Ogilvie, Daniel M. *Fantasies of Flight.* Oxford: Oxford University Press, 2004.

———. "Margaret's Smile." In *Handbook of Psychobiography.* Ed. William Todd Schultz. Oxford: Oxford University Press, 2005. Pp. 175–87.

Ormond, Leonée. *J. M. Barrie.* Edinburgh: Scottish Academic Press, 1987.

Pace, Patricia. "Robert Bly Does Peter Pan: The Inner Child as Father to the Man in Steven Spielberg's *Hook.*" *The Lion and the Unicorn* 20 (1996): 113–20.

Perrot, Jean. "Pan and *Puer Aeternus:* Aestheticism and the Spirit of the Age." *Poetics Today* 13 (1992): 155–67.

Powell, Michelle. "An Awfully Big Adventure." www.amprep.org/past/peter/peter1.html.

Robbins, Phyllis. *Maude Adams: An Intimate Portrait.* New York: G. P. Putnam's Sons, 1956.

Rose, Jacqueline. *The Case of Peter Pan, or The Impossibility of Children's Fiction.* London: Macmillan, 1984.

———. "State and Language: *Peter Pan* as Written for the Child." In *Language, Gender, and Childhood.* Ed. Carolyn Steedman, Cathy Unwin, and Valerie Walkerdine. London: Routledge, 1985. Pp. 88–112.

Rotert, Richard. "The Kiss in a Box." *Children's Literature* 18 (1990): 114–23.

Routh, Chris. "Peter Pan: Flawed or Fledgling 'Hero'?" In *A Necessary Fantasy? The Heroic Figure in Children's Popular Culture.* New York: Routledge, 2000. Pp. 291–307.

———. "'Man for the Sword and for the Needle She': Illustrations of Wendy's Role in J. M. Barrie's *Peter and Wendy.*" *Children's Literature in Education* 32 (2001): 57–75.

Rowling, J. K. *Harry Potter and the Sorcerer's Stone.* New York: Scholastic, 1997.

Roy, James A. *James Matthew Barrie.* London: Jarrolds, 1937.

Russell, Patricia Read. "Parallel Romantic Fantasies: Barrie's *Peter Pan* and Spielberg's *E.T.: The Extraterrestrial.*" *Children's Literature Association Quarterly* 8 (1993): 28–30.

Rustin, Michael. "A Defence of Children's Fiction: Another Reading of Peter Pan." *Free Associations* 2 (1985): 128–48.

Seville, Catherine. "Peter Pan's Rights: To Protect or Petrify?" *Cambridge Quarterly* 33 (2004): 119–54.

Sibley, Carroll. *Barrie and His Contemporaries*. Webster Groves, MO: International Mark Twain Society, 1936.

Smollett, Tobias. *The Works of Tobias Smollett*. London: B. Law, 1797.

Starkey, Penelope Schott. "The Many Mothers of Peter Pan: An Explanation and Lamentation." *Research Studies* 42 (1974): 1–10. .

Stevenson, Lionel. "A Source for Barrie's *Peter Pan*." *Philological Quarterly* 7 (1929): 210–14.

Stewart, Angus. "Captain Hook's Secret." *Scottish Literary Journal* 25 (1998): 45–53.

Tarr, Carol Anita. "Shifting Images of Adulthood: From Barrie's *Peter Pan* to Spielberg's *Hook*." In *The Antic Art: Enhancing Children's Literary Experiences through Film and Video*. Ed. Lucy Rollin. Fort Atkinson, WI: Highsmith, 1993. Pp. 63–72.

Telfer, Kevin. *The Remarkable Story of Great Ormond Street Hospital*. New York: Simon & Schuster, 2008.

Toby, Marlene, and Carol Greene. *James M. Barrie: Author of* Peter Pan. Danbury, CT: Children's Press, 1995.

Twain, Mark. *The Adventures of Tom Sawyer*. New York: New American Library, 1980.

Walbrook, H. M. *J. M. Barrie and the Theatre*. London: F. V. White, 1922.

Wellhousen, Karyn, and Zenong Yin. "'Peter Pan Isn't a Girls' Part': An Investigation of Gender Bias in a Kindergarten Classroom." *Women and Language* 22 (1997): 35–39.

White, Donna R., and C. Anita Tarr, eds. *J. M. Barrie's* Peter Pan *In and Out of Time: A Children's Classic at 100*. Lanham, MD: Children's Literature Association and Scarecrow Press, 2006.

Williams, David Park. "Hook and Ahab: Barrie's Strange Satire on Melville." *PMLA* 80 (1965): 483–88.

Wilson, Ann. "Hauntings: Anxiety, Technology, and Gender in *Peter Pan*." *Modern Drama* 43 (2000): 595–610.

Winter, Douglas E. *Clive Barker: The Dark Fantastic*. New York: HarperCollins, 2001.

Wolf, Stacy. "'Never Gonna Be a Man / Catch Me If You Can / I Won't Grow Up': A Lesbian Account of Mary Martin as Peter Pan." *Theatre Journal* 49 (1997): 493–509.

Woollcott, Alexander. *Shouts and Murmurs: Echoes of a Thousand and One First Nights*. New York: The Century Co., 1922.

Wright, Allen. *J. M. Barrie: Glamour of Twilight*. Edinburgh: Ramsay Head Press, 1976.

Wullschläger, Jackie. *Inventing Wonderland: The Lives and Fantasies of Lewis Carroll, Edward Lear, J. M. Barrie, Kenneth Grahame, and A. A. Milne.* New York: Free Press, 1995.

Yeoman, Ann. *Now or Neverland: Peter Pan and the Myth of Eternal Youth. A Psychological Perspective on a Cultural Icon.* Toronto: Inner City Books, 1999.

Zipes, Jack. *Sticks and Stones: The Troublesome Success of Children's Literature from Slovenly Peter to Harry Potter.* New York: Routledge, 2001.

———. Introduction. *Peter Pan: Peter and Wendy and Peter Pan in Kensington Gardens.* New York: Penguin, 2004. Pp. vii–xxxii.

www.gosh.org/peterpan. Great Ormond Street Hospital website for Peter Pan, with a gallery of illustrations and other resources.

www.jmbarrie.co.uk. Website hosted by Andrew Birkin.

www.jmbarrie.net. Website hosted by J. M. Barrie Society.

www.kirriemuirheritage.org. Website of the Kirriemuir Heritage Trust, formed to protect and develop the heritage of J. M. Barrie's birthplace and its surrounding district.

www.moatbrae.org. Website for Moat Brae House, a Georgian townhouse in Dumfries, Scotland, where J. M. Barrie played pirates while a pupil at Dumfries Academy.

About the Author

Born in 1860 in Kirriemuir, Scotland, J. M. Barrie was the third son of hand-loom weaver David Barrie and his wife, Margaret Ogilvy. His parents valued education, and their son studied literature at Edinburgh University before moving to London to launch a career as a journalist. In 1888, Barrie published *Auld Licht Idylls*, followed by *A Window on Thrums* and *The Little Minister*. These works, all based on village life in Kirriemuir, established him as a fiction writer with a flair for local color, an ear for finely calibrated dialogue, and a marvelous instinct for whimsy. The playwright in Barrie soon got the better of the novelist, and, after the success of a dramatic version of *The Little Minister*, there was no turning back. With additional theatrical triumphs to his credit—*The Admirable Crichton*, *Dear Brutus*, and *Mary Rose*—Barrie became one of the foremost playwrights of his day.

In 1894 Barrie married the actress Mary Ansell. The two never had children of their own, and they divorced fifteen years later, in 1909. But Barrie was always surrounded by children, even during his marriage, most notably when he took his St. Bernard, Porthos, for walks in Kensington Gardens. It was there that he met the Llewelyn Davies boys, who inspired him to write about a baby boy and his adventures in Kensington Gardens. These were the boys also featured in *The Boy Castaways of Black Lake Island*, a volume published in two copies that documented summer adventures on a "desert island" with a villain named Captain Swarthy (played by Barrie). Barrie transformed those real-life adventures into *Peter Pan, or the Boy Who Would Not Grow Up*, performed in 1904 in London—then continuously save for two years during World War II. He adopted the five Llewelyn Davies boys after the death of their father in 1907 and their mother in 1910. Before his death, in 1937, he donated the rights to all works featuring Peter Pan to the Great Ormond Street Children's Hospital. On the day of Sir James Barrie's death, the king of England sent a message to Peter Davies, the third of the Llewelyn Davies brothers: "His loss will be universally mourned, for his writing has brought joy and inspiration to young and old alike."

About the Editor

Maria Tatar is the John L. Loeb Professor of Folklore & Mythology and Germanic Languages & Literatures at Harvard University, where she teaches courses in the fields of German studies, children's literature, and folklore. Her fascination with the story of Peter Pan reaches back to childhood. It was reawakened when she taught a course on children's literature in Harvard's General Education Program and explored, with her students, the complex, multilayered story behind the story of Peter Pan. With each passing year, the experience of reading *Peter and Wendy* was enriched by trying to understand the many different dimensions of this famed childhood entertainment.

Maria Tatar is the author of *The Annotated Brothers Grimm, Enchanted Hunters: The Power of Stories in Childhood, Classic Fairy Tales*, and *Secrets beyond the Door: The Story of Bluebeard and His Seven Wives*, among other volumes. She served as dean for the humanities at Harvard and is the recipient of awards from the National Endowment for the Humanities, the Guggenheim Foundation, and the Radcliffe Institute for Advanced Study.